The place is Twelfth-Century China. It is the Time of Hsu Yung...

THE TARTAR

'A magnificent novel as lusty and tumultuous as the age it re-creates!

"I found it fascinating. From his first battle ... he grows against a panorama of court intrigue, warfare, and women who gave him everything from simple pleasure to betrayal and a final union that couldn't be ended even by death."

—Jeanne Williams,
author of A Lady Bought With Rifles

THE TARTAR

FRANKLIN PROUD

A KANGAROO BOOK
PUBLISHED BY POCKET BOOKS NEW YORK

Distributed in Canada by PaperJacks Ltd., a Licensee
of the trademarks of Simon & Schuster, a division of
Gulf+Western Corporation.

Another *Original* publication of POCKET BOOKS

POCKET BOOKS, a Simon & Schuster division of
GULF & WESTERN CORPORATION
1230 Avenue of the Americas, New York, N.Y. 10020

In Canada distributed by PaperJacks Ltd.,
330 Steelcase Road, Markham, Ontario.

ISBN: 0-671-81135-5

First Pocket Books printing March, 1978

Trademarks registered in the United States and other countries.

Printed in Canada

Author's Foreword

The scrolls of Hsü Yung the Tartar, which form the body of the story, span an intriguing era of Chinese and Southeast Asian history during the closing years of the twelfth century and the early years of the thirteenth century. To avoid appending an unwieldy glossary, I have taken certain liberties in the translation of the scrolls.

Throughout his text, Hsü Yung uses dates pertaining to the reigning Sung emperors, the twelve-year cycle of the Chinese lunar calendar, the months of the lunar calendar, and the time of day in accordance with the Chinese twelve two-hour segments. I have substituted corresponding Gregorian calendar dates for the Sung dynastic dating. I have left the lunar years and months and the Chinese hours of the day more or less intact, adding only descriptive references to seasonal changes or time of day for purposes of clarification.

For Chinese weights and measures, I have substituted English equivalents.

Hsü Yung's usage of family and given names, particularly with respect to the reigning emperors of the Sung dynasty, gives rise to confusion. Where the names are relatively simple, I have left them as they appear in his scrolls. In some cases I have substituted English translations of given names. With the Sung emperors I have used only their posthumous titles. With the Cham and Khmer monarchs, I use the honorific titles with the suffix *varman,* meaning Protector, by which they are known to history.

The political entities that existed in Hsü Yung's time have undergone a number of changes. Some have expanded, such as China united under the thirteenth-to-fourteenth-century Yüan (Mongol) dynasty, which absorbed the former Chin, Hsi Hsai, and Southern Sung dynasties and the kingdom of Nan Chao. Others diminished in size and importance or disappeared entirely. During the thirteenth to fourteenth centuries, the Siamese and the Lao were encouraged by the Yüan dynasty to form independent kingdoms at the expense of a dwindling Khmer empire. In the fifteenth century, the Siamese overran and sacked Angkor Thom, and the Annamites (Vietnamese) defeated the Cham. Kambuja (Cambodia) was reduced to approximately its present limits. The kingdom of Champa ceased to be a political entity. The Cham cities of Indrapura, Vijaya, and Panduranga—located respectively at or near the present-day Vietnamese cities of Hué, Binh Dinh, and Phan Rang—no longer exist. They, together with the boundaries of states as they were in Hsü Yung's day, are illustrated in the maps that precede the text.

With two exceptions, where the names of cities have changed over the centuries, I have used present-day place names. The exceptions are Vien Chang (Vientiane) and Lin-an (Hangchow).

In the scrolls chronicling his early years, Hsü Yung refers to himself as Siao Hu, Young Tartar. In later scrolls, he used Lao Hu, Old Tartar. In the main, I have confined myself to the "Tartar" throughout his memoirs.

This, then, is the story of the Tartar, in his own words:
". . . a soldier's rather than a scholar's tale."

F.M.P., September 1977

THE TARTAR

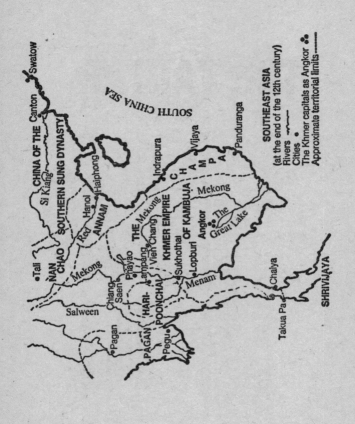

SOUTHEAST ASIA
(at the end of the 12th century)
Rivers ～～～
Cities •
The Khmer capitals as Angkor ••
Approximate territorial limits ------

CHINA OF THE
SOUTHERN SUNG DYNASTY
Canton • Swatow
Si Kiang
NAN
CHAO
• Tali
Red River
Hanoi • Haiphong
ANNAM
SOUTH CHINA SEA
Indrapura
Mekong
C
H
A
M
P
A
Vijaya
Panduranga
Mekong
KHMER EMPIRE
OF KAMBUJA
Angkor
The
Great Lake
Vien Chang
Lampang
Phayao
Sukhothai
Lopburi
Chiang Saen
HARI-
POONCHAI
Menam
Salween
Mekong
Pagan
PAGAN
Pegu
Takua Pa
Chaiya
SHRIVIJAYA

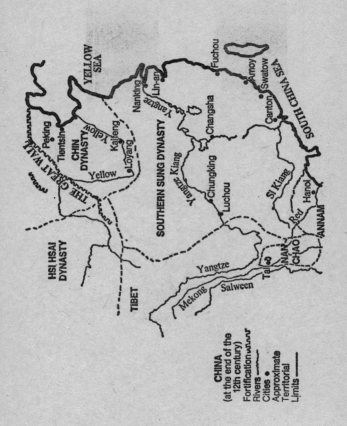

CHINA
(at the end of the
12th century)
Fortification ⌇⌇⌇
Rivers ———
Cities ●
Approximate
Territorial
Limits ———

Prologue

In mid-afternoon, the rain slackened, then stopped. Servants entered the room and opened the louvered shutters without disturbing the sleeping man. Bright sunlight flooded his sleeping chamber.

A maidservant brought tea and placed it on the matting beside the low bed. She touched the man's arm gently to rouse him from his afternoon nap. When his eyes opened, she bent low as a mark of respect and then withdrew from his presence.

The man stretched, swung his legs over the edge of his ornately carved wooden bed, and sat up. He poured himself a cup of steaming, fragrant tea. As he savored the aromatic infusion, his gaze was attracted to the familiar view outside the window closest to his bed.

He looked down on a vivid splash of color provided by a glaze-tile roofed pavilion adjoining the main residence. A trellis next to the pavilion was smothered in a cloud of mauve bougainvillaea blossoms. In the garden beyond, flowering shrubs painted a colorful contrast against the green backdrop of a screen of tall bamboo trees. At the far end of the grounds, palm trees and a giant banyan tree reared above a tangle of lesser foliage. The gilded towers of a nearby Brahman temple loomed beyond the trees. In the distance, massed gray and white clouds obscured the mountain peaks.

The scene, shimmering as it did through a vapor haze rising from the drying earth, had about it a quality of unreality. The man's attention was caught by a more distinct form of motion. Armed soldiers who had sheltered themselves beneath the banyan during the noontime deluge moved listlessly to resume their appointed stations.

The man shrugged resignedly at this irritating reminder of his present status. The soldiers, as well, had become a familiar part of the scenery since he had embarked on his self-appointed task.

Placing his empty cup beside the teapot, the man frowned, ran his fingers through his graying, close-cropped hair in a gesture of annoyance, and stood up. He presented an imposing figure: straight-backed and firmly muscled despite his sixty years.

He paused to retie the waist knot of his *sampot*, a sarong-like cloth sheath extending from his waist to his ankles. Satisfied that the garment was secure, he walked the few paces from his bed to a low table beside the main window. An old wound lent stiffness to his right leg, giving him a slight but noticeable limp.

Seating himself on cushions by the table, he examined the scroll on which he had been working before the noontime rain darkened the room. The sunlight that bathed the table, brushes, and scroll permitted a scrutiny of the work completed that morning. Satisfied that the last few characters exhibited no flaws, he nodded approvingly.

Methodically, he rubbed an ink stick on the stone and added a few drops of water to achieve the desired consistency. With the ink prepared to his satisfaction, he selected a brush from a bamboo cup and addressed himself to the calligraphy that had occupied most of his daylight hours over the last few months.

It had been an exacting task. His eyesight was no longer good, and he found he could not work by lamplight. But, as the work progressed, he had gained in speed and dexterity. Now that the end of his chronicle was but a few weeks off, the work went quickly. Perhaps, he thought ruefully, it goes too quickly; but he had pledged himself to complete the task with as little delay as possible.

Shadows chased themselves across the scroll as he brush-stroked in the logograms. He became so absorbed in his artistry that the hollow booming of ceremonial drums from the temple failed to distract him.

chapter 1

HAD SCHOLASTIC PURSUITS OCCUPIED MORE OF MY TIME
as a youth, my calligraphy would exhibit more grace and
harmony. The brushstrokes are crude because my bent
lay in other directions. I could ride before I could walk.
Those who instructed me in horsemanship and the martial
arts spoke highly of my abilities. Only the harried tutors
assigned to my classical education were driven to the
brink of despair. Had more discipline been exercised during my formative years, I might have developed along
more balanced lines.

Of course, had I been more academically inclined,
there might have been but little to chronicle. This story
is of adventure in distant and barbaric ands. It is a
soldier's, rather than a scholar's, tale. I beseech those who
peruse these memoirs to do so with charity and an eye
to content rather than to form.

It is not my intention to dwell upon my childhood, but
such background has bearing on later events and cannot
be ignored entirely. As the bamboo shoot is shaped, so
grows the stalk.

I was born in Changsha, the capital of Hunan province,
in 1162, in the sixth month of the Year of the Horse.
My father, Hsü Ta-kuan, was a Confucian classical
scholar and an administrator of mandarin rank. At the
time of my birth, he was governor of the Changsha prefecture, a position he continued to hold until I was in my

teens. I was his ninth son, the only one presented to him by my mother, his number three wife, who died a few days after bringing me into this world.

The family name of Hsü is an honored one in Chinese annals. My ancestors include the emperors of the Southern T'ang dynasty of the tenth century. My father was proud of our lineage and, although a man of peace himself, never tired of recounting the heroic deeds of our ancestors. My forebears on my mother's side are not quite so illustrious. She was of Khitan nobility. Although the Khitan tribesmen, Tartar horsemen from beyond the Great Wall, established the Liao dynasty in the extreme northeastern section of China in 947 and had been exposed to Chinese customs and culture for more than two centuries, they were still considered barbarians at the time of their defeat at the hands of Jürched horsemen in 1125, and they are considered so to this day. Perhaps it is from that wild blood that I inherited my rebellious streak and my instinctive ability to handle horses.

My maternal grandfather was attached in some capacity to the Sung court at Kaifeng. When Kaifeng was overrun by the Jürched barbarians in 1126, my grandfather escaped with the remnants of the court, which fled to the south. He was present when Kao Tsung, High Ancestor, son of Ch'in Tsung, Excellent Ancestor, was proclaimed emperor in 1127. He wandered with the emperor and his retinue for the next decade until the court settled on Lin-an as the temporary residence for the royal seat of the Southern Sung dynasty. My mother was born in Lin-an, which was where my father met and married her. At the time of the marriage, my mother was nineteen, my father forty-two. I was born a year later.

Since my mother died of complications arising during my birth, my image of her was a composite picture based on secondhand information. The servants recalled her as a beautiful girl of infectious good humor who filled the house with light and laughter. My father's number one and number two wives, both considerably older than my mother, had not welcomed her to the ménage and bore her nothing but malice. When they discussed her, it was to describe her as alien of form and features: a large, awkward, homely girl lacking in respect and social graces. It was stressed that my mother's unbound feet bespoke low station and barbaric background. My half brothers and half sisters swung between these poles of opinion and, while generally critical, seemed to remember my mother with some degree of affection.

The image I have carried with me from childhood is without doubt an overly idealized version, but it persists to this day. I have always favored the servants' viewpoint. I visualized my mother as a great beauty. I was grateful to her for her physical endowment, which bestowed on me my muscular build and above-average height. My sense of humor, a trait singularly lacking in the rest of the family, must be a legacy from her. I did not consider her unbound feet a stigma and, in fact have never been able to look with favor on that fashionable deformity.

My father was a Confucian scholar in the classic mold. He was a great friend of the moralistic reformer and philosopher Chu Hsi, even though Chu was nine years my father's junior. My boyhood memory of my father is of a stern, aloof, and somewhat forbidding figure. He was a man of uncompromising probity: strict, but scrupulously fair. He inspired confidence, but he did not invite familiarity. As a child, I was in awe of him. As I grew older, I held him in respect and high esteem, but we were never close. I cannot recall ever hearing my father laugh or seeing him smile.

My father did not marry again after my mother's death and sired no more children until taking a concubine when well in his fifties. During my childhood, I was the youngest of the family, the closest being a half brother eight years my senior. Even had my features and stature not set me somewhat apart, the age differences would have tended to isolate me from my immediate kin. This gap was to have a marked bearing on subsequent events, but it was of little consequence to me at the time.

I certainly did not lack for companionship during my early years. I do not know the exact number of aunts, uncles, cousins, and relatives of more distant ties who lived with us. Then, too, the governor's residence was palatial, demanding a considerable number of servants, guards, overseers, and clerks—most of whom lived on the premises and had growing families. There was no shortage of children close to my age, and no dearth of mischief and deviltry we could stir up. In the pranks and escapades, I fear I was more often than not the ringleader.

Just when, and by whom, I was dubbed "the Tartar" escapes me. I think the sobriquet was conferred on me by one of my illustrious half brothers, but I am not sure. Without doubt, it was intended to be a derogatory reference to my Khitan heritage. I accepted it, however, as a title of distinction and a source of pride. The nickname stuck. To my friends, relatives, the servants, and even my tutors, I became known familiarly as the Tartar. The sobriquet stayed with me into adult life. There are more people who know me simply as the Tartar than have ever known me by my family and given name—Hsü Yung.

I was fortunate as a child. With the exception of a mother's love, I lacked for nothing. I was afforded all the advantages deriving from my father's wealth and position. The city of Changsha, a bustling river port and hub of regional commerce, was a fascinating place for a boy to explore, particularly if the boy was the son of the governor. The country remained at peace and no natural disasters intruded to mar the tranquility of those years.

I accepted all this as a normal state of affairs. It was not until later, when I was forced to rely on acquired skills for survival, that I began to appreciate how favored had been my childhood.

Looking back, it is difficult to find points of significance. There were no peaks of triumph, no chasms of tragedy. Only through later experiences could I perceive the value, or lack thereof, of lessons learned in childhood. Whatever I learned as a boy that served me well in later years was achieved more by accident than by design, by absorption rather than application.

The avenue to advancement and exalted station was the successful completion of competitive examinations on the Confucian Classics. Why, then, if my father was the strict disciplinarian I have indicated, did he not exercise his authority to ensure I applied myself to my classical studies? It is not an easy question to answer.

My father was not in ignorance of my scholastic performance. In addition to the progress reports submitted regularly by my instructors and tutors, my father had even more direct evidence on which to base his opinions.

Each week he assembled my brothers, cousins, and myself. With us seated around him, he would lecture on ethics or discourse on historical highlights. At the conclusion of the session, he would conduct a sort of oral examination. My stumbling answers could have left no doubt concerning my weakness in classical studies.

That my father had a sound appreciation of my strengths and shortcomings was revealed to me somewhat later. That he allowed me to pursue my headstrong course with a minimum of restraint was probably due to considerations I could not have suspected as a child.

One thing that stands out in my memory is my boyhood fascination with ships and seafarers.

The Changsha dock area abounded with doss houses, brothels, and taverns. It was expressly forbidden for myself or the other children to visit the area unless accompanied by an adult. This was not without reason. Many a lad had disappeared, whisked from the docks to fill out a shorthanded crew aboard a departing merchant junk. Nor was it unheard of for the son of a wealthy merchant to be kidnapped and held for ransom. Still, this strict prohibition only served to enhance the area's mystery and appeal, and it turned each illicit visit into an adventure. As often as I could, alone or accompanied by one or more of my more daring cousins, I haunted the forbidden area.

My transgressions did not go undetected, nor unpunished. Since this did little to deter me, and when it was determined that I was a familiar figure to ship masters and merchants and, accordingly, relatively safe from harm, the ban was relaxed. From that point my interest in the dock area waned in favor of exploration of the river, the sandbar from which Changsha derives its name, and the surrounding countryside.

My interest in things nautical expanded my education in a number of ways. One of these was that through exposure to cargoes and cargo handling, dockside haggling, and the storage and movement of goods and produce, I absorbed the rudiments of trading and commercial practice. Another was that the tall tales spun by seafarers of fabled lands where esoteric practices were commonplace and where temples and palaces were sheathed in gold and encrusted with precious stones fired my youthful imagination and instilled in me a desire to travel and see these

strange lands for myself. The most important benefit, however, was probably that my interest in history was aroused.

Memorizing names and dates from a dusty past of Chinese history stretching back as far as the imagination
could conceive had seemed to me a pretty profitless exercise. I had acquired a basic background of the parade of
dynasties from the fabled Hsia some thirty-two hundred
years ago to the Southern Sung of today, and I had a
general appreciation of the greatness and magnificence of
the Middle Kingdom and the Dragon Throne. I had
balked, however, at learning by rote long chronological
lists of emperors, their posthumous and temple titles, their
dates of ascension and abdication or demise, and the
events of history within the confusing framework of dynastic year cycles.

True, I had listened with interest to my father's recounting of the more recent sequence of events over the past
two and a half centuries, from the collapse of the T'ang
dynasty in the early tenth century to the present. Tales of
exploits of my ancestors were woven into this history,
which gave it more meaning. The half century of near
anarchy and warlord rivalry of the Five Dynasties and the
Ten Independent States had some romantic appeal, but
the establishment of the Sung dynasty by Chao K'uang-
yin in 960 seemed pretty dull stuff. That the Tartar horsemen had swept down from the north in 947 to found the
Liao dynasty in the far northeast was much more interesting. These were the Khitan tribesmen, my mother's people.

My father was only six when the Jürched horsemen
swept in from the northeastern steppes to vanquish the
Liao and drive the Sung survivors south from their captured capital of Kaifeng. The victorious Jürched established a new Tartar dominion, the Chin dynasty. To my
father, born and raised in Nanking, those events far to
the north had seemed pretty remote until he was exposed
to the emperor and his peripatetic retinue when they
passed through Nanking. By then my father had been a
boy of fourteen, preparing for his classical exams and
subsequent service with the Sung administration. My
father had been in Nanking in 1161, the year before my
birth, and witnessed the Chin failure to cross the river and
take the city. But, as I have already observed, my
father was a man of peace who favored temporizing

and the payment of tribute to warfare, and his accounts lacked color.

With the sun-weathered seadogs of the waterfront, it was a different story. I was enthralled as they spun fantastic tales of bloody combat. I could almost hear the tumult of battle, smell burning pitch or acrid gunpowder smoke, and had no difficulty visualizing myself in the heart of the action as the hero of the day.

Some seamen I met had seen action with the one hundred twenty Sung naval vessels that had routed a vastly superior Chin force of six hundred ships in a fateful engagement off Tsingtao in 1161. Others had been with the river fleet, which had included about one hundred of the huge merchant junks making use of rockets, bombs, and fire rafts, known as "whales," that turned back the main thrust of the Chin army in its attempt to cross the Yangtze in the same year, 1161.

My tutors must have been puzzled by my sudden interest in history. I avidly read what old accounts and annals my tutors could produce. It was at that early age that I began to perceive a repeating pattern of conquest by less cultured people, generally nomadic herdsmen from the north, followed by their gradual decline as they became sedentary farmers and fell in turn to a new wave of restless horsemen. Even then I could appreciate the contention of scholars that China was a vast and placid sea that absorbed and calmed all the turbulent streams that entered it. These concepts were admittedly pretty vague, but they were to stay with me and form the basis of some of my actions and exploits of the years to come. They were to take on more substance as I gained firsthand experience in warfare and politics.

A familiarity with nautical terms and some knowledge of ship construction and developments, such as the treadmill-operated paddle-wheel vessel, were lesser benefits from my maritime interest. A negative aspect was that the time spent frequenting the waterfront was time I could have devoted to more conventional scholarship.

There are important milestones in everyone's life. The first to appear in my life did so without warning the year I turned fourteen, the Year of the Ram. In the second month of that year, 1175, my father was summoned to the

Sung court in Lin-an. He returned to Changsha less than a month later.

It was several days after my father's homecoming that I was summoned to his presence.

chapter 2

IT WAS A WEEK FILLED WITH SURPRISES.

I learned that my father had returned from Lin-an accompanied by a concubine. My informant was one of the housemaids, who embellished the account with ecstatic praise of the concubine's beauty. I affected disinterest, but I was beside myself with curiosity.

It took some ingenuity to find an excuse to visit the women's quarters of the main pavilion, an area in which I had never displayed interest. My pretext was that I was looking for an ink stone borrowed from my tutor by one of the handmaidens. It was a pretty flimsy story, believed by none, but I was rewarded with a glimpse of the latest distaff edition to the household.

She was an undeniably pretty little thing with delicate features and milk-white skin. I judged her to be not much older than myself. I was mistaken. That evening I learned from my knowledgeable informant that the girl's name was Apricot Blossom and that she was six years my senior.

The next day I was advised to attend my father at the close of the Hours of the Monkey. I confess that I wondered if my contriving to see the concubine had been reported to my father and was the reason for this summons.

At the appointed hour, I dutifully reported to the study off my father's sleeping quarters. A manservant conducted me to the balcony overlooking the garden compound. My

13

father was engaged in applying the finishing touches to a painting and did not acknowledge my presence.

I watched with interest from a respectful distance. The painting was on silk, an ink-and-color presentation of a flowering branch on which was perched a magpie. With deft strokes, my father was adding a delicate shade of pink to the blossoms.

There came unbidden to my mind an image of Apricot Blossom and my father in an amorous embrace. It was a picture I found oddly disturbing. To me, my father, who was approaching fifty-seven, seemed incredibly ancient and Apricot Blossom seemed much younger than her years. With an effort, I put these thoughts from my mind as being disrespectful to both my father and his new concubine. I hoped that my boldness in invading the women's quarters on a flimsy pretext was not to be the subject of discussion. It was no crime in itself, and I doubted if Apricot Blossom had seen me or even knew of my existence.

The evening light faded. My father carefully cleaned his brush and put it in an ivory case. He turned to me and inclined his head slightly in a nod of greeting.

"Sit down, my son."

I settled onto a low stool and gazed up at the gowned figure seated primly before me. I waited for my father to continue.

"You do not," my father said mildly, "have much aptitude for the noble classics. The fault may rest with you, or perhaps with the tutors I have employed to guide your scholastic footsteps. I fear the former is the case. This distresses me since, as you must know, your future rank and station are hinged largely upon your passing examinations on the Confucian Classics. Your chances of doing so are remote, if not impossible. To become proficient both academically and athletically should be an obtainable goal, but this doesn't seem to apply in your case."

My father paused. I waited out his silence uncomfortably.

"It is no disgrace," my father continued. "It merely reduces the options. A military, rather than an administrative, career seems indicated. Of late, you have shown a preference for things pertaining to ships and the sea. Therefore, for some months I have had in mind your apprenticeship to a suitable naval unit."

As I absorbed this revelation, my father watched me intently. It was most welcome news, yet I tried not to betray my delight. I had the feeling that in some way my father was putting me to a test. I bowed my head in acknowledgment and to indicate my acceptance of his wishes.

"It was my intention to seek out certain men of influence in naval circles during my visit to Lin-an. That I did not do so was because the emperor's wishes put a different light on the matter. I have been entrusted with a mission. I am to proceed to the capital of the kingdom of Chenla, which I believe is now known also as Kambuja, as an envoy with the express task of promoting a more active exchange of trade. This commission will probably occupy the better part of two years. I have decided that you shall accompany me. The experience should be beneficial. Two years hence will still be time enough to consider advancing a naval career."

I was dumbfounded. My secret wish to visit the exotic lands so vividly described to me by grizzled seamen was being granted. I could hardly believe my good fortune. I did my best to maintain an outward calm, but I am sure my trembling limbs betrayed my excitement.

My father dismissed me without further comment. I left, feeling as though I was floating on a cloud. Then I was struck by a chilling thought that brought me down from the cloud to the reality of the courtyard with a jarring thump. What if Apricot Blossom was the fox fairy in cunning disguise and my father was bewitched? What if the mission was a diabolical plot to disrupt our household and lead us all to our doom?

We were to set sail from Canton in the ninth month, when the winds would favor a southwesterly passage. Those items being supplied by the emperor—the transport vessel, naval escort, assigned militia, commercial counselors, horses, arms, provisions, trade goods, and gifts—were to be assembled in the southern port city by the end of the eighth month. My father dispatched his chief steward to supervise and report on these proceedings.

There was a good deal to be done in Changsha. My father had to select the guards, clerks, and servants who would form his personal retinue. He had to decide what personal and household effects we would take with us. In addition, he had to instruct a mandarin sent by the Sung court to act as governor of the prefecture during my father's absence.

To me my father gave the task of assisting the captain of the guard, the stable master, and the chief clerk in whatever capacities they considered helpful. I was an impediment they accepted good-naturedly.

I saw more of my father during those weeks of preparation than I had in almost as many years. I observed him closely. If bewitched, he showed no outward signs. This, I concluded, may only mean that Apricot Blossom could be biding her time, since she and her handmaidens were included in my father's retinue. As a precautionary measure, I religiously inserted extra joss sticks in the pewter urn of the family Confucian shrine.

I was impatient to embark on the adventure, supernatural risks notwithstanding. I begrudged the time devoted to the preparations. During the long, hot summer, the days seemed to drag by. Then, to my surprise, it was autumn, and all was in readiness for our departure from Changsha.

We proceeded upstream on the Siang River. As the navigable tributaries grew smaller and shallower, we changed to smaller river craft. Finally, the party was faced with an overland trek across the mountainous terrain separating the headwaters of the Siang from the tributaries leading to the Pearl River and Canton. With my father and Apricot Blossom in sedan chairs, and the rest of the retinue in oxcarts, on horseback, or on foot, we continued our southward progress until we could take once more to waterborne, and considerably more comfortable, transport.

The walled city of Canton provided me with a foretaste of the wonders to come. Like Changsha, it was a river port, but at that point the similarity ceased. Canton teemed with life and surged with frenetic activity by day and by night. Within the city walls, two tall pagodas—one one hundred and seventy feet in height, the other about ten feet shorter, dating back to the Sui and early Sung dynasties, respectively—loomed above narrow streets congested with cramped dwellings and open-fronted shops. We were allocated spacious quarters in the eastern section of the city. They were quarters befitting my father's rank and station.

We were in Canton several weeks, awaiting the arrival of two important commercial counselors and our final provisioning. This gave me time to explore beyond the city walls. The docks were crowded with high-pooped, ocean-going merchantmen, barges loaded with goods of every description, and foreign vessels of strange shape, and even stranger rig. For miles and miles along the riverbank, sampans and river craft were tied, stem to stern, in row after row. On these craft lived the *tankia*, the boat people, who lived their lives simply, seldom if ever putting a foot on dry land. A jumble of thatch-roofed shacks crowded against the city walls and spilled down to the waterfront go-downs. A sand flat to the southwest of the city was devoted to sleazy taverns and restaurants catering to the foreign seafarers and merchants who were not allowed within the gates of the city. I must admit, my only frame of reference being Changsha, that I viewed Canton with wide-eyed wonder, and with more than a little disgust.

In the last week of the ninth month, we slipped our lines and proceeded majestically downstream. With a following wind billowing our brown-dyed sails and the current assisting us, we navigated the eighty miles downstream in the space of a single tide. At the river's mouth, we were joined by two escorting naval vessels.

The sea was not what I had anticipated. Seafarers' tales dwell mainly on the perils of the deep. I had expected to put forth into the teeth of a raging storm. Instead, I was introduced to the sea on its best behavior.

The brown water of the river became mottled with blue-green translucent patches. These spread until all that remained of the river was a series of muddy streaks that gradually faded from view. As we left the headland and rocky islands astern, the ship's motion underwent a change. The bow rose and fell gently. The vessel heeled to starboard and rolled with a slow cadence as we rode easily to a long offshore swell. A following sea paced us with measured tread.

I was enchanted. The salty sea breeze acted upon me like an elixir. My spirit took wing to go skimming over the white-crested waves like a sea gull.

The effect produced in me by this introduction to the sea was not shared by the majority of my father's retinue. Most of them, including my father, had little or no ap-

petite and retired to their quarters, not to emerge again
until we were several days at sea. I, on the other hand,
was in my element. I roamed the ship, exploring the
huge junk above and below decks from stem to high
poop. I worked with the seamen and plagued the sailing
master with questions. Patiently, he explained to me how
the configurations of stars assisted him in determining our
course by night and how the floating needle, which always points toward the heavenly abode of the Emperor
of Jade, helped guide him by day.

For nine days and nights we sailed on a southwesterly
heading. Our escorting units stayed slightly ahead, positioned about a mile distant to windward and leeward.
Apart from an occasional overtaking rain squall, the
weather remained fair and clear, with the wind holding
steady from the northeast.

During the ninth night of our passage, the wind
dropped. Dawn of our tenth day at sea found us drifting
on the surface of a glassy sea without a breath of air to
stir the batten-extended lug sails. The upwind naval vessel had drifted down upon us during the night and stood
close on our port bow. The second vessel was almost out
of sight on our starboard beam. We stayed in the same
relative positions all through that day.

The morning of the eleventh day found us still
becalmed. The sky had taken on a brassy sheen, and
about mid-morning a long southeasterly swell made itself
felt. The battens of our slatted sails clattered against the
pole masts as we rolled to the swell, but still no breeze
ruffled the sea's surface or fanned the scorching deck of
our ship.

The crew went about their tasks wearing worried frowns
and speaking little. In the port wing of the high poop, the
sailing master gazed steadily in the direction of the swell,
his features fixed in a dark scowl. One of our escorting
vessels, the one that had stayed on our port bow yesterday, was now about half a mile astern of us. The other
ship was nowhere to be seen.

The air of foreboding pervading the ship transmitted
itself to the passengers. Even the horses, stabled below
decks, were unaccountably restive. Many of the militia,
guards, clerks, and servants came on deck to stand in
knots or pace the decks nervously. My father, who made
it a practice not to appear on deck during the heat of the

day, spent some time on the poop deck during the late morning.

I was wending my way forward in the early afternoon when I noticed Apricot Blossom standing dejectedly by the starboard midship rail. I observed her from a distance. Her pale features were beaded with perspiration. Her eyes were wide with fright, and her small hands trembled visibly. Since the fox fairy would have nothing to fear from the elements, I reasoned that she could not be such a creature in human guise. I felt a twinge of guilt at having wronged her in my thoughts. I could not but feel sympathy for her fright and bewilderment. As I passed, I touched her arm reassuringly and grinned broadly with a confidence I did not feel. I was rewarded with a tremulous smile of gratitude and congratulated myself on a convincing performance.

The swell increased appreciably during the Hours of the Goat. The sailing master issued a number of sharp orders. The sails were dropped. Lines were secured and everything movable was lashed down. Hatches were battened down. Up forward, two large objects of woven bamboo were brought from below decks. These were rigged into large cones, a large opening at one end, tapering to a small opening at the other. Crossed bamboo spars, to which were attached long lines, kept the large openings widespread.

I questioned a seaman concerning all this activity, and particularly concerning the two big cones. I was advised that the sailing master suspected the approach of a *taifung*, Great Wind, and was taking precautionary measures. The cones, it was explained, could be payed out over the bow, where they would stream out to the length of their ropes, hold the ship's head to the wind, and slow its backward drift. I felt a thrill of fear. I had heard seamen refer to the dreadful power of typhoons with nothing but awe and respect.

We were barely into the Hours of the Monkey when a ragged line of black clouds frayed the southeastern horizon. The sailing master ordered leeboards and rudder lowered to their full extents and the tiller secured in the midships position. All passengers were ordered below decks.

What prompted me to disregard those orders I will never know. I positioned myself between two bales lashed

abaft the mainmast and settled down to await the storm.
I had not long to wait.

The low, black clouds raced toward us. A chill breeze
swept the deck as cat's-paws skittered across the sea toward us. The wind struck with a sighing moan, which
changed to a throaty shriek as the full fury of the storm
hit us.

I have never, before or since, experienced anything
quite as terrifying as that typhoon. The sun was blotted
out and it became as dark as night. Waves loomed to
awesome heights in the gloom, then crashed down upon
our bow to sweep aft in foaming avalanches The crests
were whipped off the waves and sent scudding to join the
horizontally slanted rain. It was impossible to say where
the sea ended and the rain-saturated sky began. We were
in the vortex of a roaring, screaming, watery hell.

I will never know how I managed to survive the storm.
The mainmast and the two heavy bales afforded me some
protection, but time and again I was submerged beneath
the frothing sea that swept the deck. Had I not had the
presence of mind to tie myself to the mast, I would surely
have been washed over the side.

My memory of that terrible night is not very clear. I
have no idea how long the storm lasted, but I recall
that there came a point when the fury of the storm
abated and the creaking and groaning of the stricken
ship became less strident. Water no longer crashed down
upon me, but the deck was still awash and the rain had
not slackened. Exhausted, and waterlogged, I fell into a
sort of drugged sleep.

By morning the storm had blown itself out. The day
dawned bright and sparkling. Stiff, aching in every muscle and feeling as though I was returning from death itself, I awoke with the sun in my eyes. I was wedged
between one bale and the splintered stump of the mainmast. How and when the mast had broken and been carried away without my knowledge, leaving me unhurt and
still tied securely to its base, is a mystery I have never
resolved.

Of the three vessels in our small convoy, we were the
only one to survive the typhoon. There was no sign of
our escorting vessels, nor were we to hear of or see them
again.

The storm had taken an appalling toll. Our casualties

among the passengers and crew were seven dead, thirty-two injured, and five missing. Four of our seven horses had died below decks. When the inventory of damage sustained was completed, the tally was alarming. Below decks, the holds, storerooms, and cabins were a shambles. On the upper deck, two of the three masts had been carried away and almost everything that had been stowed on deck, including the furled sails, had been swept overboard. The port side of the poop was smashed and splintered, and the taffrail looked as though it had been sheared off with a giant cleaver.

Of our immediate party, Apricot Blossom had a sprained ankle and a gash on her left forearm, while my father had a number of bad bruises and a dislocated shoulder. I, who should by rights have drowned on deck, had escaped without so much as a scratch.

By noon, a small sail had been jury-rigged amidships. We were making little better than steerageway and could only sail before the wind, but we were at least afloat and making some progress.

There was some excitement the next morning when a white sail was spotted on the western horizon. When a second, then a third, sail could be made out, and it was obvious that the ships were bearing toward us, the sailing master looked anything but pleased.

From the hull design and the cut of the sails, the ships bearing down upon us were vessels of the kingdom of Champa, renowned for their piracy in these waters. Once again we were ordered below decks as the militia were positioned along the ship's rails.

chapter 3

MY VIEW FROM THE STERN WINDOWS WAS RESTRICTED, but I could see clearly the two Cham vessels closing on our port and starboard quarters from astern. The third attacking ship stood off to windward.

As the Cham ships passed beneath the overhang of our transom, I looked down on them from my vantage point. Their loose-footed sails had been let fly to reduce the ship's way. At the tillers the helmsmen inched the ships ever closer. Along the gunwales seamen crouched with grappling hooks. In the bows and raised stern sheets, archers and crossbowmen let fly flight after flight of whistling shafts aimed at our open deck and defending militia.

The Cham were unlike any group of people I had ever seen. They were brown-skinned, stocky, and coarse of features. Most of them wore their hair piled atop their heads in tight chignons. A number wore leather jacket-like garments as a form of armor, and some had head coverings with extended leather flaps to protect their necks. As weapons, they carried pikes and long, blunt-tipped swords. They were grim-faced, silent, and a truly fearsome lot of cutthroats.

Our crippled vessel shuddered as first one, then the second, Cham vessel ground alongside. The battle erupted in shouts, screams, and the clash of arms. From astern, the third Cham vessel swooped in like a falcon intent on the kill.

As hopelessly outnumbered as were our militia, the outcome of the lopsided battle was pretty much a foregone conclusion. It was not much of a surprise, therefore, that when the tumult subsided it was Cham pirates who opened the doors and motioned us out on deck. But I was not prepared for the scene of carnage that met my gaze.

The decks of our junk ran with blood. The Cham were loading their dead and wounded aboard their vessels. The corpses of our heroic defenders, and the still-moaning wounded, were being callously thrown over the side into a sea alive with thrashing sharks. In the foredeck section, a number of our militia and seamen were kneeling stoically as a Cham swordsman methodically beheaded them one by one.

A Cham, somewhat taller than the rest, stood apart, surveying the scene. He wore a *sampot* that dropped almost to his ankles, a sword in a heavily embossed silver scabbard, and a wide gold bracelet on his right upper arm. He gestured and spoke a few words to our guards, who herded us in the direction of a knot of passengers.

A guard pushed my father roughly. Without thinking, I growled a protest and launched myself at the guard. It was a futile gesture. Before I knew what had happened, I received a blow on the side of my head and was sprawled out on the deck at the feet of the tall Cham. I struggled to rise, my head ringing and my vision blurred. My arms were seized from behind.

I fully expected to be decapitated on the spot and was determined I would not utter a sound or betray any emotion. When nothing happened, I looked up into the grinning face of the pirate leader. He said something that brought broad smiles to the faces of the guards, placed his hands on his hips, and laughed. I vowed that if I lived, I would one day kill the swaggering murderer.

The Cham pirates committed no further acts of violence. A prize crew was put on board. We survivors were confined below decks and our junk was taken in tow.

It was a full two days before we were allowed on deck. Ahead lay a long line of sandy coastline with blue mountains as a backdrop. This, I assumed, was Champa, or Lin-yi, Savage Forest, as it was often referred to by seafarers and ancient chroniclers.

We entered the lagoon through a cut in the coastal sand dunes. The landward side of the lagoon was fringed with tall palms and feathery casuarina trees. Behind this screen of foliage loomed the towers of temples and the steeply pitched roofs of large buildings. We were informed this was Vijaya, the royal seat and capital of the kingdom of Champa. It was a city of considerable size and, if the gold sheathing on towers and spires was any indication, a metropolis of much wealth. From the number of merchant vessels at anchor in the lagoon, Vijaya was also the scene of a good deal of maritime commercial activity.

No sooner was the anchor dropped than boats came alongside and the prize crew disembarked. No one approached the vessel for the remainder of that day and night. The next morning, when we were beginning to wonder what was happening and my father was talking about someone swimming ashore to make our presence known, a large rowboat was seen to be heading toward us.

An official-looking party boarded us. With them was a Chinese merchant to act as interpreter. My father explained who he was and what had befallen us. There followed some discussion among the Cham officials, exchanges not translated by the interpreter, and then a request for my father to accompany the group for further discussions ashore.

Within a matter of hours, my father returned along with several boats and seamen. We were taken to the city and conducted to a palatial residence located within the grounds of the royal palace. Our personal effects and our three remaining horses were brought along later. The trade goods and the gifts of the Sung court to the Khmer king had mysteriously disappeared.

Three days after we had settled into these new quarters, my father was granted an audience with the king, Jaya Indravarman IV. As my father reported it, the meeting was most cordial. The king deplored the piratical act and assured my father that the culprits would be caught and punished. An effort would be made to locate and return the missing gifts and trade goods. A messenger would be dispatched to China to advise the emperor concerning the plight of his envoy to the Khmer court. Our vessel would be repaired at the Cham naval slipways. And, until suitable arrangements could be concluded to permit the continuance of his journey and mission, my father and his retinue were to consider themselves as honored guests.

It transpired that another matter had been discussed at the royal interview. Arrangements had been concluded whereby I was to receive instructions in the local language and customs from the Brahman priesthood. While a return to schooling was not much to my liking, I could appreciate the wisdom of my father's initiative.

Ten days after my father's royal audience, we were invited to attend public executions being conducted at the main market square. We were informed that the felons sentenced to death were the pirate leaders who had so villainously assaulted us. We duly witnessed the decapitations, but I must confess that I had difficulty distinguishing between the Cham and could not have sworn that any of those beheaded were of the pirate band. One that I was certain I could have identified, the swaggering commander, was not among those executed.

The days stretched into weeks, the weeks into months. Although we were treated with exaggerated courtesy, it was obvious that we were little better than prisoners. We had a limited amount of freedom within the royal compound, but we had to seek permission if we wished to venture beyond these confines. If authority was granted, we had to be accompanied by a large military escort. Areas such as the commercial section of the city and the docks appeared to be expressly prohibited.

For many weeks my father's only source of information was the Chinese merchant who had acted as interpreter from the time of our arrival. His visits were not frequent, and we later discovered that his information was deliberately misleading.

I had no preconceived image of Champa. In Changsha my waterfront solicitation of information had been concentrated on Kambuja, Angkor, and the Khmer people. Never expecting to visit Champa, there seemed no point in my exploring that avenue. Even had I done so, I would not have been prepared for what I encountered.

I was plunged into a totally alien world. In appearance, religion, custom, language, and even diet, the Cham were utterly foreign. The country, abounding in lush foliage and with seasonal changes consisting only of a shift from wet to dry, with little change in temperature or humidity, lacked appeal. The birds, reptiles, and beasts of the jungle were of a bewildering variety and often of great danger. It is little wonder that I found this strange new world confusing.

The Cham were an entirely different ethnic breed. Their features were sharper, their noses longer and more pronounced, their eyes larger, and their coloration darker than mine. True, much of the darker hue came from exposure to the hot sun, since well-born ladies shunned the sun and many were almost as jade-white as Apricot Blossom.

The Cham dress was simplicity itself. We had arrived during the rainy season, when many wore jacket-like garments above their sheath-draped *sampots*. When the rain gave way to sunnier days, the loose upper garments were discarded by both men and women. Such immodesty would be unthinkable for a Chinese woman, but I soon became accustomed to the sight of female breasts. I, too, took to wearing nothing but the *sampot* as the only practical answer to the climate. My father looked on this askance, but he did not criticize my lack of decorum.

The staple diet of the Cham was rice, but it was much spicier than the cuisine of South China, since the Cham included hot peppers in almost every dish. They also used a pungent sauce made from rotting fish with most dishes.

The ritualistic Hindu faith of Champa was the antithesis of the Confucian eithic under which I was raised. The cult of Sivaism was the form favored in Champa. The reigning monarch was the *devaraja*, the reincarnation of Siva, the Destroyer and the Creator, as a living god-king. In the temples, the *devaraja* was symbolized by a stone lingum, a stylized phallus. The mythology woven into the Hindu faith, and its erotic overtones, appealed to me, but the pantheon of major and minor gods and goddesses, the concept of reincarnation, and the ritual practices repelled me.

Women in Vijaya enjoyed a status unheard of in China. For example, women could choose their own mates. In the marketplaces, trading was almost exclusively the province of women. Far from being relegated to the relative obscurity of the home, Cham women were much in evidence in public. Communal bathing was one aspect of sexual free-dom that met with my approval—once I overcame my initial shock.

In view of this emancipation of womanhood, there was one ritual I found mystifying. This was the practice known as *suttee*, wherein the wives voluntarily immolated them-selves on the funeral pyres of their deceased husbands. The first time I witnessed this barbaric act I was horrified. I have since become inured to the grisly spectacle, but I find it no easier to comprehend.

My composite picture of Vijaya, the kingdom of Champa, and the Cham people was built up piece by piece over many years. My initial impressions were formed during those early months as I gained proficiency in the spoken language.

Since I was starting out with absolutely no knowledge of Cham customs or the language, I was included for in-struction with the youngest children of the palace house-hold. I must have seemed a strange creature to them and quickly became the object of their hostility. This attitude was not confined to the children, but was also shared by my Brahman mentors.

To remove myself from this embarrassing atmosphere, I applied myself with an unaccustomed diligence. Within a few weeks, my application was rewarded by my being shifted to a group more my own age. All it seemed that I had achieved was to expose myself to even more virulent ridicule, exacerbated by the fact that I now could under-stand many of the cruel jibes.

At the time, I was growing rapidly and had reached that awkward, gawky age. In height, I was already equal to most adult Cham. This served to make me even more alien to my fellow students. It also made them exercise a degree of caution, which was just as well, since even though I exercised restraint, I am not of placid tempera-ment.

A day came when I was goaded beyond endurance. Emboldened by their numbers, my tormentors cornered me in a cul-de-sac of the temple's inner courtyard and their taunts and insults turned to violence. I don't know which one threw the stone. It doesn't matter. I was struck on the cheek. The sight of blood seemed to trigger them off and turn the students into an angry mob. They set upon me with flailing fists. Grimly, I fought back.

To my astonishment, I did not fight alone. A boy who had until now been one of the chief architects of my discomfort detached himself from my assailants to become an unlikely ally. What the final outcome would have been I do not know. The appearance of two priests abruptly concluded our melee. In the face of this common enemy, we beat a hasty retreat from the courtyard.

When we considered ourselves safely beyond the reach of the priestly authority, we paused to dust ourselves off and gingerly explore our bruises. My champion caught my eye and favored me with a broad grin. I chuckled in response, and an unspoken bond was born.

His name was Sri Vidyanandana, a ranking prince of the royal house. Vidya, a contraction I found more manageable, was never able to explain what had prompted him to jump to my defense. As a result of that brief alliance in combat, we became inseparable companions. I jumped overnight from an outcast to an accepted member of the group. Of even greater benefit, when in the company of the prince, my comings and goings from the palace compound were not subjected to the surveillance of our military jailers.

Together, Vidya and I explored the marketplaces, stole fruit and sugarcane from vendors' stalls, watched with awe the performances of jugglers and acrobats, swam in the reservoirs and irrigation canals, and haunted the commercial and dock areas previously forbidden to me. From Vidya, I learned a good deal.

I discovered that all the children under instruction in the palace temple were of a common sire, King Jaya Indravarman IV. Vidya never did tell me how many wives were boasted by the king, but the number must have been considerable. Including his four brothers and three sisters and his many half brothers and half sisters, Vidya was one of the king's one hundred and sixty-four living offspring.

I was intrigued by the small but sturdy horses ridden by the Cham. The riders used neither saddle nor stirrups, guiding their steeds skillfully with pressure from knees and thighs. Vidya was almost as skilled a horseman as myself, but he had difficulty mastering our larger horses. My favorite, a bay stallion named Sa-lu-tzu, after one of the famed six horses of the T'ang emperor, Tai Tsung, was a pacer of easy gait, yet Vidya could not get used to the saddle and stirrups, and so he preferred his smaller mare. My only complaint concerning the Cham horses was that they seemed too small and frail.

With Vidya as my almost constant companion, the weeks and months sped by.

It was in our fifth month in Vijaya that my father summoned me for a private interview. I presented myself promptly at the appointed hour. For the occasion, I changed from the *sampot,* which was by now all that I normally wore, to the jacket, loose trousers, and felt slippers my father preferred.

Our meeting took place in the garden of the main pavilion. It was late afternoon. My father sat on a wooden bench, shaded by flowering vines supported by a trellis. At a nod from him, I seated myself on the grass at his feet.

Without preamble, he spoke, his eyes downcast, as though in contemplation. "My son, I am sorely troubled."

My father's face was drawn and he seemed to have aged. I felt a twinge of guilt that I had gone my way with but little thought of him over the past few months. Respectfully, I waited for him to continue.

"The king was to have dispatched a messenger to advise Lin-an of our whereabouts. More than enough time has passed for me to have received some word from the emperor. I have heard nothing. My requests for an audience with the king have been to no avail. Wang, who acts as my intermediary and interpreter in these matters, is evasive. We are not being mistreated, but we are nonetheless prisoners. We are being held here as hostages, although for what purpose I have not divined.

"Of us all, only you have attained any useful command of the language or have any freedom of movement. It may be that you have heard gossip that might shed some light on this matter."

For me, life had become so pleasant that I had dwelt but little on our predicament as a party. Still, I had heard nothing that related to our situation. Our presence seemed of little concern to the average Cham and to the Chinese merchants I had chanced to meet in the commercial district.

"Honored father, I confess that I have questioned no one on this subject. Nor has any information concerning us been volunteered in my presence. The talk in the marketplace, and throughout the city, is concerned chiefly with preparations for war with the Khmer, and little else."

My father's brows drew down and his lips compressed. "Ah. It is as I suspected. I questioned Wang on such a possibility. He assured me that no action was contemplated against the Khmer. Merchant Wang has been instructed to foster this impression. I still do not perceive the exact purpose of our detention, but it is in some way connected with the rivalry between Champa and Kambuja. In considering this, I have concluded that our capture by Cham pirates was not a matter of chance."

My father gazed upon me intently and spoke deliberately. "My son, henceforth you must be my eyes and ears in this hostile realm. In addition, I must charge you with two specific tasks.

"The first of these concerns our ship. The king assured me that it would be made ready for sea travel. Wang has advised me that this work is progressing favorably. I believe this to be a falsehood. Without arousing suspicion, I hope you can find out exactly what is being done with respect to these repairs.

"The second task requires even more discretion. I have need of the services of a captain or officer of a Chinese merchantman who can be trusted to convey a message to Canton. Whoever accepts the role of courier will be amply rewarded. I will rely on you to locate such a man in such a way that Wang has no knowledge of the contact."

My father took such a lengthy pause that I felt the interview was concluded. "I shall do my best to comply with your wishes, honored sire," I said as I rose to my feet.

My father was not quite ready to dismiss me. He looked up at me reflectively. "I have observed in you a restlessness of spirit, my son. Like the wind, you cannot be easily bound or chained. In this quality, as in appearance, you remind me much of your mother. I have no wish to change your character, but I must caution you to temper your actions with prudence. The tasks I have imposed on you are fraught with danger. I could not forgive myself if you came to harm. I counsel you to proceed with extreme caution."

I was happy to receive my father's confidence and trust but I found his parting remarks somewhat puzzling. It should not have been necessary for him to point out the dangers of my mission. It was the only time I had ever heard him refer to my headstrong nature or to my mother. This was the closest I had ever seen my father come to displaying emotion. In some oblique fashion, I felt he had tried to convey some larger message.

The first of my tasks proved ridiculously easy. Vidya and I had argued the advantages and disadvantages of Cham and Chinese ship design and sail-rigging. We had visited the shipyards on several occasions. The naval slipways adjoined the civil yards, although in the past we had paid them scant attention. It was a simple matter for me to pursue the same argument and suggest a visit to the shipyards to prove a point.

As we scrambled over the scaffolding and vessels in various stages of construction, I worked my way close to the naval slipways. From a vantage point on the deck of a merchant hull nearing completion, I had a reasonably clear view of the slipways. Our ship was nowhere to be seen on the ways. Then I spotted the familiar high poop among the number of other ships tied to a jetty on the far side of the ways. Even without a closer inspection, I could make out the stump of the mainmast and the damaged poop. No workmen were to be seen. From its outward appearance, it looked as though little or nothing had been done to effect repairs.

When I reported this to my father, he didn't seem at all surprised. It was not necessary, he said, to attempt a closer scrutiny.

My second task, that of locating a trustworthy courier, proved to be a much more difficult assignment.

chapter 4

I HAD BECOME FRIENDLY WITH MOST OF THE CHINESE merchants who acted as agents for the exportation to China of such items as ivory, rhinoceros horns, sandalwood, cinnamon, and birds of exotic plumage. Many of these traders also acted as importers of Chinese silk, porcelain, celadon, fibers, gold, and non-precious metals. It was a two-way trade of a seasonal character. The northeast monsoon winds favored maritime passage from China to Champa, Kambuja, and kingdoms to the west. The southwest monsoon reversed that trade pattern.

We had become unwilling guests in Vijaya during the early part of the northeast monsoon season. Now the winds were shifting to the southwest. More and more vessels were arriving from the island kingdoms and beyond. While this increased our chances of relaying a message to Canton, it reduced our chances of leaving Vijaya for our onward voyage to Angkor. It was a prospect that caused my father considerable concern—all the more so since, as I learned from one of her handmaidens, Apricot Blossom was three months with child. Now, unfortunately, the Cham king could claim with some legitimacy that it would be unlikely that the Sung emperor would send a naval escort, and the voyage to Angkor could not be undertaken with safety until the shift of seasonal wind some six months hence.

By now I was a familiar figure in the commercial district and along the waterfront. Vidya, who had not initially displayed much enthusiasm for commercial matters, had developed a lively interest in trade and trade goods due to his association with me in our forays into the commercial section. There was, therefore, nothing to arouse suspicion in our frequenting the docks and warehouses of the waterfront.

Through the Chinese and Cham merchants, Vidya and I had ready access to ships in the harbor. Arab, Indonesian, and Indian merchantmen were now arriving in increasing numbers. Though these were not suited to my purpose, they could not be neglected. Wherever possible, however, I concentrated on Chinese vessels. The problem, I soon discovered, was how a fourteen-year-old youth could establish a close enough relationship with the masters and officers of these ships to broach the delicate matter entrusted to me. Finding a trustworthy courier began to look like a hopeless undertaking.

Several weeks elapsed and I was beginning to despair. Then one morning I was hailed by name from the deck of a large junk tied to the dock. I looked up into the beaming countenance of a weather-beaten sailing master who had befriended me and regaled me with many a tall tale in Changsha.

Vidya and I scrambled aboard the vessel. In response to the mariner's questions, I related the events that had brought my father and myself to these shores. Even though Vidya understood very little Chinese, I did not divulge that my father and his entourage were other than honored guests in Vijaya. When Vidya was out of earshot, I told the sailing master that I had an important message from my father that required the utmost secrecy. The puzzled seafarer agreed to treat the matter as confidential. It was arranged that I would meet him on board the following morning.

My father had prepared two messages: one was addressed to the emperor in Lin-an; the other was to be delivered personally to the governor of Canton. The second message contained instructions for the speedy dispatch of the first message and also specified that the courier was to be handsomely rewarded. Wrapped in a cloth, the messages were tied securely to the inside of my thigh and hidden from view by my *sampot*.

Vidya was watching cargo being loaded amidships.

Screened from view by the high poop, I passed the messages to the sailing master. I stressed the urgency of the mission and swore him to secrecy, adding that he would be well rewarded by the governor of Canton for performing this service for my father.

As Vidya and I disembarked, I paused at the bottom of the gangplank to wipe perspiration from my brow with the cloth that had concealed the messages. I dropped it into the lapping water next to the dock piling.

The merchant ship set sail a day later. When a week had gone by, and there was no sign to indicate local knowledge of my guilty secret, I breathed easier. My father, I was relieved to note, looked much less harried.

The weakening of the northwest monsoon produced a marked change in the weather. The rain was reduced to an occasional evening thundershower, then ceased altogether. The days grew hotter and hotter as the sun beat down mercilessly from a cloudless sky.

There were several ornamental lakes within the palace grounds. I started to spend an hour or two each evening bathing in the lake closest to our pavilion. While I was the only one in our compound to avail myself of this opportunity, I was by no means alone in the tree-shaded pool. Many of the Cham royal household made it a practice to refresh themselves in the pool. In the cool of the evening, the girls and women were well represented.

I must admit that a good part of the attraction for me was the spectacle of the nude girl bathers. I was beset by speculative fantasies, but I lacked the nerve to translate them into reality. This was not so with my male companions, who joined the women in contests of splashing and mock struggle. As darkness descended, many couples detached themselves to seek the privacy of the surrounding shrubbery. Throaty laughter and low giggles coming from the leafy bowers inflamed my already overwrought imagination.

One evening I lounged against the stone facing at the side of the pool. Suddenly something seized my ankle beneath the water. I cried out, lost my balance, and fell sideways into the water. When I floundered to the surface, I found myself looking up at the laughing countenance of White Lotus, a younger half sister of Vidya.

White Lotus was an attractive and spirited girl a year or so younger than myself. I had noticed her often on the palace grounds. We had exchanged smiles and I would have liked to become better acquainted with her, but I could not get up my courage to the point of approaching her. Vidya had been amused by my timidity, claiming that White Lotus was attracted to me and needed just a little encouragement.

Now she stood before me, a vision of radiant loveliness. She was chest deep in the water, her firm young breasts immersed to their pert nipples. The rays of the dying sun glistened on her wet hair and sparkled from the droplets of water clinging to her upper body. She was bathed in a red-gold nimbus.

When I recovered my senses, I rose to my feet close beside her. She laughed and pushed me playfully. Catching her arm, I pulled her off balance and pushed her under the water. When she rose, sputtering and laughing, I reached to submerge her again, but she ducked beneath my extended hand to catch me around the waist in a tight embrace. Her breasts pressed against my lower chest and her legs were twined around mine.

It was as though fire flooded my loins. My manhood rose unbidden to press hard against her flesh. Her lips parted in an odd smile. She looked up into my face. Then, beneath the water, I felt her small hand slide up my inner thigh until it clutched my swollen penis gently but firmly. Then, with a tinkling laugh, she twisted loose from my circling arms and was gone.

For the next three days I sought her in vain at the small lake. I concluded, sadly, that for her our meeting had been some kind of game, and I was angry that my body had betrayed my quick passion. I tried to put her out of my mind, but with scant success.

On the fourth evening after my brief encounter with White Lotus, I emerged from the lake after darkness had fallen. A pale moon lit the grass and foliage as I absently knotted my *sampot* in a clearing by the pool's edge. Although I heard no sound, a sudden motion caught my attention. I whirled around to find White Lotus standing at the edge of the clearing.

She advanced, took my hand, and wordlessly led me into the screening bushes. I followed her along a small footpath for several hundred yards. We came to a small clearing in which stood a tree-screened pavilion. At her heels, I ascended the steps.

She threw open the shutters. Moonlight flooded the single room of the interior. It was simply furnished. A stone statue of Siva stood in one corner on a wooden pedestal. The only other item of furniture was a low bed strewn with tiger and leopard skins.

I heard a faint rustling as White Lotus let her *sampot* slip to the straw matting. Proudly, she stood before me lithely naked. She moved to me and deftly untied the waist knot of my garment. As it slid to my ankles, White Lotus gave a throaty chuckle as my swelling manhood was exposed to the moonlight. She pulled me down on the bed at her side.

Once again I had cause to curse my tumultuous passion. It seemed that I had no sooner penetrated her warm, tight receptacle when I exploded in an unrestrained burst. I rolled away from her and lay on my back upon the soft skins. The only sounds were my hoarse breathing, the hum of nocturnal insects, and the chirping of wall lizards.

A new sound intruded. She made a low crooning sound as she bit my neck and shoulders. Her small hand caressed my chest, belly, and loins. Under these tender ministrations, it was not long before my prowess was fully restored.

My second performance was more satisfactory. White Lotus restrained my impetuous assault with softly murmured instructions that subsided into low moans as the rhythm increased in tempo. Wave after wave of ecstasy swept over me. Finally, in one great lunge, which she met with an upward thrust, the waves crested in a crashing, foaming breaker. With a shuddering sigh, she went limp beneath me.

With our sweat-streaked bodies locked in embrace, we slept, oblivious to the insects of the night.

During the next few weeks, White Lotus introduced me to ecstasies I had not dreamed existed. She explained to me that a mutually fulfilling conjugal relationship was a basic tenet of her Hindu faith. As was the practice, she had been deflowered by a Brahman priest when she had attained puberty. Thereafter, her instruction in erotic practices had been taken over by the older women of the royal household. There was, she assured me, a Brahman scripture, the *Kama Sutra,* which outlined in detail the nuances of lovemaking and an infinite number of variations in intercourse. There were no orifices of our bodies left unexplored under her tutelage. In me, she found a willing pupil. It did not occur to me at the time that she displayed consummate skill in the practice, as well as the theory, of her art.

When I was with White Lotus, I was enraptured, my appetite as insatiable as her own. When we were apart, I was miserable. I am sure that Vidya noticed my distraction, but he said nothing. My nocturnal meetings with White Lotus were in the seclusion of the small pavilion I had come to think of as our exclusive property. In public, bathing in the evenings or when I encountered her on the palace grounds, I treated her with studied indifference. Such was my infatuation that I had eyes for no other young maidens and did not notice their giggles or appraising glances.

When White Lotus informed me casually that she was to accompany a royal party on a journey to the south, I was plunged into the depths of despair. She was to be gone for two weeks or more. I couldn't see how I was to survive such a lengthy separation. Fortunately for my sanity, other matters intruded to distract me from my abject grief.

Early in the eighth month of our sojourn in Vijaya, my father was summoned to the presence of the king. On his return from this audience, my father assembled the official members of his entourage. I was flattered to be included in their company.

The king, my father stated, had informed him that a message had been received from the Sung court advising that a naval escort was being assembled at Canton and would soon be dispatched to Vijaya. The Cham king was most happy that we could now continue our interrupted mission to the Khmer captial. The king regretted any inconvenience we might have experienced during our long wait and added that his shipwrights and riggers had been unable to repair our vessel. The king would place one of his own ships at our disposal. In closing, the king had added that it was his wish that his son, Sri Vidyanandana, accompany us to the Khmer court in order that the boy's education could be completed under the high priest of Angkor Wat.

At the news that Vidya and I would be able to continue our friendship, I was elated, but the thought that I was to be parted from White Lotus brought me to the verge of utter dejection.

I had little time to dwell on my sorrow. Our military guards had not been withdrawn and the restrictions of our movements continued. I alone had the freedom of movement I had enjoyed over the months. Consequently, my father commissioned me to act in the capacity of a liaison agent between the merchant Wang and himself in making preparations for the forthcoming voyage. I went about my duties with a heavy heart.

I was advised of White Lotus' return by a message relayed through a servant. That night we met at our trysting place. It would have been a joyous reunion if it had not been for my knowledge that we must soon part. I kept this from her, though she chided me on my seeming indifference after our long separation.

The day that the six Sung warships appeared off Vijaya marked our ninth month in the Cham capital almost to the day. I should have been overjoyed at the sight of the proud junks, but I was, in fact, steeped in misery. I sought out Vidya and confided to him my love for his sister and my grief at the prospect of our parting.

I had expected sympathetic understanding from my friend, and I was ill-prepared for his reaction to my disclosures.

"Do you believe yourself to be in love with White Lotus?" Vidya asked incredulously.

I nodded dejectedly. "We love each other."

"By the gods, do you think you are the only one to share her favors?"

I turned angrily on Vidya. He held up his hand and looked concerned. "Tartar," he said rapidly, "I am sure she is fond of you, and she is very skilled at making love. She has bragged of her conquest of you and claims you to be a marvelous lover, but she cannot return your love. While she may have some freedom of choice concerning a husband, it must be within her caste. You are of royal lineage, but not of a reigning house . . . and you are not of our blood. Has she not told you the purpose of her recent visit to the south? It was to arrange for her marriage to a prince of the realm of Panduranga. She should have told you this. She has been betrothed to him for some years."

I was shaken. My thoughts were in turmoil. Vidya had no reason to lie. He must be speaking the truth, yet I could not bring myself to believe him. I mumbled something, then left hurriedly before he could see that my eyes were clouded by tears.

That evening I angrily confronted White Lotus with my newfound knowledge. Desperately, I wanted her to deny my charges. She did not, and she seemed surprised that I should be enraged. She took my hand, but I snatched it from her grasp.

"Do not be angry with me, my Tartar. I *do* love you. I really do. No one has brought me the pleasure you have in our lovemaking. Perhaps no one else ever shall. But it could not last."

"Why not?" I snapped. But I felt sick inside due to her tacit admission that she had had other lovers.

"Surely you knew that I have to marry within royal circles. Then, too, we both knew you must someday leave Vijaya. Even before I left for the south, I knew that day was soon at hand. It is now upon us. Why, then, are you angry?"

I had no answer for her simple logic, yet I felt betrayed. I brought myself to look at her. She sat before me, naked upon the low bed. She looked so small and helpless that my heart melted.

We made love that night with a ferocity and passion unmatched in our previous lovemaking. Spent, I lay on my back, gazing into the darkness. White Lotus snuggled up to me and spoke soothingly.

"My husband-to-be is over thirty. I am sure he cannot match your strength, my love." Then she giggled softly. "He does not know I am with child. Our firstborn will be of your seed."

My throat was dry. I could not bring myself to answer.

chapter 5

ALTHOUGH OUR PARTY EMBARKED EARLY, IT WAS ALMOST midday before Vidya and his attendants joined the ship. The lines were slipped. As we pulled away from the wharf, I scanned the faces on the dockside. White Lotus was nowhere to be seen.

As we emerged from the lagoon into the open sea, we were joined by the Sung warships that had been anchored offshore. We set a southerly course in the early afternoon.

The winds, though mainly from the southwest, were light and variable. Our progress was slow. Our Cham ship could sail closer to the wind, and this gave us a somewhat faster speed than the Chinese junks. By nightfall our escort was dropping astern.

The next morning, the Chinese warships were far distant on our port quarter. In the early afternoon we rounded a steeply rising headland and altered our course to the southwest into a freshening wind. By dusk, our escorting ships were completely out of sight.

The morning of our third day at sea found us off a coastline of forbidding cliffs. Two ships put out from this rocky shoreline, which appeared to offer no haven. The vessels bore down on us, then shaped their courses to parallel our own. A Cham officer told me that a large bay, its dogleg entrance hidden by an offshore island and almost impossible to detect from seaward, lay securely hidden behind the rugged foreshore. The Cham ships, he advised, were warships assigned to augment our escort. I noted with interest that although no oars or oarsmen were in evidence, oar ports extended along the sides of the Cham warships.

For the next four days we proceeded along the coast. On the morning of the fifth day, one of our Cham escorting vessels was detached to continue to the mouth of the Mekong River and upstream to alert the Khmer capital of our coming. Our ship and the remaining Cham escort closed a shoreline marked by two prominent hills. We anchored in a shallow bay to await the arrival of our Sung escort.

For the first few days of the voyage, I had had little interest in the passage. The memory of White Lotus haunted most of my waking hours. Her disclosure that she was with child weighed heavily upon me. I had little appetite, and I slept poorly. Until now I had considered marriage too far in the future to merit serious thought. Fatherhood had been a vague concept. Now all that had changed. My thoughts were in turmoil.

That White Lotus could have invented the story of her pregnancy occurred to me. Even if she was with child, had not she had other lovers? How can a woman know with certainty who fathers her child if she has taken many lovers? I did not know the answers to these questions. They troubled me.

For several days I avoided the company of my fellow passengers. Vidya, noting my distraction, left me to my own devices. Gradually, however, my mood of depression lightened. White Lotus was never far from my thoughts, but I began to take more interest in things around me. I sought out the companionship of Vidya. We speculated on Angkor and the Khmer court. If he noticed that I studiously avoided any reference to his half sister, he neither remarked on the omission nor raised the subject himself.

About noon of our second day at anchor, the characteristic lugsails and high stern poops of junks were sighted. By evening all six ships of our Chinese escort rode at anchor alongside us in the bay.

At first light we weighed anchor. With the Cham escort leading the way, we proceeded through waters that gradually changed from blue-green to brown as we neared the Mekong delta. How the pilot could determine at which point to enter the unbroken expanse of mangroves that marked the outer limits of the delta was a mystery.

The delta was flooded as far as the eye could see. We were surrounded on all sides by a flat expanse of brown water broken here and there by clumps of trees. The pilot, determining the navigable channel by fringing, partially submerged palmetto fronds, guided our upstream course unerringly. It was slow work. Anchoring at night and during the ebbing tide, and sailing only when the flooding tide assisted us, it took the better part of five days to reach a point where four branches of the river converged. We passed close to a fishing village on the western bank to enter a fork leading to the northwest.

A sluggish current assisted us, and by nightfall we emerged into a vast, inland lake. We sailed all through the night. At dawn we were joined by a number of Khmer warships. It was an impressive convoy that sailed majestically northward.

Sometime during the dark hours, we dropped anchor near the head of the lake at a point where a small river emptied into the Great Lake. It had taken us ten and a half months to complete our voyage from Canton. I was a year older, and much wiser, than when we left Changsha to venture into the unknown.

I surveyed the shoreline with curiosity. Grass-roofed huts, dwarfed by a backdrop of towering trees, straggled along the lakefront. Nowhere could I see anything that even faintly resembled the descriptions of fabled Angkor. My heart sank. Surely this collection of dilapidated dwellings couldn't represent Yasodharapura, the present Angkor capital of the Khmer empire.

A Cham officer laughed when I voiced my bewilderment. The capital and old city-states of Angkor were situated some thirteen miles inland from the lake, he assured me, adding that the huge temples would probably surpass any description I had been given. I would see them for myself soon enough, he stated, pointing to a flotilla of small and large craft putting out from the lakeshore and heading toward us.

As my father's party, and Vidya and his retinue, disembarked, larger craft were coming alongside our Cham ship and the Sung warships to unload our effects, militia, and horses.

The voyage had been a series of surprises piled one atop another. They were not yet at an end.

As our craft was rowed past the Cham escort, which had been detached to bring word of our coming, I glanced up toward the bow of the vessel. Standing in clear view, and looking down at me with an amused smile, was a Cham I was not likely to forget. The face was that of the pirate commander I had sworn to kill. I was about to bring this to my father's attention, but we slid beneath the bow of the anchored vessel and the grinning Cham was blocked from view. What was this murdering cutthroat doing on board the Cham warship? It was a question I resolved to put to my father, but it was several days before an opportunity presented itself.

We were met at Yasodharapura with incredible pomp. High officials of the court and temple hierarchies were on hand to bid us welcome. Nobles rode caparisoned elephants. Slaves shielded the aristocrats and officials from the sun with parasols of scarlet silk. Flags and banners fluttered in the breeze. Musicians with drums, cymbals, and flutes added a festive touch. Soldiers, both mounted and on foot, were in serried ranks, holding back a throng of curious spectators.

My father, Apricot Blossom, and Prince Vidya were provided with slave-borne palanquins with golden litters. I was transported in a horse-drawn chariot. The rest of our respective retinues were on foot as we proceeded slowly along a route crowded on both sides by spectators in a holiday mood.

Vidya and his attendants, accompanied by Brahman priests and a military escort, separated from the procession, while our party was conducted to the quarters allocated to my father.

That my father enjoyed a position of honor and respect was reflected by the palatial dwellings and outbuildings provided us. The main residence, fronted by a stone-paved courtyard, was a splendid structure with a steeply pitched roof of bronze-glazed tile. The eaves and roof ends were ornately decorated. The portals and lintel were of gilded wood, and the doors and shutters were inlaid with mother-of-pearl and precious stones.

With the exception of the stables, all the buildings were elevated to a one-story level. This kept them well clear of the soaked earth during the rainy season and provided a circulation of cooling air in all seasons. Tall shade trees and spacious grounds with ornamental pools also helped to make the heat and humidity less oppressive.

An eight-foot wooden wall enclosed the property. The massive main gates facing south led from the avenue to the main courtyard. A smaller set of gates on the north side led to a boat landing on the two-hundred-foot-wide water basin that surrounded the rectangular two-mile wall encompassing the temple of Angkor Wat.

On our arrival, we encountered an added feature we had not anticipated. More than one hundred slaves were prostrating themselves face-down in the courtyard. Our own servants were sufficient to minister to our wants and needs, but my father could hardly reject this Khmer gesture of hospitality.

The Khmer called the slaves by the collective term *chung*. The slaves were considered subhuman and held in such contempt that even sexual intercourse between master and slave was unthinkable. While quarters were provided for our servants, the *chung* had to make do as best they could on the hard-packed earth beneath our dwellings. Four slaves—two girls of about my own age, a young boy, and an older man—were assigned to me as personal servants. I was not unkind to them and, frankly, could find few tasks for them to perform. Like everyone else in our household, I soon came to accept the presence of the slaves as normal and was barely aware of their existence.

In religion, language, culture, customs, cuisine, and dress, there are many similarities between Champa and Kambuja. Our nine-month sojourn in Vijaya was of assistance to our adjustment to Angkor. That no restrictions were imposed on our movements made the settling-in process all the more pleasant.

A full week went by after our arrival before my father was summoned to present his diplomatic credentials to the Khmer king, Tribhuvanadityavarman. On his return from the audience, my father requested my presence. Among other matters discussed at the palace had been a continuation of my education. The services of a suitable Brahman tutor had been contracted.

Before taking my leave of my father, I recalled the incident of seeing the pirate captain on board the Cham ship of war. I told my father of the encounter. He received the news with no outward sign of agitation.

"You may remember, my son, that I suggested some months ago that the pirate attack might not have been a matter of chance. Evidence points more and more in that direction. What you have just disclosed is added confirmation that our capture was arranged by the Cham king to serve some purpose.

"As you know, the trade goods and gifts for the Khmer king, which were lost at the time of our capture, were not recovered. They were not even mentioned again by the king. In my estimation, they were part of an agreed-upon fee. The Cham king seemed amused when I suggested this, and he made no attempt to deny my allegation."

It was not my place to question my father's judgment, yet I could not see what purpose would be served by our detention in Vijaya.

"The Cham king used us as hostages. Our safety was used as a bargaining factor. As I am an official representative of the Sung court, that court was naturally concerned for my well-being. I was an envoy to the Khmer court, which gave the members of that court some interest, as well. I do not know of any overtures to the Khmer court, but through the messages I received by the hand of the Sung naval commander I am aware of the negotiations at Lin-an.

"The Cham king was to have sent a messenger to the Sung court to advise the emperor of our fate and whereabouts. He did better than that. He sent one of his top ministers—not as a mere messenger, but in the capacity of an envoy. In return for our safe conduct to Angkor, the Cham wanted Chinese participation in a war against the Khmer.

"Emperor Hsiao Tsung, Filial Ancestor, wisely rejected the proposed alliance, since Sung interests favor foreign trade, not military adventure. As a guarantee for our safety, he detained the Cham envoy. I am advised that the envoy was not at all concerned at this treatment, which leads me to two conclusions. The first is that the Cham did not expect the Sung to sponsor their plans to attack Kambuja, but they *did* want to assure themselves of Chinese neutrality in the event of war. The second deduction is that we were never in much danger and that the Cham king fully intended to release us in his own good time.

"When my message, thanks to your excellent efforts, reached the emperor, he acted promptly to assemble a naval escort and to resupply us with militia, trade goods, and royal gifts. The Cham king was advised of this development and promptly displayed every evidence of full cooperation."

My father paused, extending his hand from the sleeve of his gown in order to pour himself a cup of tea. While he sipped the steaming liquid, I digested what he had told me. If his assessment was correct, all the events of the past eleven months were linked together and the presence of the pirate leader on board the warship was no mere coincidence. But, try as I might, I could not see a clear pattern to the events. I voiced this to my father.

He nodded. His hand once more disapppeared into his sleeve as he folded his arms across his chest. "What emerges from all this, my son, is extremely interesting. We have been given a glimpse of the complex character of an ambitious man, King Jaya Indravarman IV. Yet it is only a glimpse. The king is an opportunist of infinite guile.

"I am convinced, for example, that, with or without the arrival of the Sung warship, we would have been conducted here to Angkor . . . although I think it might have been a month or so later, when the seasonal floodwater subsided somewhat. We would have arrived almost as we did, on board a Cham vessel escorted by Cham warships . . . and with your friend, the young prince, as an addition to our party. The only changes were in timing forced upon the king by the arrival of the Sung escort, and that escort itself. Had the Sung warships not appeared, I think that our original trade goods and gifts might have been produced as miraculously as they disappeared.

"How does your mortal enemy, the pirate, fit into this picture? I do not know, but I suspect he is more than the pirate he appears to be. But of this I *am* sure: he fits into the scheme that has shaped our fortunes since the typhoon—the resolve of the Cham king to wage war on his Khmer neighbor."

The months following our arrival were busy ones. Apricot Blossom gave birth to a son: a half brother more than fifteen years my junior and younger than his oldest half brother by more than thirty-five years. The rainy season ended. The dry season was upon us and within three months the Great Lake shrank almost sevenfold in volume. The Year of the Monkey yielded to the Year of the Cock. As I explored Angkor and its surroundings, the sharp and painful memory of White Lotus dimmed.

Angkor is not a city. It is a limited region where a series of Khmer kings have established their royal capitals over the past three and a half centuries. On ascending his throne, each king is obliged to embark on a public works program. With this undertaking launched, the king is free to devote himself to the design and construction of one or more temples to commemorate his reign. At Angkor the result is an astonishing concentration of awesome stone structures within a relatively confined area.

Seafarers are prone to exaggeration, but in the case of Angkor their descriptions had fallen far short of reality. Such barbaric splendor, such prodigious works in stone, beggar description.

The city that received us, Yasodharapura, was the third capital at Angkor to bear that name. More than twelve miles in perimeter, it was bounded by a wooden stockade. At its center, a temple named Bakheng was perched atop a two-hundred-foot-high hill. This temple was constructed along with the first city to be called Yasodharapura and dated from the early tenth century.

The urbanized portion of the capital consisted of a concentration of buildings and dwellings around the royal palace and royal residential compounds and the various temple complexes. The remaining area within the fortifications was given over to rice fields and rural hamlets clustering along the network of canals.

Beyond the city, farmland, dotted with bustling communities and laced with roads, irrigation canals, and busy waterways, stretched as far as the eye could see. Two immense reservoirs stood just outside the capital, each more than four miles in length and about a mile and a half in width. These artificial lakes stored the abundant water of the rainy season for controlled release during the dry season.

The most prominent landmark within the city was the

huge central tower of the pyramidal temple, Baphuon.
Constructed about a century ago on a man-made promontory, the temple is the largest of the Angkor complex. But
by far the most impressive temple was the most recently
constructed, Angkor Wat, which received its finishing
touches less than ten years before my birth. In truth, I
have never before or since seen anything to compare with
the beauty and symmetry of the temple. Dedicated to
Vishnu, and serving as a mausoleum for its builder, King
Suryavarman II, there is scarcely a square inch of the
portals, supports, and galleries that is not carved. The
temple group is truly a symphony in stone. If I close my
eyes, I can see it now as I saw it then from the window of
my sleeping quarters, its gold-sheathed central tower
and flanking towers rearing gracefully against the dawn
sky.

As I have already said, there are many similarities between Champa and Kambuja. There are also many differences. I would have liked to explore the city and
surrounding countryside with Vidya to make comparisons,
but I saw him infrequently now that he was under instruction at the sanctuary. My observations will have to suffice.

While Brahmanism was the prevailing state religion of
both kingdoms, it was the cult of Siva that was favored
in Vijaya, and that of Vishnu was dominant in Angkor.
Sanskrit, which I had not yet mastered, was the written
language of state in both countries. There were many
variations in the spoken tongues, but there was enough in
common that I could follow Khmer from the outset. The
climates of both kingdoms were tropical, but the wet- and
dry-season cycles were reversed. Champa's rainy season
was governed by the northeast monsoon winds, while the
rains in Kambuja came from the moisture-laden winds
of the southwest monsoon and served to temper somewhat
what would normally have been the hottest months.

The major difference was in the people. The Khmer
were of different racial stock from the Cham. The Khmer
were shorter, stockier, and darker. Their faces were
rounder and their features coarser than those of the Cham.
Khmer hair, worn in a plait atop the head, was frizzier
than that of the Cham. In all, apart from the fact that
Khmer women tended to have larger breasts, I found the
Cham the more appealing to my tastes.

I learned something of the realm's more recent history.

Suryavarman II, the builder of Angkor Wat, was succeeded by a cousin in 1150. The new king, a devout Buddhist, reigned ten years before his own demise. His eldest son and rightful heir, Jayavarman, was away on a military campaign, and a younger half brother took advantage of the situation to ascend the throne. Jayavarman, a devout Buddhist like his father, renounced the throne rather than plunge the country into a bloody fratricidal war and went into self-imposed exile in Champa.

The new monarch, Yasovarman II, reigned only five years before being challenged by an ambitious upstart. Hearing of Yasovarman's troubles, the legitimate heir, Jayavarman, hurried from Champa to Angkor but arrived too late to save his half brother's life or the throne, which had already been seized by the usurper. For a second time, Jayavarman went into voluntary exile to avoid bloodshed.

The usurper, King Tribhuvanadityavarman, an unwieldy name that I found difficult to pronounce, let alone remember, was the reigning monarch at the time of our arrival. Fearing plots against his life, he seldom ventured from his closely guarded palace. I never did, in fact, see the king.

The Khmer were well aware that their bellicose neighbor, Champa, was preparing for war. There was much gossip concerning this in the marketplaces. Strong Khmer forces were deployed to the east of the capital, along the probable line of Cham advance, and the people were confident that a Cham thrust would be turned back as it had been a decade earlier.

When the Cham struck, it was from a totally unsuspected direction.

chapter 6

EARLY IN THE YEAR OF THE COCK, 1177, THE TENTH DAY of the second month was a day that could never fade from my memory.

I awoke in the predawn Hours of the Tiger. What had aroused me was unaccustomed noise. In the compound there were the sounds of running feet and terse orders. From a greater distance, I could make out a muffled beating of drums and the rise and fall of shouting. The mournful blare of conch shells intruded above the other sounds. The square of sky visible through my window was suffused with a wavering pink.

Jumping up from my sleeping mat, I hastily donned a *sampot*. Even before I went to the window, I realized the city must be under attack. Flames flickered against the northwestern skyline, and from the window the distant tumult of battle could be heard more distinctly. Below me, the shadowy figures of our armed guards hurried to take up their posts on the compound walls.

I rushed from my sleeping quarters and bounded down the steps to the courtyard. I made out Horse-master Chang and hailed him.

"Where is the fighting?" I queried.

"We are not sure, Siao Hu. Some cavalry officers rode by a few minutes ago. They said that the main attack seems to be directed against the section of the royal palace and northwestern temples, but the cavalry was on its way to reinforce the garrison at Angkor Wat."

"Is it an attempt to overthrow the king?"

"It is an invasion by the Cham army."

"How? How could they approach without warning?"

"They came by ship. The Cham officer told us that a Cham fleet appeared as if by magic in the Great Lake."

Impossible, I thought. It is almost three hundred miles from the mouth of the Mekong to the head of the Great Lake. How could an invasion fleet travel such a distance and not be detected in time for Khmer craft to warn of its approach? But it had happened; that was obvious. And then I knew how it had been accomplished. In my mind's eye I saw again the Cham warships and recalled the rows of oar ports on their sides. Using wind, tide, *and* galley slaves, the fast Cham ships could easily have outpaced sailing craft in the approaches and on the Tonle Sap, the Great Lake.

The seriousness of the situation struck me. The major part of the Khmer forces were to the east. Caught unaware, the Khmer warships in the lake would have been no obstacle to the Cham fleet. The defense forces of Yasodharapura would have been unprepared for an assault, and the wooden stockades could not have withstood an attack in force. Unless Khmer reinforcements could be brought back to the city without delay, the capital must surely fall.

"Has my father been advised of the situation?" I asked Chang.

"Yes. The captain of the guard has done so."

It suddenly struck me that both Horse-master Chang and I had been conversing in hoarse whispers, as though loud conversation would bring the Cham invaders down upon us. The sounds of battle still came to us from a distance, yet within the compound sounds were muted and voices were subdued.

Assembling us in the courtyard, my father addressed us from the residence balcony. He had dressed in his ceremonial robes and was an imposing figure. His bearing, tone, and words had a calming effect.

He reminded us that he was an official envoy of the Dragon Throne. All within the confines of the compound were, accordingly, subjects of the Sung emperor; the compound itself was Chinese soil and strictly neutral in this struggle. We must, he cautioned, avoid any act of provocation. He counseled us to be vigilant, but to go about our daily chores calmly.

The senior staff members were invited to my father's quarters for detailed instructions. Here his briefing was more explicit and less sanguine. He observed that no emergency provisions for flight had been made. We had no choice but to remain where we were and hope for the best. We could offer sanctuary to armed forces of neither side lest we invite attack by pursuing forces. If attacked, we must try to parlay with the belligerents to point out our diplomatic status. He suggested, however, that this course of action might not be possible, since the attacking forces would probably be Cham troops flushed with victory, intent on rape and pillage, and unlikely to be swayed by reason. We could not hope to hold out for long against a sustained attack and must resist the initial onslaught with sufficient vigor to discourage a prolonged engagement. We were instructed to prepare for a siege as rapidly as possible without spreading alarm among the household and staff.

As we went about our tasks during the morning, the sounds of battle seemed to be drawing closer. A pall of smoke hung over the capital, partially obscuring a coppery sun. There was a scattered movement of Khmer troops on the roadway fronting our compound. This military traffic became heavier as the morning progressed.

At noon I learned by questioning an officer that the palace and surrounding compounds had been overrun and the Khmer king had been killed in combat. The Khmer defending forces were falling back and regrouping at the temple complex of Angkor Wat. There was no news of Khmer relieving forces from the east. It was rumored, in fact, that a Cham army was advancing overland from the east.

In the early afternoon, gray-black smoke billowed skyward from the west. Throngs of peasants, their possessions loaded in horse-drawn carts or being trundled in hand carts, started to move along the roadway in a steady stream to the east. Women, carrying babies and further laden with shoulder-stick paniers, mingled with farmers pushing carts and children driving cattle. We were told that the Cham troops were sweeping forward from the west and setting fire to the ripening fields of rice in their path. The fleeing peasantry had no clear idea of where they were going other than a vague impression that safety lay in reaching the Siemreap River, to the east of the city. The Cham tactic seemed to be to clog the roads and waterways with refugees to hamper the further movement of Khmer troops.

Early in the Hours of the Monkey, at about four-thirty P.M., Cham forces launched their assault against the low outer walls of the Angkor Wat complex. From the windows of my quarters, I had a view of part of the southern wall on the other side of the moat-like basin. Cham troops, on rafts and sampans, crossed the waterway into a hail of arrows. Soldiers falling from the craft had little chance for survival in the crocodile-infested moat.

I watched with fascination as wave after wave of Cham troops reached the far bank and advanced on the perimeter wall. Forming a decorative delineation, rather than performing any defensive function, the wall did not long deter the attackers, yet it was just high enough to cut off my view of the battle.

From the earlier sounds, the initial attack on the complex was from the west, where fierce fighting must have taken place for control of the stone causeway bridging the basin at the main entrance portal to the complex. Now that the battle was joined in earnest within the complex grounds, it was close enough that I could distinguish individual sounds in the overall din—the shrill trumpeting of war elephants, the clash of arms in hand-to-hand combat, the hollow booming of drums, the blare of conch-shell signals, the hoarse shouting of combatants, and the screams of wounded animals and men.

This being their last redoubt within the city, the Khmer forces fought with desperation. The battle raged for well over three hours, seesawing backward and forward, but drawing ever eastward. Dust swirled within the temple grounds and mingled with the smoke that hung over the city like a shroud. As darkness approached, the sounds grew less distinct. I assumed that the fighting was now taking place within the galleries and on the tiered terraces of the temple itself.

When night blanketed the embattled city, the fighting had become localized within the temple complex, but it had not yet abated throughout the city. From the diminishing sounds, however, I assumed the daylong battle was lessening in intensity. Flames flickered along the northern and western skylines and leaped heavenward from within the grounds of Angkor Wat. The dancing flames were reflected eerily from the gilded towers and cast a red glow on the underside of the low-hanging pall of smoke.

With the coming of night, we breathed a little easier in our compound, but we did not relax our vigilance. It was assumed that an attack, if it was to come, would not be mounted until dawn. I cannot say why, but I did not share this sentiment. I heartily agreed with my father's order that no lights were to be shown and that all cooking fires were to be extinguished.

I had given thought to what role I could best play in a battle for our compound. With sword or spear, I could add but little to our militia defending the perimeter walls. One more crossbow would not serve to much advantage. But as an archer of some skill, even though I had had little practice for some time, I could perform a useful function. I could speed five shafts for every bolt fired from a crossbow and, at long range, with much more accuracy. What I needed was a vantage point that commanded as large an arc of fire as possible.

None of the outbuildings suited my purpose. The north-facing windows of the main residence looked over gardens where large trees obstructed the path of an arrow's flight. Still, if we were attacked on the northern wall and fighting spilled over into the gardens, the window of my sleeping quarters would prove useful. The long veranda at the front of our residential pavilion, commanding as it did an unbroken view of the courtyard and main gates, provided my best firing platform.

During the day, in slow stages in order not to alarm the servants, I assembled an ample stock of arrows in my quarters. When darkness descended, I positioned a strung bow at each end of the veranda and distributed filled quivers of arrows at intervals along the balustrade. I buckled on my sword and put on the jade thumb ring that had been a parting gift from my Jürched archery instructor in Changsha. With these preparations completed, there was nothing to do but await an attack I felt sure was imminent.

In the second hour of darkness, the sounds of battle had

all but subsided. Night sounds filtered through the darkness of the compound. Beyond the gates, the stream of families fleeing eastward had become a thin trickle. There were no signs of attack developing, and I began to doubt the reliability of my instincts. Restive, I left the shadows of the veranda and went to seek out Horse-master Chang. I found him by the stables.

It had occurred to me that at least some of our horses should be saddled. It was true, as my father had pointed out, that there was no place to flee. Yet, should the necessity of flight arise, a mounted man would stand a better chance of escape than would a man on foot. I found that Chang had anticipated me and that four steeds, including my favorite bay, were already saddled.

My intention was to advise my father that some of our horses were in readiness. I was ascending the residence steps when I heard shouting coming from the direction of our western wall. The attack had come. There was no point now in trying to hide under cover of darkness. Soldiers with lighted torches were running to assist our beleaguered defenders.

I hesitated for a moment on the steps. My first instinct was to join the running militia. Then reason prevailed. I could be of little help at the western wall. I mounted the remaining steps two at a time, ran the length of the veranda, and took up a position at the end closest to the fighting. It was as well that I did so.

Even before I had adjusted a quiver at my back, an attack came from another quarter, this time directed against our main gates. Torches wavered beyond the gates. Shouted orders rang out. Then, before my astonished eyes, the gates bulged inward, creaked, and groaned, then collapsed with a crash. The Cham had commandeered a war elephant. It came crashing through the wreckage of the toppled gates. Close on its heels came Cham foot soldiers.

The first arrow I ever shot in combat caught the Cham soldier who was guiding the elephant squarely in the throat and toppled him from his lofty perch. The big beast, confronted by our spearmen and with no mahout to guide him, hesitated. Trumpeting shrilly, the ungainly animal backed up, turned ponderously in panic, and started back through the gates, trampling Cham infantrymen in its path. This brief respite of confusion in the enemy ranks gave our militia time to form a defensive front.

As fast as I could draw the bowstring and take hasty aim, I let fly arrow after arrow. I picked my targets in the thickest of the fighting. My eyes searched out their next target even before the whistling arrows reached their marks. I lost all track of time and was wildly exhilarated.

It has never ceased to amaze me how the senses function in the heat of battle. I was conscious of the entire scene, as though the milling combatants were moving in slow motion, yet my eyes caught and my mind recorded minute details: an arm was lopped off; a prostrate Cham clawed at an arrow in his chest; blood spurted from the stump of a severed leg; old Horse-master Chang roared in anger as he swept his halberd in a singing arc. One part of my mind registered the fact that the din of battle in the western part of the compound was drawing closer. And I recognized that we were badly outnumbered and slowly giving ground. Yet I felt no fear as I changed quivers and moved my firing position several times, my arm moving with tireless precision.

For most of the day the smoke-laden air had rasped my throat and made my eyes water. When it was that I noticed the acrid smell was much stronger and my eyes were smarting, I cannot tell. Then I heard the crackling and noticed a wavering light at my back. Even before I confirmed it with a glance, I knew the residence was on fire.

Smoke billowed from the shuttered windows. Flames licked at the eaves and the roof overhang. Then, to my horror, I saw the figure of my father standing at the far end of the balcony. He stood calmly, viewing the fighting below him with an air of detachment. Behind him, dancing flames illuminated him clearly.

I shot a glance downward. A knot of Cham swordsmen had broken through our thinning defenses and was nearing the bottom of the steps. Barring the approach were Horse-master Chang and two militiamen.

It hadn't rained for more than five months, and all wooden buildings were dry as tinder. It would be only a matter of minutes before the residence became a blazing inferno. If the pavilion was not to become our funeral pyre, I must somehow get my father safely away from the building.

Those thoughts ran through my head as I dropped my bow. Running toward my father, I drew my sword. I neither reached my father nor exercised my swordsmanship in a bid to escape the burning residence.

A flaming roof beam dropped to bar my path. One end smashed through the balustrade. The other end bounced off the porch flooring and caught me in the chest. I was catapulted backward. Clawing helplessly at the air, I went over the broken balustrade and into space.

The last thing I remember was falling through a curtain of descending sparks.

chapter 7

Awareness returned slowly and painfully. I was being subjected to a swaying, jostling motion. It was pitch dark. From the sounds, smell, and feel, I deduced I was in some sort of horse-drawn vehicle filled with rice straw.

I tried to sit up. I sank back with a sharp gasp as a searing pain knifed through my head.

Something rustled in the straw close to my right ear. I hoped it wasn't one of the giant rats that infested Angkor. On that happy thought, I must have slipped back into unconsciousness.

I awakened for the second time to find that the straw had been removed from on top of me. I stared up through a screen of bamboo leaves at blue sky.

Recalling my earlier experience, I sat up cautiously. I winced as pain stabbed my throbbing head, then spread rapidly to my chest and down my left side. Probing gingerly, I discovered a large lump at the back of my head, and there was an encrustation on my neck and shoulder that I assumed to be dried blood. Continuing my inventory, I found that my chest was black and blue with bruises and that my left side, from waist to mid-thigh, was badly burned and suppurating. I was completely nude, a mess, and to add insult to injury, my pubic hair had been singed off.

Memory flooded back—the embattled city, our compound under attack, the residence in flames. The image of my father as I had last seen him came sharply into focus. And I remembered a shower of sparks as I fell toward the hard-packed earth below the veranda. Nothing more. It left many unanswered questions.

What had happened to my father and the rest of the household? Who, besides myself, had survived the slaughter? Why had we been attacked at all, and why by such a large and determined force? Where was I, and how had I arrived here?

With considerable effort, I raised myself high enough to survey the immediate surroundings. My conveyance, a two-wheeled farm cart, stood in a grove of thick bamboo. The only animal in evidence was my stallion, Sa-lu-tzu, tethered to a small tree. A girl was crouching over a small fire, her firm breasts quivering as she vigorously stirred something in an earthenware pot. I recognized her as the youngest of my two female slaves.

Settling back into my bed of straw, I pondered this scant evidence. The girl couldn't have lifted me into the cart without help, so there must be at least one other person somewhere close by. My big bay was not what you would call a draft animal. It would have been next to impossible to fit him between the shafts of the small cart. Therefore, there must be another horse not too far away. I could have saved myself this exercise in deductive reasoning. My conclusions were erroneous.

Carrying the cooking pot, and with a folded *sampot* over one arm, the girl appeared at the back of the cart. She noticed that I was awake, and she lowered her eyes as she scrambled into the cart.

The pot contained a smelly, gray-green concoction. She liberally smeared this mucky substance over the burned parts of my waist, rump, and upper thigh. Even though she was gentle, it was painful. I said nothing to distract her.

When she considered me sufficiently smeared, she bandaged the coated areas with strips of cloth cut from the *sampot*. The remainder of the garment she gave to me. Normally, my nudity would not have concerned me, especially before a slave. My singed crotch looked peculiar, almost obscene. I fashioned a crude loincloth. As I awkwardly fastened it around my bandaged waist, I questioned the girl.

"Where are we?" I asked.

"Two, perhaps three, miles past Banteay Srei," she answered in halting Khmer, her eyes downcast.

That meant we were about fifteen miles northeast of Angkor. We must have traveled the better part of the night. Under the circumstances, however, it didn't seem a great distance to put between myself and the hapless city.

"Who else is with us?" I questioned.

"No one."

Her answer astonished me. "What? . . . How? . . ." My voice trailed off.

Slowly, with a good deal of prompting on my part, she supplied me with the missing pieces. Not once during the interrogation did she look into my face.

With other frightened slaves and servants, she had huddled in the shadows of the supports beneath the residence. Then, with a shower of sparks and dropping fragments of burning wood, I had fallen almost at her feet. My loincloth had been ablaze. With the help of a servant, she had pulled me beneath the pavilion. They had ripped off my burning garment. They had at first taken me for dead, but then they had discovered I was only unconscious.

The heat and the rush of air being sucked up by the fire had made it impossible to stay beneath the blazing pavilion. The servants and slaves had fled in confusion and terror. Why the girl had not abandoned me was not clear, but she had not and had managed to drag me clear of the burning building. It had been there, at the rear of the residence, that the stable master had found us.

"Old Chang?" I queried.

"Yes, that is what he is called."

"What then?" I prompted.

"I helped him carry you to the stables . . . to the back of the stables where there were some carts. He ordered me to fill two carts with straw and told me to get some things we would need. He brought your horse to the rear of the stables. The horse would not fit." She moved her hands to describe the cart shafts and pointed to the front of the cart. "He fixed that. Then I helped him put you in the cart and cover you with straw. He told me to wait. He left. I waited a long time. Then I heard Cham soldiers talking in the stables. They are going to kill the horses and burn the stables. I cannot wait longer for the old man.

As quietly as possible I leave, leading the horse. In the north wall I find a big hole."

"You were not seen . . . not stopped?"

She shrugged. "I led the horse along the water's edge, under the big trees. It was dark. Then I joined some farm people on the road. As we left the city, I was stopped. But the Cham soldiers were tired and I am a *pnong*. One soldier wanted the horse. The officer said the horse was too big. I was not stopped again until just after dawn."

She had described herself with the Khmer word *pnong*. It meant "savage," and it was applied to all hill-tribe people. The Cham adopted the same attitude toward the mountain dwellers. It was only logical that she had not been molested. That the cart had not been searched was another matter and probably only due to the fact that the soldiers were bone-weary after almost twenty-four hours of fighting.

"Who stopped you the second time?" I asked.

"I was not stopped," she explained. "I saw Khmer soldiers taking food and other things from people ahead of me on the road. I led the horse off the road into some brush. I stuck to the woods until I found this place. I would have had to stop anyway to find the roots and things I needed to heal your burns."

What she said concerned me. If Khmer soldiers were robbing the fleeing refugees, it meant a collapse of discipline, a breakdown of authority. Under such conditions, we had as much to fear from the Khmer as from the Cham soldiers. We would have to be careful and most likely travel only by night. Then it suddenly struck me that I had no idea where we were heading.

"Where are we going?" I questioned.

"To the mountains, to my people. It is far, but you will be safe there."

Her primitive tribe probably lived in the trees, or in holes burrowed in the ground, I thought. It wasn't much of a choice, but there was little I could do about it until I improved a bit and could fend for myself.

I was loath to ask my final question. I think I knew the answer before I posed the question.

"What happened to my father?"

For a moment, she did not answer. When she did, her

voice was almost inaudible. "He is dead. The stable master told me he saw your father perish in the fire."

Although I ached in every muscle, I managed to sleep fitfully during the day. It was late afternoon when the slave woke me up. She gave me some boiled, unseasoned rice containing some green vegetables I did not recognize. A newly cut bamboo joint held some brackish water. I was so ravenously hungry that the Spartan fare tasted like a feast.

She arranged the straw so that I was half-seated and facing forward. As she gathered our meager store of possessions—a Khmer battle ax, a not-so-sharp bronze knife, the earthen cooking pot, and three bamboo joints filled with water and plugged with clay and leaves—I noted how Horse-master Chang had solved the problem of the cart shafts. He had notched a heavy plank at both ends, pushed it between the shafts to spread them apart, and tied the spreader securely in place. The stallion could now fit quite easily between the shafts, which were made fast to a rope yoke secured to the saddle.

With the evening sun at our backs, we started off in an easterly direction. The girl trotted alongside the big stallion, her hand on his halter.

I never did learn the secret formulation of the stuff she applied to my burns. I wish I had. It was most effective. Within two days the pain had almost disappeared. Two days later, when I removed the bandages and washed off the caked salve, the flesh beneath was pink and unscarred.

If my physical recovery was rapid, the same could not be said for the country. Refugees bore tales of horror concerning the fate of Angkor.

Cham soldiers had roamed the streets raping, looting, and killing. Treasuries, palaces, temples, and residences had been methodically cleaned of valuables. The gold and silver sheathing had been stripped from the temples. Prisoners by the thousands had been used as beasts of burden to transport the loot to the naval vessels in the Great Lake. The ships were so laden with captives and booty that they could barely stay afloat. Then, when the city had been denuded of everything of value, the systematic killing started.

Khmer who had survived the initial onslaught and the sacking of the city were rounded up and sent to gather timbers from the city stockade and other material of an inflammable nature. Those who resisted or tried to escape were killed on the spot. Logs, timber, straw, matting, and cloth were piled around the market squares. Then the surviving population was herded into the marketplaces, which were then put to the torch. Screams emanated from the gigantic bonfires, which smelled of burning flesh. Tens upon tens of thousands were incinerated alive. When no Khmer man, woman, or child was left alive within the city, the Cham withdrew. Only the silent towers of stone loomed above the smoking rubble, from which even the rats had departed.

The Cham must have considered the devastation they had visited upon Angkor sufficient to break for all time the will and fighting potential of their rival. When the forces withdrew, taking with them the wealth of Kambuja and the elite of the realm as captives, they left behind a modest army of occupation.

That a powerful state can collapse almost overnight seems improbable, yet that is what happened. Some semblance of order may have persisted for a time in the far reaches of the realm, but in the demoralized region closer to the capital the sudden removal of authoritative control resulted almost immediately in anarchy.

Armed groups of renegade Khmer soldiers roamed the countryside robbing and killing. Families left their vulnerable hamlets and sought protection in stockaded villages. These walled villages barricaded themselves against any and all strangers. No hand was raised to help the urban refugees. They wandered about aimlessly and turned to preying upon one another in desperation. Even the monasteries barred their doors to wayfarers.

The girl and I fared better than most. By traveling at night and staying clear of the main thoroughfares, we avoided encounters with the soldiery. By the third day of our flight, even the side roads were no longer safe and our farm cart became an encumbrance. We abandoned the cart and set out cross-country. We followed paths and trails, detoured to avoid centers of habitation, and managed to skirt the swamps and marshes in our path. As we moved deeper into the savanna and scrub jungle of higher ground, we traveled by day instead of night.

I am guilty of oversimplification. It was by no means as easy as I make it sound. Without assistance, few city dwellers could have survived more than a few days.

I was fortunate. The girl knew the haunts and habits of the dangerous beasts and reptiles. She was adept at snaring lizards, birds, and small game. She knew every edible root, leaf, flower, and fruit in the plains and forest. Even more important, she knew which plants must be avoided. Without the help of this child of nature, I would probably have joined my ancestors while still a youth.

My body mended quickly. My spirits lacked the same resiliency. I was subject to periods of black depression. My nights were haunted by disturbing dreams.

I did not blame myself for my father's tragic death. Fate had willed it so, and nothing I could have done would have prevented it. Yet I felt strangely cheated. My father and I had not been close, but had he lived, I felt we would have approached a broader understanding and a deeper affection.

In other moments of melancholy, I speculated on the fate of Apricot Blossom, the baby half brother I would never see again, and the rest of our household. True, I had no positive knowledge of their passing, but I had scant hope that any had survived.

Some vexing questions returned again and again. To the best of my knowledge, no other residential compound near ours had been under attack on the night of the battle. Why not? Why us? Why, in the face of our determined defense and their heavy casualties, had our attackers persisted? Why had a two-pronged assault in strength been mounted against a neutral target in the first place?

There was another perplexing matter that slowly began to dominate my thoughts. This was my relationship with my companion in flight. I found myself questioning some of my most basic beliefs. At least on my side, it was a confusing and uncomfortable situation.

Slavery was not a Confucian principle per se, but the levels of authority from the emperor downward were clearly defined. The upward fealty and downward responsibility were basic tenets of the Confucian ethic. The lower echelons of this time-honored structure, the servants and landless peasants, were not too far removed from serfdom.

The rigidly codified Brahman caste system of Champa and Kambuja had seemed to me a logical extension of the stratified structure I had always known. My father, as a Confucian scholar, equated quite fittingly with the highest caste of Brahman literati. I accepted the caste structure and considered an "untouchable" class only natural. It was a bit more difficult for me to accept the fact that birth, not attainment, dictated the caste, a status that could not be altered during the life-span of the individual.

Slaves, I readily accepted, were a subhuman breed. As such, they were beneath contempt and fitted for only the most menial of labor. I did not agree that they should be abused. In my estimation they would respond to detached kindness, the same treatment I would accord a well-mannered horse, with devotion.

My initial reaction to the fact that I had been snatched from almost certain death by a slave was that her action was only proper. When I had time to examine this reasoning, I found a number of flaws and became less and less sure of its validity.

In dragging me from beneath the burning pavilion, hiding me in the straw-filled cart, and spiriting me from the beleaguered city, she had done so at considerable risk to her own safety. Without me, she would have attracted little attention and could have escaped with ease. She could hope for no reward from my rescue. Now that the fabric of the social system that supported slavery had been ripped apart, she need fear no punishment if she abandoned me.

A master has few, if any, obligations to his slaves. He is free to discipline them as he sees fit, even to kill them without compunction. He may feel a responsibility to protect them from the whims and caprices of outsiders. As matters stood, I was in no position to exercise even that obligation. The reverse was the case. I was the one being shielded from harm.

There were other disturbing aspects to this new relationship. In Yasodharapura, it had not escaped my attention that the girl was attractive. I had found this pleasing, nothing more. Now that we were cast in such close daily contact, she ceased to be a nonentity and I became increasingly aware of her physical charms.

She was slim-waisted and graceful of movement. Her face was both lovely and expressive. Her thrusting young breasts, with their pert nipples, fired my imagination. With some astonishment, I discovered that she was not only human, but highly desirable.

It had not troubled me before, but now I recognized that I knew nothing about her. I did not know to which hill tribe she belonged. I didn't even know if she had a name.

I felt that our relationship should be changed, but I didn't know quite how to go about it. I thought of a number of approaches, and then I discarded each before putting it into action. I did not wish to appear a fool, nor did I want to risk being rebuffed. I need not have concerned myself. Fate was to intervene in an unexpected manner.

chapter 8

TOWARD THE END OF THE SECOND WEEK OF OUR JOURNEY, we came to the Mekong River. The girl called it by its Khmer name, Thonle Thom, Big River. At the point where we reached it, well to the northeast of Angkor, it bore little resemblance to the broad waterway on which I had sailed inland from the sea to reach Angkor. Here the muddy river fanned out in myriad channels over a rocky plateau. It dropped toward the plains in frothing rapids and tumbling waterfalls.

It had not rained for many months. Now was the hot, dry season preceding the monsoon rains. The river was at its lowest seasonal level. Many of the channels coursing down the rocky expanse were mere trickles, or altogether dry. Yet, even in this season, the river carried a huge volume of water to the distant sea, and several of the many branches looked to be both deep and treacherous. But since our destination lay to the east, we had no choice but to cross the forbidding terrain, an expanse I judged to be almost ten miles that included a number of hazardous water-courses.

We moved north along the western edge of the rock-strewn riverbed. At a point where the plateau seemed relatively flat and free from precipitous drops, we started our crossing.

The shallow channels presented no difficulties. The girl, who was out of her element and could not swim, approached each crossing with hesitant reluctance, but as the day progressed without incident, she followed my lead with increasing confidence.

Having been brought up in the river port of Changsha, I was familiar with river currents and was a strong swimmer. This was a vastly different river, and while I had no fear, I proceeded with caution.

At each crossing, leading the stallion, I went in advance. With a long pole, I probed in front of me beneath the turbid water for firm footing. When I encountered deep water, I tried upstream and downstream until I located a shallower stream bed. The girl waded alongside the horse, clutching one end of the rope yoke slung across the saddle. In this manner, we negotiated the various stream branches without too much trouble.

We came to the first of several channels where I was unable to locate a fordable crossing. When the water became too deep, I moved back alongside the horse. Grasping the other free end of the yoke, I urged the stallion forward. He at first balked, then floundered ahead into deep water, trailing us along head-high as he struck out for the far bank. When his flailing hooves found footing, all three of us scrambled into safer depths.

The going was painfully slow. By early afternoon we had crossed less than half the rocky expanse. It was not my wish that nightfall would find us still in this bleak area of jagged, water-scoured boulders, scrub-crested sandy hummocks, and the bleached skeletons of big trees deposited on rock pinnacles by the retreating waters of the last flood season. The sun beat down on us mercilessly from a cloudless sky. The rocks were sharp underfoot. Land crabs, lizards, and snakes, in particular the black-and-yellow-banded kraits, scuttled or slithered away as we approached. The horse snorted and shied away from the snakes and had as little liking for the terrain as myself. I grew less cautious as the day advanced.

Late in the afternoon, we came upon the widest stream we had encountered thus far. I waded forward. The bottom dropped away within yards of the bank. I should have explored to find a more suitable point of crossing, but I was anxious to press ahead as quickly as possible. Taking up my position on his right, I slapped Sa-lu-tzu on his flank. He plunged ahead.

The current was strong. It struck me that this must be

the main channel. Despite the stallion's efforts, the opposite bank drew closer only slowly as we were carried
downstream and around a curving bend. I became aware
of a dull roaring. Ahead, the stream narrowed and I could
make out white water. There was no point in dwelling on
my folly. All I could hope was that the horse would find
solid footing before we were swept into the rapids.

We were perilously close to the roiling water before the
horse found purchase. As he lunged ahead, he stumbled.
As he struggled to regain his footing, I heard the girl cry
out. She had lost her grip on the rope. Caught by the current, she was carried around the horse's rump. Her eyes
were wide with fright as she was swept past me.

Releasing my hold, I struck out after her bobbing head.
An overfall sucked me beneath the surface and tumbled
me over and over. When I broke the surface, she was only
a few yards from me. Only the top of her head was visible, sliding down a race toward a huge boulder that split
the stream into two forks. To the right of the rock, a mist
of spray hung above the surface. A steady roar indicated
a cataract. In a frenzy of desperation, I thrashed to narrow the distance that separated us.

I caught her scant seconds before we reached the boulder. Pulling with my free arm and kicking frantically, I
managed to steer us into the left-hand fork. The rock
scraped down my right side. We were catapulted into a
boiling maelstrom, buffeted by water-capped rocks, then
flung into a froth-topped backwater formed by a projection of shelving rock.

I pushed her partially clear of the water, scrambled out,
and pulled her inert body up onto the rock shelf. The
swirling waters had ripped off her *sampot* and she was
completely nude. I could detect no sign of life as I
stretched her out face-down on the rock.

Astride her, I pressed down on her lower rib cage, then
released the pressure. Water gushed from her mouth as I
repeated the rhythmic pressure and release again and
again. Silently, I prayed to my ancestors that she would re-
vive. It could not have been long, but it seemed like an
eternity before my prayers were answered and she was
seized by a paroxysm of retching coughs. I breathed another prayer of thanks.

She was breathing again, but she had not regained consciousness. A thin trickle of blood oozed from beneath

her wet hair at the right temple. I examined her and found a shallow cut where her head had been struck.

When she was breathing easier, I cradled her in my arms and carried her up the bank to level ground. Not far distant, a sandy hump topped with stunted trees offered a haven of shade. I set off in that direction. Not far away, the stallion stood on the riverbank. He followed in response to my whistle.

I laid her down gently in the shade of some low bushes. Gathering leaves and dry grass, I made her a more comfortable bed, then set about examining her wounds. The cut at her temple was crusting over but was still bleeding. Two deep gashes on her left thigh seeped blood upon the pallet I had fashioned for her. I removed my still-damp *sampot* and cleaned her wounds. With a strip torn from the *sampot*, I bound her head wound. I compressed the edges of the ragged gashes on her thigh, and with a wider strip of cloth I bandaged her upper leg tightly.

She stirred. I glanced up to find her eyes upon me, wide, questioning. She struggled to sit up, but I pushed her gently back. Her eyes still held mine, the first time, I think, that she had not lowered her eyes in deference. A smile trembled on her lips. Then her face took on an expression of concern and she raised her hand. Her fingers softly touched my right shoulder where my flesh was torn and scraped and oozed blood.

I was astonished. She was recovering from a close brush with death and her first instinct was to comfort me. I reached down and gathered her into my arms, holding her in a tight embrace. She gave a shuddering sigh. Her small arms circled my neck and she brought her cheek to mine in a soft kiss.

Fire seeped into my loins. She felt my manhood swelling against her stomach and pressed against it. Her nipples grew hard against my chest as she lay back and pulled me onto her. Her legs spread wide to welcome my thrust.

As I forced an entrance, she gave a sharp cry of pain. When I started to withdraw, her fingers dug into my buttocks and she thrust upward to force a deeper penetration.

It was a spontaneous act of lovemaking born of need and hunger. It was both a gesture in defiance of death and an affirmation of life. It was a release of pent-up

emotions and a fulfillment of fantasies. Regardless of the
circumstances that brought her to me as a virgin, hers
was a gift bestowed willingly and with joy. From that
feral mating grew a bond that coupled us more surely
than could have been achieved by any ceremony devised
by man.

I had wished for a change in our relationship. The
metamorphosis surpassed my wildest imaginings.

Out destination was still her hill-tribe village, but much
of the urgency had gone out of the journey. The farming
communities were by now well behind us and with them
the scavenging bands of renegades. As the terrain grew
less hospitable, habitations became smaller and more
widely scattered. For some days we had seen no sign of
human intrusion. The Cham army that had been rumored
as advancing from the east was nowhere in evidence.
In moving to the northeast, toward the mountain range
that lay to the north of Angkor, we may have removed
ourselves from the path of Cham forces, but I suspected that the Cham king had never intended an overland assault.

From the eastern bank of the Mekong, our route lay
toward the blue line of distant peaks. We entered a region of jungle-matted hills, valleys, and gorges choked
with tangled foliage, scrub-clad slopes, and tumbling
mountain streams. It was a region into which few low-
landers had penetrated, a primeval region of rain forest
and grassy uplands inhabited almost exclusively by wild-
life.

The flowering trees were a riot of white, pink, red,
and orange. The jungle air was heavy with the perfume
of the blooms. The forest echoed to the chattering of mon-
keys, bird calls, and the drowsy humming of bees. The
sky was a brilliant blue; the air warm and bright. We
were filled with the sheer joy of living and in no hurry to
reach our ultimate destination. We followed the courses
of streams, stopping for days at a time in glades or Alpine
meadows that struck our fancy.

In the light of the love I now experienced, I recognized that my romance with White Lotus had been nothing but infatuation. The memory of White Lotus had all
but faded, but I owed her a debt of gratitude. From
her tutelage in the art of love, I had acquired the skill

and patience to bring to this new union pinnacles of ecstasy.

With each passing day, we discovered more about each other. I learned that her name, in her native tongue, was Mun Guah, Morning Mist. Her people were called Jarai. Her father was the *khoa bon*, the headman of her village. She told me of her childhood and village life as she remembered it. She was at first reluctant to tell me of her mother. Why this was so became clear to me the day she disclosed the events that had brought her to Angkor.

Four years earlier, when she could have been no older than eleven, her mother had taken her to a lowland village. They had been with a Jarai party trading mountain produce for salt. The lowland community had been attacked by Khmer soldiers. Morning Mist and her mother had been among those taken captive.

When they arrived at Yasodharapura, after a long and arduous journey, Morning Mist had been given to a high-ranking official as a household slave. Her mother had been assigned to a labor battalion. The girl had neither seen nor heard of her mother again and knew not whether she was alive or dead.

In my turn, I told Morning Mist of my boyhood in Changsha and the adventures that had befallen me since setting sail from Canton. I omitted any reference to White Lotus. Morning Mist listened with rapt attention, even though there was much she did not understand. She had never seen the sea. She had not even seen the Great Lake near Angkor, and my recounting of our voyage, the great storm, and the attack by Cham pirates could have meant but little to her.

This was Morning Mist's country. She was intimately familiar with the terrain and its flora and fauna. She delighted in sharing her knowledge with me and taught me a good deal, including the Jarai names for the trees, shrubs, animals, birds, and reptiles we encountered. She also solemnly instructed me concerning the Father God in which she believed and the myriad good and evil spirits that pervaded the mountains, streams, and forest.

My Confucian and Mahayana Buddhist upbringing denied the existence of spirits, yet I must confess to being of a superstitious nature. Sailors are a superstitious breed, and from seafarers I had acquired a healthy respect for ghosts and phantoms. Despite my early training, I more than half believed in the spirits described by Morning Mist. It is not difficult to accept their presence in the hush of high jungle, or at night when one hears the roaring of tigers and the rasping cough of a hunting leopard.

That predators were often close, or actually stalking us, we were aware from pug marks in the soft sand by streams or in the dust of the game trails we followed. We made no attempt to track the big cats. They, in turn, did not molest us. Nonetheless, I was uneasy. Our only weapons were the Khmer ax and a blunt knife, hardly adequate in my estimation for our protection and utterly useless for hunting game. I decided to add to our slim arsenal. In this resolve, I think I was prompted by pride as much as anything else. Up to this point, we had subsisted solely due to Morning Mist's skills in snaring small game. I was anxious to make some contribution to our larder.

The second day after our Mekong crossing, we came upon a grassy, tree-shaded glade beside a small stream. We made camp and I decided we would not move on until Morning Mist's leg was fully healed With the girl's help, I found a tree of tough and springy wood suited to my purpose. I made first a spear some eight feet in length, its sharpened point hardened in our campfire. My second fabrication was more ambitious.

The stave bow I produced was crude by comparison to the composite Chinese bows with which I was familiar. For a bowstring I used plaited strands from the rope yoke. Arrows I fashioned from thin bamboo fletched with feathers from a bird Morning Mist had snared, their tips fire-hardened. For a quiver I used a bamboo joint on a rope sling. The contrivance was primitive, but I was proud of my handiwork.

Having lost my thumb ring, I adopted a two-finger pull. In range and accuracy, the bow left much to be desired. At close range, however, I developed a reasonable accuracy after several hours of practice.

The next morning, not far from our campsite, I dropped a barking deer with my first shaft. When I returned to place my prize casually at Morning Mist's feet, I was rewarded as she clapped her hands in delight. For the rest of that day, I basked unashamedly in her praise.

After a few days at our first campsite, we moved on in an easterly direction. A day later we forded a sizable stream and set up camp again on the shore of a small lake.

We stayed by the lake more than a week. Game was plentiful and so unaccustomed to hunters that, unskilled as I was at tracking, I had no difficulty in providing meat. I took advantage of the lake to teach Morning Mist to swim, and we spent long hours splashing happily in the cooling, crystal-clear water.

Had it not been for the memory of my father's tragic death and the sadness that came upon me when I thought of all those who had lost their lives in Angkor, I could not have asked for a more pleasant life. We had a noble steed, an ax, an earthen cooking pot, a crude but effective bow, a bountiful forest, and each other. These seemed to me the only ingredients needed for happiness, and I was loath to leave our sylvan haven. Yet, while Morning Mist shared my happiness of the moment, she was understandably anxious to return to her people. Then, too, she pointed out that the rainy season would be upon us before many weeks and that the jungle and uplands were not as pleasant in that season. For one thing, she explained that the chilling mists and drenching downpours would demand more clothing than the breech-clouts she had fashioned from the remnant of my *sampot*.

At a leisurely pace, we continued our journey toward the far mountains.

I think that Morning Mist may have sensed their presence. As she stirred the embers beneath the cooking pot, she paused every now and then to scan the foliage at the edge of the clearing. The stallion, grazing at the far side of the clearing, was restless. I was honing our knife when the horse whinnied. I glanced up to find them standing motionless in the slanting rays of the morning sun.

There were three of them: stocky men wearing calf-length trousers and loose jackets of black cloth. Two carried cocked crossbows aimed at us. The third had a strung bow over his shoulder and wore a short sword. They stood just inside the clearing.

Morning Mist had seen them at the same instant that I had. Her face lit up with a happy smile of recognition and she called out something in her language. The faces of the three men registered surprise. One of them made some sort of answer. The menacing crossbows were lowered. Like wraiths, two more men appeared from the screening bushes to join their companions. Two of the men, the one with the bow and one of the crossbowmen, advanced toward Morning Mist.

Morning Mist shot me a reassuring glance. "Jarai," she said simply.

Soon all five men squatted on their haunches close to the fire. Morning Mist spoke to them at length, accompanying her account with gestures. The men nodded and from time to time interjected guttural comments. Curious glances were directed at the stallion and myself as Morning Mist's animated saga unfolded. The hunters grew relaxed and dipped into the cooking pot, yet I noted that their crossbows remained cocked and close at hand.

They were a hunting party. They had been aware of our presence in the area for several days and had tracked us for the last two days. They were not from her village, but they were familiar with it. In response to her questions, they traced a map on the ground and gave Morning Mist detailed directions. In mid-morning, the men melted into the shrubbery as silently as they had arrived.

It was three days later that I caught my first glimpse of the Jarai village that was to be my home for the next four years. It consisted of twelve thatched, stilt-raised longhouses clustered on a gently sloping upland meadow. In the background rose forest-mantled hills. In the foreground, between us and the meadow, the trail wound through a shallow gorge.

By what means I do not know, but the villagers knew of our coming. They were assembled in knots on the packed earth between the longhouses. Children and barking dogs ran between the groups.

Before descending into the gorge, I had Morning Mist mount Sa-lu-tzu. I walked at the stallion's head, my hand on his bridle. Why I was prompted to do this I do not know. Morning Mist had been a child when captured. She was returning as a young woman, together with an awesome beast and an alien stranger. To her kinfolk, it must have seemed as though she were returning from the grave. I felt she should make an impressive entrance.

She understood my theatrical gesture. That I walked while she rode proudly in the splendor of her semi-nudity was a mark of my love and respect. She laughed gaily and looked fondly down on me as we started our descent.

chapter 9

MY ADJUSTMENT TO LIFE IN THE JARAI VILLAGE WAS not an easy process. It hardly could have been otherwise.

It was a closely knit community in which I was a grotesque intruder. My few words of their language made communication all but impossible with anyone other than Morning Mist. I knew next to nothing of their culture or customs. The men were skilled trackers and hunters, attributes of which I had acquired only the barest rudiments. My association with Morning Mist, the daughter of the village headman, did not endear me to the unmarried men. I evoked resentment and ridicule.

On my side, I found the smoke-filled interior of the longhouse irritating, though when the rainy season brought clouds of insects, I came to appreciate the protection afforded by the smoke. The smell of the chickens, pigs, and dogs housed beneath the longhouse was at first offensive to my nostrils, but in time I grew used to this, as well. I found the presence of the twenty people housed in the longhouse an abrasive intrusion on my privacy. To me, the short, wiry men were as alien as I must have been to them. The religious ceremonies were at first meaningless to me; even when I understood them better, they appeared primitive and childish. It would be many weeks before I was included in the simple pleasures of festive occasions or the storytelling sessions that were an integral part of longhouse life.

77

The period of adjustment was not much easier for Morning Mist. Her long absence from her kinfolk made her a stranger in their midst. That she had chosen me to be her mate placed her in an unenviable position of censure. She was pointedly rebuffed by the wife her father had taken during her absence.

That we were considered outsiders only served to draw us closer together. Morning Mist was my constant companion, my mentor, and my solace. For her sake, I endured the ridicule and impositions with as good grace as I could muster. If any jibes were leveled at me in her presence, she sprang to my defense with the ferocity of a tigress.

As often as possible during the first few weeks, we went off by ourselves into the forest. There we would make love, walk with our arms around each other, and discuss the situation. I was for leaving the village and striking out to the east toward the coast and Vijaya. She considered the journey too perilous, with the clouds starting to build over the mountain peaks and the rainy season not far off. If our position with her people had not improved by the end of the coming season, she agreed to accompany me wherever I chose to lead.

That we were mated by mutual consent was acknowledged but not accepted. The village *pojao,* the shaman who interceded with the spirits, dispensed medicine, and guided the community in spiritual matters, insisted that our union must be sanctified by tribal ceremony before we could be allocated a marital cubicle in the longhouse. If we were to share a conjugal sleeping mat, we had no choice in the matter.

The ceremony consisted of a feast of chicken and roast pig, provided for the occasion by Morning Mist's father. After the feast, drums, lutes, and reed pipes supplied music for tribal dances that went on well into the night. My impression was that the ceremony was only an excuse for the festivities. I was soon disabused on this score.

Marriage demands a bride's price. Grooms, like myself, who come empty-handed are required to donate their services to the family of the bride for a period of a year. Normally, this means contributing their share of the hunt to the family larder. In my case, not being considered worthy of inclusion in hunting parties, it meant menial

tasks assigned with relish by Morning Mist's stepmother.
I helped the women and older men with work in the
distant hillside fields and with such tasks as fetching firewood. I endured these demeaning chores without rancor.
They not only involved me in community life, but they
were a small price to pay for the hand of Morning Mist.

I found a felled thornwood tree among a pile of cut
brush. The wood was suitably seasoned for my purpose,
and I cut a seven-foot length of what I considered to be
the proper size and curvature. It was not until the rains
came that I had time to devote to the task I had in mind.

The heart of the longhouse is the communal living and
working area around the log-sided, earth-filled firebox,
with drying racks extending upward to the ridge pole. I
chose a spot well clear of the cooking activity and started
the long hours of painstaking work. I was no craftsman. My knowledge of the construction of a *kung*, the
Chinese composite bow, had been imparted by my old
archery instructor. To him, each part of a bow held mys-
tical properties and each stage of its crafting was a sacred
rite. I worked from the memory of his lessons.

Working outward from the center grip, I shaped, bev-
eled, and smoothed the limbs. While this was being done,
Morning Mist procured the materials I would need: deer
sinew, gumlac, animal glue, and the horns from a young
couprey, a breed of long-horned, wild cattle native to the
upland savannas.

As I labored each afternoon and evening, I attracted
spectators. At first these were children; later they were
joined by curious young men of the longhouse.

To the inside curve of the limbs, which would be the
back of the strung bow, I applied sinews in layers of
gumlac mixed with glue. This would lend resistance to
the pull. I then softened strips of couprey horn and
glued them to the outer curve, the bow's belly. This was
designed to reduce the compressibility and give whiplash
resiliency. At the limb ends, I scarped in the inward-canted
hardwood ears with bone inserts for the bowstring nocks.
At the string fulcrum point of the limb ends, I inlaid sections of horn to absorb the slap of the string knots. I covered the grip with doeskin.

While Morning Mist made me a rawhide quiver with
a wide band of cotton as a sling, I selected three-foot

lengths of slim, jointless bamboo and set about making arrows fletched with trimmed feathers and tipped with the black steel arrowheads favored by the tribesmen. Morning Mist braided several bowstrings of cotton. These I measured carefully, knotted the loops, and rubbed the strings with beeswax. All that remained was to carve myself a thumb ring from deer horn. Morning Mist made me a soft leather ring pouch with a rawhide drawstring.

It was finished. It may not have presented the appearance of a *kung* crafted by Chinese artisans, but it was a reasonable facsimile. When I strung it into its reverse curve, I was well pleased with the smooth curve of its belly. All that remained was to test the weapon.

The next morning, when the sun had burned the thick mist from the meadow, I tried the bow. Children and some of the village men clustered around as I fitted the thumb ring, selected an arrow, canted the bow upward, drew the bowstring back smoothly to its full extent, and let fly. The bowstring twanged and the arrow sang as it arched heavenward. The gasping of surprise from the assembled tribesmen was music to my ears.

I followed the flight against the sky and clouds with slitted eyes. The arrow dropped into some low shrubs far down the meadow. When I paced it off, the distance was a bit more than three hundred yards. It was far from being a record, but I was elated. The tribesmen, who had followed and counted off my paces, were dumbfounded. No Jarai bowman, even the strongest among them, could have achieved much more than half that distance.

In the days that followed my initial test, I set up target marks at distances of twenty-five, fifty, seventy-five, and one hundred yards. When the mornings were clear, before the building clouds brought the noontime deluge, I practiced hour after hour, improving my speed and accuracy at varying ranges.

When I was satisfied that I had mastered the weapon, I saddled Sa-lu-tzu. At full gallop, the stallion thundered back and forth across the meadow, wheeling sharply in response to pressure from my knees, while I loosed shaft after shaft at the passing marks.

Throughout these practice sessions, I was attended by a growing audience of tribespeople. The young men shouted encouragement as I drove arrows unerringly into the targets. The older men were silent, but they nodded approvingly as the arrows found their marks.

I was, as I have noted, a bowman of considerable skill. The practice was necessary, but I admit to showing off shamelessly. My only excuse for this display of vanity is that it was for a good purpose.

What I had anticipated happened ten days after my first performance to demonstrate the bow's capabilities. I arrived back at the longhouse late one afternoon to find the headman and four of the tribe's most skilled huntsmen squatting beside the fire pit. They were sipping fermented rice liquor through thin bamboo stems from a large earthenware jug. Morning Mist and women of the household were serving them from bowls of rice, meat, and peppers. I was invited to join the circle.

As I squatted beside the men, I caught Morning Mist's eyes upon me. They shone with love and pride. I drank sparingly of the potent brew and listened respectfully as the men discussed various matters pertaining to the season and the crops. Then, casually, one of the hunters invited me to join a hunting party on the morrow. Without allowing my face to betray emotion, I nodded my acceptance. Inwardly, I breathed a prayer of thanks to the crusty old Jürched archer who had trained me as a boy.

The hunt was a success. I brought down a magnificent stag with a single shot at a range of about forty yards. There was an element of luck, I must admit, but it was a beautiful shot that entered his left eye, penetrated his brain, and dropped him like a stone.

Our return from the hunt was a triumphal procession. In the longhouse we ate and drank well into the night. I listened with becoming modesty as my marksmanship was extolled.

Later that night, as Morning Mist lay pressed close to me, she informed me she was with child.

The seasons melted into each other with astonishing swiftness. We had arrived at the village at the beginning of the wet season in the Year of the Cock. Early in the following dry season, Morning Mist presented me with a beautiful baby daughter. The following wet season, in the Year of the Dog, she gave birth to a sturdy boy. The Year of the Dog gave way to that of the Pig, then the Rat.

Late in the wet season of that year, Morning Mist announced proudly that she was again pregnant.

Unquestionably, those were the happiest years of my life.

My bowmanship had earned me acceptance into the tribe, but it also imposed on me certain obligations. I taught the tribesmen how to fabricate the composite bow. I instructed them in archery and taught them how the use of the thumb ring and the Mongolian release gave added weight to the pull and increased the effectiveness of the weapon.

Our village was at peace with its neighboring hill tribes. Nonetheless, in the second year I added instruction in the martial arts and swordsmanship, as I had been taught them in my youth. I did this more to keep myself in practice than to instill warlike qualities in the Jarai. To my surprise, the weekly sessions became surprisingly popular with the youth of the village.

In turn, I was a pupil. My companions of the hunt taught me the haunts and habits of the jungle beasts, how to stalk game silently, and how to avoid situations that could lead to danger. There were, I learned, no hard and fast rules to this game. Often the hunter becomes the hunted. I learned to have a healthy respect for the big cats and never to underestimate the cunning of a wild boar. Yet, despite the skill and caution of my teachers in this age-old lore, my companions and I had many a close call. It is not a game for weaklings, the infirm, or the faint of heart. From many a hunt, we returned bearing dead or wounded comrades.

While I seemed to bear a charmed life, I did not escape entirely unscathed. Toward the end of the second wet season, I came down with a raging fever. My companions carried me back to the village in a raving delirium.

Morning Mist, who was still nursing our son at the time, never left my side. While the fever raged, she bathed my body constantly. When chills gripped me, she warmed my body with her own. The village *pojao* concocted an evil-smelling and exceedingly bitter brew that was forced on me; this was the only thing besides water that passed my lips for several days.

The fever finally left me, but it was another week before I regained my former strength. During my illness, the rains had ceased. I proposed that Morning Mist leave the children with her stepmother and that we take the stallion and explore the high country to the southeast. The idea appealed to her, but she protested that she could not leave the nursing baby.

Two days later she informed me that her cousin had agreed to look after the little girl and wet-nurse the baby. Early the next morning we set off gaily toward the rising sun.

We found that much had changed since our odyssey of two years earlier. Then, our emotions had been heightened by fear and uncertainty. Now, I was as at home in the jungle element as she was. In many ways, I was her superior. Our roles were reversed in that I was now both protector and provider.

We had changed physically. I was an inch taller and much broader in the chest and shoulders. Her figure had ripened into maturity, though she still retained the slim appeal of youth and the natural grace of adolescence.

Emotionally, we were different from the days when we had groped to find each other and found love in one blinding revelation of mutual need and surrender. Our relationship had taken on depth and meaning through our shared experiences of tribal censure and parenthood. Our love was like a deep river nourishing us both.

None of the early passion had gone from our love-making. If anything, we were more confident and more responsive to each other's needs. Her breasts were still heavy with milk, and at night as we lay by the dying embers in each other's arms, she sighed in contentment as I sucked the sweet liquid oozing from her swollen nipples.

We explored ridgeline game trails, splashed and swam in cold mountain pools, and ascended through high-canopy jungle to pine-clad mountain passes. Eventually, we descended onto a highland plateau. We had encountered Jarai and Rhade villages. On the plateau, we came across a Cham community, a Buddhist enclave.

I talked with the priests. They were more surprised that I could discourse with them in their language and knew of Vijaya than they were by our bizarre appearance. They told me that Vijaya lay not much more than a week's journey to the southeast and gave me directions that would lead us through the eastern mountain range to the coastal plains.

Two years earlier, I would have welcomed such directions. Now I hadn't the slightest inclination to follow the route they indicated. When we left the Cham village, we circled slowly to the southwest.

Early one afternoon, with Morning Mist mounted and myself on foot, we broke through a screen of foliage into an Alpine meadow. Suddenly the stallion whinnied and shied, very nearly unseating Morning Mist. Not twenty yards in front of us a mother rhinoceros and her ungainly calf eyed us uncertainly.

She lowered her twin-horned head and pawed the earth nervously. Avoiding any abrupt movement, I fitted an arrow to my bow. My heart was in my mouth. Like an elephant, a rhino is almost impervious to an arrow. If she charged, I would need luck and all the skill at my command to stop her. Then, to my relief, the big beast wheeled and crashed off into the low shrubs, her calf lumbering along at her heels.

It was too early to breath easy. The rhinoceros is unpredictable and she could well come thundering at us from another direction. Morning Mist dismounted. Leading the horse, we circled cautiously downwind and went toward higher ground. When I judged us safe, I grinned broadly.

"Among my people," I said, "the rhinoceros horn is highly prized. Ground into powder, it is eaten by Chinese men with their food. It is said to give the strength of a bull in lovemaking."

Morning Mist giggled. She circled my waist with her arms and looked up into my face. "If I am impaled, I want only to be gored by you . . . and you have no need of a rhinoceros horn."

On our return to the village, we were given a tumultuous welcome. The shaman gave thanks to the spirits for our safe return. Our homecoming was the excuse for a feast and dancing.

As I danced to the slow cadence of drum and pipes, my eyes rested on Morning Mist as she fed our hungry young son. How different, I thought, is this welcome from the one we received on her first homecoming.

Our journey had taught me something. Morning Mist and I were complete unto ourselves and our children, but we were also part of a larger whole. This was our village.

Our home. My home. The past seemed remote and not of much importance.

By the time that Morning Mist announced she was again with child, I had turned nineteen, our daughter was three, and our son was two. The dry season would soon be upon us and the Year of the Bull was not far off.

A year earlier, we had moved into a newly constructed longhouse where I had ample room to set up an area devoted to the fabrication of composite bows. I was not only the tribe's best bowman, but I was rapidly becoming one of its most able trackers and hunters. I had been honored with a place on the village council. I had many staunch friends. I had come a long, long way from my days as a social outcast. Morning Mist shared the esteem in which I was held. Our position in the community was comfortable and secure.

We were a hunting party of seven that set out late in the first month of the Year of the Bull. Our destination was a remote valley where gaur, elephant, and rhinoceros were thought to be plentiful. Because of the distance, we were mounted. We expected to be gone from the village no more than ten days.

There was nothing on the golden morning of our departure to presage the tragedy that was to overtake our peaceful community.

chapter 10

IT HAD BEEN A SUCCESSFUL EXPEDITION. THREE OF THE
wiry mountain horses were being used as pack animals to
carry our spoils. We were returning with a set of elephant
tusks, the carcasses of two bull gaur and a wild boar,
deer haunches, and a leopard skin. Only the rhinoceros
had eluded us.

Anxious to get back to the village, we broke camp before dawn. If we made good time, we could be home early
in the afternoon.

A strange sensation of impending peril came over me
about mid-morning. Riding Sa-lu-tzu, I was a short distance ahead of the rest of the hunting party. The stallion,
as well, seemed to sense something and whinnied softly.
The danger, whatever it was, did not seem close at hand.
Some instinct warned me that it was Morning Mist and
the children who were threatened. Cold fingers of dread
clutched my heart. I knew with certainty that something
was amiss at the village.

I reined the horse to a halt. He pawed the ground
impatiently while we waited for my companions to catch
up with us. When they did, one look at their strained
faces told me that I was not alone in my premonition.

We held a hurried conference. It was agreed that those
of us who were mounted would ride on ahead at our best
speed. The three whose steeds were being used as beasts
of burden would unload their horses, cache the tusks,
hides, and meat, and follow as quickly as they could.

Pressing my heels into the stallion's flanks, I set off at a gallop. In the mountainous terrain, such a pace could not be sustained. Nonetheless, I gradually drew well ahead of my companions.

Even before I topped the final ridge, the distant din was audible. It was, I concluded with alarm, the sound of battle.

The descent was steep. The village, still more than two miles away, was screened from view by the heavy rain forest until the trail leveled briefly on a lower ridgeline. Muffled though it was by foliage, the unmistakable sound of conflict grew ever more distinct. I pushed the stallion beyond the limits dictated by caution.

When we broke out onto the ridgeline, I had a relatively clear view of the village and much of the meadow. The scene that met my gaze instilled fear and horror.

The village was encircled by an attacking force. The attackers were soldiers, but at this distance I could not make out whether they were Cham or Khmer. Bodies and debris between the far gorge and the village attested to the fact that the Jarai defenders had put up stiff resistance. The fighting was now within the southern portion of the village and five of the longhouses were ablaze.

When we broke through the trees onto the meadow, Sa-lu-tzu was in full gallop. I appraised the situation at a glance. Fighting still raged within the village, where more than half the longhouses were now on fire. To the north of the village, a knot of children and elderly noncombatants were being fiercely defended. I could make out Morning Mist at her father's side in that latter ring of defense. Sword in hand, she was making a stand against an advancing arc of soldiers. The attackers were Khmer. They appeared to be a disciplined force heavily outnumbering the Jarai defenders.

My uppermost thought was my family. Guiding the stallion with my knees, I headed for Morning Mist, yelling defiantly as I closed the distance.

My bursting upon the scene caused only momentary wavering in the Khmer ranks. A sharp command rang out and four spearmen ran to bar my advance. My whistling shafts dropped two and winged a third even before I had narrowed the distance to fifty yards. Five more soldiers were detached to replace their fallen comrades.

I heard shouts behind me. A quick glance confirmed

that my three mounted companions had arrived on the field of combat. Hoping that they would recognize my tactics, I veered to the left. My plan was to draw as many attackers as possible in my direction and thin the Khmer ranks to a point where the Jarai could break through and flee toward the safety of the tree line.

It was a slim chance, but it might have worked. Two more of my arrows found their mark and more Khmer soldiers were running forward to form a line against myself and the charging horsemen to my rear. I swung toward the running Khmer, hoping to cut into their ranks before they could form a solid line. As I did so, Sa-lu-tzu stumbled and I was flung headlong over his neck.

I hit the ground and rolled. I was on my feet in an instant. Weaponless, I faced a Khmer swordsman.

As the sword arced downward, I pivoted and caught the soldier with a kick to the head. He reeled. Before he could recover, I was upon him, had wrenched the sword from his grasp, and driven it to the hilt in his stomach.

I fought my way forward. Not far away Morning Mist was cutting her way toward me. Not many yards separated us when I caught a crashing blow on the head. Before the blackness of unconsciousness claimed me, I saw Morning Mist clearly, her face a twisted mask of grief and hate.

That image will be with me always. It was the last time I was to see my beloved in this world.

When I struggled back to consciousness, I was lying on trampled grass, my hands securely bound behind my back. My head throbbed. My vision was blurred by pain. With some difficulty, I managed to sit up and look around me.

What met my gaze was a scene of carnage. The longhouses were reduced to smoking embers. Dead bodies lay everywhere. The sickly sweet stench of death hung thickly in the air.

Not far from me, a group of horses was tethered, among them my bay stallion. Somewhat closer, Khmer soldiers were stuffing squawking chickens into baskets and trussing squealing pigs. Guards lounged close to the small group of prisoners, of which I was one.

Apart from myself, there were eight Jarai tribesmen. Like myself, all had their hands tied. The closest to me was one of the hunting party, the only one of that group in evidence.

"How many escaped?" I questioned.

He looked at me bleakly. "None," he said dully. "We are all who live."

All! Nine men out of a village that had numbered more than two hundred and sixty tribespeople this morning. Why? Why such senseless slaughter?

I turned to the man squatting on my right. Blood welled from an untended wound on his upper arm. "How . . . when did they come?"

For a moment, he looked at me uncomprehendingly. When he answered, it was haltingly, as though he did not wish to remember. "Early . . . they came just after dawn. It was a small band. We killed some. They fled. They came back later . . . many soldiers. You saw. We tried to get the children to the forest. We were cut off. We fought until we could fight no more. . . ." His voice trailed off.

"The women . . . children?" I prompted.

"Dead. When the fighting was over, they killed the old people first. Then the women. The children were last. All dead."

I sank my head onto my knees. Thoughts slowly churned through my numbed brain. No more would I watch my children romping in carefree play. I would not see my lovely daughter grow to womanhood. I would not teach my son to ride, hunt, or master the bow. I had taught them nothing of their proud heritage. I never would. Our unborn child would never see the light of day.

Slowly, painfully, the final realization intruded. Never again would I hold Morning Mist's warm body to my own, nor would I smell the tantalizing, musky scent of her flesh. Why had I not died with her? I felt empty, drained of all feeling.

Numbed by grief, I paid little heed to the activities of the Khmer troops as they methodically collected the weapons of the fallen, tended their wounded, and cremated their dead. The Jarai dead were left where they lay: carrion, to be devoured by insects, birds, and scavenging beasts at their leisure. Mercifully, the mounds of corpses at the site where the executions had taken place were to the north of the village and beyond my vision.

Late in the afternoon, we captives were prodded to our

feet. Our hands were untied and we were pressed into service, carrying litters of Khmer wounded.

As we left the meadow to wind down into the gorge, I did not give even a backward glance. Within days the predators would have picked the Jarai bones clean. Within a season, scrub jungle would have reclaimed the meadow and nothing would remain but the charred stumps of longhouse stilts hidden in the long grass to testify that a thriving community had once existed at the site.

A chapter in my life had closed. What lay ahead I neither knew nor cared.

chapter 11

A SAGE ONCE SAID: "A JOURNEY OF A THOUSAND *li* STARTS with a single step." My first step along the long course of a military career came when I was brought into the presence of the Khmer king.

A few days earlier, the Khmer troops that had overrun our village had rejoined their main force, an army on the march. I was surprised at the size of the force. In this remote region, where had it been assembled? It was coming from the east, its line of march to the southwest. It could have been gathered together only in the far highlands. A number of Cham units within its ranks seemed to confirm my supposition, but I had little time to speculate on the matter.

My Jarai companions and myself were put to work as slave labor. By day, we loaded and unloaded the baggage train, carried heavy burdens ourselves, under the watchful eyes of guards, gathered firewood, and fetched water. In the evenings, we collected fodder for the tethered war elephants and horses. We were not fed; we had to forage scraps as best we might. If we lagged at our labors, we were beaten unmercifully. At night, we were shackled and roped together to sleep on the bare ground.

The second day, the wounded Jarai I had questioned back at the upland meadow died in his sleep. His shackles were removed and his corpse was tossed casually to one side of the trail.

At dawn on the fourth day, I was roused by the guards and untied from my companions. In fetters, wearing only my ripped and stained Jarai trousers, I was led away by a rope halter.

The king was seated beneath a high canopy of scarlet silk. He sat cross-legged on a woven mat upon a raised platform. To his rear, a semicircle of noblemen and military commanders was seated. A royal retainer held a gold-handled parasol of white silk above the monarch's head.

I was led forward and halted some yards before the platform. A violent shove and a heavy blow to my head sent me sprawling face-down on the dust. My head ringing, I struggled to a kneeling position.

A smile on his thick lips, the king looked down at me. He spoke mildly, but his voice was deep and resonant.

"We are told you rode a stallion of foreign breed, a horse that once graced the stables of an emissary to the court at Angkor. How came you by this steed?"

"He is my property," I answered. Drawing myself as erect as my position allowed, I continued. "I am Siao Hu, the Young Tartar"—I translated for his benefit—"son of Hsü Ta-kuan, most noble envoy from the Dragon Throne to the court of Kambuja."

"It is as we suspected. How did you come to be with the *pnong* dogs, Young Barbarian?"

"I escaped from the capital when it was overrun by the Cham," I said simply.

"Obviously," the king commented dryly. He did not pursue the subject. The smile had not left his lips, but his eyes, beneath their heavy lids, were cold and appraising.

One of the king's military advisers leaned forward and whispered something to the king, handing him as he did so a composite bow. The king examined the weapon, canted it at an angle, and tested its pull. Placing the bow across his knees, he returned his attention to me.

"This is a weapon common to your country. Is it you who taught these savages to make such a bow?"

"Yes."

"Then you, Barbarian, are responsible for their resistance to our authority. It is because of you that we found it necessary to teach the curs a lesson . . . and came away with a paltry handful of slaves. It was a costly lesson.

Apart from the soldiers you killed personally, and we are told it was no small number, you owe us for the lives of all the soldiers lost in the punitive encounter."

I said nothing. What could I say against such reasoning? Had the Jarai no right to defend themselves and their homes and families? In the king's estimation, they had no such right.

"Had not the soldiers needed some slaves to transport their wounded, you would have been killed along with the rest of the rebellious herd. It is an oversight that we can easily rectify. Because we have been told that you fought well, and because you are not a *pnong*, we are disposed to be lenient. We will give you a choice. You can join your illustrious ancestors now, or you can discharge your debt to us, and at the same time avenge your father's death, by joining our cause. What say you?"

Had I been given this choice a few days earlier, I would have opted for death. I still cared little whether I lived or died, but destiny had spared me for some other purpose. Only a fool flies in the face of destiny.

"I will serve your cause."

The king's smile broadened slightly. "A prudent choice." His next remarks, addressed to the captain of the guard, were in a crisper tone. "Strip him of his rags. Clothe him, arm him, return to him his horse . . . and teach him proper respect."

A second blow to my head knocked me prostrate at the king's feet.

Life underwent an immediate change. I lived with a cavalry troop and rode in the vanguard of the advancing army.

I was not accepted in the unit with good grace, but none could dispute the king's command. I did not blame my fellow cavalrymen for their distant attitude and open hostility. I was a freakish stranger in their midst. I was more than a head taller than the average man. Mounted on my big stallion, I stood out like a beacon on a barren foreshore. While I did carry a Khmer battle ax in a loop on my saddle, unlike my companions I rode with stirrups and was armed with a strange-looking bow rather than the customary cavalry spear. No friendship was offered me, and I sought none.

I felt guilty that my former Jarai comrades were in the

slave ranks, but there was little that I could do about it. Several times I tried to take them food, but each time I was prevented by the guards from completing my mission. During the day, their labors in the baggage train and my position in the forward units prevented my seeing them. In the evenings, when they brought fodder for the horses, I sometimes encountered one or more of my former companions. When this happened, they averted their gaze. Conversational attempts on my part met with silence or mumbled responses. Whether I wanted it or not, a master-slave relationship had intruded to separate us. In one sense, I was grateful for the infrequency of contact and growing rift. The presence of the Jarai was a constant reminder of my personal loss.

During the long days and nights, I tried not to dwell on my immediate past. I concentrated on the moment and my present situation. Predominant in my speculations were my impressions of King Jayavarman VII—Jaya, the Protector.

In Angkor, he had been pictured as a devout and saintly Buddhist, a man of peaceful convictions. That he had twice renounced his rightful throne to prevent bloodshed had been held up as proof of piety and humility. Devout Buddhist he may have been, but there was little in his bearing during our brief encounter, or as he stood proudly erect beneath the royal parasol in the swaying howdah of his war elephant during the daily march, to indicate humility.

There were contradictions. The king wore no crown. His only ornament was a wide gold bracelet on his right wrist. His elephant was unadorned. His only trapping was the white parasol of state.

Other aspects disturbed me. From all accounts, the king was in his middle fifties. His physical appearance was that of a much younger man. He was short, but powerfully built. His neck was thick, his torso and arms well muscled, his belly flat, and his face unlined. No gray flecked his carefully plaited hair. He exuded an aura of strength and power.

What I found most disturbing, however, was something not easily defined. Living close to nature, as I had over the last few years, one acquires an inner sense that warns of danger. It is the instinct for self-preservation. It cannot be ignored if one wants to stay alive in the jungle. I had experienced this warning in the presence of the king. It had not come from the threat of death in the choice I'd been offered. It had not left me when that threat had been lifted. The king had turned on me a smiling countenance, but the smile had not extended to his coldly appraising eyes. In the king, I sensed an implacable foe. Yet it went deeper than that. It was as though some sort of bond had been established between us.

I went over the conversational exchange that had taken place between us. There hadn't been much to my side of the exchange, and the king had used words sparingly. What he had said and what his words implied were significant.

In my mind, I was almost sure that the king had known my identity before I was brought into his presence. I am convinced also that he understands the Mandarin dialect I speak. Siao Hu, translated into Khmer phonetically, has no meaning. Only to the Chinese has Tartar the connotation of "barbarian." That the king had understood this and chosen to derogate my nickname indicated to me that he held my father's rank and station, and, by implication, the Sung court and the Chinese people, in disdain. There could be no other explanation. It would be absurd for the Khmer, who had come so recently upon the scene, to consider the Tartars barbarians.

In his reasons for offering me my life, the king had made the fine distinction that I was not a *phong*—a savage. In Khmer, the shades of meaning between "barbarian" and "savage" are, at best, indistinct. The king left no doubt that he considered mountain tribespeople on the same level as animals, and myself as only slightly above that category. When the Jarai resisted the slave-gathering force, the king was infuriated and ordered the annihilation of the tribe. That my Jarai companions and myself had escaped this edict was due solely to the force commander's need for litter bearers.

As we wound slowly through the foothills and onto the plains, I had much to ponder.

The army, which seemed to me at the time to be of considerable size, was a comparatively small force. I learned something of its composition and genesis as the days passed. I also gained new insight into the character of the king.

When his father died in 1160, Prince Jayavarman was thirty-five and commanding a Khmer force campaigning in Champa. For some reason, he chose not to oppose the succession of a half brother to the throne. Until 1165, Jayavarman remained in Champa, campaigning now on behalf of the new monarch.

In 1165, learning that the throne was threatened, Jayavarman marched his forces toward Angkor. He arrived too late to prevent the takeover and was in something of a quandary.

As the usurper did not, Jayavarman knew that the Cham were preparing for an invasion of Kambuja. If he launched his forces against Angkor, the country would be so weakened that it would fall easy prey to Cham attackers. Jayavarman again renounced the throne and retired eastward with his army still intact.

The Cham armies launched their invasion in 1170. That they were defeated was due in large measure to the entrenched forces in Jayavarman blocking their path in the northeast. Jayavarman's army followed the retreating Cham forces into the highlands. Lacking sufficient strength to continue on and attack the Cham capital, he established a redoubt in the highlands and remained there.

It was this period in the life of the Khmer prince that gave birth to the rumors that he had gone into self-imposed exile in a monastic retreat. It was a romanticized version of the actual facts. True, he was virtually in self-exile, but he had no intention of remaining in that condition. It is also true that he devoted a good deal of energy to the construction of Buddhist temples in his highland retreat. From what I learned, there must have been many in Angkor who knew the facts and the prince's intentions.

Jayavarman meant to march on Angkor and claim his rightful throne. He lacked two things needed to ensure success. He had been so long removed from the capital and court circles that he needed time to muster support among the factions opposed to the usurper. His highland retreat was so distant that it placed severe limitations on troop replacement and recruitment. In 1177, he had overcome most of the obstacles and was preparing to march. Then came the lightning thrust of the Cham seaborne invasion. In Kambuja, what was not in the hands of the Cham conquerors was thrown into anarchy. Jayavarman's carefully laid plans were thwarted once again.

Now, in 1181, he had claimed the throne that had been his by right of inheritance for twenty-one years. Many of the veteran campaigners with him now had been with him for more than twenty-two years. Others were more recent recruits from the remnants of the Khmer forces defeated at Angkor. The Cham mercenaries were the most recent additions. He expected to pick up support along our path. Our destination was Angkor; our objective was to purge the land of Cham forces of occupation.

We reached the Mekong well to the south of the rocky plateau where Morning Mist and I had crossed it years before. Here the stream was divided into several channels and raced past rocky islets. For two days of marching, we followed the river south until we reached a point where the channels joined and the river flowed placidly between high levees it had built for itself through countless centuries of flooding the surrounding plains. A considerable force, nearly the equal of our small army, awaited us at this point of rendezvous. Large rafts were tied to the riverbank, waiting to ferry us across.

The river behind us, our path lay almost due west. Angkor was no more than a five-day march ahead, but our pace was slowed as more and more Khmer units appeared from the nearby towns and villages to swell our ranks.

With Angkor still a two-day march away, the army, by now of formidable size, was divided into two bodies. My cavalry unit was attached to the army escorting the monarch. We swung to a northwesterly route.

The Cham army awaited us some miles east of the razed city of Yasodharapura. Had their intelligence advised them of the size to which the Khmer forces had grown, the Cham might not have chosen to make a stand. Still, they had little choice. Our army blocked them to the east and northeast. The Khmer army moving up from the south cut off that line of retreat. No Cham fleet rode at anchor in the Great Lake to succor them. The only avenue of escape remaining was to the west, where each step took then deeper into hostile country and farther from their homeland.

There was another factor. The Cham believed they had crushed the Khmer for all time. The lack of organized resistance over the past four years had reinforced that belief. Even had they known they were heavily out-numbered, overconfidence probably would have overridden prudence.

The day of battle dawned bright and clear. The armies were drawn up facing each other across a grassy plain dotted with stubbled paddy fields. Not a breath of air stirred the scorched grass and our battle pennants hung limply. We had been joined during the night by elements of the southern army and presented a front that must have dismayed the Cham commanders.

A cinnabar sun hung low on the eastern horizon, painting the scene in red-gold hue. Conch shells blew the advance. Our army started to move ponderously forward and now the pennants stirred with the motion. It was an awesome spectacle as the war elephants, spearmen, crossbowmen, and archers closed the gap with measured tread to the cadence of drumbeats. The conches blared again and the pace quickened, the war elephants going into a shuffling gait and trumpeting shrilly. The drums took up a faster beat. The Cham Army started to move slowly forward, and as the distance narrowed, clouds of arrows arched in both directions.

Since the disposition of the cavalry was on the flanks, my view of the advancing lines was considerably restricted. I could make out the white parasol of the king in the forefront of the advance, but only the commander riding the elephant closest to the northern flank was clearly visible. Dust, rising in choking clouds and hanging in the still air, further obscured the scene.

From the swaying platform on the elephant's back, the commander shouted orders and encouragement to the foot soldiers flanking his lumbering mount. The officer wore a helmet of braided leather with long flaps to protect his neck and shoulders. As armor, he wore a leather vest-like garment. His weapons were a short bow and a long cavalry spear. The foot soldiers, bareheaded, wore leather jerkins. The spearmen, armed with eight-foot spears or halberds, carried rectangular leather shields. The bowmen, both those who had crossbows and those with the short Khmer bows, had no shields and would fall back behind the line of spearmen once the hand-to-hand combat started. Most of the foot soldiers carried either swords or battle axes in addition to their primary weapons.

In the early stages of battle, the role of the cavalry was restricted. Our mounts would not survive a charge against a line of spearmen. Our task was to ride down and dispatch foot soldiers once the ranks were broken and we could pursue targets of opportunity. We rode in loose formation, fanned out over a wide front. Once the battle was joined, we would attempt to sweep around the opposing flanks. At the same time, we had to prevent such out-flanking tactics by the enemy cavalry.

Most of the cavalrymen carried circular leather shields. They were armed with cavalry spears, varying in length from fourteen to eighteen feet. A few had crossbows, essentially a one-shot weapon since, once fired, the rider had to dismount to re-cock the bow by means of a belt hook. Secondary weapons—swords, battle axes, or both—were looped to their saddles.

With one exception, the cavalrymen wore protective leather jerkins. The exception was myself, since none of the available jackets were large enough to fit me. Nor did I carry a shield. I was armed with two six-foot Jarai bows, three quivers of arrows, and a battle ax. The long arrows, and the thumb ring I wore, I had made myself during the long march.

In the swirling dust, I did not see the armies meet. I was aware of the fateful moment by the shouting and clash of arms. With the pressure of my heels, I urged Sa-lu-tzu forward into the fray.

chapter 12

THE ASSAULT ON MY FATHER'S COMPOUND FOUR YEARS earlier and the attack on the Jarai village were my introductions to conflict. Bloody though those encounters had been, they were mere skirmishes compared with the clash of armies.

This was my first encounter with large-scale warfare. It should stand out vividly in my memory. It doesn't. I recall certain incidents with clarity, but, for the most part, the action has become blurred by the passage of time. One reason is that the loss of Morning Mist and the children was still fresh in my mind, to the exclusion of other emotions and sharpened awareness. I fought instinctively, with little regard for personal safety. My major concern was to preserve Sa-lu-tzu from injury.

I was not consumed by a desire to avenge my father's death. The pain in my heart gave me more reason to vent my anger on my Khmer companions than on the Cham soldiers opposing us. My instincts now were those of the hunter who kills only according to his needs and has no stomach for wanton slaughter. But there was no choice. It was a simple case of kill or be killed.

In the confusion, deafening din, and choking clouds of dust, I had but two thoughts. I must avoid the serried ranks of enemy spearmen to keep my stallion from being impaled, and I must keep myself beyond the range of crossbow bolts. Arrows did reach me, but they were mostly spent, and although I was grazed, none found its mark. On my part, I had a distinct advantage in the superior range and accuracy of my composite bow. From a comparatively safe distance, I picked my targets at will and sent my shafts singing into the milling throng with devastating effect.

Of the entire battle, only two encounters are etched on my memory.

At one point, I found myself close to two war elephants locked in a titanic struggle. One I recognized as that of the Khmer king. Trunks intertwined and tusks locked, the ponderous beasts swayed in a deadly dance. Seated behind the ears of their mammoth steeds, the mahouts slashed at each other with halberds. The king, with his parasol bearer to his rear, sat calmly, his long spear poised at the ready. As I wheeled not far from the plunging elephants, I winged an arrow at the Cham mahout. The distance was not great. The arrow caught him in the chest, penetrating his leather armor with ease. Clutching frantically at the shaft protruding from his breast, he toppled from his perch. Advancing pikemen forced me on a divergent course and I saw no more of the action.

The second incident occurred late in the battle. It taught me the worth of the Khmer ax and is indelibly impressed on my memory.

I had exhausted my supply of arrows. With my bows slung over my shoulder, I rode with ax in hand. A Cham spearman loomed in my path, his spear braced and extended to spit the stallion. Sa-lu-tzu responded instantly to the pressure of my knees and slid past the lethal point with only inches to spare. As the Cham lunged forward, my descending ax neatly sheared through his spear shaft. As the ax continued its swing, I twisted my wrist and brought it down to split the spearman's skull.

I was familiar with the Khmer ax, but I had given little thought to its efficacy as a weapon. I had used one to good advantage in clearing brush and felling trees and in the shaping of my first crude bow. It consists of a three-to-four-foot wooden half that is curved at the top. A wedge of steel is set and firmly secured to the outer side of the curve. It is light and a remarkably effective weapon. From the day of the battle, it became an indispensable part of my personal armory.

It was a fierce battle, but one of relatively short duration. The remainder of the Khmer army arrived from the southeast to join the fray shortly after the initial clash. The Cham forces, hopelessly outnumbered and outmaneuvered, were cut to ribbons.

One moment the air was filled with the tumult of battle; the next moment a strange hush descended. The dust started to settle to reveal the trampled fields strewn with the dead and dying. The day and the field were ours.

Khmer soldiers went stolidly about their tasks of dispatching the Cham wounded and collecting weapons and our own dead and wounded. A trembling Sa-lu-tzu, his sides heaving, stood stock-still. I noticed blood oozing from a gash in his foreleg and dismounted to examine the wound. I experienced no elation at our victory, no surge of relief that I had come through the ordeal unscathed. My only reaction was an immense weariness.

As I stood beside the stallion, my mouth was dry and my eyes smarted from the abrasive dust. Slipping my ax back into its saddle loop, I glanced upward at the sky. The sun still stood well short of its midday zenith.

The king selected a site about half a mile north of the rubble of the destroyed capital for his temporary residence. Although it was nothing more than a sprawling collection of tents and silken pavilions, it was formally named Jayasri. Within days, however, river craft bore timber from the forest and distant hills and a more permanent city started to rise on the plain. An army of slaves and artisans was put to work and peasants from the surrounding rural communities were pressed into service.

The cavalry unit to which I was attached was bivouacked on the eastern fringe of the construction activity, but we did not long escape its inroads. Foremen, guards, and gangs of slave labor appeared one morning and work started on the building of stables, barracks for the troopers, and dwellings for the officers. Not far away, heavy timbers were used to construct stockades for the war elephants.

For the next two weeks, I exercised Sa-lu-tzu and attended to such matters as refurbishing my stock of arrows and acquiring a leather jerkin. Beyond that, I went through the days listlessly, caring little for food, drink, or the activity around me. There were women aplenty to

satisfy the appetites of my fellow cavalrymen, but I had
no inclination in that direction. In barracks life, however,
it is next to impossible to isolate one's self completely from
one's comrades-in-arms. And, in my case, there were
practical considerations that made some of the troopers
seek me out.

Although no cavalry units had been involved in the
punitive action against the Jarai village, word of the bowmanship of the tribesmen and my small part in the encounter had reached the cavalrymen. No doubt my
actions were embellished in the telling. It also appeared
to be common knowledge that the introduction of the
composite bow to the Jarai was my doing.

Then came the battle with the Cham. Our cavalry had
suffered heavy losses, yet I, despite my lack of shield or
jerkin, had come through without a scratch, my horse
but lightly wounded. There were those, both officers and
troopers, who had witnessed my battle tactics and had
seen firsthand the effectiveness of the composite bow.

I do not recall who was the first to approach me, but
in my third week at Jayasri I found history repeating
itself. As I had four years earlier, I found myself demon-
strating the range of the bow and its accuracy at varying
ranges. I explained how the thumb ring gave added pull
and distance, and how the use of stirrups imparted stability and permitted more flexibility in archery from horseback. Within a week, I found myself once again cast in
the role of an instructor, in both the fabrication and use
of the Chinese *kung*. I did not, I fear, have much success
in selling the concept of stirrups.

I rapidly gained converts from my own troop and other
cavalry units. It was absorbing work that helped to lift my
spirits from the black despondency that had been with
me for months. The memory of Morning Mist and my
loss did not fade, but the pain receded somewhat as I
lost myself in work. And, as they had with the Jarai, my
skills gained me the respect of and a measure of acceptance by my Khmer fellow cavalrymen.

I still did not count myself a craftsman in the making
of a composite bow. My skill at archery, however, must
have very nearly rivaled that of a Chinese *kung shou*,
expert archer. I would have welcomed a chance to compete against a bow master of my own race. But it
mattered little. There were none in Kambuja to match

my skill. In the land of the blind, the one-eyed man is king.

Early in the fourth month of the Year of the Bull, we received word that our cavalry unit was assigned to a force undertaking a mission against the southern kingdom of Malyang. The king of that vassal state of the empire had refused to acknowledge the sovereignty of Jayavarman VII and was to be taught a lesson.

Malyang was not a large state. The army assembled for the punitive expedition was relatively small. Only four cavalry units were attached to the force that marched westward to skirt the Great Lake before turning to the south. As we rode in the van, banners fluttering, I was pleased to note that almost half my unit had forsaken their traditional cavalry spears in favor of composite bows, and a sprinkling of bowman rode in other units.

It was not until the second day of the march that I received the surprise. I had not known who commanded the force. There was no reason why I should have been curious on that score, and my position with the forward units was well in advance of the command elephants. On the evening of the second day, however, as I rode back to tether Sa-lu-tzu for the night, I saw the commanding general being assisted from his kneeling elephant. Imagine my shocked surprise when I recognized my old friend and boyhood companion, Sri Vidyanandana.

"Vidya!" I shouted, unable to contain myself.

The Cham prince turned toward me, a frown on his face. For a moment he regarded me without apparent recognition. Then a smile lit his handsome face and he inclined his head slightly before turning toward his silken pavilion.

That night I was summoned to the prince's pavilion. Vidya had lost none of his taste for luxury. The matting of his pavilion was strewn with furs. A low table bore the remains of a sumptuous repast. He was attended by six slaves, three of each sex, all young and comely. It was then I received my second surprise of the day, for I recognized one of the male slaves as a Jarai, my former companion of the hunt.

Vidya ordered the remains of his meal removed and commanded that rice wine be brought. When the jar of wine appeared, he dismissed the servants and the guard who had ushered me into his presence. The slaves withdrew with downcast eyes. By neither glance nor gesture had the Jarai indicated recognition, yet I was sure he knew who I was and I experienced a twinge of guilt.

On my arrival in the pavilion, Vidya had acknowledged my presence with nothing more than a perfunctory nod. When the slaves had withdrawn, however, his face was split by a wide grin as he bounded to his feet and advanced to me. He embraced me lightly, then moved back with a mock grimace.

"You stink of horses, Tartar. But then you always did. I'll never know how my dear sister could have tolerated your intimate embrace."

"You are wearing enough perfume to disguise the odor of both elephants and horses," I retorted dryly.

Vidya grinned. "You've grown. I hardly recognized you. In fact, I recognized that brute of a stallion before it struck me it was actually you." He sobered. "I thought you were dead. How did you escape when Angkor was destroyed?"

I gave a brief account of my escape to the safety of a hill-tribe village. For some reason, I did not indicate that the slave assisting me was a girl, nor did I tell Vidya of my marriage or murdered family. It was not disloyalty to the memory of Morning Mist. It was that I felt such a relationship would be beyond Vidya's comprehension. The only real interest he displayed was when I recounted the Khmer slaughter of the villagers and my recruitment into the Khmer cavalry.

As I talked, I observed Vidya. He, too, had changed. He was shorter than myself by half a head, but he was tall by Khmer standards. His hair was carefully coiffed. His arms and torso were oiled and perfumed. He wore several flashing rings on his fingers and wide gold bracelets on each arm. The hem of his *sampot* was richly embroidered with gold and silver. There was about him an imperious air, as befitted royalty, but his smile was open and disarming. He had matured into an unquestionably handsome man. I could find little trace of the carefree youth I had known in the days we prowled the Vijaya waterfront together.

"Come," said Vidya when I had concluded my account, "I am forgetting my manners. Join me in a cup of wine." When we were seated, I questioned Vidya. "When I watched the temple of Angkor Wat under attack," I said, "I wondered if you would be safe, even though you are of the Cham royal house. What actually happened?"

Vidya frowned. He hesitated a moment before answering. "I wasn't there. I didn't even know about the attack until some weeks later. Had I known of it in advance, I would certainly have warned you."

"Where were you?"

"Preah Vihear. Do you know of the sanctuary?"

"I've heard of it. It's in the mountains to the north, isn't it?"

"Yes. It's about eighty-five miles northeast of Angkor in the Dangrek Range. Fantastic temple. Built right on the edge of a thousand-foot cliff. Pretty secluded. I'd been taken there for instruction and meditation. It's ideal for that. It's cut off from the rest of the kingdom, and, frankly, it's damned dull. We didn't learn about the attack on Angkor until some priests who had escaped from Angkor Wat found their way to the sanctuary weeks later. They told us some frightening stories concerning the unstable state of the countryside through which they'd passed. Even though I am Cham, my mentors felt it would be better for me to stay where I was."

"You stayed there four years?" I questioned incredulously.

"No, two years. By then I couldn't take much more of the peace and solitude. I went to Lopburi, in the west. There I undertook some military training. It's a bit livelier than Preah Vihear, but it was still too rustic for my tastes.

"When I heard through couriers that King Jayavarman was mounting an assault to retake Angkor, I mustered some troops and set out to join him. I caught up with his army at Kompong Thom and offered him my services. I was commanding units of the southern force, but I arrived in time for the last part of the battle."

"But they were Cham. Didn't it bother you that you were fighting your own people?"

Vidya grinned. "Not at all. My father could have told me of his plans. I could have had a command. But then I'd have ended up on the losing side in that battle. It's better to be with the victor than the vanquished."

Vidya's attitude and lack of loyalty astounded me. "And now?" I queried.

"And now," Vidya said, with a sweeping gesture of his hand, "I'm entrusted with this mission. The king assures me I have a brilliant military future. He is arranging a royal marriage for me when this little operation is concluded."

We drank some wine. There was a little more conversation of a general nature, but I sensed that Vidya was becoming restive. In truth, wearing nothing but a frayed *sampot*, I felt awkward in his illustrious presence. I am sure he was relieved when I excused myself and took my leave.

Vidya accompanied me to the pavilion flap. For a moment his hand rested lightly on my forearm.

"We must see to it, my dear Tartar, that we find something a bit better for you than being a cavalry trooper."

The way he said "trooper" made it sound like something one step removed from a horse. I nodded and smiled.

The remaining week of our march to the south was uneventful. I was not summoned again to Vidyas's presence. I had not expected to be, and I gave it no thought.

There was only one thing I found puzzling. Each evening slaves and a number of the foot soldiers were sent into the surrounding countryside armed with long-shafted, forked sticks. Their task was to hunt for poisonous snakes. Before the week was out, one wagon in the baggage train was piled high with woven baskets filled with cobras, pit vipers, and krait. I ascertained that the order for this collecting of venomous reptiles came from the commanding general himself, but there was no hint concerning his purpose.

chapter 13

I WILL NOT DIGNIFY THE ACTION THAT TOOK PLACE BY calling it a battle. It could be described more properly as a rout.

In a shallow valley on the approaches to the Malyang capital, we were met by an undisciplined force consisting mainly of foot soldiers. They had no cavalry support and only four war elephants. We formed into battle array. The conch shells sounded their wailing signal for the advance and our elephants started forward in a shambling gait. But before the front lines met in combat, the enemy broke and fled in disorder, yielding the field without a fight. There were a few scattered skirmishes where the fleeing enemies were trapped and had no choice but to make a stand, but there was nothing even remotely approaching a battle.

Our orders were to take no prisoners. It was killing ground. I pursued a few spearmen, dropping them in their tracks with ease, but I had no stomach for this kind of warfare. On a larger scale, it was a repetition of the slaughter inflicted on the Jarai village. My fellow cavalrymen, under no such moral constraints as myself, killed everyone in their path.

The city was enclosed in a wooden stockade. It was breached with ease and with very little loss of life on our side. Once within the city, our soldiers raped and pillaged without let or hindrance. The only restraint placed upon them was that the city should not be put to the torch until the palace and temples were stripped of valuables and the royal granaries were emptied of foodstuffs. No injunction was placed on the taking of life, and the cries of the victims and wailing of mourners went on throughout the afternoon and well into the night.

The next morning the surviving townspeople were assembled in the market square. Under the supervision of our soldiers, some were put to work gathering the spoils of the city and loading this plunder into bullock carts. Others, by far the largest number of the populace, were marched to the sun-baked paddy fields beyond the city where they were directed to dig an immense pit. Small details were given yet other tasks: the gathering of stockade timbers to build a funeral pyre for our dead; the fabrication of a huge trellis of bamboo poles.

I did not grasp the purpose of the bamboo construction, but the object of the pit was not hard to fathom. Many of the laboring townsfolk must have deduced the purpose of the pit as it grew in size, yet few resisted the commands of our military guards. Those who did, who threw down their mattocks or refused to carry the baskets of earth from the digging site, were dispatched on the spot.

I learned later that while many of the noblemen and their families had fled the city when news of our approach reached them, the king, his family, and some of the noblemen had stayed behind. No doubt the king had hoped to bargain for his safety by pledging belated fealty to the Angkor court. If so, he was quickly disabused on this score.

On our entry into the city, the palace grounds had been surrounded and all within taken prisoner. Our war elephants had been turned loose to forage in the gardens. With the exception of the king, the male members of the royal and noble households had been assembled in the palace courtyard. There, before the horrified eyes of their wives and daughters, they had been summarily executed by decapitation.

Vidya ordered a victory feast prepared at the palace for himself and his senior officers. The king and the women of the royal household were guests at the festivities. At the conclusion of the banquet, Vidya and his commanders took their pleasure with the women. I was

informed that Vidya played a prominent part in the orgy
and that later he retired with two of the young princesses
to the royal chamber to conclude his revelry.

In the morning, the slaves, servants, and women of the
household were supplied as live targets for a company of
crossbowmen. The king, stripped naked and confined in a
bamboo cage so small that he could neither stand nor sit,
was a witness to this scene before being borne away on
the bed of a farm cart commandeered for that purpose.

In the late afternoon, the pit beyond the town was
deemed sufficiently large to serve its intended purpose. It
was about ten feet deep, some twenty feet in width, and
it stretched the length of two paddy fields. The inhabitants of the capital and the nearby rural communities
were rounded up. Men, women, children, babes in arms,
the aged and the infirm—all were herded to the yawning
hole. To most, it must have been obvious by this time
that the pit was intended as a mass grave, yet they shuffled
toward their fate with the docility of farm animals being
led to the slaughter. The sympathy I had entertained for
their plight waned.

When the populace was all gathered at the pit's edge,
they were prodded into jumping into the hole. This they
did with the same sheep-like resignation they had displayed in assembling. Babies were passed downward. The
aged were assisted. It was as though the earth was swal-
lowing them into its gaping maw before my eyes, and in
silence broken only by a low undertone of muted complaint. It was an awesome spectacle.

Finally, all but three trembling youths who had been
singled out from the throng and held to one side had disappeared into the pit. It was now that I discovered why
the snakes had been collected during our southward march.

The wagon loaded with its baskets of reptiles was
brought to the edge of the pit. Slaves gingerly carried
the baskets with their deadly contents to points indicated
by guards. At a signal, the slaves removed the lids and
dumped the writhing serpents into the open pit. Immediately, screams rose up from the shadowed depths.

Now another mystery was resolved. Slaves carried the
sections of bamboo trellis and set them in place over
the pit. Moving cautiously out onto the swaying bamboo,
they lashed the sections together to form a giant grating. I
had assumed the Malyang peasants and city dwellers were

to be buried alive. This was not the case. They were to suffer more protracted agonies as they slowly perished from lack of food and water in their below-ground prison. Those who died from snakebite within the next few hours would be the lucky ones.

An encampment was set up to the north of the city. In the evening, the city was set aflame by our withdrawing troops. As I prepared to bed down for the night, I watched the flames soar skyward. There is a magic in the spectacle of fire that unlocks the floodgates of memory and triggers the imagination. My random thoughts dwelt on the events of the long day and also went skipping backward in time.

I am neither fascinated nor horrified by snakes. I have a healthy respect for them, particularly the virulent species that abound in these regions. My first reaction when I watched the reptiles being showered downward into the prison pit was one of revulsion. Then the significance and symbolism of the act struck me.

From the Buddhist religious training of my boyhood, I associated the cobra with the *naga,* the multi-headed mythical serpent that gave the Enlightened One his first bath and sheltered him from the seven-day storm raised by his enemies to prevent his Enlightenment. From my exposure to the Hindu mythologies of Champa and Kambuja, I knew the *naga* played an important role. The *naga* king is usually depicted as a patron of fertility, wealth, justice, and spiritual enlightenment. In the animistic beliefs of the peasants and hill tribes, the cobra is usually thought to represent retributive justice.

It mattered little to the unfortunate captives in the pit whether they died quickly from snake venom or starved slowly beneath a blistering sun. The end result was inevitable—in either case, death. It was their *karma,* their fate, for having been the subjects of a rebellious monarch. Vidya had been motivated by neither sadism nor mercy. To him, the fate of the captives was a matter of supreme indifference. As an example to other Khmer subject states, Malyang must be punished. How its people perished did not concern Vidya. What concerned him was that the manner of their passing and the fate of their kingdom have impact on other vassal states that might be contemplating revolt.

In this light, Vidya's refinement of torture was purely

theatrical. It was for the benefit of his troops, which would spread the word, and for the three young men who had been spared the pit so that they could witness the death throes of their people and convey the message to nearby communities. In this context, the poisonous snakes represented the wrath and swift justice of the Khmer god-king in distant Angkor. If it was Vidya's idea, it was effective symbolism, and I could not but applaud his imaginative initiative.

What surprised me most, however, was that I had identified with the captives and sympathized with their plight. True, this sympathy had diminished when they had failed in their halfhearted defense and accepted their fate without demur. But my identification, however fleeting, had existed. I made an effort to fathom this weakness in my character.

The Confucian principles under which I'd been brought up dictated unquestioning fealty to one's father and unswerving allegiance to superior authority and, ultimately, the emperor. It was a stratified social order I had never questioned. Nor had I questioned my position in the structure. Why should I? It was preordained by birth, as was the position of those less fortunate than myself. And, by diligent application to study of the Classics and the successful completion of competitive examinations, it was always possible to improve one's position. In theory, one could rise from buffalo-boy to emperor.

My exposure to the cultures of Champa and Angkor had reinforced rather than eroded my beliefs. There were differences between these Indianized cultures and my own, such as the status of women and the rigid caste system that bound one, in this life, to the position attained by birth, but the hierarchical structure was essentially the same as in China. I saw no reason to question these values.

There was certainly no softness deriving from my Khitan heritage. The fierce, nomadic Tartars from the bleak steppes were not noted for pity.

The only thing I could conclude was that my four years of life with the Jarai had altered my viewpoint in some subtle fashion. Still, I could not see how this could be so. I had accepted the intimacy of longhouse life and the village decision-making process by council debate as essentially a family structure. Authority had been vested in the village headman, the shaman, and the council of elders. I had been accepted into the family circle and had earned a position in the council by competitive process. It was not a complex structure, but one admirably suited to survival of a small group in a hostile wilderness. I had always considered that if the society had expanded to include other villages and taken on the trappings of a civilized society, the village authority would have evolved into something very similar to the Confucian system prevailing in my native land. The headman might not become an emperor, of course, but he would become a minor monarch. The shaman would graduate to high priest, the superior huntsmen would emerge as an elite group of military commanders and nobility, and a master-servant relationship was bound to follow.

Yet, without question, my sojourn with the Jarai had changed some of my thinking. I looked upon the simple tribespeople as inferior—due to the fact that they had not experienced the benefits of civilization—but not as savages. They were bound by superstitions and lacked formal education, but they were wise in other ways. They had learned to live in harmony with Nature, who could be a cruel and capricious mistress. And they had earned nobility in my mind and heart through their spirited defense of their village.

This was the crux of the matter. Since I now looked upon the Jarai, and by extension, other hill tribespeople, as human beings, it was only natural that I should extend this to the commoners among the Khmer. I was measuring people by a new yardstick. Was this weakness? It could not be. I had learned these values through Morning Mist, who had given me nothing but strength. It was not weakness; it was a new insight. If I did not allow this to degenerate into sentimentality, the insight could serve to give me added wisdom and strength.

I was not accustomed to deductive reasoning of this nature. I felt I had grasped a major truth, but my thoughts were still confused. There were other perplexing questions, but I would leave them to the morrow.

With my head resting comfortably on my saddle, I closed my eyes and shut out the ruddy glare of the burning city. Within minutes, I drifted into a deep and dreamless sleep.

We remained encamped to the north of the burned-out city for three days. On the second day, I visited the pit site. The stench of rotting corpses was overpowering. The noontime sun beat straight down into the depths. I could see some movement among the bodies and there were faint sounds of moaning, but thousands were corpses already bloated with their burden of foul-smelling gases. I did not visit the charnel pit again, and I was thankful that my duties as a cavalry trooper exempted me from guard duty at the site.

In the afternoon of the third day, crossbowmen were sent to the pit to shoot anyone still moving. Then the guards were withdrawn and preparations got under way to break camp the following morning.

I had bathed in the shallow river, partaken of the evening meal, and was about to take a look at Sa-lu-tzu before retiring when I received a summons to Prince Vidyanandana's pavilion. I arrived to find Vidya in the company of three of his commanders. They were all slightly intoxicated. Vidya was in an ebullient mood.

"Tartar," he said expansively, "the campaign went well, did it not? We have taught the dogs a lesson they will not soon forget."

I didn't consider that our expedition to Malyang was much of a campaign, and the "dogs" he referred to were in rather short supply to benefit from his instructive technique. Still, I could not dispute the fact that when word spread concerning the fate of the rebellious kingdom, it could not fail to have the desired impact. I smiled and nodded.

"To other matters." Vidya beamed. "You once demonstrated to me your prowess with your Chinese bow. I was impressed. I now find that you have shared your skill with a number of my cavalrymen. I have been advised that they performed very well with their new instruments."

"Thank you."

"The captain of the Sixth Cavalry Troop met with an unfortunate accident in the city. A vacancy exists. I am promoting you to his command."

The captain of the Sixth Cavalry Troop had indeed met with an accident. He was a roistering bully who had been killed by one of his own men in a dispute over a girl. I wondered if Vidya knew the facts of the episode. The trooper had not been punished for his mutinous act. It was the general consensus of opinion among my comrades-in-arms that the captain richly deserved his fate. The field promotion was an honor, but I was not at all sure I wanted to take over that particular command. Yet, what choice did I have?

"I am honored to accept the commission," I said.

"Good. You have our permission to leave."

On that curt dismissal, I turned and left. Still, I had no cause for complaint. With no previous military experience, and in only a bit more than four months of service in the Khmer army, I had risen to the rank of captain.

The camp was astir well before dawn. Leading Salu-tzu, I joined the Sixth Cavalry Troop to assume command. The news of my appointment had preceded me. While I was received with civility, it was not difficult to perceive that my posting did not meet a consensus of approval. I had not expected it to be otherwise. I was not only alien of form and figure, but I had been promoted over the heads of veteran troopers of long standing. I would have to earn the respect of my troopers and fellow officers. I did not expect this would be an easy achievement.

The army formed into a long column and moved northward shortly after sunrise. The cavalry led the procession, with myself at the head of Sixth Cavalry Troop as the second cavalry unit in the line. Behind the cavalry, and ahead of the columns of foot soldiers, the farm cart bearing the caged king of Malyang swayed and bounced over the uneven track. Behind the infantry, the elephants with their escorts of spearmen were strung out in loose formation. The pack train, swollen with added carts bearing the plunder of the fallen city, brought up the rear under the watchful eyes of guards.

It would take us slightly more than a week to make the return journey. I had ample time in which to plan the future of Sixth Cavalry Troop.

chapter 14

WE ENCOUNTERED A GOOD DEAL OF ACTIVITY WELL BE-
fore reaching Angkor. When the army rounded the northwestern extremity of the Great Lake, we were met with
the spectacle of an ant-like army of laborers repairing
the great road leading to the west and clearing mile after
mile of irrigation canals. The closer we got to Jayasri, the
more frenetic the activity became. I noted that although
the rice seedbed plantings were emerald-green, few peasants labored in the stubbled paddy fields preparing the
soil for planting.

We had been gone from Angkor less than a month. I
was astonished at the changes that had been wrought in
our absence. Glazed tiles glistened on the steeply pitched
roof of the new royal residence at Jayasri. Around the
palace, a number of imposing wooden buildings graced
the changed skyline. Some two miles southeast of Jayasri,
on the eastern bank of the Siemreap River and just south
of the East Baray reservoir, the stone foundation of a
new temple had taken shape. In the center of Jayasri
itself, another temple foundation was taking shape. Much
of the rubble of the destroyed city of Yasodharapura had
been cleared away. Immediately north of the looming hill-
top temple of Phnom Bakheng, which had been the geo-
metric center of Yasodharapura, a square with sides of
about one-and-three-quarters miles had been marked out

as the site of the new royal capital. Already, just outside this marked perimeter, excavation was in progress on
a wide ditch that would be the city's protective moat. We
had known that Jayasri was intended as a temporary
royal seat. The king was certainly wasting no time in
putting his plans for a more permanent capital into effect.

We Chinese are an industrious people, yet I have never
heard of or witnessed anything in my homeland to match
the feverish activity in progress at Angkor. The air rang
with the sounds of adzes and axes on wood and the chip-
ping of stonemason's chisels. Smoke belched from brick
kilns both day and night. Huge mounds of earth reared
next to the excavation sites. The waterways were choked
with river craft bringing heavy timbers and blocks of
sandstone and laterite cut from distant quarries. Dust rose
in clouds and hung thickly in the air. Everywhere one
looked, there was bustle and motion.

In this frenzy of construction, there seemed little labor
for other tasks. This undoubtedly accounted for the fact
that I had seen little activity in the fields. Yet in one area,
work was progressing hand in hand with the construction
projects.

The wellspring of Kambuja's strength and power is the
fantastic fertility of the alluvial soil of the plains surrounding the Great Lake. To stem the annual flooding of the
lake and to store the monsoon rains for use during the
half a year when no rain falls, the Khmer had developed
an ingenious and incredibly complex system of flood control and irrigation. It consists of a combination of dyking,
reservoirs, sluice gates, and mile upon mile of canals and
ditches lacing the countryside for many square miles in
the vicinity of Angkor. The Cham are nearly as skilled
as the Khmer in hydrological engineering. They fully appreciated the value of these waterworks to the Khmer
economy. During their four years of occupation, the Cham
deliberately neglected the irrigation system, allowing it to
fall into a sad state of disrepair. Now an army of laborers
equal to or surpassing in size that engaged in construction
was hard at work bringing the system back to working order.

I had never noticed any shortage of slave labor in
Angkor, but the immensity of the present projects meant
that the communities surrounding the capital must have

been stripped of all available manpower. I assumed that this was a temporary levy in order to accomplish as much as possible before the rains, which were now only a matter of weeks away, forced a slowdown in construction. When the rains softened the sun-baked soil of the paddy fields, much of this labor force would be diverted to the essential tasks of rice cultivation. Logical as my assumption was, it was only partially correct. A portion of the labor force was returned to the outlying villages when the rains came, but the majority remained in the capital on a shift-work basis that took full advantage of the periods during the day when the rains ceased or slackened. The king was determined that his plans would proceed without interruption. He had made provisions, as we in the military were to learn, to supplement the food supply from other sources.

On our return from the Malyang operation, we in the cavalry had another surprise in store for us. On our departure, construction of stables and barracks had been well under way to the east of Jayasri. During our absence, there had been a change of plan. The area we had formerly occupied was now being excavated to form a third reservoir to supplement those of the East and West Baray. Our quarters had been shifted about a mile to the south, in the vicinity of the eleventh-century temple of Ta Keo. With the East Baray just east of us, and the Siemreap River forming our western limit, it was in fact a better location than our former campsite and somewhat removed from the heart of the construction activity. On our arrival, the barracks blocks, officers' quarters, and stables were nearing completion.

I was allocated a modest dwelling in the officers' quarters. It was mounted on stilts and consisted of a small porch and two rooms. The only furnishings provided were a straw mat in the larger of the two rooms and a smaller, sleeping mat in the second room. It suited me admirably and was vastly superior to the cubicle I would have had to share with three other troopers in the barracks block. I found that I had also acquired two slaves along with my officer status.

During the march north, I had given a good deal of thought to my new responsibilities and had arrived at a number of conclusions. The troopers of the Sixth Troop resented me. There was not much I could do on that score at the moment. But if I was unpopular now, I was sure it was nothing compared with the unpopularity I would earn in the weeks ahead. I had resolved that the sixth troop would be the finest unit in the entire cavalry, if it killed them—or me.

The troopers were in for a number of surprises. For one thing, I intended to make the troop's primary weapon the composite bow. It had proved its worth in the Malyang action, and I did not anticipate too much objection from other than diehard traditionalists.

The other measures I had in mind could hardly be expected to gain ready acceptance. Objections notwithstanding, the Sixth Troop would ride with stirrups. I intended to try out battle tactics that were radical departures from accepted practice. All this would call for arduous weeks of training and iron discipline. These innovations would not endear me to the fiercely independent cavalry troopers. Without a shadow of a doubt, I also would be earning the contempt and ridicule of my fellow cavalry officers.

I allowed three days for the troopers to settle into their new quarters before assembling them to apprise them of my plans for their future. My disclosures met with black scowls. At the conclusion of my address, I indicated I would entertain applications for transfer. Before the Hours of the Snake were out, I had received and approved eight such applications. Included in that number were those of the second-in-command and the trooper who had killed the former captain of the troop.

I promoted a grizzled veteran to the position of second-in-command. The vacancies could have been filled by conscripts, but I preferred to let the troop remain below strength for the time being. It would take time for craftsmen to fabricate the required bows and long-shafted arrows and for saddlers to fit stirrups. Until that was done, training in earnest could not begin. Those troopers who had elected to stay with the Sixth Cavalry Troop had yet to learn what was in store for them.

On our return from Malyang, we received a tumultuous welcome. It was much more, I thought, than the operation warranted.

The Malyang king, dust-smeared and crippled from his hunched posture in the cage, was to suffer added indignity. The cage was suspended from an arch in the market square, where the deposed monarch was placed on public view. The cage remained in that position for two weeks despite the fact that the king was dead within three days.

The army was disbanded. The foot soldiers not pressed into labor battalions returned to their villages and crops.

Honors were heaped on Prince Vidyanandana. It was announced that he had been promoted to the command of the Army of the West. Vidya publicly proclaimed his conversion to the Buddhist faith, and shortly thereafter it was announced that he was to be married to a ranking princess of the Khmer royal house.

I did not begrudge Vidya these honors, even though I could not see how they had been earned. Frankly, I was nonplussed. I put it down to my lack of understanding of the Cham and Khmer.

The Army of the West, based at the western capital of Lopburi, had remained virtually intact and undefeated all during the Cham occupation of Angkor. It had not attempted to retake Angkor since it had been fully occupied, holding together the western provinces of the empire. Command of that force was a position of prestige and grave responsibility. In the Khmer king's position, I would have hesitated to appoint a man to a command of that magnitude who had already demonstrated that he was prepared to switch his allegiance and turn against his own people. How could the loyalty of such a man be relied upon?

In all fairness to Vidya, I recognized that I was judging him by the standards instilled in me by my upbringing. In his position, I do not believe I could have turned against my own father and taken up arms against my own race, no matter what the provocation. True, I had accepted service with the Khmer king, but I had not sworn allegiance to the monarch and still considered myself loyal to the Dragon Throne of the Sung emperor. In all honesty, I had to admit that it was highly unlikely that my loyalty would ever be put to a test. The Sung court was opposed to military conquest on foreign soil.

That Vidya had proclaimed himself a Buddhist did not

astonish me. As in China, a degree of religious tolerance existed in both Champa and Kambuja. The religion of state depended on the personal preference of the reigning monarch. In thise case, it was the Mahayana Buddhism of King Jayavarman VII that was replacing the Vishnu cult of Hinduism practiced by his predecessor. Vidya was merely acknowledging the new state religion. It did not necessarily indicate his personal convictions. In any case proclaiming himself Buddhist was probably a necessary prelude to his pending nuptials.

Vidya had expressed delight at the prospects of a royal wedding of state. It should strengthen his position with the royal house which was obviously also the desire of the Khmer king. Although the king's reasoning escaped me, I could only conclude that Sri Vidyanandana had been singled out by Jayavarman for exalted station.

It was the second week of the fifth month. The wind had changed to the southwest and we now received our daily quota of rain. I had worked out a training program to take full advantage of the mornings, before the building clouds unleashed their burden of moisture. Admittedly, this was the opening phase, and the easiest. It was going better than I had anticipated. So far, the troopers had accepted the regimen with a minimum of grumbling. In fact, had there been no grousing, I would have been concerned. What was even more satisfying was the fact that four of the troopers of my former unit, the four who had shown the most promise with the Chinese bow, had requested transfers to the Sixth Troop.

The mornings were devoted to archery instruction and practice. It didn't look as though I had any expert marksmen in the making, but the troopers, with few exceptions, were making good progress. A competitive spirit was developing. The unfamiliar Mongolian release, utilizing the thumb ring, had presented less difficulty than I had expected. Now the troopers of the Sixth Cavalry Troop could be readily distinguished from cavalrymen of other units. Each trooper of my troop now had a ring pouch hanging at his waist. These had drawn ribald comments from troopers of other units. Yet I now noted with quiet satisfaction that many of my troopers were decorating their pouches with hand-tooling.

Even though the initial phase was progressing better than I had hoped, it was much too early to congratulate myself. The next step would be the crucial test. I was far from sanguine and time was crowding in on me. Two days earlier, I had been advised that the stirrup-fitted saddles would be ready within the week. As yet, I had formulated no firm program. A religious festival on the morrow would give me an added day, but I could no longer ignore the problem.

It was mid-afternoon, the Hours of the Ram. The noontime deluge had passed, giving us temporary respite before the evening rain. My troopers were exercising their horses on the grassy field bordering the river. I sat in the main room of my dwelling, turning over in my mind the instructional approaches available to me. Thinking was not easy. Carpenters were at work on the roof above my head. From the field came the broken rhythm of horses' hooves. Suddenly a new sound intruded.

In broken Khmer, someone was questioning one of my slaves. I could not be mistaken. I would know that grating voice anywhere. Bounding to my feet, I rushed out onto the porch. Beneath me I viewed a gesticulating ghost from my past. Standing in the steaming compound, his black trousers sodden and streaked with mud, stood Horsemaster Chang.

"Chang!" I shouted joyously as I descended, taking the steps two at a time.

His unruly shock of gray hair tilted back as he raised his head. His weathered face broke into a wide grin, displaying his stained and broken teeth.

We stood ankle-deep in the mud of the compound, embracing each other. Then Chang moved back to arm's length and subjected me to searching scrutiny.

"Young Master," he said, "I heard that you had returned from the dead. I could scarcely believe it. Then Sa-lu-tzu was described to me. Then I knew it to be true and thanked my ancestors." He paused and looked me up and down once again. "Wherever the fates led you, they did you no harm."

"Young Master?" I repeated chidingly. "Since when have I ceased to be Young Tartar and become a master in your eyes?"

"Since your honored father died," Chang said simply.

"Come, Old Stallion. A servant you have never been. An old and trusted friend you are; a servant you shall never be, to me or any man." I threw my arm over his shoulder and turned him toward the steps. "We need not stand here in the dung and mud. Join me in my palatial quarters."

We had much to tell each other. We talked through the afternoon and into the evening, when the rain drummed on the roof and walls. We shared a simple meal of rice and fish, and we continued our discourse well into the night.

Chang told me first of the death of my father, emphasizing that he had stood proudly erect until the end and had not cried out even when the flames had enveloped him. There was reverence in his voice as he recounted those final moments. My heart swelled with pride, even while sorrow flooded me.

Chang had witnessed my fall from the flaming balcony. He had been too occupied in the defense of the stairway to come to my assistance. When the intense heat of the blazing pavilion had driven the Cham attackers back from their objective, he had searched for me. He found me at the rear of the residence, my inert body guarded by a slave girl. With the girl's help, he had taken me to the rear of the stables. While the girl, on his instructions, loaded the two farm carts with straw, Chang had spread the cart shafts to accommodate our horses.

With me safely stowed beneath straw in the cart bed, Chang had returned to the outbuildings in the hopes of finding others he could lead to safety. Most of the buildings were aflame. Outside the women's quarters, he found Apricot Blossom. Her hair was burned from her head, her clothing was smoldering, and the exposed parts of her body were charred and blistering. In her arms she cradled the corpse of her baby, which she had somehow retrieved from the nurse's room.

When Chang carried Apricot Blossom to the stables, it was to find that the Cham soldiers had set fire to the buildings. Those horses still within the stables were screaming in agony. At the rear of the stables, Chang found only one cart. The slave girl had fled with the stallion and the other cart.

Having no horse for the second cart, Chang had carried Apricot Blossom in his arms. She was barely conscious, but she refused to release her precious burden, the dead baby.

Chang had discovered the gap in the northern wall that Morning Mist had found. He knew the cart had passed that way from the wheel tracks, but he saw no sign of it. On the bank of the moat, he had found an abandoned sampan.

Shielded from view by the overhang of a banyan tree at the water's edge, he had waited out the long night. When Apricot Blossom had slipped mercifully into unconsciousness, he had taken the corpse from her arms and let it float out into the moat. It had not been anywhere in sight in the morning. He assumed the body had been consumed by a crocodile.

In the morning, he had sculled northward on the moat until he reached the feed-in canal connecting it with the river. He had seen some Cham patrols, but he had not been stopped.

Chang had drifted downriver until he came to the Great Lake. In a small Chinese trading community, he had found shelter and medical assistance for Apricot Blossom. They had been there ever since.

For some time, Chang had hoped to hear that I had escaped safely. When there had been no word for more than a year, hope had waned. When four years had gone by, he had given up hope altogether. My reappearance, he stated, was like a miracle.

In response to my questions concerning other survivors, Chang shook his head bleakly. A few servants and four or five Chinese militiamen had made good their escape. The rest had perished. Two of the militiamen had found berths on Chinese merchantmen. The other two had married Khmer women and were living in the same lakeshore community as Chang.

I questioned Chang about Apricot Blossom. He was hesitant in his answers. I gathered that she was terribly disfigured from her burns. She lived almost entirely in the seclusion of a darkened room. The merchant who had given them sanctuary was honored to have the concubine of the respected envoy as his guest. Chang, in order to repay the merchant's kindness, was in his employ as an overseer of cargo handling.

Apricot Blossom knew of Chang's journey to Angkor in search of me. She was, he stated, thrilled at the prospect of seeing me. He cautioned me, however, that while she had recovered to some extent physically, she had scars of the mind that were unlikely to heal. He quoted one example. She had never accepted the fact that her baby had died in the holocaust; she believed the boy was now a child of five. She was looking forward to my reaction on my first meeting with a half brother I would never see.

When Chang had finished his story, I embarked on my saga. I told him of my long journey with Morning Mist and of my awakening love for the courageous girl. In as much detail as possible, I told him of my life with the Jarai, my marriage with Morning Mist, and my family from that union. At many points in my account, he nodded approvingly. When I told him how I had introduced the Chinese *kung* to the tribesmen, he grunted in satisfaction. As I relived the terrible day of the Khmer attack, my voice became choked with emotion. Tactfully, Chang made no comment.

I would have brushed lightly over the last few months and my exploits as a cavalryman, but Chang prodded me with questions. When I brought up the subject of Prince Vidyanandana and his rapid rise in the king's favor, Chang snorted. From the day he had overheard Vidya make some disparaging comments about Chinese horses, Chang had disliked the prince intensely.

"So the young popinjay is riding high," Chang commented.

"He seems to prefer war elephants, but I would not dispute that he is well elevated," I replied lightly. "At any rate, I have him to thank for my field promotion."

"You would have made it without his help. It just might have taken a little longer."

It was a flattering observation, but I doubt if Chang believed it any more than I did. I let it pass.

I became enthusiastic as I explained my plans to convert the Sixth Cavalry Troop into an elite unit of mounted bowmen. Chang looked dubious. When I outlined the innovations I was planning with respect to mounted battle tactics, he was openly skeptical.

"It is no easy matter to break with tradition," Chang

observed. "You have had some success in introducing the *kung*, but I would not be too optimistic about converting your troopers to stirrups. The Khmer horses are tough, but too small. They have not been trained as pacers. It would be difficult to change their gait. And unless the gait is smoothed, your troopers will have a bad time of it . . . and curse you roundly for your efforts."

"You could train Khmer horses," I said innocently.

"Perhaps."

"Would you like to try?"

Chang laughed. "No. Then I would be the one cursed by your troopers." Then he sobered. "We might be able to do it, if we took it in easy stages . . . and if we didn't get murdered by horse-soldiers with sore backsides. It might be worth a try."

"Would you accept a posting as riding master of the Sixth Troop?"

Chang grinned ruefully. "To keep you from getting killed, I'll probably have to."

"Then it's settled. Tomorrow we'll journey downriver so I can pay my respects to Apricot Blossom, thank your merchant friend for all that he has done, and arrange for him to receive payment for her stay in his home. The next day we'll return here together. I will introduce the troopers to their ugly new taskmaster . . . and we can plan out a firm training program. I'm sure you will be happier with your beloved horses than you are nursing cargo."

"That may well be true," Chang replied. "I will agree, but only to the training of horse and rider in simple horsemanship with the added benefit of stirrups. I will leave to you the tactics you have outlined. Such coordination has never been successful, even with Chinese cavalry."

"Has it ever been attempted?" I asked.

"I'm not sure. I've never heard of it, and I've lived a good deal longer than yourself."

"If you can train the horses and teach these barbarians to ride with stirrups, I think I can achieve the rest."

"We will see," Chang grunted. "You have reached man's estate, Tartar. With the help of your illustrious ancestors, you may yet attain wisdom."

Chang stayed the night. As I lay on my sleeping mat,

waiting for sleep to claim me, I breathed a prayer of thanks to the spirits of my father and my ancestors. They had seen to it that I was reunited with Horse-master Chang when I sorely needed his guidance and help.

chapter 15

As I was to learn, warfare in these regions affected by the monsoon rains is seasonal in character. This holds particularly true in the Kingdom of Kambuja and the lands to the west that comprise the Khmer empire. The governing factor is the moisture-laden southwest monsoon that blows from the fifth to the eleventh months of the year. This season turns all roads not paved with stone into quagmires. The fields are flooded and the ground is soft and marshy. War elephants cannot maneuver under such conditions. Supply trains become mired and an army becomes hopelessly bogged down. It is, accordingly, the season for growing, not for conquest.

When the harvest is in and the rains cease, nobles gather together their able-bodied men from the fields and villages. These peasants are pressed into service to form the units of the armed forces used for conquest. They are largely untrained. It is for this reason that the crossbow, which is of deadly accuracy at short range and requires very little in the way of training, is a favored weapon. Correspondingly, it takes little practice to wield a spear or halberd. Under normal circumstances, cavalry units are hastily recruited and consist of nothing more than mounted spearmen acting independently. The limited role played by cavalry in combat is, therefore, understandable.

As the dry season drew to a close, or as otherwise

dictated by the planting and harvesting cycles, the peasant armies were disbanded and the men returned to till the ancestral fields of their liege lords. Command in battle was based on birthright rather than on ability. Some nobles had acquired martial skills, but many more were as ill-equipped for combat as the peasants they commanded. Given these prevailing conditions, victory normally depended on sheer weight of numbers.

This is not to say that there were no professional soldiers. The militia protecting the persons and properties of the landowning nobles were in the nature of permanent forces, as were the elite units of the palace guard. The latter forces acted as training grounds for the nobility. True, some soldiers of exceptional ability, though not of noble birth, had risen to positions of tactical, if not nominal, command, but these were the exceptions rather than the rule.

Those familiar with the customs and practices of the region and the times will say that I should have known all this from the outset. They would say that my plan to train an elite cadre of mounted archers was overly ambitious and doomed to failure. I can only advance in my defense the facts that my reasoning was based on my limited experience under somewhat peculiar conditions and my then lack of knowledge of the rigid strictures imposed by the terrain and climate. And, although it would not be proved out for some years, my concepts were not as unsound as they at first appeared.

One factor that misled me was the character of the Khmer forces that then existed. Jayavarman VII, due to his long years of self-imposed exile and his campaigning in Champa, had built up and retained a force resembling a standing army. This nucleus had not been disbanded after the defeat of the Cham army. This encouraged me in the belief that the king intended to build a permanent army on this base of experienced veterans. In this assumption, I was not entirely incorrect, but it was not of much help to me at the time.

In considering the capabilities and limitations of cavalry, I had arrived at certain conclusions. Fortunately, or unfortunately, these were based in part on my experience during the battle against the Cham. The limitations of cavalry were self-evident. Horses could not charge into solid lines of spearmen without inviting almost certain destruction. By extension, cavalry was virtually useless against a fortified position. Moreover, horse and rider could be readily picked off if they ventured within the range of crossbowmen. These factors dictated the existing tactics whereby the advantage of mobility only came into play in mopping-up operations of a disorganized and fleeing enemy.

In the battle against the Cham forces, my composite bow gave me firepower coupled with mobility. The range and accuracy of the weapon had permitted me to keep beyond the range of crossbow bolts, avoid closing with the ranks of spearmen, and still wreak havoc in the enemy ranks Thus, I had been able to utilize my superior mobility in the initial stages of the battle. If, I reasoned, this advantage could be multiplied through a number of mounted archers on a coordinated basis, it was theoretically possible to turn the flank of an opposing force in the early stages of a battle and influence its final outcome.

This was my basic concept. I would first introduce the composite bow, next the stability imparted by stirrups, and then, when I considered they had acquired sufficient proficiency in bowmanship from the saddle, I would embark on the final phase of training. This I visualized as the troop sweeping in line formation past targets in serried ranks and coordinating their fire to maximum effect.

Simple It was to prove otherwise. Horse-master Chang had assessed the obstacles more accurately than myself.

It proved much more difficult to train the sturdy little Khmer horses as pacers than I had expected. Chang, assisted by cursing troopers, kept at the task for weeks, which dragged into months, before anything even vaguely resembling a smooth gait was achieved.

From the beginning, the veteran troopers balked at the use of stirrups. It was only by imposing tough discipline that I managed to keep them training. Morale was at a low ebb. As Chang had correctly foreseen, the troop was almost at the point of open rebellion. It would not have surprised Chang if I had been murdered. That an attempt was not made on my life was probably due to caution imposed on the troopers by my size and strength and the sure knowledge that if the attempt failed, the guilty party or parties would be subject to swift and final discipline.

I also had erred on another count. The monsoon rains are consistent. The nights and mornings are generally clear. Clouds mass during the morning, then deliver a deluge that lasts for one or two hours at midday. It usually clears for several hours during the afternoon before the evening buildup provides a second torrential onslaught of two or three hours' duration.

I had counted on the morning dry periods for training purposes. I had not legislated for the cumulative effect of the rains. The exercise field soon resembled a swamp. I shifted to another site, which quickly became a trampled mire. Finally, I found some relatively solid, rising ground near the base of the hill on which Phnom Bakheng towers above the plain. Unfortunately, the distance between the stables and this site almost halved the time available for instruction.

The sixth month of the year gave way to the seventh, then the eighth. What little headway we were making was painfully slow. A haggard and disgruntled Chang suggested that we abandon the project, at least until the onset of the dry season. It made sense, but I stubbornly rejected his counsel. In the ninth month, frustrated by the lack of results, I decided to accept his advice.

When I told Chang of my decision, he unaccountably reversed his stand. He had noted a subtle change in the attitude of the troopers that I had not yet detected. Since he spent a good deal of time with the troopers in the stables and barracks block, he was in a better position than myself to gauge their mood and temper. Still, I should have noticed the shift myself, had I been more observant.

The men had put up with a good deal of ridicule from troopers of the other cavalry units. Shortly after the training sessions with the horses got under way and the stirrups made an appearance, the troopers of the Sixth stopped wearing their ring pouches. The gesture of defiance was not lost on me, yet, when they again started to wear the pouches about midway through the ninth month, I must have been too distracted to notice it.

The trouble was that I had expected too much of the troopers. I had underestimated the resistance they had displayed toward departure from traditional methods. I had anticipated a certain amount of resentment, but not the sullen compliance with orders that stopped just short of mutiny. In my keen disappointment at their response to the training, I had failed to notice a gradual improvement in horsemanship, marksmanship, and general attitude.

Just when it dawned on some of the troopers that they had acquired a measure of competence in a new field is difficult to say. Chang claimed he had detected the beginnings of pride in their new achievements a full week before the ring pouches again put in an appearance. There is a rapport between horse and rider, and the horses responded to the new attitude with improved performance. A spirit of competition reentered the training sessions. The change, when it occurred, was as dramatic as it was sudden.

The Sixth Cavalry Troop was a long way from the elite force I had visualized. The troopers were not yet ready for the introduction of coordinated tactics. But they were unlike any cavalry unit in the army. They knew it, and they took pride in the difference. Even the horses seemed to sense that they were now unique among their breed, and they held their heads proudly.

I compromised. I concentrated on bowmanship from fast-moving mounts. There would be time enough, when the rain slackened about a month hence, to introduce group tactics.

The about-face on the part of the troopers did not mean that I became a popular figure. I was considered a harsh taskmaster and did nothing to alter that image. I passed out no praise or reward for their improvement. On the contrary, I lengthened the instructional periods to make up for lost time. There was a good deal of grumbling, but I drew satisfaction from the fact that I was now treated with deference and respect. It amused Horsemaster Chang.

When I had accompanied Chang downriver to pay my respects to Apricot Blossom and express my gratitude to the Chinese merchant for his generosity, it had not been an altogether happy occasion. The merchant, who had profited from Chang's services without remuneration, had not been overjoyed to learn that he was about to lose Chang. He had been somewhat mollified when I had given him two bars of silver, a portion of my share from the loot of Malyang, and a sack of rice. I had promised the merchant that there would be similar contributions in the future, and we had parted on good terms.

I don't know exactly what I anticipated from my reunion with Apricot Blossom. Chang had cautioned me in advance that I must not expect my father's concubine to be as I remembered her. She was, he stated, not only a mass of scar tissue from her burns, but she had all but lost the sight of one eye. She had, he said, a somewhat distressing tendency to dwell on memories of happier times and was divorced from reality. She seemed to have no memory of the fateful night of the Cham attack. Above all, if she talked of her dead child, I was to humor her with the pretense that the boy still lived.

With this background at my disposal, I approached the meeting with misgivings. That I was ushered into a room so heavily curtained that it was almost as dark as night served to increase my uneasiness.

The room was close and uncomfortably hot. The scent of jasmine, which I had come to associate with my father's concubine, could not mask a strong odor of medication. As my eyes became adjusted to the gloom, I made out a shawled figure seated on a low bed piled high with cushions. Since as yet no words had passed between us, I could not have attested to the fact that the dim outline belonged to Apricot Blossom.

A servant girl silently served tea. Seated on a cushion on the floor, I sipped the steaming liquid. Still, the silence was unbroken. I was beginning to find the atmosphere of the bedchamber oppressive.

"Stand up, Tartar." The soft voice was unmistakably that of Apricot Blossom.

In response to her command, I rose to my feet. After a minute or so of more silence, I began to feel restive and decidedly uncomfortable.

A soft chuckle came from the dim figure on the bed. "You may be seated," she said. "You have grown and filled out well. Your father would be pleased. I'm sure your honored mother would share his sentiments. Now, tell me of the adventures that have befallen you in the four and a half years since last I saw you."

Without preamble, I launched into an abbreviated version of the account I had given Horse-master Chang. My recounting of my love for Morning Mist, our marriage, and our children gave me pain, but I found the words flowed more freely in this second telling. I played down the horror of the attack on the Jarai village, simply stating that my wife and family had been killed in the encounter. I concluded with a brief sketch of the more recent events and my promotion to officer status.

Apricot Blossom did not interrupt during my discourse. She remained so quiet and still that I was not sure she had followed the entire account. Her words, when I had finished, assured me that she had listened attentively.

"I grieve with you for your loss. Yet I am happy that you learned the meaning of love in its fullest measure . . . and at an age young enough that you will recognize it when it again enters your life."

I did not respond to her remark. In my heart I felt that I could never recapture the love that had been so cruelly taken from me.

"Your father would be very proud. You have done well. You have become the man he would have wished." Her voice softened as she continued. "Of all his sons, he loved you most. He loved your mother much as you loved your Morning Mist. He, too, was stricken with grief when your mother joined her ancestors at an early age. For him, you were an extension of that love."

Her disclosures concerning my father startled me. I had never thought of my father as a sentimental man. And, for some reason, I had always considered that a man's relationship with a concubine was physical in character and did not involve the confidences shared between man and wife. Obviously, at least insofar as my father and Apricot Blossom were concerned, this had not been the case.

Her eyes were more accustomed to the semi-gloom than mine. She must have noticed consternation mirrored in my face. She laughed softly.

"Does it surprise you that your father and I shared such intimacy? It should not. I loved your father very much. I could not hope to replace your mother in his heart, but in a different way he loved me in return. We were very close. He was as overjoyed as myself when I bore him a sturdy son. My loss, Tartar, is as great as your own. I shall mourn your father until the day I die."

There was nothing for me to say. A silence lengthened between us. It was Apricot Blossom who picked up the thread of conversation once more.

"We often discussed you. Your father was worried that he had been remiss in his paternal duties in your case. He felt that he should have been much stricter with regard to your studies of the classics. His leniency, he feared, would leave you ill-prepared for a career in the service of the emperor. His decision to have you accompany him to Angkor was based on your father's wish to broaden your experience through exposure to diplomatic proceedings.

"I think that your disregard for your own safety during the storm at sea and your jumping to his defense in our encounter with the pirates startled your father. It also pleased him Until then, he had looked upon you as a boy. He suddenly saw in you the makings of the man you have become. He decided to take you more fully into his confidence although I believe he found this more diffi-cult to do than he had anticipated. The fault lay not on your side but in the set pattern of his ways. He entrusted you with a delicate mission during our captivity in the Cham capital, and he was elated by the way you handled the trust he placed in you.

"When we reached Angkor, your father had come to a decision concerning your future. He abandoned his plan to have you join the naval service. He intended to peti-tion the emperor to have you trained for diplomatic service. You knew nothing of this. He had, in fact, dis-patched a scroll on the matter and would have advised you upon his receipt of an answer from the Sung court. Unfortunately, fate intervened to decree another course.

"Yes, Tartar your father would have been well pleased by your conduct over the last few years."

Apricot Blossom had given me much food for thought. I had sensed my father's desire to communicate with me on a more equal footing. It had seemed out of charac-ter. I understood him better now, and some of his re-marks that had seemed cryptic at the time now made more sense. That we had not grown closer during our enforced stay in Vijaya was not my father's fault. Had I not been so blindly infatuated with White Lotus and oc-cupied with pleasures of the flesh, my father and I might have bridged the gap with less difficulty. That he had planned a diplomatic career for me was indeed news. I was about to question Apricot Blossom further in that regard when she pulled a cord suspended above her bed and addressed me.

"Please forgive me, Tartar, but I tire so quickly. Old Chang may have told you that I have not been well."

"Yes."

"You will visit me again?"

"As often as my duties permit."

The young servant girl appeared silently from beyond the heavy curtains that screened the entrance doorway. I turned to take my departure, but I was stopped by a question from Apricot Blossom.

"You have met your young brother. Does he resemble your father?"

Even though Chang had warned me, I was not prepared for the question. I hoped the gloom masked my consternation.

"A truly remarkable likeness," I lied, I hoped convincingly.

On the upriver journey, my thoughts were chiefly about Apricot Blossom. I had no way of judging the extent of her disfigurement, but I assumed it must be extensive, or she would not choose to live in isolation and almost total darkness.

I realized that I actually knew very little about her. Her position as my father's concubine had precluded familiarity. It had come as something of a surprise to find she knew so much about me, that I had been the subject of much discussion between herself and my father.

Had it not been for her disconcerting reference to her child at the close of our conversation, I would not have thought her divorced from reality. I voiced some of my thoughts on this score to Chang.

"You were right. She did not mention the night of the Cham attack. Yet she accepts the fact of my father's death. She must associate his death with that night."

"Perhaps she does. She chooses not to relive the horror of that night. I can't say that I blame her," Chang replied.

"Nor I. I am glad you warned me about the child. As I was leaving, she questioned me about the boy. I pretended he was still alive."

"That is well. It is a delusion of harm to none."

"One thing struck me as strange. She is attended by a servant, a young girl. Not once did the girl utter a sound."

Chang chuckled. "It would have been more strange if she had. The child is one of the merchant's daughters. She has tended your father's concubine from the day we arrived and is devoted to her. The girl has been mute since birth."

chapter 16

In the tenth month the prevailing wind shifted to the northeast and the dry season was upon us. While carpenters, bricklayers, stone-cutters, and stonemasons had continued their labors on various construction projects during the months of precipitation, the rains had slowed road construction and irrigation system work almost to a halt and forced a total suspension of excavation. Now work was resumed on all phases of the king's projects. In addition, recruitment got under way to mount military campaigns on the far-flung frontiers of the empire.

I received orders for the Sixth Cavalry Troop to attach itself to the Cavalry of the Golden Banner, which was assigned to support an army being raised to campaign in the north under the command of Prince In, one of the king's oldest sons. In the few weeks remaining to me before the army could be assembled and made ready to move out, I concentrated on my long-delayed tactical training.

The troopers grasped the essentials much more quickly than I had anticipated. The targets I now set up were serried ranks of upright planks affixed to wooden bases by a leather hinge. The marks were held in the upright position by sticks. Hit squarely, the target would snap the stick and topple backward. The marks represented ranks of enemy foot soldiers—bowmen, spearmen, and crossbowmen. In single file, and at full gallop, the troopers swept down the target ranks at a distance calculated to render them safe from enemy crossbow fire. Until they got the feel of it, I allowed independent fire. Then I introduced coordination by allocating target segments, each man to take out the marks left standing by his predecessor before moving to targets in his own sector. In an amazingly short period of training, the marks were toppling with incredible swiftness. The troopers could now see where the months of training had been leading them and the devastating effect that could be achieved through teamwork.

I explained the variables as I visualized them. The troop might be called on to move out from its position in the wing of the battle formation to sweep along the line of advancing enemy foot soldiers creating havoc in the enemy ranks before the lines clashed. If the enemy had strong cavalry units, our initial objective could be to neutralize that force through our advantage of weapon range, then sweep around the exposed flank. Or a situation might develop where we would concentrate our fire on an already weakened position, chewing it to shreds from a relatively safe distance.

The essential difference between these tactics and those formerly practiced as mounted spearmen was that, given the superior accuracy and range of the composite bow, cavalry archers could spearhead the attack instead of being held in reserve for mopping-up operations. Once their arrows were expended, the cavalry would revert to its former role of using hand weapons. The men would be involved in the battle from the sounding of the attack until the last enemy straggler was cut down and could well influence the outcome from the battle's outset.

The troopers saw that their expanded role could be crucial Their morale, which had improved during the closing month of the rainy season, now soared to astonishing heights They swaggered as they walked, and they openly boasted of their mastery of horsemanship with stirrups and their prowess with the Chinese bow. They were not as good as they thought; on the other hand, they were much better than I had expected.

During the final weeks of our training sessions, we found that troopers and officers from other cavalry units came as unbidden spectators. We were asked a number of questions concerning the training of the horses, the value of riding with stirrups, the attributes of the composite bow, and the battle tactics we were putting into practice. Many officers who had been openly derisive might still have been skeptical, but they at least were now withholding comment. This unsolicited interest pleased me. But what I found most gratifying of all was that Horsemaster Chang no longer seemed to find the tactics a source of amusement.

It is, of course, one thing to practice marksmanship against fixed targets, yet quite another to face an armed and moving foe. I had predicated my safety factor on the range of crossbow quarrels. The common bow in the hands of enemy archers still posed a threat, and I had deprived my troopers of the protection afforded by shields. Then, too, in the mopping-up phase of a battle, the long cavalry spear was probably more effective than a sword or battle ax. Only battle experience would prove whether the advantages I had bestowed upon my reluctant troopers outweighed the disadvantages I had inflicted upon them.

I was anxious to put my theories to the acid test of conflict. Here I was to be taught a badly needed lesson. It is one that I should have suspected from the punitive mission against Malyang. Battles, if they occur at all, rarely develop as expected.

We were a force of some size. On the march, with our support train straggling along to the rear, we stretched out over a distance of some miles. To hide the presence of such a body, even in sparsely inhabited country, is no easy matter. We moved slowly, made no secret of our intrusion, and advertised our coming well in advance of our arrival. Initially, at least, there was no reason for us to do otherwise since we were proceeding through regions firmly under Khmer domination.

We crossed over a mountain range well to the west of the sanctuary of Preah Vihear, where Prince Vidya had fretted out a couple of years of unwelcome isolation. We emerged onto a vast plateau carpeted with scrub jungle, tall grass, and dotted with jungle-matted hills. The red soil of the plateau seemed fertile and the plain was well-watered with shallow rivers, but it supported a relatively small population. The villages we came upon were few and far between. We did not encounter what could be termed an enthusiastic welcome.

The reasons for our lack of popularity were obvious. A year earlier, heavy demands had been made on these rural communites in terms of manpower and produce. The able-bodied men had not been returned to their native villages; instead, they had been kept in Angkor, either as military or labor conscripts. Consequently, the crop yields of most of these communities had suffered due to labor shortages. Now an army sat on their doorstep, demanding provisions and additional levies of manpower and produce. The demands could not be gainsaid. The size of the armed force was a grim reminder of the might of Angkor and of the fate of the kingdom of Malyang.

Depending on the community, the army stayed encamped at its gates anywhere from two to four days. Garrisons were relieved. In some cases, administrative officials were changed. Arrangements were concluded for the transporting under guards, generally portions of the relieved garrison, of the produce and labor conscripts to Angkor. During this interval, the soldiers took their pleasures with the young maidens of the town or village. While this latter activity was an added cause for complaint by village elders, the girls of the man-short communities did not appear to be averse to the procedure. On the contrary, they gave every indication of welcoming the servicing.

We sallied forth with pennants flying in the second week of the eleventh month of the Year of the Bull. We reached the City of Sandalwood, the town called Vien Chang in the local tongue, well into the first month of the new year—the Month of the Tiger of the Year of the Tiger. I reckoned the northeasterly distance traveled to be not much more than three hundred miles. We had averaged about six miles a day. The northern limits of Khmer suzerainty were still some one hundred miles distant. Prince In did not seem in any great hurry to extend the northern frontier.

Prince In called a halt in the City of Sandalwood. Here, in this tree-shaded town on the eastern bank of the Mekong, he established a temporary headquarters, preempting the residence of the local governor for his personal quarters. It would be more than a year before

Prince In vacated the premises to embark on a leisurely return to Angkor.

The army was divided into two forces. The larger of the two was to proceed to the northern frontier and beyond into the thickly jungled mountainous terrain. The second force, to which the Sixth Cavalry Troop was attached, was to probe upriver on the Mekong to the west and into a little-known region of mountain ranges and valleys. The objectives of both forces were the same: to annex territory in the name of the king and to return to the City of Sandalwood bearing plunder and captive slaves.

It took more than a month to settle on the composition of the two forces and assemble the stores thought needed for the two-pronged campaign. When the force to which I was attached finally rafted across to the western bank of the Mekong and headed west, the dry season was half over. I left Horse-master Chang, who had accompanied me from Angkor in the capacity of sergeant at arms, in the City of Sandalwood to supervise the training of more horses and the fabrication of a supplementary stock of bows and long arrows. I reasoned that the probing actions would lead to prolonged campaigns of conquest. In this assumption, I was once again proved wrong.

Apart from three significant events, there is little worthy of recounting over the period of the fifteen months from the time our force headed westward from the City of Sandalwood until the combined army of Prince In returned to Angkor in the sixth month of the Year of the Hare. During that time, we encountered no military forces to oppose us. There were no battles, large or small. Some of our units were ambushed, skirmishing actions were undertaken, and we burned two villages to the ground, more in frustration than in anger. My tactical concepts went untested.

It would not have surprised me if the Sixth Cavalry Troop had abandoned their bows and stirrups to return to their traditional weapons and methods. That they stayed with both bow and stirrups throughout the campaign led to an interesting development.

I cannot pretend to inventing the employment of cavalry I hit upon. They were not practices adopted by the Chinese, Khmer, or Cham, but they had been utilized for centuries by my nomadic forebears from the northern steppes. In Chinese, Khmer, and Cham armies, cavalry was tied to the main force by the necessity of supplying their needs. With the Tartar horsemen, their herds, homes, families, and supplies went with them. With their felt tents mounted on great flat-bedded wagons, the herdsmen and fighting horsemen were never far removed from their base of operations. In their case, the mounted bowmen were the military force with their supplies constantly keeping pace.

How it came about that I was reminded of tales of Tartar exploits was due to the limitations imposed on our cavalry. When not used in battle as secondary forces, cavalry were used for advance reconnaissance and communication link.

The Sixth Cavalry Troop, riding well in ad the main force by day, had come upon a numb lages hidden in fertile valleys. These were repor force commander, but by the time the main body the villagers, with the exception of oldsters, had fied into the surrounding hills. Time and again, populations simply melted away before the arrival of the army. Plundering the granaries and burning the cottages of nearly empty communities gave us little satisfaction.

Early one afternoon, riding ahead of the troop, I topped a ridge and viewed below a small village nestling in ripening fields on the valley floor. Screened by foliage, I was not detected. In the fields and village streets, life went on at a normal pace. As far as I could see, the village boasted no defense. It was then that the idea struck me.

I rode back and halted the troop well short of the ridge. I explained my plan. With three troopers I would remain where we now were. The remainder of the troop was split into two parties. Spacing themselves at intervals of approximately one hundred yards, the parties were to encircle the valley from opposite directions until the lead troopers made contact on the far side of the valley. They were then to stay hidden and await developments.

I would allow about an hour for the troopers to reach their positions. Then, with my three companions, I would ride over the crest of the ridge. When I was certain the villagers had seen us, we would retreat back across the ridge as though our mission were to report to an advancing force.

If the villagers reacted, as had been our experience of late, they would gather their essential belongings and children and flee toward the sanctuary of the hills. Once this exodus was under way, the troopers were to break from their tree-line cover and close in around the village at full gallop. Myself, and my three troopers, fanning out to cover a wide arc, would ride down from the ridge to complete the encirclement.

As widely spaced as we would be, most of the villagers could elude us and still make good their escape to the safety of the forest. I was counting on them to react differently. In all likelihood, seeing riders converging on themselves from all directions, they would believe us to be part of a larger force and themselves hopelessly trapped. In their confusion and panic, they were most likely to flee back toward the village. Once we had them herded into the town, they could be contained until the main force caught up with us.

It worked out even better than I had expected. The villagers reacted as I had anticipated. We pursued them, picking off a few of the stragglers. We rode a containing circle on the outskirts of the village, cutting down any who attempted to escape. I dispatched a rider to guide the force commander to our location.

Less than an hour after the departure of my dispatch rider, a small group of men appeared at the edge of the village. They had their hands clasped above their heads to indicate they were unarmed. I had them conducted to me. They were the village headman and some of the village elders. One of their number spoke halting Khmer. Their purpose, it transpired, was to surrender the village. I gravely accepted the surrender in the name of King Jayavarman VII.

As evening shadows started to engulf the valley, war elephants plodded down from the ridge, followed by cavalry and streams of infantrymen. They entered the town to find myself and my troopers calmly eating at food stalls in the village market square. The force commander was delighted that I could turn over to him a small but relatively intact prize.

I saw no reason why our success could not be repeated. That evening I outlined my plan to the force commander. He was skeptical, but the Sixth Troop's achievement of the afternoon was a convincing argument. He finally agreed to detach the Sixth Troop and two other cavalry troops, together with an appropriate backup supply, as an independent mobile force. The Sixth Troop, by virtue of its superior firepower, would spearhead the force. Even though I was the junior cavalry captain, I was placed in command of the strike force.

We ranged several days and, finally, more than a week ahead of the main force. We moved quickly, chiefly at night, our supply units catching up with us by day. By achieving the element of surprise, we took four villages in much the same manner as the Sixth Troop had captured its first prize. Our final assault of the campaign was against a stockade township of some size. This we placed under siege until the army joined us to overrun the defenses. We lost only four troopers in the engagements, and two more succumbed to fever. Our captives numbered in the thousands.

While it was not an original concept, I consider my employment of cavalry units as a mobile task force as the first significant event of the campaign. The second incident worth a passing mention was of a more personal nature.

The loss of Morning Mist and our children had been a terrible blow to me. In the battle against the Cham, and in the action at Malyang, I had cared not whether I lived or died. In fact, now that I look back on those days, I may have deliberately courted death.

At Jayasri, throughout the rainy season of the Year of the Bull, I had thrown myself into the training program, driving myself even harder than I had the cavalrymen under my command. Whether I had known it or not, this had been an attempt to ease the pain of my grief. I believe old Chang had suspected this, but he had said nothing.

In all that time, I had not had the slightest inclination for female companionship, although it was readily available. I firmly believed I would never again find love, and I found the thought of bedding a woman repugnant. To yield to temptations of the flesh, I felt, would be a disloyalty to my memory of Morning Mist.

During the northern campaign, however, my attitude underwent a change. Hot blood courses through my veins. My sexual appetites could not be stilled forever, no matter how much I may have wished them quieted. The campaign imposed few pressures and few outlets for my energies. I became bored and restive. More and more, as the months progressed, I found my thoughts turning to sexual fantasies. Guiltily, I suppressed these urges, but they returned unbidden again and again. Finally, on the afternoon the Sixth Cavalry Troop took the village in the action I have described, the demands of my flesh could no longer be denied. As a right of conquest, I claimed a pretty girl from among the captives.

That night, when I returned to my tent after my meeting with the force commander, the girl squatted on her haunches beside the tent. To be truthful, in my preoccupation with plans for the cavalry strike force, I had forgotten about her. At the sight of her, however, there was a compelling stirring in my groin.

She rose to her feet at my approach and submissively followed me into the tent. She wore a simple garment similar to the Khmer *sampot*, except she wore it higher to cover her breasts. I ripped it from her. She stood naked before me, trembling slightly, her firm young breasts rising and falling with her rapid breathing. I unknotted my *sampot* and let it fall to my feet. She gasped as her eyes beheld my swollen manhood.

It wasn't lovemaking. It was simple rape. I was astonished at the savagery of my assault. She was young, no more than sixteen, but not a virgin. My brutal thrusting must have hurt her, but she did not cry out.

I fully expected to feel remorse, yet I did not. I took her a second time before the fire in my loins was quelled. I lay on my back, bathed in sweat and breathing heavily. She lay at my side, perfectly still, exuding a musky odor of stale sweat and spent juices.

My thoughts turned slowly. Oddly enough, I did not think of Morning Mist. The image conjured up was that of White Lotus.

I took the girl with me. She walked with the supply unit, joining me in my tent at night only when bidden. She never complained and seemed to find my aggressive lovemaking natural and not unwelcome. It was more than a week before I learned her name. In her native tongue, Siamese, it was Dang.

With the rainy season imminent, my independent strike force rejoined the main force for the return march to the City of Sandalwood. I took Dang with me. She stayed with me through the wet season in the City of Sandalwood and accompanied me on our second campaign in the north-western mountains.

In time, I grew more gentle in my lovemaking. I was kind to Dang, but there was never, at least on my part, love between us. I became accustomed to her tending to my needs and sharing my bed and looked upon her with some affection.

Why, in the many months we were together, Dang did not conceive, is a mystery to me. At the time, I considered that the fault lay with me. I recalled that it had taken Morning Mist well over a year to become heavy with child after my bout of fever in the Jarai village. The fever returned to plague me while in the City of Sandalwood, although it was of less severity than in the first attack. I considered that there must be some connection between the ailment and my apparent infertility, although the fever, when it passed, certainly didn't lessen my desires or impair my performance.

chapter 17

THE THIRD SIGNIFICANT EVENT OF THE CAMPAIGN WAS one of the most frightening experiences of my life. To this day, when memory transports me back to that morning, I fee again the chill of fear that assailed me then.

It took place in the final week of the second westerly thrust from the City of Sandalwood. Our force was returning to join with the task force that had been dispatched to the northeast. Then, as one army, we would march south toward Angkor. The campaign was over for this season which suited me. It was the fourth month of the Year of the Hare.

Unlike his father, Prince In was not a forceful character. He was given to vacillation and was swayed by first one argument and then another. The composition of forces to campaign in the second dry season should have been determined before the rainy season drew to a close. That it was not done was blamed on the fact that the Mekong spilled over its banks to flood both sides of the river just at the end of the rainy season. This was certainly a distraction. It necessitated moving our encampment to higher ground. It forced Prince In to temporarily abandon the comfort of the governor's residence. We had to wait for the floodwaters to recede before contemplating a campaign. But this cannot excuse the fact that we did not get under way until the first month of the Year of the Hare, leaving us at best four months of active campaigning before we had to start our return march for Angkor.

This time the force dispatched to the west was the larger. Its commander was a nobleman almost as irresolute as Prince In. The commander of the Cavalry of the Golden Banner attached himself to the force. He was a sour little man who made no secret of his contempt for my new techniques and innovations.

No cavalry strike force was formed on this campaign. My troop was employed chiefly on long-range patrols.

We reached the northernmost part of an arcing swing to the west and north at the end of the third month of the year. With the exception of overrunning several hill-tribe villages that offered little resistance, it had not been a successful operation. Now, on the western bank of the Mekong, we took a stockaded village that produced but few captives. Some of the prisoners told of Siamese kingdoms and princely states that lay not far to the west and of a walled city not more than two to three days' march away.

The force commander hesitated. Not far upstream from our position, the Mekong emerged from a formidable gorge. The rocky cut through the mountains extended for some thirteen miles, according to our captives. The walled kingdom, which they called Chiang Saen, lay a little more than a day's march farther upstream. It was the force commander's decision that, since no easy passage presented itself along the riverbank and the dry season would soon end, there was not sufficient time to mount an attack. We turned our faces to the south. Any chance of a major battle during this campaign evaporated. I consoled myself with the thought that the vinegary cavalry commander would probably not have allowed me to put my tactical theories to the test, even had a battle developed.

As we moved over a mountain pass and into a valley running almost due south, our supply train was harassed by hit-and-run attackers. To discourage these ambushes, cavalry units were deployed on the flanks.

The climbing sun had burned away the mist. The day promised to be hot and sultry.

I was a short distance in advance of the troop. I could not see them, but I heard them scrambling up the rocky defile I had just negotiated. I broke clear of the confining rocks onto a flat ledge. In front of me, the mountain dropped away in a sheer cliff.

From my coign of vantage, I had a clear view of the valley. A thin ribbon of river shimmered in the sun. Our army, with its supply train and columns of captives strung out to the rear, looked like an army of slow-moving ants.

I gazed around me. To my right, the ledge shelved gently to a fold in the rock face, which provided enough shelter to support some stunted foliage. Treetops visible beyond the outcropping suggested less severe slopes with a mantle of denser jungle ahead. If any would-be attackers lurked in this forbidding terrain, they would stick to forest cover and shun exposed positions such as the one I now occupied. I urged Sa-lu-tzu toward the rock face on my right.

We rounded the outcropping. Suddenly the stallion froze in his tracks. I eased the battle ax from its saddle loop as I scanned the thin bushes directly in front of us to find out what had alarmed the bay. At first I could see nothing and tried to urge Sa-lu-tzu forward. The stallion refused to budge. He stood rooted to the spot, trembling violently.

There was no breeze, yet I thought I detected a slight swaying motion in the bushes in front of us. Then I saw it clearly. Cold fear gripped my heart.

It was a giant cobra, almost the same color as the dry, sun-browned shrubbery. Its hood was flared. Its body, which I had taken for the slender trunk of a tree, was thicker than my forearm. It rose to a height that must have exceeded six feet. For a moment, the scene seemed suspended in time; then it dissolved into a blur of action.

The cobra struck. Its chewing teeth fastened on Sa-lu-tzu's neck. The stallion screamed, reared, and struck out with flashing hooves in an attempt to dislodge the writhing attacker. I was flung from the saddle, landing heavily on the rocky ground.

Dazed by the fall, I scrambled painfully to my feet. Sa-lu-tzu, still screaming in terror, had slipped and fallen on his side.

The serpent detached its bloodied mouth from the struggling bay. It swung its flat head, and its lidless eyes fixed themselves on me. It slithered across the stallion's lashing forelegs and headed directly toward me. As it came, the forward few feet of its body lifted clear off the ground. I stood as though transfixed. It was a few seconds before my stunned brain registered what was happening.

The ax had been knocked from my grasp by my fall. It lay almost at my feet. I scooped it from the ground and poised myself to meet the oncoming monster. I would have only one swing; there was no room for error, no second chance.

I mentally calculated the serpent's distance from me and its speed of advance. Wait. Wait. *Now!*

My hand responded to the command flashed by my brain. The ax swung in a downward arc. The blade caught the snake just behind the head, shearing it from the body and sending it flying into some coarse grass. The serpent's body continued its forward advance. Blood gushed from the headless neck and splashed my leg.

When my second in command rounded the outcropping, he found me seated on a rock, bathed in sweat and shaking. The deadly neurotoxic venom had done its work; my valiant Sa-lu-tzu was dead. The dusty coils of the decapitated snake still writhed not far from me.

That was my first encounter with a king cobra. It was not to be my last, but it was unlike any other meeting and impressed itself on my mind for all time. In my superstitious awe, I thought I had met the storied *naga* king in the flesh. Why I had been singled out for the king's attack I did not know. But one thing I did know was that ordinary snakes, even cobras, will, unless cornered, flee from a man. This was no ordinary snake. In length it measured over twenty feet. Its attack against me had been deliberate. I cannot be blamed for believing I had incurred the wrath of a god-demon.

Later, Dang explained to me that the male king cobra is cannibalistic. During the month when the female is giving birth, the male stays constantly close by in order to enjoy the tasty morsels, those of his offspring that cannot escape. In anticipation of his infanticidal feast, the male king cobra will attack, instantly and fearlessly, anything he feels might rob him of this pleasure.

I believed Dang, because I wanted to believe her, but it was many years before I accepted this explanation as fact.

The month when the female cobra gives birth to her

wriggling young is the fourth month of the lunar year. Appropriately, it is the Month of the Snake.

When we reached the City of Sandalwood, I told Dang that she could have her freedom. In the bustle of forming for our march to the south, she could make good her escape without detection and return to the safety of her village after our departure. To my astonishment, she did not want to leave me. Using the small command of her language I had gained, I tried to explain that if she accompanied me she would be reduced to the status of a mere slave. I am not too sure how much of this she understood, since she still seemed to want to stay with me.

During his stay in the City of Sandalwood, Horse-master Chang had taken a shrewish Annamite to tend his bodily needs. He did not intend to take her with him on his return to Angkor, and she seemed quite content with this arrangement. With her help, Dang was persuaded that she could not accompany me. When I left her with Horse-master Chang's woman, there were tears in Dang's eyes. I came close to relenting. Later I was glad that I had not. A simple country girl, she would have found nothing but unhappiness in the artificial urban world of Angkor.

Our return march to Angkor was uneventful. The rains had started in earnest by the time we had reached the mountains marking the southern limits of the plateau, but to our delight we found that a stone-paved road, complete with rest houses at intervals, had been pushed north from Angkor and through the mountains during our absence. Despite the rains, we made good time.

The changes that had taken place at Angkor in the time we had been in the north were startling. Obviously, there had been no letup in the pace of construction, nor did the rains appear to be slowing the projects. The king seemed determined that Angkor was to be transformed during his reign as it had never been altered during the reigns of preceding monarchs.

Much that had been the temporary royal capital of Jayasri had disappeared. The site, with the exception of the temple of Preah Khan, and an island where a new temple called Neak Pean was in the foundation stage of construction, was given over to the artificial lake that had been under excavation at the time of our departure.

Preah Khan, while not completed, was rising rapidly. To the east of the lake-reservoir, yet another temple was being laid out. To the south, not far from our cavalry quarters, the first temple project of King Jayavarman VII, Ta Prohm had progressed to a point where it was nearing completion.

As if this frenetic construction of monolithic Buddhist sanctuaries was not enough, the tower of the eleventh-century temple of Phimeanakas had been freshly gilded. In addition, the more recent temples of Preah Palilay and Baphuon all within the perimeter of the capital under construction, were under repair.

The three-hundred-thirty-foot-wide moat encompassing the new royal capital, already named Angkor Thom, Angkor the Great, was not only fully excavated, but it was in use, since it was needed to bring the massive laterite blocks that would form the ramparts. The wall was rising steadily.

A new royal palace was being constructed near the temple of Phimeanakas. The king, in fact, was already in residence in a completed wing, and other palaces were taking shape in the royal compound.

In terms of other military achievements over the same span of months, our campaign in the north had not been much of a success. The captives and plunder we brought back were nothing by comparison with the spoils of war that had streamed into the capital from Prince Vidya's Army of the West and from an Army of the South that was campaigning in a mountainous peninsula in the remote southwestern region of the empire. The latter army, in fact, was to continue campaigning for at least another year and then be relieved by a newly recruited force.

With the amount of continuing construction in and around Angkor Thom, the network of stone-paved roads that was being pushed to all corners of the realm, and with two armies that were virtually standing armies to support, it was not difficult to see why huge manpower reserves were necessary. Captives from military conquest were essential to feed the insatiable maw. Under these circumstances, our rather poor showing from a year and a half of campaigning in the north must have angered the king.

The army of Prince In was disbanded. The Sixth Cavalry Troop moved back to its quarters, barracks, and stables east of the river. I scarcely had time to settle in before I received word of my promotion.

I learned of my good fortune from the commander of the Cavalry of the Golden Banner. He summoned me and curtly informed me that I had been promoted to the command of the Cavalry of the Scarlet Banner. He neither congratulated me nor indicated how or why the promotion had come about.

The Cavalry of the Scarlet Banner is attached to the Army of the West. Apart from the palace guard, the Army of the West is the closest thing to a permanent force, and professional officers covet postings to it for experience and as avenues to further promotion. Suddenly, as commander of its cavalry, I held an important position in the command structure of that army. I could not blame the commander of the Cavalry of the Golden Banner for his churlishness. It was probably a post he had sought himself.

I had just turned twenty-two. I had less than two and a half years of experience in the Khmer forces. I had just been promoted over the heads of a good many senior officers probably more deserving than myself. I felt I had Vidya to thank for this. It was unlikely that Prince In had had anything to do with it. I doubted if he knew of my existence. And certainly the commander of the Cavalry of the Golden Banner had had no hand in the matter.

I perceived that my promotion was a mixed blessing. I had a friend in high places, but I was also earning powerful enemies. Not the least of these was, without doubt, the commander of the Cavalry of the Golden Banner.

Horse-master Chang was elated when I told him of the promotion and contended that it was no more than I deserved. He agreed that I would be unpopular with many of my fellow officers, but he pointed out that I wasn't engaged in any popularity contest. He advanced a suggestion, putting into words something I had been vaguely considering myself.

I was almost six feet in height, tall even by Chinese standards, and a full head taller than the average Khmer. My features had a distinctly Mongolian cast. According to Chang, I took after my Khitan mother in appearance, and my nickname was aptly applied. I would stand out in Chinese society and could not avoid attracting attention in these barbaric realms. Although few, if any, knew its derivation, I was known as the Tartar by my troopers and fellow officers. With my promotion, the name would soon be known throughout the armed forces. In fact, Chang asserted, it was already known more widely than I suspected. Since I was already distinctive, I should, without posturing, exploit the differences. For example, I had always worn my hair close-cropped, contrary to the local fashion, and I should continue to do so. I should, he suggested, stop plucking my moustache and cultivate it in the drooping fashion of my nomadic forefathers. He had, he hinted, other embellishments in mind, but he would leave them for a later date.

The Cavalry of the Scarlet Banner was not quartered at Angkor but at the western capital of Lopburi. I was not expected to join the force until the close of the present rainy season. Since I had in mind a number of radical changes for the Cavalry of the Scarlet Banner, the time in Angkor could be put to good advantage.

From my experience with training the Sixth Cavalry Troop, and from the mistakes I had made as well as the results achieved, I knew that the Khmer cavalrymen could be converted to mounted bowmen, that Khmer horses could be trained to a suitable gait, and I knew just about how long the process should take. It was not my intention to retrain the entire Cavalry of the Scarlet Banner, but I wanted, within a year, four troops of mounted archers trained in the battle tactics we had tried out with the Sixth Cavalry Troop. These units, when trained, could also spearhead mobile striking forces as required.

It would have simplified matters if the Sixth Cavalry Troop could have been transferred intact to the Scarlet Banner command. This, I learned, was out of the question. I did the next best thing. The veteran I had appointed my second in command of the sixth troop had taken over the command. He agreed to release four of his best troopers to me on a temporary basis. Volunteers were called for, and I was pleased that the troop, almost to a man, volunteered their services. Of the four selected, two had been my cavalry companions from my own days as a trooper prior to my field promotion.

The troopers were given the task of training new horses. I would oversee the crafting of bows and arrows. Horse-master Chang, who was reluctant to leave, was commissioned by me to go to China to purchase on my behalf a number of stallions and broodmares, and a quantity of composite bows. He was also to recruit the services of four stable masters, a skilled saddler, two bow craftsmen, and four archery experts.

I turned over to Chang what little gold and silver I had managed to accumulate. It was by no means enough to cover the purchases and recruitment. I also gave Chang a scroll to take to my family in Changsha, instructing them to advance sufficient funds from my patrimony to underwrite anything Chang required. My father had several times mentioned this patrimony. I did not know what monies, goods, and properties he had bequeathed to me, but he was, at the time of his death, a very wealthy man. The patrimony should be more than enough to meet my requirements.

A large residential pavilion and outbuildings within the military compound in the new city of Angkor Thom went with my promotion. I moved in, acquiring in the process six servants and thirty slaves.

There was one more important matter to be attended to. I selected a large, airy sleeping chamber with an adjoining room. The sleeping chamber I had fitted with heavy curtains that could be drawn across both windows and entranceways. The chamber and adjoining room I furnished with everything I thought Apricot Blossom and her personal servant would require, and I assigned four slaves as their personal retinue. The final touch was the installation of a bell in the adjoining room that could be rung by pull cords in the sleeping chamber.

Everything was in readiness to receive my father's concubine under my roof. I think he would have wished it so. What I did not know, as yet, was whether it would meet with her wishes, and, if it did, if the Chinese merchant would agree to his daughter accompanying her mistress to my residence.

Chang went with me when I journeyed to the trading community on the Great Lake. For one thing, he had to arrange his passage to Canton. For another, I felt he would be in a better position than myself to persuade the merchant to part with his mute daughter.

The news of my promotion to exalted rank must have preceded us. The merchant received us with great deference. He was, in fact, nothing short of obsequious, which hugely amused Chang. As my friend, factotum, and trusted sergeant at arms, Chang had acquired almost as much status as myself in the eyes of his former master. The merchant assured us that he would be honored to have his daughter become a member of my household staff.

When I put my proposal to Apricot Blossom, she at first demurred. She was, she said, comfortable and well looked after where she was and had no wish to be a burden on me. I assured her that this was far from the case. My residence was too large for my use alone. By being my honored guest, she would be doing me a favor by acting as the mistress of the house during my absences, which were bound to be lengthy. I think what finally persuaded her to accept the invitation was when I said that I knew it would have been my father's wish that I do everything in my power to further her well-being. If she preferred, I stated, I could arrange for her to return to China and her own people, together with her son. She had few living relatives, she said, and no desire to return to China. My father's home she did not consider as her own without his presence. She would be honored to accept my hospitality and thanked me on behalf of herself and her son.

It was not until later that I realized there had been no mention of the boy up to the point of my introducing him into the conversation.

chapter 18

WHEN HORSE-MASTER CHANG WAS DUE TO EMBARK, I went with him to the lake port to see him safely installed on the merchant junk. Accompanying us were my four troopers as a mounted escort, a slave-borne curtained palanquin, and a horse-drawn cart. We had proceeded only a short distance before more riders joined us. Under the command of their new captain, the Sixth Troop had turned out to a man to bid farewell to the crusty old riding master who had earned their respect and affection. Although Chang would have died rather than display emotion, I could tell he was touched by this show of esteem.

When the junk had cast off her lines and her high-pooped stern was well offshore as the vessel shaped a southeasterly course, my party went to the home of the Chinese merchant. The Sixth Troop, logically, should have returned to Angkor at this point. They did not. They stayed at a respectful distance while a heavily veiled Apricot Blossom, mincing along on her bound feet, was assisted into the palanquin by her maidservant. The servant, together with a small amount of baggage, occupied the cart.

As we moved off, the Sixth Troop formed as an escort. Although the proceedings must have piqued the curiosity of the troopers, no questions were asked and nothing was said to indicate this was other than an everyday occurrence.

The procession drew curious glances as we clattered into the city. The Sixth Troop did not take its leave until we were within the flagged compound of my residence. It was a gesture of respect I will long remember.

I believe that was the first time it occurred to me that I had the ability to inspire loyalty in those under my command. It was a quality possessed by my father to a marked degree, a gift he had bestowed on me. I was wise enough to appreciate that Chang had recognized this latent talent within me and had steered me on a course best suited to develop it to its best advantage. His guidance, I now realized, had started when I was a small boy and had never ceased. He had been gone but a few short hours, and already I missed the Old Stallion.

Supervision of the composite bow fabrication and the training of the horses did not make heavy demands on my time. I was able, during the months of the rainy season, to devote a good deal of my time to Apricot Blossom. It was a rewarding experience.

Apricot Blossom, I found, was a remarkable woman. I discovered qualities in her that made it easy to understand why my father had been attracted to her and why she commanded the devotion of her mute handmaiden.

Chinese girls of breeding were normally isolated from the boys of the household at the age of seven. At that point, the binding of their feet to achieve the prized "golden lotus" perfection started. Their education consisted of training in spinning, sewing, embroidery, music, and polite conversation. For the most part, they could neither read nor write. Secluded from the world, they generally had little or no knowledge of happenings outside the household. Their redeeming virtue was their chastity: they would go to the wedding bed as primary wife, secondary wife, or concubine in virginal purity. They were taught to be subservient to patriarchal authority: their father, husband, and, on the death of their husband, their eldest son. Their function was to ensure the "filial piety" demanded by the Confucian ethic by bearing sons.

This was how it had been with my half sisters in our household. It had been so with the daughters of our friends and neighbors. It was, I had believed since childhood, the ordered and accepted pattern of the civilized world.

My mother, with unbound feet, had been an exception in that respect. Apricot Blossom, even though her feet were bound, had not been cast in the normal mold. She had both wit and wisdom. I was to learn much from our discussions.

Apricot Blossom's father had been a Confucian scholar and a minor official at the Sung court in Lin-an. His religious persuasion had been the Taoism of Lao-tzu, a more hedonistic faith than the Mahayana Buddhism of my father's house. According to Apricot Blossom, her father had been repelled by the prudery and hypocrisy he had seen on every side in the capital city. This had caused him to turn away from many of the accepted Confucian practices. In the education of his daughters, he had adhered strictly to the principle of chastity, but he had been liberal in other areas.

In addition to spinning, sewing, embroidery, and music, Apricot Blossom and her sisters and half sisters had been taught to cook and had received instruction in chess. An even greater departure from convention had been that the girls had been taught to read and write, and a large number of texts and scrolls had been made available to them for the furtherance of their education.

I was to find that Apricot Blossom was well versed in a wide variety of subjects. In Chinese history, her knowledge was superior to my own. She was particularly conversant with the role women had played throughout the course of history, a subject I could neither dispute nor debate.

It may have been due to the fact that our conversations took place in a darkened room, or that when she walked with me at night in the garden her face was hidden by a veil, but I found we could touch on the most delicate of subjects without embarrassment. Our discussions were astonishingly frank. I was, I discovered, naïve despite my experience in sexual matters. Through Apricot Blossom, I received a liberal education that might otherwise have been denied me. One such discussion stands out vividly in my memory.

Apricot Blossom claimed that there were a number of ancient Taoist texts that dealt explicitly with the "Flowery Battle." The term was unfamiliar to me, and I asked her to explain it. She laughed. The texts, she explained, gave details and instructions concerning techniques and variations of the sexual act. The books were liberally illustrated and, with the exception of some intricate positions, easy to follow. She had read these texts as a girl. Thanks to them, she said, she had come to my father's bed a virgin but with a knowledge of erotic practices that had brought pleasure and delight to their subsequent lovemaking.

"How," I asked ingenuously, "could you remember the techniques without having put them into practice?"

She laughed softly. "I had the foresight to bring one of the books with me from my father's house. Your father was kind enough to indulge my wishes. I did not long lack for practice. But, even had I not had the text to refer to, I am sure the positions were sufficiently impressed on my memory to assist in improvisations."

The mental picture conjured up by her words did not, strangely enough, detract from my image of my father. It gave him an added dimension and made him seem less austere and more human. The more I talked with Apricot Blossom, the better I came to know the man who had sired me. My train of thought was interrupted by Apricot Blossom's next, unexpected, statement.

"The Taoist text was, I understand, similar to the *Kama Sutra*, from which your charming young Cham princess drew her inspiration. In her case, however, unencumbered by chastity, she must not have lacked for practice."

I was startled. I had not thought my affair with White Lotus was known to any member of our household. I was thankful for the darkness, which hid my flush of embarrassment.

"I . . . ah . . ." I stammered in confusion.

Apricot Blossom's laugh tinkled. "Tartar, Tartar," she said, "did you believe your love affair with the girl was a secret? There are few secrets in a household of many servants. You were observed on several occasions in your hidden pavilion. Your activities were reported in lurid detail. Your father did not approve of Cham mores or customs, but he was delighted that you were receiving such expert tuition."

"We . . . I thought myself madly in love with her. I was heartbroken when we left," I said lamely. Then, without knowing why I did so, I disclosed what I had told no one up to then. "On the night before our departure, she told me she was carrying my child."

Apricot Blossom did not reply for several moments.

When she finally spoke, her voice was serious. "She may have been with child; however, she may not have been, but merely told you that she was to reaffirm the hold she knew she had over you. Women sometimes do strange things. If she was pregnant, you could well be the father. But the promiscuity of the Cham women matches that of Chinese women in ancient times . . . before Fu Hsi founded the institution of marriage during the Chou dynasty. In those matriarchal days, a child knew only its mother. The girl had other lovers, did she not?"

"Yes," I said glumly. "Her brother told me that she had. She boasted of the fact herself."

"Then you must not concern yourself. If she was indeed pregnant, she could not possibly know whose seed stirred the life in her womb."

As the weeks progressed, I came to know Apricot Blossom better and better and appreciate her company more and more. It became my habit to spend some time with her each afternoon, partaking of tea and touching on a wide range of topics. Although I did not take my meals with her, I often returned in the evening to continue our discussions. Weather permitting, we walked at night in the garden several times a week.

When we talked in Apricot Blossom's curtained chamber, we were alone unless her maidservant was summoned to perform some service. When we walked in the garden, however, the mute girl was invariably present to be available at a moment's notice in case she was needed. The girl was more than a handmaiden to Apricot Blossom; she was also a companion, a confidante, and a friend.

A congenital defect had robbed the girl of her voice, but her hearing was unimpaired. Apricot Blossom conversed with the girl, who answered by means of a simple sign language they had evolved between themselves. I discovered that Apricot Blossom had taught the girl calligraphy. Her communication with her mistress was not limited to sign language.

To say that we walked in the garden is not an entirely accurate description. Apricot Blossom tripped daintily along on her lotus feet, with myself matching my stride to her mincing gait as best I could. The mute girl brought up the rear at a discreet distance. Apricot Blossom tired easily. We spent the better part of these nocturnal outings sitting in a pergola at the foot of the garden.

On one such evening, as we sat on a wooden bench in the grape arbor, I watched Apricot Blossom's tiny feet as she swung them in time to a melody she was humming faintly. The little feet, encased in silken slippers, looked like those of a child. While the practice of foot binding had been mentioned in some of our discussions, the references had been only in passing. They had been enough, however, for me to appreciate that Apricot Blossom had no liking for the practice and found the subject distasteful. As I watched the slippers peeping out from beneath the hem of her gown, fluttering like butterflies, curiosity overcame my discretion.

"Was it painful?" I questioned.

"Was what painful? Does my singing disturb you?"

"Not at all. I was thinking of the shaping of your lotus feet. Did it hurt much?"

"Not particularly. If the binding is expertly done, the process is uncomfortable but not too painful. If it is inexpertly done, I understand it can be excruciatingly painful. If the binding is too tight, the circulation is cut off and the feet become infected. If an attempt is made to compress the feet beyond the limits of physical tolerance, bones can be broken. I have heard of such cases. I have heard that many times the toes that have been curled under have dropped off. Fortunately, none of this happened in our household. Nonetheless, it is a crippling and degrading custom that I deplore. Had my child been a girl, I would not have allowed her feet to be bound. In this, your father was in agreement with me, and he would have opposed any attempt on the part of his principal wife to impose foot binding on our daughter."

I should have dropped the subject, but now that it had been broached, I pursued it.

"You say the toes are curled under. I always thought the binding just prevented the normal growth of the foot."

"You have never seen a lotus foot without its binding?" she asked incredulously.

"I have not had that pleasure. It is a fashion not followed in this region."

"I shall not satisfy your curiosity by displaying mine," she said tartly. "I find them loathsome, misshapen objects. The binding does, of course, stunt growth, but it is designed to reshape the feet, as well. Only the big toes remain normal. The remaining toes are curled under the soles to make the feet appear slimmer. To shorten the feet, the balls of the feet are forced toward the heels until the exaggerated arches finally become nothing more than deep creases. It is a monstrous imposition forced on my sex in the name of fashion."

"Do most women feel as you do about the custom?"

"Alas, no. Were that so, the custom could not have prevailed as long as it has. There are many who take great pride in their tiny feet. The bound feet are considered a mark of distinction. Obviously, a woman with bound feet cannot work in the paddy fields. It is also considered to denote subservience. A woman cannot hobble far from home and hearth in this condition, and she is thus looked upon as a pampered creature symbolizing the wealth and station of her husband. It is largely the male ego that has prompted and sustained the custom." She paused, then added dryly, "Well-bred women somehow overlook the fact that bound feet are as common in the brothel as they are in the genteel bedchamber."

"Are we Chinese the only people who have adopted this custom?" I asked.

"To the best of my knowledge, it is not a practice followed beyond the confines of the Middle Kingdom. It has been borrowed by races that have ventured south of the Great Wall bent on conquest and have stayed to settle in our realm. These newcomers ape us in all things until it becomes next to impossible to distinguish between conqueror and conquered. The Tangut of the northwestern Hsi Hsia dynasty have adopted foot binding as a mark of gentility. Your forebears, the Khitan of the Liao dynasty, followed the practice. It was a mutilation that your mother somehow escaped. I am told that women of the Jürched of the new Chin dynasty in the north are accepting the practice. So, it is not a custom confined to us Chinese . . . but it does not seem to have gone beyond our borders. For that, barbaric races such as the Cham and Khmer can thank their gods."

"Has the custom always been with us? I don't mean for those who till the soil and tend the herds, of course, but with the nobility and women of high station."

"Legend would have it so, but legends are not always

based on fact. A number of stories date foot binding to the Shang dynasty of more than twenty-five hundred years ago. One story is that a Shang empress had a club foot. She persuaded the emperor to decree bound feet for all women of the realm. I believe, however, that the practice started only about two centuries ago in our own Sung dynasty.

"My reason for assuming this is that women of the T'ang dynasty indulged in horseback riding and sports involving kicking a ball. They could hardly have engaged in such activities with bound feet.

"What I have heard, and what I believe to be the origin of the custom, is that in the early years of the present dynasty temple dancers started to bind their feet to achieve a bird-like step. Men seemed to find the dainty feet inordinately attractive. Women not of the dancing sorority started to imitate the temple entertainers to vie with them for men's affection. From that start, the custom spread, and in the process it acquired its own mythology. Today I am the victim of a foolish vanity of that era."

I had listened attentively to Apricot Blossom's views on the subject and was much impressed by her fund of knowledge. It was obviously something to which she had devoted thought and study. There was one aspect, I noted, that she had studiously avoided. It was of a delicate nature, yet I ventured to question her further.

"You say men found the bound feet of the temple dancers fascinating. As a boy, I heard it said that men were sexually aroused by lotus feet. It was also rumored that women derive great pleasure and stimulation from having their tiny, tender feet squeezed or nibbled during intercourse. I suppose if I had stayed in China, I would know by now whether those assertions were true or false. Perhaps you can enlighten me."

Apricot Blossom hesitated before answering. "I do not know if I can give you a satisfactory answer," she said. "Many men appear to become aroused by bound feet. I have known women who claimed that they achieved the heights of ecstasy from the activities you mention. But I can only speak from my own experience. I derived no pleasure from having my feet caressed. Your father, when he knew this, avoided such gestures. On his part, he claimed that bound feet did not stimulate him in the least. I believe he spoke the truth, but he could have been influenced in his thinking by his love for your mother. I, as you may have gathered by now, have been prejudiced against foot binding since childhood. My belief is that the erotic appeal of lotus feet and the sexual stimulation credited to them are delusions, but I may not be in a position to judge fairly. Someday, when you return to your homeland, you must answer these questions for yourself."

It was an admirable arrangement, for me a comfortable and satisfying one. Apricot Blossom ran the household from her curtained bedchamber, using one of the servants as housekeeper and intermediary. It was Apricot Blossom who planned the meals and gave instructions on the ordering of food and drink. The household ran smoothly. The servants and slaves were not mistreated.

I learned to my amusement that Apricot Blossom was thought, by the servants, to be blessed with psychic powers. Any infractions of her rules, any deviation from her laid-down routines, or any squabbling among the servants or slaves was known to her almost as soon as it took place and the culprit was promptly disciplined. The mute handmaiden acted as Apricot Blossom's eyes and ears. Neither the servants nor slaves knew the girl could communicate with her mistress in writing.

During those months there was one thing about Apricot Blossom that puzzled me. Not once since her arrival in my house had she made a reference to her son. She had not questioned me concerning his whereabouts, state of health, or activities. I was almost positive she knew the child was dead, but I could not bring myself to confirm the suspicion.

chapter 19

Prince Vidyanandana considered Lopburi provincial and rustic. He spent as little time in the western capital as possible, much preferring the gaiety and excitement of the royal capital at Angkor. His duties as the general commanding the Army of the West were not as arduous as one might imagine. He left the day-to-day running of the army to the professional soldier who was his second-in-command and took personal command of only those dry-season campaigns calculated to enhance his reputation as a commander of skill and daring.

Vidya had advanced his career considerably since our Malyang expedition. He was a popular and much sought-after figure in court circles. The Army of the West had enjoyed a good deal of success in campaigns against the Mon kingdoms, victories for which Vidya took the credit. On the social scene, Vidya's primary wife, the Khmer princess of the royal house, had been augmented during my absence by two secondary wives, the daughter of a highly placed Brahman official and a Mon princess. A fourth wedding, I learned, was being planned for a few months hence.

Vidya entertained royally at his palatial residence within the royal compound. Enjoying as he did the favor of the king, Vidya was surrounded by sycophants. Nonetheless, due to his charm and wit, he commanded a following in court and ecclesiastical circles in his own right.

167

I was anxious to pay my respects to Vidya and to thank him for arranging my promotion. I wished, as well, to request that my date of joining the Army of the West be advanced so that I could initiate a training program prior to officially assuming command of the cavalry. The sweeping changes I had in mind would also require Vidya's approval. I was confident that I could bring him over to my point of view. I was prevented from approaching Vidya when I received notification of my promotion due to the fact that, in spite of the onset of the rainy season, he had not yet returned from Lopburi.

The Month of the Ram, the second month of the rainy season, was well advanced before word reached me that Vidya was a day's march from Angkor and should arrive in the royal capital the next morning. I rode out along the western road early the next morning to witness Vidya's triumphal return.

Two troops of cavalry, with scarlet pennants fluttering from the tips of their upright spears, led the procession. They were followed by a company of crossbowmen. Next came seemingly endless lines of captives, many of whom were in chains. To the rear of the captives was a military band beating a cadence with drums and cymbals. Next marched a company of spearmen. Behind the spearmen, escorted by a cavalry troop, the caparisoned war elephant of Prince Vidya plodded in ponderous majesty.

Vidya was seated in the howdah. His scarlet *sampot* was richly embroidered. Bracelets of gold adorned his upper arms and wrists. Gems flashed on his fingers. His extended right arm grasped a gold-tipped spear. His handsome face was set in an expression of studied indifference. Above his head was the scarlet silk parasol of his rank, to each side of which were white parasols that were once the property of Mon monarchs now dead or among the captives.

A second company of spearmen marched behind the war elephant. Behind these infantrymen, a long line of creaking carts and wagons groaned under their loads of booty from the campaign. A fourth troop of cavalry brought up the rear.

I smiled. Vidya had not lost his theatrical flair.

I waited a few days before presenting myself at Vidya's residence. I was kept waiting more than an hour before being ushered into his presence.

Vidya greeted me with the offhanded hauteur I had come to expect of him. He had been bathed and scented and his hair was groomed, but his reddened eyes betrayed a night of roistering from which he had not fully recovered even at this late hour of the morning.

"It is a pleasure to see you, Tartar," he said with little convinction. "What brings you here?"

"I came" I said affably, "to congratulate you on your successful campaign in the west. I witnessed your return to the capital It was an impressive spectacle."

Vidya grinned boyishly. "It was quite a victory . . . several victories, in fact. We did much better than Prince In's campaigns in the north. The only trouble is that it took longer than I had planned, and then I was detained by . . . ah . . . personal affairs in Lopburi. Dreary place. But that you will find out for yourself, since you are soon to be my commander of cavalry."

"That is the second reason for my visit," I said, seizing the opportunity. "I came to thank you for interceding on my behalf."

The smile left Vidya's face and was replaced by a slight frown. He eyed me speculatively. "The present commander is due to retire in four months. In my discussion with the king concerning a replacement, your name was mentioned."

I had not expected such modesty from Vidya. I let it pass. "With your approval, I intend to make a number of changes in the Cavalry of the Scarlet Banner. If you have time, we could discuss these now. If not, I shall await your pleasure."

Vidya waved his hand brusquely. "I leave such matters to my second-in-command. He is responsible for anything to do with tactics and training. I command in the field. It is his responsibility to see to it that the army is in a state of preparedness such that my strategic objectives can be achieved. If you have changes in mind for the cavalry, they must be discussed with him and receive his approval."

I was dismayed. Delegation of authority is the hallmark of a good military commander, but what Vidya's comments suggested was that he had no interest in administrative matters or tactical planning. If what I had just heard was correct, if I was not misinterpreting his meaning, he had absolved himself of all responsibility other than field command.

My thoughts must have been reflected in my expression. Vidya laughed. "Tartar," he said, "you take life . . . and warfare . . . much too seriously. The Army of the West has proved itself invincible. I assure you that my second-in-command is an able and competent soldier. Were it not so, I would have had him replaced."

"Have I your leave, then, to discuss these matters with him directly?" I asked stiffly.

Vidya waved his hand absently. It was obvious that he was becoming bored with the conversation. "By all means," he said. "Do so at your leisure. You will find him rotting away in Lopburi with his beloved troops."

When I reflected on it, I don't know why I should have been dismayed by Vidya's attitude. Field command in the Khmer Army was a sinecure bestowed by the king as royal patronage. It had little or nothing to do with competence. Prince In, during our campaign in the north, had not even bothered to retain field command beyond the City of Sandalwood. Why should I expect more of Vidya?

The truth was that I *did* expect more of Vidya. Although he had cooled toward me and made it patently clear that he considered me of vastly inferior station, I still looked on him with affection due to our boyhood association. I had expected him to take an interest in my tactical theories. I had been vain enough to think that Vidya must have heard of my exploits with the mobile strike force in the north, and that this had been the reason he had been responsible for my advancement. Now I doubted that this was the case. Why else would he have sponsored my promotion? Did he feel some sort of obligation toward me because of our boyhood friendship? If so, he took great pains to hide it in our infrequent meetings.

Another thing defied explanation, now more than ever. Vidya had spoken of his strategic objectives in the west. They were not strategies of Vidya's conception. They were strategic objectives devised by only one man, King Jayavarman. Vidya was charged with their execution in his particular theater of action. Yet the king did not seem to object to Vidya spending more time in Angkor than at his base of operations in Lopburi. As a mark of the king's favor, Vidya's forthcoming marriage was to another young princess of the Khmer royal house. Why was the king disposed to lavish this indulgence on a turncoat prince of the kingdom of Champa?

I voiced many of these thoughts to Apricot Blossom. Her comments were interesting.

"You are a man of action, Tartar. You have wisdom, an inquiring mind, and ingenuity, but intrigue is foreign to your nature. Policies of state are often baffling and rewards for service to the throne are uncertain. General Yüeh Fei's thanks from High Ancestor for victories against the Chin was prison and strangulation."

"Are you suggesting that Vidya is destined for execution?"

"Not at all. But I have no doubt that the honors the king is heaping upon Vidyanandana are for some purpose. From what I have heard, King Jayavarman is no fool, nor is he easily fooled."

"You do not hold Vidya in high esteem?"

"I do not. Your father and I thought him a spoiled and self-centered youth. Neither of us could understand why the prince devoted so much attention to you, nor why you seemed attracted to him."

"At least I have him to thank for my promotion and improved station."

"Perhaps. If so, he has displayed more wisdom than I gave him credit for. But, Tartar, do not be blinded by your friendship for the prince. I do not believe he can be trusted. I have a strong feeling he will one day try to do you harm."

The road distance from Angkor Thom to Lopburi is about two hundred and fifty miles. The stone-topped road is raised above the marshy ground and flooded fields. There are rest houses along the route. River crossings are made easy by raft ferries. Without pushing my Khmer horse, I completed the journey in less than a week. Had I been riding my faithful Sa-lu-tzu, I could have cut two days off that time.

It was the Month of the Monkey, a few weeks after my inconclusive discussion with Vidya. There was little point, I had concluded, in proceeding with the training of the horses, the fabrication of stirrup-attached saddles, and the manufacture of composite bows if the Army of the West rejected my proposals. I regretted that my initial rash of enthusiasm had prompted me to send horse-master Chang on a procurement mission that could well cost me my patrimony to no avail. Accordingly, despite the discomfort of the rains, I was on my way to try and sway the general of the second rank, Vidya's second-in-command, to accept my views. I was not too sanguine. From past experience, I knew my theories were considered unorthodox and impractical by veteran professional soldiers. I did not expect the second-in-command to be any exception. As I rode along, I marshaled my arguments.

I had ample time on the journey to dwell on other matters. The roadway itself, and the traffic that moved upon it in spite of the season, turned my thoughts to King Jayavarman and the changes he had wrought in less than three years of reign.

The Cham had thought that when they cut off the head by their razing of Yasodharapura, the limbs would wither and die. They thought they had smashed forever the power of Kambuja. How wrong that rash assumption had been. The will and energy of a single man had proved them wrong. It was now less than eight years since the sacking of Angkor, and the Khmer capital already was, or would be soon, stronger than at any time in its history. The limbs, far from withering, now extended farther to the north, west, and south than they had prior to the Cham invasion. In less than three years, King Jayavarman had raised the kingdom from the ashes of its defeat and set the empire on a path toward greater glory. It was a prodigious feat—and it looked to be but in its infancy.

I pondered the king's achievements—this road, for example. It had existed for many years, perhaps centuries. But under the king's construction program it had been raised, widened, its surface vastly improved, rest houses provided along its route, and with each dry season it was being extended farther west. And this was just one road of many. The king's intention was easy to discern. Surfaced roads would be pushed into every part of the realm so that no corner of the empire would be isolated by the seasons. Troops, produce, and labor crews could be shifted at will, regardless of the rains that had formerly paralyzed the empire for six months of the year. It was an ambitious program that would take years, perhaps generations, to complete.

The intricate system of flood control and irrigation in and around Angkor was rapidly nearing its former efficiency. As slave labor flooded into the capital as the fruits of conquest, many of the peasants recruited for the labor force in the capital who had come from the rich croplands near Angkor were being returned to their fields, at least for planting and harvesting. There was a good deal more agricultural activity in evidence in the plains close to Angkor today than there had been in the growing season two years ago. Still, even had this not been so, there would have been no shortage of foodstuffs in Angkor, since produce poured in from the heavily taxed outlying communities and from newly conquered regions. Granaries in Angkor Thom were bursting with stored foodstuffs. More granaries were under construction. The renowned rats of Angkor were sleeker and fatter than ever. It was almost as though King Jayavarman were preparing the city for a lengthy siege.

The construction projects at Angkor staggered the imagination. There had been no letup and there were no signs that a slowdown was contemplated. On the contrary. No sooner did one project near completion than architects and builders were embarking on another. When the supplementary lake-reservoir north of Angkor Thom and the wide moat around the city had been completed, the army of laborers employed in their excavation had been diverted to the widening and deepening of existing canals and the digging of new waterways. Even before the gleaming roof tiles were affixed to a palace in the royal compound, another royal residence was rearing at its side.

Of all the projects under way, it was the orgy of construction in stone that most impressed me. Four massive temples were in various stages of construction. The foundations of a fifth, Banteay Kdei, had been started close to the first temple complex Jayavarman had commissioned, Ta Prohm. And it was common knowledge that the royal architects were working feverishly under the critical eye of the king to complete plans for the most magnificent temple of them all. It was to be constructed on a site at the geographical center of the new capital.

The six temples would take decades to complete, but they were not the only stone construction in progress. At the moment, priority was being given to the stone ramparts of the city, the causeways that would span the outer moat, and the five gates that would give entrance to the walled city. If the Cham armies came again, Jayavarman did not intend that they would find easy access to his royal seat. If they managed to cross the wide, crocodile-stocked moat, they would smash themselves on the stone walls like seas breaking against a foreshore cliff.

These musings covered many days of my journey, but it was not until I neared my destination that I discerned what I thought to be a dovetailed pattern to the king's planning. What had appeared to be glaring inconsistencies started to fall neatly into place.

One feature of the frenzied construction at Angkor that had concerned me was its implication in a military sense. The gigantic projects in progress or those projected at Angkor demanded an almost limitless supply of slave labor. Unless the projects were scaled down, which did not appear to be the king's intention, the needed manpower could only be provided by military conquest. Armies of conquest themselves make heavy demands on the available manpower as more and more conscripts are required for the far-flung operations and to fill the gaps created as professional soldiers are siphoned off to govern and garrison conquered territories. As my experience in the sparsely populated northern regions indicated, captive manpower was not limitless. In conquest, therefore, a point of diminishing returns should be reached eventually.

Peasant armies recruited on a seasonal basis are not suited to continuous military operations. Permanent forces are called for. The Army of the West was one such professional force. The new Army of the South looked to be a permanent fixture. The campaign in the north appeared to have been a mere probing action to confirm that the region constituted no threat, nor did it provide fertile fields for conquest. That army had been disbanded.

Powerful armies can pose threats to the monarchies that create them. On ascending the throne, King Jayavarman had acquired an intact standing army in the west. He probably considered its loyalty questionable. How was he dealing with the situation? He had replaced the commander of the Army of the West with a candidate of his own choosing. As a counterbalancing force, he had brought into being the Army of the South, its command structure composed of trusted veterans from his previous campaigns.

In the king's place, what sort of man would I select to command the Army of the West? I would not seek a man of conspicuous military skills. I would look for a man unlikely to engender strong loyalties in his subordinates, possibly a man of foreign birth. The man would hold his rank and position not through professional competence or the support of his troops, but solely through royal patronage—just such a man, in fact, as Prince Vidyanandana.

What were the king's probable courses of action? In my estimation, when he was satisfied that he had achieved a stable military power base, he would reduce his commitment in the field and consolidate his territorial gains. Then, when the flow of captive labor lessened, he would reduce the heavy commitment to his projects in order to strike a better manpower balance throughout the realm. Labor battalions would be confined to slave labor and many Khmer farmers would return to agricultural pursuits.

The question was: Which of the various ongoing projects could be profitably scaled down? The causeways, gates, and walls of the city would be completed in the not-too-distant future, but the labor force involved would probably be diverted to the construction of the temple planned within the city. It was unlikely that work would be slowed on any of the other temples since they represented projections of the king's religious fervor. Projects such as road building, irrigation, and the excavation of waterways could be spread over a longer period. It was in these latter areas that I considered the king would moderate his demands on labor.

One thing I found puzzling was the number of temples simultaneously under construction. When completed, they, too, would be a drain on the populace in the supply of acolytes, temple dancers, and the continuing support of the priesthood. Then an explanation came to me.

For centuries, the Brahman ecclesiastical hierarchy had exercised administrative authority throughout the realm. They had grown immensely powerful in the process. Due to his many years of absence, Jayavarman was a stranger to the religious cabal. He probably had reason to doubt the sincerity of Brahman support. Since the hierarchy was too deeply entrenched to be eliminated, the best that could be done would be to weaken its hold. Whether his deep devotion to Buddhism was real or feigned, Jayavarman was using his persuasion to calculated advantage. As rapidly as possible, he was building an administrative elite of Buddhist priests who, owing their position of privilege to their god-king, could be expected to give him their undivided loyalty. He was wasting no time in providing them with temples of worship.

There could be, I thought, a parallel with the nobility. With the exception of his immediate family, Jayavarman was virtually unknown to the Angkor court circle and might harbor doubts concerning the allegiance of his nobles. In this case, he was likely to build an inner circle of noblemen who owed their station to his favors. This could explain Vidya's rapid rise in the social order.

King Jayavarman, I concluded, was doing more than extending the borders of his empire. He was in the process of reshaping its entire social structure.

In these speculations, I came reasonably close to the truth in some areas. In others, I fear, I was way off the mark. What I had not allowed for, and at that time had no way of assessing, was the character of the king or the magnitude of his driving ambitions.

chapter 20

I ARRANGED FOR AN APPOINTMENT WITH THE GENERAL and arrived at his quarters at the agreed-upon hour. I was ushered directly into his presence. He was not alone. A second officer was seated on his right.

The general was an older man than I had anticipated. His hair was gray. He bore a number of scars. One shoulder seemed slightly higher than the other. I judged him to be in his early sixties. The second officer was much younger, probably in his mid-forties. He, too, had a furrowed scar running from his collarbone obliquely across his chest.

"I have taken the liberty," the general said, "of requesting my cavalry commander to be present at this meeting. Since he is the officer you will be replacing, it will give you an opportunity to meet each other. Undoubtedly, some of our remarks will be of interest to him."

"Thank you, sir," I replied respectfully.

"Why," the general asked mildly, "have you arrived so far in advance of your date of takeover?"

I chose my words carefully. "I presented myself to your commanding general in Angkor Thom. I had in mind some proposals concerning cavalry tactics and training, some of which would benefit from advance preparation. There was no point in my initiating action without command approval. He advised me, sir, that you have full authority in these matters. I have come to present these proposals for your consideration."

"Please proceed."

As concisely as I could, I outlined my concepts, starting with the capabilities of the Chinese composite bow. Both officers listened attentively. When I sketched in my theories concerning battle tactics and recounted my modest success in the training of the Sixth Cavalry Troop, I candidly admitted that the training had yet to stand the test of combat.

The general smiled thinly. "It has been some time since we have been opposed by forces of sufficient strength to give your novel theories any kind of fair test, but I find them interesting. Do you propose to convert the Cavalry of the Scarlet Banner into a glorified version of the troop you commanded?"

"No, sir, only four troops on a trial basis."

I then went on to describe our experiences during the northern campaign, when the Sixth Troop had been used to spearhead a mobile strike force, and the results achieved. If, I stated, four troops could be trained to be sufficiently competent in bowmanship, one or two mobile strike forces could be effectively employed in long-range operations well in advance of the main force.

The general nodded thoughtfully. "It would appear to have merit. The element of surprise should work in your favor. It seems to have worked in the northern campaign."

"Then, sir, do I have your approval?"

"On a trial basis, with no more than four troops, yes . . . unless the commander objects."

The cavalry commander smiled. "Any objections I might have would only have force for the next three months. My colleague of the Golden Banner does not share your enthusiasm, but I am of the opinion, and have been for some time, that the cavalry can and should play a larger part in warfare. The Chinese bow you describe looks like it could provide the firepower answer that will elevate the cavalry to the position it should occupy. I heartily agree with your proposals and wish you luck."

The general smiled broadly. "Then I will leave it to you to get to know each other and work out the details."

The cavalry commander and I left together. When we were a short distance from the general's quarters, the commander said, "So you are the Tartar. News of your exploits during the northern campaign preceded you here. I expected you to be older."

The moustache that drooped thinly down each side of my mouth obviously did not yet disguise my youth. I grinned apologetically.

The commander chuckled. "You're audacious. I like your concepts. I'm glad you are the one relieving me in my command. When do you want to get the training of your special troops under way?"

"As soon as possible."

"Good. I'll help you all I can in the selection of the units and officers I consider best qualified for your training. You'll find some good men among them."

"I'm sure I will."

We walked a few paces in silence. There was something that I didn't understand. Finally, I could no longer contain my curiosity.

"If I am not being impertinent," I said, "you do not seem of retirement age."

The commander frowned. "I'm not. Retirement is not my wish. It is at the request of the commanding general."

"Might I inquire why?"

"In return for favors received, our noble commanding general promoted a lad to the rank of captain of cavalry. I refused to accept the simpering stripling. The result is that I am being retired . . . and the young misfit commands the Ninth Cavalry Troop."

I was shaken by this revelation. "Didn't General Dom support your rejection of an unqualified officer?" I asked in shocked disbelief.

"As far as was prudent. He is a fine man and an excellent officer. You have seen that he is no longer young. He is, in fact, past due for retirement. He feels, and I agree, that at this time the Army of the West needs his steadying influence. Supporting me strongly could have meant his dismissal. We talked it over and he agreed to endorse my retirement.

"Frankly, Tartar, I'm glad you came here as you did. Rumors travel fast in the army. What we heard about you was confusing, to say the least. Many were critical of the changes you introduced into the Sixth Troop, but the scoffers were silenced by your subsequent performance. You are earning an enviable reputation among the cavalry. On the other hand, it is known that you received a field promotion from Prince Vidyanandana, and it is rumored that you are old friends. Now that General Dom and I have had a chance to meet you and listen to your views, we are much more at ease in our minds concerning your posting."

"The prince has been a friend of mine for about eight years," I said thoughtfully, "since I was a captive hostage in the Cham capital. I am just now beginning to know him."

"If he was responsible for your promotion," the commander said "he may be wiser as a military commander than we thought."

The selection of the four units to undergo training took two days After discussing my intended training program with the commander, I returned to Angkor.

I dispatched my four troopers to Lopburi to begin the archery instruction. I would have liked to accompany them but I did not. I wanted them to feel they had my trust and confidence. In addition, I did not want to appear to be interfering in the running of the Cavalry of the Scarlet Banner before assuming my command. The troopers were instructed to report to the cavalry commander for assignment Another sound reason to keep me in Angkor for another month or two was that the training of the horses was not yet completed. I borrowed another two troopers from the Sixth Troop to assist me in this task.

I have learned a good deal more about homosexual practices, both within and outside military service, than I knew at that time. Homosexuality has no appeal for me personally. I have never been able to condone the practice, nor accept it as natural, but I have come to live with it without the revulsion I experienced at the time.

Homosexual practices must have existed then, as they do now. in the Chinese forces. I have observed that when soldiers are deprived of women they will fornicate with anything that walks, crawls, or flies—including each other. As I mentioned earlier, however, there was rarely a time when the Khmer forces experienced any shortage of willing, or unwilling, female companionship, yet homosexuality, if not rife, was by no means uncommon in the Khmer Army. As I was to learn later, this was equally applicable in the Cham forces. The practice, in fact, seemed to be an accepted part of Khmer and Cham life.

The reverse was the case in the China of my youth, and, in fact, throughout my lifetime. There have been permissive periods in Chinese history, the lusty T'ang dynasty being a point in case. The Sung dynasty, however, saw a resurgence of the teachings of K'ung Fu-tzu, the philosopher and teacher who formulated the Confucian ethic some seventeen hundred years before my birth. This puritanical doctrine holds homosexuality to be an unnatural act and a great evil. I was taught this as a boy. Our household may have been more rigidly puritanical than most, due to the influence of the Confucian reformer, Chu Hsi, who was my father's friend.

These early teachings were reinforced by those of my instructors in the military arts. They held that masturbation, sodomy, and homosexuality were evils to be avoided since they resulted in the dissipation of *ching*, the male essence, and sapped physical vigor. Their arguments lost some weight when they advocated total abstinence to conserve the *ching*, since this was contrary to the Confucian principle of filial piety.

I confess that I have not strictly followed the admonitions of my martial arts instructors. When sexual fantasies have crowded in on me and the pressures have grown too strong in periods of abstinence, I have been known to "gallop my war horse" in the solitude of my tent or quarters. But if I have been guilty of masturbation, I have adhered strictly to the rest of my boyhood instruction.

As I have already noted, the Hindu cultures of the Cham and Khmer were permissive, excessively so by my standards. Homosexuality, in both men and women, while not encouraged, was accepted and seemed to carry no particular stigma.

My first encounter with homosexual practices was during my stay in Vijaya. Boys and girls displayed interest not only in each other, but in attractive members of their own sex. At the time, however, when I was discovering the pleasures of heterosexual activities, I gave little thought to other behavior.

If homosexuality existed in the Jarai community, I saw no evidence of the fact. Male companionship on the hunts produced strong friendships but no sexual attachments.

Perhaps the exhilaration of the hunt was a sufficient outlet in itself.

My first real awareness of homosexuality came when I was rudely thrust into the Khmer forces. Probably due to my size and strength, men of homosexual tendencies are attracted to me. I received advances almost from my first day as a cavalry trooper. The first amorous cavalryman to make his desire known to me received a split lip for his pains. I meted out a like measure to the second one who tried his luck. Thereafter, I was left alone and have rarely been bothered since.

I do not set myself up as a moral arbiter. If the aberration does not impair fighting efficiency. I overlook it. In one area however, I take strong exception to homosexuality. When it involves officers and subordinates, the practice is dangerous. I see no reason why officers should not be friendly with those under their command, but familiarity destroys discipline. There can be nothing more familiar than homosexual relationships. I have never given a position of responsibility to a man or officer known by me to be a homosexual. Where I have found such a man in a responsible position under my command, I have removed him from it.

I had known Vidya to have a voracious sexual appetite, but the revelation of the cavalry commander was the first indication I had that it extended to both sexes. I was shocked and appalled. But Vidya's unforgivable sin, in my eyes, was that he had allowed his attachment to intrude to the detriment of his command.

Had I discussed the incident with Apricot Blossom, whose views were more liberal than my own, she might have influenced my thinking. Had I at that time the tolerance I have since developed, my judgment and subsequent action might not have been so harsh.

I assumed command of the Cavalry of the Scarlet Banner on the fourth day of the Month of the Boar, the first month of the dry season.

One of my first acts was to request from General Dom full disciplinary authority over the cavalry. I explained that this would not extend to field operations, but that I considered it necessary during the period of intensive training I had in mind. The general reluctantly granted my request.

The training of the four troops as mounted archers was progressing favorably. Now that the horses had arrived from Angkor, the troopers were adapting to stirrups with a minimum of protest. Much of this acceptance was due to the troopers I had selected to conduct the training. They talked from experience and amplified their instruction with anecdotes culled from the Sixth Troop's actions. On only one occasion did I take an active part in the instruction.

Mounted, I watched the Sixth Troop awkwardly firing at marks from the saddle. I was about fifty yards away and thought I had gone unnoticed until the instructor detached himself from the trainees and rode toward me. Grinning, the trooper handed me his bow and quiver of arrows. I tested the bow for weight of pull, slipped on my thumb ring, and motioned to the cavalrymen to clear my field of fire. I put my horse into a canter on a line parallel to the marks, and as fast as I could pull and release, I sent shafts winging unerringly into the marks. At the far end of the field, I wheeled outward to a distance of another thirty or so yards. I brought the horse to a full gallop. Standing upright in the stirrups, I thundered down the line, sending arrows singing into the marks without a single miss.

At the end of the sweep, I reined in and came back to the instructing trooper at a trot. As I handed the bow to him, a ragged cheer went up from the trainees. I grinned back at the laughing instructor. It had been as shameless an exhibition as the performance before the Jarai tribesmen seven and a half years earlier. Still, it does no harm to demonstrate one's skill before one's command. The instructors from the Sixth Cavalry Troop were rapidly turning me into a legend. I derived satisfaction from lending an element of credence to their exaggerated tales.

We received word from Vidya in Angkor that the campaign to the west, scheduled to get under way two weeks hence, was to be postponed. The Army of the South was facing stiff opposition from a Shrivijayan force that was being reinforced from an island kingdom to the west of the peninsular theater of action. We were ordered to send half our force to bolster our hard-pressed comrades in the south. In his message, Vidya indicated he would arrive in Lopburi shortly to discuss revised plans for our forth-coming operations.

Half my cavalry went along with our reinforcing units. For the next four or five months, my units would be at-tached to the Cavalry of the Silver Banner. I remained in Lopburi and was glad for the lull, which would give me an opportunity to complete the training of the mounted archers. Among the other units I kept back was the Ninth Cavalry Troop.

I had observed the unit closely. Morale of the Ninth Troop was low. Discipline was almost nonexistent. The young captain promoted to the command by Vidya was a posturing caricature. It was rumored he was involved sex-ually with one of his troopers. I could not allow this condi-tion to continue. I had no intention of doing so. Yet I must, I appreciated, show good cause for disciplinary ac-tion. His flagrant homosexuality was not in itself grounds for such action.

It was said later that I arranged the incident. I did not, but it couldn't have worked out better had I planned it.

The young man believed that he enjoyed a position of immunity. This worked to my advantage. I knew that, sooner or late, he would commit a breach of regulations. If I pressed the Ninth Troop, it was likely to be sooner rather than later.

Fate played into my hands. We received notification that a labor battalion recruited in a western province re-quired military guards for its journey to Angkor. I dis-patched the Ninth Cavalry Troop to discharge the mission. The time I allowed the troop to reach its western destina-tion required pushing the horses to their limit. I was con-fident that the captain would not be able to force such a killing pace and would falter somewhere along the way. My written orders called for the troop to be ready to move out at dawn the following morning.

Accompanied by an aide, I was at the Ninth Troop's parade square before dawn. The bleary-eyed troop was assembled, with the exception of one trooper and its cap-tain.

Ordering two troopers to attend us, with my aide I went directly to the captain's quarters. We found him curled in the arms of his cavalryman paramour fast asleep on his sleeping mat. The two men were rudely awakened and placed under arrest.

Three hours later the offending parties were brought before me. The trooper said nothing in his own defense. The captain stammered out a story of having been taken ill during the night and having requested the trooper to attend him. I listened coldly to this obvious fabrication, then summarily sentenced both men to be publicly executed at sunup the next morning.

Before sunrise the next morning I rode to the exercise field where the cavalry units were drawn up to witness the carrying out of the sentence. I was surprised, and pleased, to see General Dom standing on a knoll close to the field. He eyed me thoughtfully as he answered my salute, but he said nothing. His presence indicated his tacit approval of the sentence.

The red ball of the morning sun limned the three towers of the nearby temple in a red-gold aura. The drums rolled. The two prisoners, their arms pinioned behind them, were brought onto the field. The trooper walked resignedly to the marked position. The captain, sobbing wretchedly, had to be dragged onto the field by his guards.

When the headsman's sword flashed downward, the captain was still blubbering and slobbering. He couldn't even *die* like a man.

chapter 21

Vidya's interpretation of "shortly" was elastic. We were well into a new year, and more than halfway through the dry season, and he had not yet put in an appearance in Lopburi. There eventually must be some sort of confrontation between us over the execution of his one-time favorite. I was not looking forward to this, but I was anxious to have it over and done with. For that reason, and for no other, I wished him to be on the scene.

In the third month of the new year, auspiciously the Month of the Dragon in the Year of the Dragon, word reached me that Horse-master Chang had completed his mission and returned to Kambuja. He was not yet at Angkor. The Great Lake was at its lowest seasonal level, in some places no more than three feet in depth, and the approaches on the Tonle Sap River were treacherous. The horses had been unloaded downstream and were being herded overland to Angkor Thom. I set out at once, hoping to be on hand in Angkor to welcome the Old Stallion.

When I clattered into the courtyard, it was Chang who welcomed me. I leaped from my horse and embraced the grinning gargoyle. A familiar voice called my name. With one arm still over Chang's shoulder, I looked up to where the curtain fluttered at the window of Apricot Blossom's bedchamber. I waved with my free hand and called a joyous greeting. We three, all that remained of my father's party that set forth from Canton nine years ago, were reunited once more. It was a good feeling.

Horse-master Chang's mission had been a success. He returned with the horse handlers, craftsmen, and archery instructors I had requested, a large stock of arrows, and enough bows to arm six troops of cavalry. The horses, which were stabled at the cavalry stables east of the river, consisted of broodmares and enough stallions to provide for two troops with a dozen mounts to spare. The sea voyage, he assured me, had been uneventful and all the horses were in excellent condition.

It turned out that not all the horses were at the cavalry stables. The next morning Chang conducted me to my stables, where five of the finest stallions awaited my inspection. From these, I was to select a mount for myself. It was not an easy choice. They were all magnificent steeds.

Among the horses was a bay about half a hand higher at the withers than my faithful Sa-lu-tzu. Somehow, probably out of respect for Sa-lu-tzu, I could not bring myself to choose the bay. Instead, my choice fell to a strongly muscled piebald stallion. The selection of a name for the stallion was easy. I called him Ching Chui, which had been the name of a piebald steed among the six famed mounts of Emperor Tai Tsung.

Chang had other surprises in store for me that morning. When I had selected my mount, Chang took me to what I assumed to be an empty stall. There, laid on a bed of straw, seven objects gleamed in the sunlight slanting through the stable door.

The first article to catch my eye was a *chien,* a double-edged sword with an iron blade and a bronze hilt. Although it was only partially withdrawn from its red leather scabbard, I judged the blade to be about forty inches in length. The pommel and guard of the hilt were jade, as were the chape fitting and sling fittings of the scabbard. The cord lashings between the hilt rings were dyed crimson to match the scabbard.

Next to the sword was a circular shield of polished bronze. Its face was emblazoned with the head of a dragon. Beside the shield was a thornwood *kung* of superb craftsmanship. The back of the bow was veneered with birchbark stained red, as were the sharkskin handgrip and the braided silken bowstring. Complementing the bow was a quiver of tooled red leather with a scarlet silken sling. In the quiver were arrows with various types of arrowheads—whistling heads for signaling, incendiary heads, moon-toothed heads, chisel heads, spinach heads, mint-leaf heads, and, of course, the *hei kang,* the common black iron arrowhead.

Beside the bow and quiver were two articles of wearing apparel. One was a bowl-shaped helmet of polished bronze attached to which were leather flaps to protect the ears and the nape of the wearer's neck. Atop the helmet was a scarlet plume. The second article of body armor consisted of a hip-length cuirass of heavy crimson silk to which thin, overlapping leaves of iron were riveted.

The last article was something I had heard of but had never seen. It was a mantle of iron plates affixed to a silken undercloth. This barding was intended to be slipped over a horse to protect it from spears and arrows during battle.

Horse-master Chang handed me a handsome ring pouch of scarlet leather and a thumb ring of rose quartz in which was inscribed the double *hsi* character. "These," he said, "complete the ensemble."

I could not think of words with which to thank Chang for the weapons and trappings. I made light of it by saying, "I hope I don't get transferred from the Cavalry of the Scarlet Banner. You seem inordinately partial to red."

"It is a bold color that suits you well. Your moustache is filling out and gives you a suitably fierce countenance. With these," he said with a sweeping gesture, "you will cut a figure the likes of which has never been seen in this barbaric land."

"And," I added dryly, "they will make me the target of every enemy archer and spearman."

Chang laughed. "You will be, anyway. You might as well have some protection."

It was not until later that day, when I questioned Chang concerning an accounting, that he broke the bad news to me. When he had gone to Changsha, my father's wives had not received him. He had persisted and eventually had been received by the eldest of my half brothers who remained in Changsha. My brother had advised Chang that, unfortunately, my father had made no provisions for me and that no patrimony existed.

I was stunned by this piece of news. My father had never indicated the extent of my patrimony, but he had made specific mention of two houses in Nanking and riverfront property in Changsha that would be mine upon his death. There was nothing to be gained in calling my half brother a liar. I am sure Chang knew this as well as I did.

"Then how did you make payment for all that you have brought back?" I queried.

"I journeyed to Canton and presented myself to an old friend of your father's, the governor of the prefecture. He readily agreed to finance the undertaking and cautioned me to employ only the best of men and purchase nothing but the finest in the way of weapons and horse-flesh. I gave him what remained of your gold and silver as a show of good faith . . . and I followed his advice to the letter."

My ability to meet this obligation did not concern me. In my new rank, I was amply provided for. But that my family had disowned me, and divided my patrimony among themselves, came as a surprise. Without doubt, on learning of the razing of Angkor, they had thought me dead, which could justify their action. Yet, when Horse-master Chang had appeared and they had learned that I was alive, they should have come to my aid. They had not, and it appeared they had closed ranks against me. This should have bothered me, but, oddly enough, it did not. I had always been an outsider, and now I was under no obligation to the family that had cast me out.

I clapped Chang on the back. "You are fortunate, Old Stallion. It is a Tartar custom to behead the bearer of ill tidings . . . but today I am disposed to be lenient."

That evening Chang accompanied Apricot Blossom, her handmaiden, and myself as we walked in the garden. At the grape arbor, Chang perched himself on the rim of the well that stood in front of the pergola. There, we three talked well into the night, recalling incidents from the past and planning for the future. The mute girl, while she could not contribute to the conversation, listened attentively and smiled appreciatively at our sallies.

There was magic in the night. It was the season of the "mango rains," a week or so of rain during the second or third month, a precursor of the monsoon rains some two months off. A light rain during the afternoon had tempered the oppressive heat. Now a cooling breeze from the direction of the river stirred the leaves of the arbor. The breeze carried a faint scent of night-blooming jasmine. A waning moon rode high in the heavens, bathing the garden in shimmering silver.

My thoughts wandered. My mother's face appeared briefly on the screen of my mind, then was replaced by the image of myself seated at the feet of my gowned father. I saw briefly the face of Morning Mist and the laughing faces of my dead children. Then my thoughts drifted lazily back to the present.

I had not been listening. Chang was relating an anecdote concerning an incident during his voyage. I looked at the group around me. These two, I thought—no, three, for the mute maidservant was an alter ego to her mistress —were my family. I needed no others.

I had been in Angkor Thom three days before being summoned by Vidya. I arrived at the appointed hour and found him pacing back and forth in an anteroom.

Upon my entrance, Vidya whirled to face me. "You have exceeded your authority," he snapped, dispensing with any form of greeting.

"I think not," I answered calmly.

"You executed an officer without reference to my second-in-command or myself."

I noted that Vidya had made no mention of the trooper. "Full disciplinary powers were vested in me by General Dom. This applies, of course, only to the cavalry other than in field operations. I exercised that authority in sentencing a cavalry officer and a trooper to death for disobeying an order."

"Orders can be misinterpreted."

"Not written orders," I said coldly.

Vidya's voice was shrill with anger. "You knew the officer was a protégé of mine, that I held him in high regard. You gave him no chance to appeal the sentence. The matter should have been referred to me before carrying out the sentence."

"Your protégé, as you call him," I retorted scathingly, "might have been qualified to command a troupe of dancing girls. He was *not* qualified to command a cavalry troop. Had he not died by the headman's sword, he would have died in his first taste of battle . . . if not by the hand of the enemy, then by the hand of one of his troopers. If you held him in such high regard, you should not have placed him in that position. It is you, and you alone, who must bear the responsibility for his death."

Vidya's face reddened in anger. With his fist clenched, he took a step toward me. I thought he was going to strike me, and I found myself hoping that he would and provide me with an excuse to thrash him. I regretted the impulse immediately. Of the two of us, I was by far the stronger. A fight between us would only prove that fact and resolve nothing. Vidya's thoughts must have run along parallel lines. He stopped where he was and some of the color ebbed from his face as he slowly unclenched his fist.

"I will be the judge in such matters," he said gratingly.

"No," I replied evenly, "you will not—not unless you assume the responsibility for the battle-preparedness and fighting efficiency of the Army of the West. That responsibility now rests with General Dom and, subject to his authority, with me as far as the cavalry is concerned. Rest assured that everything I have done, or intend to do, was or will be in the best interests of the Cavalry of the Scarlet Banner. As commanding general, it is, or should be, in your best interest, as well."

It was quite a little speech. I had prepared at least part of it on my way to this meeting on the assumption that our discourse would develop much as it had. Now that I had delivered the lines, they sounded pompous to my ears.

Vidya's face was still suffused with heightened color. His hand trembled slightly as he raised it to point his finger at my chest. "Tartar," he said thickly, "tend to your cursed cavalry, but do not cross me. You do so at your peril."

That afternoon, sipping tea in Apricot Blossom's darkened room, I sketched in the background of the executions for her benefit and told her of my morning's confrontation with Vidya.

"So," she commented, "he has shown you his true face."

"The face of a fornicator, a corrupter of young men. Such a man could not hold a position of responsibility in China," I retorted heatedly.

"Could he not, Tartar? Your upbringing in Changsha, and in your father's house, was relatively sheltered. Had you lived in Lin-an, you might hold different views. In the capital, there are many male prostitutes. My father contended that supply cannot exist without demand. He considered male prostitution a mark of the moral bankruptcy of Confucian officialdom. There were even, he told me, men who rouged their cheeks, dressed as women, and had bound feet. Those poor misfits, he said, should be pitied rather than exploited."

This ran counter to everything I had been taught. I found it hard to credit. "You have seen such men?" I questioned.

"No," she said rather testily, "I have not seen them, or if I have, I have not known it. But my father was not given to lying or invention. If, one day, you visit the capital, you can confirm it for yourself."

"I did not mean to imply that your father lied. It is just that I find it hard to believe. Your father could have been misled. You are right. I will have to see it with my own eyes before I can accept it."

"Tell me, Tartar," she queried hesitantly, "would you have meted out the same punishment to those men had they not been homosexuals?"

It was a question I had asked myself. I answered her as truthfully as I could. "Yes, had the circumstances been the same, I am almost certain I would have given the same sentence to non-homosexuals. The commander I relieved was a good officer, one of the best I've encountered in the Khmer forces. But his forced early retirement took the heart out of him. In his last six months of command, he allowed the discipline to slip badly. When I took over, I needed to reassert authority as quickly as possible. That's why I requested full disciplinary powers. It was not, as I think both General Dom and Vidya believe, designed to trap that particular cavalry officer. I intended to punish drastically the first major offenses to come before me as an example of what the cavalry could anticipate under my command. I will admit that

I was paying special attention to the Ninth Cavalry Troop. The captain, with good cause, believed himself above censure or discipline. His conduct was outrageous. The discipline in the Ninth Troop had eroded to a point where it hardly existed at all. This situation was infecting other units. I naturally preferred that whatever offense arose have its origin in the Ninth Troop. But it was chance that placed those miserable wretches in my hands. They would have been executed, but I will confess that their homosexuality speeded their death."

That is how I rationalized my harsh justice at the time. It was, in fact, no harsher than justice I have since administered. Yet, on looking back, I am not certain that homosexuality was not the crime I was punishing. I am not sure that I convinced Apricot Blossom of my impartiality.

I rose to take my leave, but Apricot Blossom detained me.

"Do not leave just yet. There is something else I want to talk over privately."

"What is that?"

"The other night, when we discussed the future, you did not once mention the possibility of a wife and children. I have no wish to open old wounds, but it is more than three years since you lost Morning Mist and the children. You should have sons. I think you should take a wife. Your household needs more than a shadow mistress, even though I am happy to serve in that capacity."

"I have given the matter passing thought," I admitted. "The memory of my happiness with Morning Mist is still with me, but the pain of my loss has eased. I have taken other women. I do not intend a life of celibacy. But I am young. There is a lot of time ahead of me in which to consider marriage."

"The years slip by quickly," Apricot Blossom said with a sad inflection in her voice. "I think you should give the matter consideration without too much delay. It is the advice I am sure your father would give. There are many suitable young ladies in the court circle who would welcome the thought of marriage to a man with your promising future. It should not be difficult for you to make a selection."

"I will give it thought," I promised without conviction. The truth is, I *had* given it thought and had decided the time was not yet ripe for such a step. Had I known that the matter would be taken out of my hands before much more than a year had passed, I might have displayed more initiative.

chapter 22

THE REMAINING MONTHS OF THE DRY SEASON PASSED UN-
eventfully. Before returning to Lopburi, I arranged with
the captain of the Sixth Cavalry Troop that the four troopers on temporary loan be transferred to the Cavalry of the
Scarlet Banner on a permanent basis. All four had done
an excellent job, and I intended to reward them for this
devotion to duty with promotions.

Horse-master Chang came with me to Lopburi as my
sergeant at arms. The horses, and the party Chang had
recruited together with the equipment, followed a week
later.

Before the rains set in, the units we had detached to
assist the Army of the South returned to Lopburi. They
had suffered casualties and related tales of heavy fighting and inconclusive battles. The Army of the South had
based itself in a former Shrivijayan stronghold and trading center called Chaiya. Reinforcements had been sent
to Chaiya from Angkor and the Army of the South was
engaged in training and preparation for a new offensive
in the next dry season.

The commander of the Cavalry of the Silver Banner
sent a message with my returning forces congratulating
me on my promotion, thanking me for my assistance,
and praising the performance of my cavalrymen in action. He also expressed his regrets concerning our heavy
casualties. I sent to Angkor for replacement trainees, and

with the gaps to be filled in the officer ranks, I had no difficulty retaining my four troopers from the Sixth Troop of old within the four new units of mounted bowmen. Three of them were promoted to seconds-in-command of the Third, Fifth, and Eighth troops. The Fourth, the one I considered the most promising, became captain of the Eleventh troop. The four former troopers were popular with the cavalrymen they had trained, and the promotions were well received by their former trainees. I attended their promotion party and got mildly drunk on rice wine.

The season of the monsoon rains is normally a slack period for the military. The wet season of the Year of the Dragon was no exception. I spent most of the season in Angkor, returning to Lopburi in time to prepare for the projected dry season campaign in the west.

In Angkor Thom, I watched the walls of the city grow higher by the day. Inside the walls, rammed-earth galleries were rising to facilitate the defense of the massive ramparts. Work on the five temples outside the city walls went on apace. The central tower of Ta Prohm reared against the eastern skyline.

One day I found myself drawn to the site of my father's compound. Without telling anyone where I was going, I rode out of the new city by way of the southern causeway, past the looming hill of Phnom Bakheng, and down the broad avenue leading to the temple complex of Angkor Wat.

It was not difficult to locate the site, since parts of the sagging wall still stood, but to recognize it as ever having been a collection of splendid residential pavilions and outbuildings was next to impossible. The big trees had grown even taller and the charred remains of the buildings were mercifully cloaked by a tangle of foliage.

I pushed my way through the bushes to the moat surrounding Angkor Wat. Along the water's edge, a colony of thatched huts had sprung up. Standing close to the lapping water, I gazed across the moat at the soaring towers of Angkor Wat. From my angle of view, the five towers, representing the sacred Mount Meru of Hindu mythology, merged into a silhouette of only three. The damage the complex had sustained during the Cham invasion had not been repaired. The gold stripped from the towers had not been replaced. It was, I knew, still the center of Brahman religious activity, but it had about it an air of neglect.

I pushed my way back to the roadway, mounted Ching Chui, and rode slowly back toward the city. It was the last time I undertook the pilgrimage to the weed-choked shrine of my father's cremation.

To my surprise, I was becoming something of a minor celebrity in the capital. Exaggerated tales of my exploits were being circulated in court circles. In the streets of the city, my height and appearance made me an easily recognized figure, as did my stallion, Ching Chui. I found I attracted curious glances and even smiles of greeting from total strangers. There was, I think, also an air of mystery attached to me. It was known now that I was the son of a Chinese envoy to the court and that I had miraculously escaped the slaughter of the Cham invasion. It was also common knowledge that I was unmarried and that a woman, whose face none had seen, presided over my bachelor establishment. Without doubt, it was curiosity that prompted the many invitations I received during those months.

I attended some of the functions out of a sense of obligation. I was not comfortable in that atmosphere, having had little practice in the social graces and no inclination toward polite and meaningless conversation. I discovered, however, that Apricot Blossom was correct—there were a number of attractive young ladies who made it quite obvious that they would look with favor on a proposal of marriage. Men approached me to extol the virtues of daughters who had expressed an interest in me. Although I did nothing to encourage these advances, the invitations persisted.

It was with a feeling of relief and a lifting of my spirits that I rode through the uncompleted western gate on my return to Lopburi. At my side, Horse-master Chang also seemed more at ease now that the city was behind us.

There was nothing remarkable about that season's campaign. No large-scale battles developed, although they certainly could have, had we pressed north after crossing the mountains and challenged the powerful Burman armies of Pegu and Pagan. Instead, we ranged down the coast on a southerly route before recrossing the mountains to return to Lopburi.

Although it was a relatively short campaign of less than five months' duration, it was a success in terms of captives and plunder. We overran a number of Mon cities of fair size and considerable wealth. It was not, on this campaign, our intention to annex territory. We stripped the palaces, and the *chedis* and *stupas* of the Buddhist temples, of their jewels and precious metals, seized the contents of granaries, herded most of the inhabitants into captivity, and put the pillaged cities to the torch. The cavalry took an active part in the campaign. A mobile striking force, composed of the four troops of bowmen augmented by four spear-armed troops, operated well ahead of the main force. For several weeks, until I was confident that the command could be entrusted to a subordinate, I led the strike force personally.

The tactics I employed, with one refinement, were similar to those I had used in the northern campaign. Since I had more units at my disposal than in the earlier campaign, I divided the force into two groups, each consisting of two troops of spearmen and two of mounted archers. The groups advanced on parallel courses separated from each other by about a mile. It enabled them to converge on an opposing force or village objective from two sides and rapidly effect encirclement. Command signals were passed between the groups by means of whistling arrows.

These tactics proved very effective against small communities. For larger engagements, the strike force rejoined the main body. I was gratified when General Dom announced at a staff meeting that the bow-equipped cavalry was to be considered a permanent arm of the mounted forces.

I rode with the strike force with my shield slung from the left side of the saddle pommel. From the cantle, my Khmer ax hung in a loop on the left. My sword, which I had dubbed Kan Chiang, in honor of the legendary blade produced for King Ho Lu, was slung in a loop on the right side of the cantle. These might have been encumbrances for a Khmer steed. They didn't bother Ching Chui in the least.

With the strike force, I considered my leather jerkin as adequate armor. When we were drawn up before the gates of the first city we besieged, I donned my full trappings for the first time. When I appeared before the mounted troops wearing my plumed helmet and gleaming cuirass, and with Ching Chui barded in metallic splendor, I was greeted with a spontaneous cheer from the troopers. In his lofty perch on his war elephant, General Dom smiled broadly. Since we would soon face a shower of arrows from the city's defenses, the garb was practical. But, as Horse-master Chang had intended, it also presented a striking appearance.

Mounted on a mottled gray, Chang sat not far from me beaming with pride. I caught his eye and winked. The Cavalry of the Scarlet Banner had the distinction of being led by the youngest, tallest, and now the most flamboyantly attired cavalry commander in the Khmer forces.

Prince Vidyanandana did not join us to take over command until we were effecting our first mountain crossing. In his party he had with him a young prince of the royal house who would be a spectator to the forthcoming actions.

I didn't see much of Vidya during the campaign. It was General Dom who gave the staff briefings. On the few occasions when we were together, Vidya was distant and I was coolly correct.

I do not know if the young Khmer prince learned anything from the actions of the campaign. He seemed indifferent to military proceedings. He was, however, fascinated by the Buddhism practiced by the Mon, and he spent a good deal of time in the company of captive monks.

The Buddhism of the Mon is the Theravada sect, as opposed to the Mahayana Buddhism prevailing in China, Annam, and those who adhere to the Buddhist faith in the kingdoms of Champa and Kambuja. Both faiths are rooted in the teachings of the Enlightened One, but they differ in their interpretations of those teachings. In Mahayana Buddhism, the person of the Buddha has been deified. In Theravada Buddhism, this is not the case. The latter is a gentler faith, having wide appeal for the common people. The former is a court-imposed faith in Kambuja, where the king, as the Buddharaja, represents the reincarnated living Buddha. Theravada Buddhism was introduced to the Mon by the proselytizing monks of India's Emperor Asoka some thirteen centuries ago and has undergone little change since that time. Unlike Mahayana Buddhism, where the scriptures are in Sanskrit, the Theravadan scriptures are written in Pali, the canonical script of a far-off island called Ceylon. I learned later that the young prince became a convert to Theravada Buddhism during the course of our campaign.

My interest during the campaign was more in secular than religious matters. Determined to broaden my military knowledge, I placed myself under the tutelage of General Dom.

When I first questioned the general concerning various aspects of warfare, he was reserved and stiff. Gradually, however, when he became convinced that my interest was genuine, he unbent.

Initially, my sessions with the general were brief. As the campaign progressed, however, they grew longer as the old warrior warmed to the task of instruction.

Our discussions covered a wide range of subjects. The general discoursed at length on the deployment of forces, the advantages and disadvantages of war elephants, infantry tactics, siege tactics, and problems associated with the discipline, training, administration, and supply of an army both at its home base and in the field. I learned how the Army of the West gathered and acted on military and political intelligence supplied through a network of spies both within and outside the realm, how it garrisoned and fortified strategic locations, and how it dealt with unrest within the area under its jurisdiction. I learned as well that the general believed me to have engineered the incident leading to the execution of the cavalry captain and the trooper, but he fully approved of my sentence and its speedy execution.

General Dom was scornful of those who referred to warfare as an art. It was, he contended, a simple matter of common sense. It was his thesis that, given competent leadership, trained and seasoned troops, sound intelligence, and adequate supplies, a determined and resourceful commander should win even if pitted against a much larger force.

An empathy developed between the old general and myself. I found myself relating to him incidents from my boyhood in China and my experiences over the last few years. He, in turn, had a wealth of stories and anecdotes culled from a lifetime of military service. He had served

under a number of commanding generals during the reigns
of four successive monarchs. Although he didn't actually
say it, I gathered he considered Prince Vidyanandana one
of the most incompetent commanding generals he had encountered in a career spanning more than forty years.

There is one thing I learned above all else from General Dom's instruction. Warfare may not be an art, but
it is an incredibly complex business. The more I learned,
the more there was to learn.

We reached Lopburi some weeks ahead of the change
of season. Prince Vidyanandana, anxious to reach Angkor
before the rains set in, wasted no time in preparing his
procession for the march to the capital. I had no desire
to be part of his theatrical performance, nor did he seem
to wish me to be part of the road company. I sent Horse-
master Chang with the escorting cavalry, but I stayed
behind in Lopburi.

I busied myself with administrative matters and instituted a series of training programs. This could have
been accomplished in short order, but I managed to drag
it out for more than a month. I was anxious to see Apricot Blossom, but I was reluctant to become involved in
the social life of the capital. Moreover, exercising my
privilege of rank, my selection of female slaves from
among the Mon captives had been most gratifying. They
had relieved the tedium of the campaign. Now, installed in
my official residence in Lopburi, they were a pleasant and
satisfying diversion. Marriage looked less attractive than
ever.

Nonetheless, I was preparing to depart for Angkor
when a messenger from the capital arrived to present me
with a summons to attend the king ten days hence. Escorted by two troops of cavalry, I set off at once.

I timed my arrival at Angkor Thom to take place
early in the Hours of the Dragon, a time of morning
when I could expect the day to be clear and bright. With
this in mind, we set off early on the last day at a brisk
pace, leaving our baggage train to follow in slower time.
For my entrance, I donned my plumed helmet and polished cuirass. Scarlet pennants were affixed to the tips
of the upright cavalry spears. I sent a rider on ahead to
advise my household of my coming.

We were still about a mile from the city when a cavalry troop appeared riding toward us. Golden pennants identified them as a troop belonging to the Cavalry of the Golden Banner, yet one scarlet pennant fluttered in their midst. When they drew closer, I smiled broadly. It was Horse-master Chang with my old unit, the Sixth Cavalry Troop.

With the captain of the Sixth Troop on my right, Chang on my left, and the Sixth Troop formed up between my Scarlet Banner units, we trotted sedately over the stone causeway, through the high arch of the western gate, and into the city. It was an impressive and colorful entrance.

News of my coming had preceded me, but I had not anticipated the crowds that lined the roadway both outside and within the city. I would be less than truthful if I did not admit to a thrill of pride as I smiled in response to the cheers of the welcoming throng.

chapter 23

ON THE DAY AND HOUR OF MY APPOINTMENT, I PRESENTED myself at the royal palace. A guard conducted me along ornate passageways to a spacious, high-ceilinged room in the western wing.

The room was large, yet a clutter of tables and other objects, together with the people crowded within it, made the room seem smaller than it actually was. The wall on the side of the room nearest me was broken by a series of tall, wide windows that flooded the room with daylight. Along the far wall, wooden models of various structures were ranged on tables and pedestals. A long trestle table took up most of the floor space in the room's center. The table was piled high with papers I assumed to be architectural plans and strewn with drawing instruments. This, I thought, must be the focal point of project planning. It was, I later learned, but one of many such rooms.

The king stood by the table, absorbed by a large drawing spread out in front of him. People crowded around the monarch: robed priests, gowned dignitaries, uniformed men, and others I took to be architects and technicians. The king, though I knew him to be in his sixtieth year, looked little changed from the day I had first seen him.

The guard who had brought me to this room approached a general standing close to the king. When he caught the general's attention, the guard spoke a few words and then retired to stand stiffly at a respectful distance. The general moved to the king's side. The king, his finger tracing a path on the drawing, turned and spoke sharply to a harried-looking man on his left. When the king turned his attention back to the drawing, the general leaned forward and spoke to him briefly. The king nodded absently, but he did not look up from the drawing.

I moved to the closest window. The king knew of my presence. The guard would be sent to fetch me when the king was disposed to receive me. For the hundredth time, I wondered for what reason I had been summoned by the king. It was fruitless speculation. I would soon know the answer. Gradually, I became absorbed in the view before me.

This was my third visit to the royal compound, the previous occasions having been my visits to Vidya's residence. On neither of those visits had I had an opportunity to see much of the compound.

The royal palace was on the northern side of a wide, rectangular terrace. Other palaces and residences of state dignitaries lined the terrace, the whole of which was enclosed by a laterite wall. I thought I could make out Vidya's residence on the far side of the rectangle.

To my left, I gazed down on a newly erected sandstone facing to the terrace. Stone-workers were carving the face from their perches on bamboo scaffolding. On my right, from this height, I could make out the ceremonial square to the west of the compound and the city wall beyond. This section of the wall had reached its ordained height of twenty feet. Elephants were at work ramming the buttressing earthworks on the inside of the wall.

Directly in front of me within the rectangular enclosure, but closer to the southern terrace than to the royal palace, stood the temple of Phimeanakas, "Palace of Heaven." This temple, I had been told, had been erected some two hundred years ago during the reign of King Jayavarman V. It rose majestically on a pyramidal base of three high laterite terraces. Steep sandstone steps led up to a sandstone gallery that ran around the top courtyard. From the center of that courtyard rose the single, gilded tower. The tower glittered in the sunlight filtering through building clouds. I could make out workmen employed on some task in the gallery.

I was reminded of a legend connected with Phimeanakas. Each night, it was said, the Snake Princess, daughter of the *naga* king, appeared before the Khmer king in the form of a beautiful woman. The king was obliged to spend the first part of the night with her before visiting his wives and concubines. Should the king fail to consort with the Snake Princess, disaster would befall the empire. On the other hand, if she failed to put in an appearance, this heralded the imminent death of the monarch.

So caught up was I in these musings that I did not hear the king's approach. The first intimation I had that he was by my side was his resonant voice addressing me.

"Interesting spectacle, is it not, Barbarian?"

"Sire," I stammered, startled by his sudden appearance. I started to bow clumsily.

The king stopped me with an impatient gesture. "There is less formality here than in our throne room. Besides, as we recall, you prostrate yourself reluctantly and awkwardly."

The king turned his gaze back to the view from the window. He pointed toward the city wall beyond the ceremonial square. His eyes glittered as he observed, "The city will be impregnable. The walls will withstand the most determined attack of any army. Angkor Thom will endure forever as a monument to our genius." The king moved his arm in a sweeping arc and pointed toward the southeast. "There," he said, "in the very heart of the city, soon will rise the most magnificent temple of all time, to commemorate our reign . . . and glorify the Bodhisattva Avalokitesvara."

The king, I thought, could not be accused of modesty. As he talked, I observed him closely. There was not a fleck of gray in his hair. Apart from a few creases around his eyes, his face was unlined. His neck, shoulders, arms, and torso were strongly muscled. It was almost impossible to credit this vigorous man with being sixty years of age. His son, Prince In, a man of forty, looked older than his father. If the king was discharging his nightly obligation to the Snake Princess, as well as servicing his numerous wives and concubines, the regimen must have been beneficial.

As for the city enduring for all time, I made no comment. We Chinese have had some experience in building protective walls and fortifications. The Great Wall, constructed some thirteen centuries ago during the Han dynasty to hold back the northern barbarians, had been breached by wave after wave of intruding conquerors, including my mother's people, the Khitan. There seemed little to be gained in pointing this out to the king.

The monarch turned to face me. His face wore an enigmatic smile. His manner was easy and informal. "We have brought you here," he said, "to advise you personally of your reward for services rendered us."

Since I had no idea what services he alluded to, I said nothing.

"You came to our attention during the battle against the Cham. Since then we have taken an active interest in your career. Your field promotion met with our approval. Your subsequent actions justified that confidence. When a command vacancy arose in the Cavalry of the Scarlet Banner, it seemed suited to your talents. We had you promoted to that command, over objections from Prince Vidyanandana."

I often found the king's reference to himself in the plural, intended, I presume, to indicate that he spoke for both deity and monarch, disconcerting. In this instance, however, he had made it abundantly clear that he, and not Vidya, had been responsible for my promotion. Again, I advanced no comment.

"The prince," the king continued, "had someone else in mind as a candidate for the post. His objections to you were that you were not of noble birth. We pointed out that his father is a usurper and that the prince's nobility is of recent vintage, whereas you trace your lineage to emperors of the T'ang dynasty. But that is a matter of small importance, and, once again, your subsequent performance has justified our selection."

The king dwelt briefly in thought. He observed me closely, then continued in the same affable manner. "General Dom, an able officer in whom we have great trust, speaks well of you. He is overdue for retirement. As of now, we are promoting you to general of the second rank. Three months hence you will replace Dom as second-in-command and tactical commander of the Army of the West."

This time I was too dumbfounded to utter a word. The king seemed amused by my consternation.

"Barbarian," he said, "you appreciate that this is a command of grave responsibility. We would not have chosen you had we not believed you qualified. Your friend, Prince Vidyanandana, is overly fond of pleasure and given to excesses. He will continue to be your commanding general, but it is you who will wield the real power and provide the steadying influence."

It would be useless to protest that I did not feel myself qualified for the command. "General Dom . . . the prince . . . do they know of this change of command?"

"They do not. We will announce it in a few days when we advise the court of our arrangements for your marriage."

"Marriage!"

"Certainly. You will have social obligations. Your house requires a more suitable mistress than the disfigured concubine of your late father. We have selected a princess of the ruling house of Annam. We think you will be pleased with our choice. The wedding will take place at the temple of Preah Khan in two weeks' time."

A saffron-robed Buddhist priest approached us. His manner betrayed agitation. A fleeting frown of annoyance passed over the king's features, but by the time the priest reached us, the king's countenance was composed in a benign expression.

"Sire," the priest blurted, "the chief architect states that unless the gallery is shortened it will meet the face of the northern wall without sufficient space to allow free access."

The king's expression did not change in the slightest, but I noticed that the fingers of his left hand tensed against his thigh momentarily. "He is not here to tell us what we cannot do," the king said mildly. "His task is to translate our vision into plans the artisans can follow. We must impress this upon him."

I did not immediately discuss what had befallen me with either Horse-master Chang or Apricot Blossom. I needed time to consider what the promotion and arranged marriage meant and what they were likely to entail.

It was the Year of the Snake—the sixth month, the Month of the Ram. Within a few days I would turn twenty-four. I had been the youngest commander of cavalry in the Khmer forces. I was now the youngest general of the second rank. The king had been directly responsible for both promotions. I had been advanced over the heads of practically every professional officer in the forces.

When my advancement would be announced by the

king in a few days, along with the fact that a marriage to
a royal personage had been arranged for me, it would
be immediately apparent that I enjoyed the king's favor.
What would this mean? My rapid advancement would
be bitterly resented, but none would openly dispute it.
It would mean also that false friends would seek me out,
believing that I had the confidence of the monarch and
was in a position to advance their causes. Only the king
and I would know this had no substance in fact.

I viewed the king's honors as invidious. Overnight I
would be thrust into the limelight, gain a host of enemies,
and be plagued by fawning friends. Why had the king
chosen me, a Chinese, for these questionable honors? I
did not delude myself that his selection had been on the
basis of my military expertise. Many Khmer officers were
more capable than myself, and most, if not all, of my
former rank had more experience. I had the uncomfortable feeling that I was being promoted because I *was*
Chinese. I also felt that the fact that an Annamite princess
was to become my primary wife was of some significance.

The king, I was learning, was not given to wasting
words. He had gone to some pains to let me know that
Vidya had opposed my promotion to commander of the
cavalry, which probably meant the king knew I believed
Vidya to have been the author of my good fortune. In
his disclosures, the king had revealed that he knew a good
deal more about my background than I had suspected,
was aware of Vidya's excesses and held him in contempt,
and that the position of Apricot Blossom in my household
was known beyond the confines of my residence. To
know these facts, the king must have informants within
my household and, undoubtedly, in that of Vidya, as well.
That being the case, the king knew of the rift between
Vidya and myself and had wittingly provided me with information that would widen rather than bridge our differences. Then, having set us against each other, the king
had advised me that, despite Vidya's ineptitude, he would
continue in the capacity of commanding general, but that
I, in effect, would be responsible for my "friend's" actions.

Another unpleasant thought struck me. General Dom
had not been advised of his pending retirement and my
takeover. He would believe that my interest in military
matters stemmed from foreknowledge of the change of

command. If so, it was likely to cost me his friendship. The thought saddened me. I wondered if the king had intended this, as well.

I was, I realized, becoming enmeshed in a web of political intrigue. Apricot Blossom's words came back to me: "Policies of state are often baffling . . . and rewards for service to the throne are uncertain. . . ." A vision of the victorious General Yüeh Fei, imprisoned and strangled in his cell on the orders of the emperor, rose up to haunt me.

When I told Horse-master Chang of my imminent promotion, he was jubilant. When I voiced my concern and doubts, he sobered. He perceived what had escaped me.

"The king may expect you to fail in this undertaking . . . and to destroy both the prince and yourself in the process."

"Yes," I said thoughtfully, "that could be it—a Cham and a Chinese sacrificed on the altar of Khmer pride. We could have been raised high only so that our fall would be all the more of an example."

"Then," Chang said gruffly, "you must not fail. You are young, Tartar, but you are a born leader. You are much better qualified for this command than the king suspects."

They were heartening words, but they failed to dispel my misgivings.

That same evening I discussed the situation at length with Apricot Blossom. I recounted for her the king's exact words, leaving out only his reference to herself. I told her most of the conclusions I'd reached and ended up by giving her the possibility Chang had advanced that afternoon.

"Well," I said wryly, "the king has at least granted your wish to see me married."

"It is not *my* wish," she said reprovingly. "It is your duty to have sons."

Any doubts I had harbored concerning my impotence had been dispelled by the fact that two of my Mon slave girls in Lopburi were pregnant. This I had not disclosed to Apricot Blossom. "If the Annamite is fertile, the women's quarters will soon ring with childish laughter," I said jokingly.

"It is not a matter for levity," she said. "Your house can only grow and prosper through obedient sons. As for your concern that the princess is an Annamite, I believe you are seeing ghosts where none exist. The fact that Annam was a province of China for a thousand years and now bears little love for its former overlord is of no concern to the king. Annam borders on the northeastern frontier of the Khmer empire. The king may have in mind an alliance, which could augur well for you in this arranged match. She is, after all, a princess of the royal house."

"A signal honor," I said dryly.

For some time, she remained silent, an immobile shape in the shadows of the arbor. She spoke at last, slowly and deliberately.

"The king, I am told, is a skilled chess player. I cannot agree with old Chang that you could be an expendable piece in the game the king plays. Prince Vidyanandana may well be but a pawn, but you, I think, represent a knight or a rook in the king's eyes and will not be traded off lightly. You are right, there will be danger on every side, but I don't think you will be needlessly sacrificed. The king is playing a bold game. It is too early for me to see his end game, but I am firmly convinced you will still be on the board when his game reaches mate . . . or stalemate."

It was a day later that I learned how the chief architect's folly had been impressed upon him. In chains, he had been suspended between two working elephants facing in opposite directions. Screaming, he had been ripped apart.

I was glad that I had not protested my posting to tactical command. To do so would have been to dispute the king's judgment, quite obviously an unwise course to follow.

chapter 24

IN THE MONTH OF THE MONKEY, ON A DAY DETERMINED
by the court astrologers as favorable for our marriage
and in the auspicious Hours of the Monkey, Princess Ngo
Thi Linh and I were wedded in a Buddhist ceremony conducted in the temple of Preah Khan. The king himself led
the nobles and dignitaries attending the ceremony in pouring lustral water over our extended palms. And, though he
stayed but a short time, the king attended our wedding
feast. In this way the monarch demonstrated that our
union had his blessing and approval.

The consummation of our nuptials took place in my
chambers that night. It was, for both of us, a new experience.

Although I had not expected it, Princess Linh came to
the wedding couch a virgin. She did not whimper when
deprived of this distinction. Then, to my astonishment,
she started to respond to my thrusts with an animal ferocity and moans that reached a crescendo in hoarse
screaming. When I spurted in climax, she gave every indication of wanting to continue the passionate encounter.
At her insistence, the performance was repeated again and
again. When dawn streaked the shutters, I was spent,
bruised, and exhausted. At my side, Linh slept, purring in
her sleep like a kitten.

I could not fault the king on taste. The Annamite princess was an exquisite creature of seventeen. She had jade-

white skin, raven tresses that fell below her waist, luminous eyes in a lovely oval face, a slim, long-waisted figure, and small, taut breasts with nipples that became rigid at the slightest provocation.

We undertook a journey in celebration of our new status, Linh by palanquin and I on horseback. We stayed a week at Banteay Srie in a royal lodge placed at our disposal by the king.

I have never, before or since, met anyone like Linh. I thought her sexual ardor would cool as the weeks went by, but it did not. Her approach to the sex act had about it the ferocity of an animal in heat, and much the same urgency. She enjoyed both inflicting and being the recipient of physical pain. She favored a superior position for herself, which I did not discourage, since I found it less enervating, but my chest soon was a mass of deep scratches from her raking fingernails.

The "Flowery Battle," Apricot Blossom had called the act of lovemaking. With Linh, it resembled a battle in earnest, as my scars attested. I had considered myself a vigorous sexual partner, but I began to wish for respite. Then, one day, Linh was listless and irritable, wanting no part of lovemaking. It was her menstrual period, during which she suffered agonizing cramps and excruciating headaches. Within a few days, however, this affliction passed and she returned to the fray with renewed vigor.

Although I satisfied her demands and derived much pleasure myself from the servicing, Linh had no love or even much liking for me. She was one of the vainest creatures I have ever encountered. She spent hours admiring herself in her bronze mirror. Her thoughts, when they were not on sexual gratification, centered around clothes, jewels, and exotic perfumes. In her narcissism, there was no love left for other than herself.

She was, as represented, a princess of the royal house, but only of the ruling royal house through her maternal line. Her father hailed from nobility stemming from an earlier dynasty. She was, accordingly, a minor princess. She gave herself the airs of a queen.

Linh scorned Khmer women and treated them with disdain. She refused to adopt Khmer dress, staying with her flowing Annamite garments. I did not object, since I found her native costumes suited to her lithe, slim figure. She would not join the women of court circles in communal bathing at the ornamental lakes. Taking great pride in the whiteness of her skin, she had an abhorrence of direct sunlight. I discovered that she had a habit of slipping into the garden in the dead of night to refresh herself by bathing in the lotus pond.

Her attitude toward Apricot Blossom I thought odd. Linh did not wish to meet or speak with her, yet she was fully aware that Apricot Blossom saw to the day-to-day running of the household and allowed her to continue in that capacity. I confess that, during those first months of marriage, I neglected Apricot Blossom shamefully.

Linh had other attributes of which I was to learn in time. She was ambitious, cruel, vicious, and utterly devoid of compunction or remorse. And, as I should have known, one man could not hope to slake her unquenchable sexual thirst.

I may have suspected some of these qualities in her, but at the time they had yet to be confirmed. When she proudly informed me she was with child on the eve of my departure for Lopburi, I was overjoyed.

I was unhappy that in my new rank I would have to trade my horse for a mobile command post—a war elephant. I was not looking forward to turning over my cavalry command to the officer assigned to relieve me, the former commander of the Cavalry of the Silver Banner of the Army of the South. Least of all did I relish the thought of the exchange of command between General Dom and myself. As things turned out, I needn't have worried myself on any of those counts.

I was to turn over the command of the Cavalry of the Scarlet Banner, but I had no intention that Ching Chui would be included in the takeover. I left the big piebald stabled at my residence in Angkor. When Horse-master Chang and I set out for Lopburi, I rode an unfamiliar mount.

My first act on reaching Lopburi was to present myself at the quarters of General Dom. It was a sprawling residence I knew well and that would be mine when the exchange of command became official in a week's time. I had expected the general to be formal and distant, but I found myself welcomed cordially.

General Dom's initial reaction on hearing I was to

replace him had been much as I had visualized. Then, when he had had time to think it over, his attitude had changed. He explained to me that he had realized that, whether or not I had had prior knowledge of my posting, the long hours we had spent together would be of benefit to me in my new position of authority. He maintained that, youth notwithstanding, he could think of no one more suited to the command than myself. All I lacked, he observed dryly, was experience, and *that* I would certainly acquire in the years ahead. Having reached these conclusions, the general had found, somewhat to his surprise, that the idea of retirement from active duty had appeal. He was, he said, looking forward to divesting himself of the responsibility.

I told General Dom the circumstances of my wholly unexpected promotion and of my reservations and doubts with respect to my qualifications for the post. He listened sympathetically. As we discussed various aspects of the position in which I found myself, the rapport that had existed between us during the last campaign was reestablished.

When I told him of Horse-master Chang's interpretation of the king's motives, the general nodded gravely.

"It could be much that way," he said. "Without cause, the king fears the Army of the West. In his mind, the loyalty of the army to himself is suspect. When he ascended the throne, he would have disbanded us had he been able to do so. He could not because our authority in the western and northwestern provinces was too firmly established and any radical changes could have resulted in chaos. I am convinced that his appointment of Prince Vidyanandana as commanding general was the king's first move toward reducing our effectiveness. You could be his second. He moved you in as commander of cavalry as a logical prelude to tactical command. I would have been dumped long before this were it not for the fact that the king dare not move too quickly. He undoubtedly thinks that if the Army of the West realizes what's happening, it could move against him before it is sufficiently emasculated, or before he has had time to build up a strong enough counter-force."

"That's about the way I see it," I said, "with the Army of the South created as a permanent counterbalance. He probably didn't expect that army to run into the stiff opposition it is experiencing with the Shrivijayan forces. Had the Army of the South not been fully occupied, he might have introduced key officers from that force into the Army of the West to strike a balance he considered loyal." It was remarkably close to the conclusions I'd reached two years earlier, except at that time, believing Vidya to be the instrument of my advancement, I hadn't seen myself as part of the monarch's master plan.

"You may not be familiar enough with our structure to have noticed what else is happening," the general said. "With the king as supreme commander, the military high command has always been centered at Angkor. The palace guard was, and is, an officers' training school that provides the forces with young officers. Angkor was also the recruitment center and acted as a training command for the conscripts. When King Jayavarman arrived from the east with his own standing army, all that started to change. Using his forces as a nucleus, he has built up not only the Army of the South, but he is building a third permanent force at Angkor. I call it the Army of Angkor. When it is strong enough, and when his network of all-weather roads extends more fully into the west and north-west, I can see the day coming when the Army of the West will become nothing more than a large garrison directed by the Army of Angkor."

In my earlier musings, I had dimly perceived some of this, but certainly not to the extent General Dom had portrayed. Reminded now of my previous conclusions, I ventured a question.

"What happens if the supply of conscripts dries up?"

"That," the general said, "is really the crux of the matter. It must give the king quite a headache. He needs the steady stream of captives generated through campaigns of conquest. As long as that requirement exists, the Army of the West must be maintained . . . unless . . ." General Dom paused and rubbed his chin reflectively. "But we skirt the issue," he continued in a firmer tone. "It is how you fit into the picture that concerns us. If the king expects to weaken our command structure through your inability to command loyalty and sustain Prince Vidyanandana as an alien and unpopular commander, the objectives assigned over the coming campaigns will be difficult ones. The king will place the Army of the West under stress to hasten your collapse. The nature of the campaigns should give you an indication of the king's thinking."

"Such as?" I queried.

"A campaign against the Burman armies could end up in a disaster he could ill afford. I think we can rule that out. A campaign against the Siamese in the extreme north, which could stretch your supply lines to their limits, would be my guess.

"But I happen to believe the king has made a mistake. He must know, from my reports and his spies within the ranks, that you command the loyalty and affection of your cavalry units. It must be his belief that the specialized nature of the cavalry, and your talents in that area, make it a special case and that you could not, as an alien whose accelerated promotion has generated envy and resentment among your fellow officers, command that loyalty if placed in overall tactical command. I believe otherwise.

"Unlike Prince Vidyanandana, you have made no attempt to masquerade as a Khmer. Instead, you have exploited your racial differences to great advantage. As the Tartar, you are known and respected throughout this command. This soon should hold true throughout the realm. You will encounter jealousy, perhaps passive resistance, but I have every confidence you will overcome those obstacles to bring the Army of the West to greater victories and glories than it has enjoyed in the past."

I deeply appreciated the general's confidence and hoped fervently it was warranted.

"I shall retire to some property granted me by the king's late brother, King Yasovarman the Second," the general continued in a casual tone. "It is situated close to the mountain where the sapphire mines are located; it is an easy ride from here. If you require advice or assistance . . . or a retreat to escape the pressures . . . I am at your disposal. My house is your house."

I thanked the general warmly. It was gratifying to know I had not lost his friendship and that I could count on his help—assistance I was sure I would need.

"I wonder," the general said musingly, "what will happen when the king discovers his error."

If the king *had* erred, I wondered the same thing.

The officer posted to command the Cavalry of the Scarlet Banner was named Imre, but he was known familiarly as Long Ax. The sobriquet derived from his favored weapon, a Khmer ax of larger than normal-sized blade and a handle more than four feet in length. He was taller than the average Khmer, lean, firmly muscled, and one of the ugliest men I have ever seen. He was in his early forties and had campaigned with Jayavarman in Champa. I could not help but wonder if he was being groomed as my eventual replacement.

Commander Imre was a dedicated cavalryman. He displayed keen interest in my innovations of troops of mounted archers and the mobile strike force, of which he had heard a good deal. Within weeks of taking over command of the Cavalry of the Scarlet Banner, he requested permission to expand the mounted bowman units by two additional troops and requested procurement of more Chinese-bred steeds.

The day I saw Long Ax mounted on a Chinese stallion and riding with stirrups, even though he had no bow, I knew I had made a convert and gained an ally.

Prince Vidyanandana appeared in Lopburi several weeks before the end of the rainy season. He had never been known to arrive in the western capital this much in advance of a seasonal campaign. My sudden appointment to tactical command must have worried him, but he said nothing to betray his concern. In our daily afternoon meetings he was scrupulously correct. I noted with amusement that, while he did not actually defer to me, he was careful to avoid anything in speech or manner that might antagonize me. Vain and arrogant Vidya might have been, but I have never accused him of being a fool. By this time I am sure he had grown to hate me, but he had enough wisdom to appreciate that his position of command depended on my administrative and tactical capabilities. He did not like it, but he had to accept it. He believed, like practically everyone, that I stood high in the king's favor.

Our objective for the coming campaign was to be the kingdom of Haripoonchai. This Mon kingdom lay in a mountain-ringed valley about three hundred miles northeast of Lopburi. It had enjoyed immunity from Khmer conquest due to the difficulties entailed in the approaches through rugged terrain.

The line of march I selected was north to our vassal

domain of Sukhothai and from thence west over a low range of mountains until we reached a western tributary of the Menam River. Following the western fork of this tributary would lead us through the mountains into the valley kingdom. The distance by this route was close to four hundred miles, and in the narrow defiles of the up-river approach, we would be vulnerable to ambush.

My intelligence sources informed me that Haripoonchai did not boast a standing army. With advance warning, the Mon kingdom could muster a considerable peasant army to oppose us. In the more than a month that it would take us to reach our objective, they would have ample warning.

My answer to this problem lay with the cavalry. At Sukhothai, Commander Imre would be detached as an independent strike force of twelve troops of cavalry. They would cut north through the mountains and then west to reach the valley by a more direct route than that taken by the main force. They should reach their destination weeks ahead of the main body.

Once in the valley, the strike force would split itself into two forces of equal size. These would sweep through the valley, overrunning the poorly defended villages and laying waste to the countryside. They were not to attempt to hold captured communities. Their purpose was to wreak havoc and cause disruption over as wide a rural area as possible to forestall, or at least hamper, the formation of a peasant force of any appreciable size.

The drawback to this strategy was that the strike force would outpace its supply train, yet it must be self-sufficient until it could rejoin the main force on its arrival. Commander Imre addressed himself to this problem. He contended that, once in the valley, the units could live off the country. I agreed, but there were still the additional stocks of arrows and the mountain crossings to consider. These problems were overcome by the inclusion of spare mounts that would serve as pack animals.

Commander Imre appreciated the trust I placed in him. He welcomed the opportunity to prove the worth of his cavalry in tactics as yet untried.

During the campaign, I came to know a good deal about the capabilities and limitations of war elephants. Appreciating that the elephant is not native to China and not featured in Chinese battle tactics, General Dom had devoted quite a bit of instruction to the subject. It is one thing to discuss war elephants, yet quite another, I found, to translate the knowledge gained through instruction into planning action.

A war elephant is selected from adolescent bulls on the basis of size, strength, and tusk length. The selection is confined to bulls because the cows do not develop tusks and are smaller than the bulls. After selection, the bull is trained to respond to the mahout handler's goad-prompted guidance.

To sustain its massive bulk, the elephant consumes about two hundred pounds of fodder each day, washing this down with as much as fifty gallons of water. This means that approximately sixteen hours of the elephant's day is devoted to eating. In planning the army's march, this must be taken into consideration. The route selected must provide ample forage and water, and the length of the day's march must allow feeding time. In addition, the army's speed of advance is dictated by the elephant's shambling gait. All this is further complicated by the fact that an elephant is not sure-footed and negotiates mountainous terrain with difficulty.

There is yet another problem with the bull elephant. From adolescence onward, it secretes an oily fluid from a glandular opening situated between the eye and the ear. This happens twice each year, giving rise to a condition known as "musth." When in musth, the beast is either hopelessly lethargic or excited to the point of madness. In the latter case, the bull must be stockaded or securely chained to prevent him from hurting himself or doing lethal damage to those around him.

Offsetting the disadvantages is the fact that the war elephant is the most formidable fighting machine I have ever witnessed in action. No creature, other than another elephant, can stand before a trumpeting, charging war elephant. Its flailing trunk, sharpened tusks, and pounding feet create death and havoc in enemy ranks. Its tough hide is a natural armor almost impervious to spears and arrows. And, notwithstanding its awkward, shuffling stride, the huge beast can attain the surprising speed of about fifteen miles per hour on level ground.

The mount I inherited from General Dom was a magnificent twenty-two-year-old bull in his prime. He stood slightly more than ten feet in height at the shoulder, weighed some eight tons, and had tusks a shade over six feet in length. His broad back supported with ease the mahout perched behind his ears, the howdah that was my command post and fighting platform, and the soldier who held aloft my crimson parasol, together with all our assorted weapons and equipment.

It is, I have often thought, a great pity that elephants are not used by Chinese armies. In time, I grew to have great affection and respect for the ponderous creatures.

I have heard from Arab traders that there exist, in a land where they trade for ivory and black slaves, elephants that run a foot or so higher at the shoulder than our war elephants, outweigh ours by about a ton, have tusks that run two to three feet longer, and both bull and cow are tusked. If this is true, if these are not sailors' exaggerations, such elephants must be fearsome creatures.

If King Jayavarman intended Haripoonchai to be a severe test for the army and myself, he was sadly mistaken. We encountered some harassment in the approaches, but once in the valley we rolled forward unopposed until within sight of the capital of the realm. The lightning-swift sweeps of the cavalry strike forces had created panic throughout the realm. The ragged force drawn up to challenge us at the capital had few elephants, no cavalry to speak of, and was composed of an ill-trained rabble. When our battle line was set in motion, the enemy broke ranks and fled. The city capitulated without further resistance.

We garrisoned the capital and some of the larger communities, stripped the realm of its wealth and produce, and exacted a heavy tribute in captives. The Mon king and his royal family were among the long lines of captives as we set forth on our return march. Vidya had one more white parasol to add to King Jayavarman's impressive collection.

Administrative duties should have kept me in Lopburi for some weeks, but on the shrewd advice of Chang, I joined Vidya's triumphal procession to Angkor Thom.

When I advised Vidya of my decision to accompany him, he scowled darkly but raised no objection.

Cheering crowds lined the roadway on the approaches to the city. My richly caparisoned elephant was behind that of Vidya, separated from his by a troop of cavalry. We were close enough together, however, that it would have been difficult to determine whether the tumultuous welcome was to honor him or myself.

As we neared the causeway, I rose to my feet in the swaying howdah. The sunlight was reflected from my polished cuirass in golden shards. On my right wrist I wore a wide silver bracelet, and on a finger of that hand shone a black star-sapphire ring. My right hand rested on the hilt of my unsheathed sword. When I stood up, the cheers of the crowd rose to a roar.

In our absence, the stone balustrades of the causeway— seven-headed *nagas* supported by gods and demons from Hindu mythology—had reached completion, as had the magnificent gateway the causeway led to. The archway rose straight-sided to the twenty-foot height of the city walls, then angled inward to meet at a point some ten feet higher. On each side of the gate, the heads of the three-headed elephant of the Hindu god Indra were carved in sandstone, their trunks dropping to the base-plinth like slender columns. Above the archway, a central tower rose to a point at a height of some seventy feet above the paved roadway. Facing outward at the cardinal points of the compass were the smiling stone visages of the Avalokitesvara of Mahayana Buddhism. Each face was about ten feet in height and crowned with a diadem. The features were those of the god-king, Jayavarman VII.

When my elephant plodded through the archway, I glanced back to ensure that my mounted escort was still properly formed. The east-facing stone visage of the king stared blankly down at me. The cheers of the crowds lining the avenue within the city washed over me in waves. Each of us, I thought wryly, achieves self-aggrandizement in his own fashion—the king in effigies of stone, myself parading in battle finery before the multitude.

I wondered if the visitors to the city, or the urban dwellers who gazed daily on the gateways, grasped the significance of the king's symbolism. The Buddhist imagery of the stone faces gazing serenely toward the four

corners of the world dwarfed the pantheon of Hindu imagery beneath them on the archway and incorporated in
the balustrades of the causeway. The faces were of
Jayavarman VII, who had imposed his Buddhist faith on
the Hindu sects and his will upon the populace.

chapter 25

HAD I KNOWN WHAT DOMESTIC STRIFE AWAITED ME, I might not have been so anxious to share the homecoming honors with Vidya.

Linh had given birth a few weeks prior to my return. On my arrival I was presented with a daughter instead of the son I had hoped for. I tried not to show my disappointment, but I could not have been very successful. Linh flared up, stating angrily that if the child was a daughter rather than the son I wished for, it was my fault. It was the male seed, she said, that determined the sex of the child. This I did not believe, but I did not dispute her.

Linh had a host of complaints with respect to her pregnancy and the birth of the child. Pregnancy, she claimed, had ruined her figure. I could not notice much, if any, difference, but I held my peace on this, as well. The birth, she insisted, had been a frightful ordeal that she had no intention of repeating. I retorted as gently as I could that she had sons as well as daughters to produce. For this remark I was treated to a withering glance, but no response. But, worst of all, she wailed, was that she had been told that childbirth would put an end to her misery during menstrual periods. She had not yet had a menstrual flow, but this was the time it would have come normally, and the cramps and headaches had returned.

She was somewhat mollified when I presented her with

the gifts of silks, jewelry, and lacquerware I had brought from Haripoonchai. She did not ask where I had obtained the gifts. I had been absent for more than nine months, yet not once—neither then nor subsequently—did Linh question me about what had befallen me in that time, nor did she express the slightest interest in anything I volunteered with respect to Lopburi or the Haripoonchai campaign. Her life revolved completely around herself. My only value, as far as I could make out, was to give her sexual gratification and shower her with gifts.

On that first night of my return, Linh pleaded a headache and did not share my bed. To be truthful, I was not displeased. It had been a long journey and I was too tired to meet the demands she normally made on me. I was so tired, in fact, that though I did visit Apricot Blossom, it was only for a moment to exchange greetings.

Prior to my marriage, mine had been a happy household, a haven of peace and contentment. All that had changed. The servants and slaves no longer went about their chores with smiling faces. There was an atmosphere of resentment, even fear, among the servants.

I remarked on this to Linh. She flew into a rage.

"You do not know what they are like when you are absent," she said angrily. "They are lazy . . . shiftless . . . disrespectful. I have had to punish many of them to teach them proper respect. I have replaced some of the slaves with others who speak *my* native tongue."

I had noticed some new faces. That had not concerned me. Linh's attitude and actions did. "Madam," I said coldly, "you will discipline no one within this compound without my approval and consent. I, and I alone, will mete out punishment when and if required."

"I am not to run your household?" she snapped. "I suppose that . . . that *concubine* is to be mistress under your roof!"

I was angry. It showed in my face and voice. "The unfortunate woman you refer to was my *father's* concubine. She held an honorable position in his household. She is now my responsibility. You do not owe her deference, but you will treat her with civility and respect. You, not she, are mistress of my household, but you will run it in accordance with my wishes. Is that clearly understood?"

Linh was startled by my vehemence. Her eyes widened.

"I . . . I," she said, then lapsed into silence, completing what she had been about to say by nodding meekly.

That afternoon I made it a point to spend some hours with Apricot Blossom.

She wanted to know how my promotion had been received in Lopburi and how we had fared on the campaign. She expressed satisfaction when I gave her the gist of my discourse with General Dom. As I recounted the planning and execution of the campaign, she questioned me closely on a number of points. She was pleased that the campaign had gone as well as it had and that our casualties had been light.

Eventually, I brought the conversation around to matters of the household.

"Has my wife mistreated you in any way?" I asked abruptly.

"No," she answered with a humorless laugh. "She has ignored me. I have not even seen her. I am told she is very beautiful."

"She is . . . and very spoiled."

"Have patience with her, Tartar," Apricot Blossom said chidingly. "She is young. Her pregnancy was not an easy time for her. She will yet give you sons."

I snorted. "She blamed *me*. She told me it is the father who determines the sex of an unborn child."

"There are some who hold that to be true."

"Do you?" I questioned incredulously.

"I do not know," she answered, "but it does not matter. It is the woman who carries the child within her. It is the woman who will be blamed for any defects."

"The child is sound and healthy," I said defensively. "A daughter is not a defect."

"No," she said with a trace of bitterness, "but she is considered of little worth."

A silence grew between us as we both became absorbed in thought.

"There are important matters I must discuss with you," Apricot Blossom said, breaking the momentary silence. "They should have been talked of before this. The fault is mine. I intended to discuss these things before your wedding, but I kept putting it off. Since the wedding, we have seen little of each other."

"That," I said, "is my doing. I have neglected you. My

thoughts have been on my own pleasures. Can you forgive my selfishness?"

"Do not reproach yourself. It is as it should be. Your wife must take precedence."

"What are these important matters?"

"The first is of the least importance. It concerns the terrible night the compound was attacked and set ablaze. I rushed to the nurse's quarters. I fought my way into the burning building, only to find both the nurse and my infant son dead. I took the dead child from the nurse's arms and somehow managed to escape from the building, even though my clothing and hair were afire. Old Chang found me. I was hysterical and incoherent. Out of my mind with grief, I would not release my hold on the dead child."

"You knew the baby was dead. . . . Then why? . . ."

She laughed mirthlessly. "Why did I pretend the child lived? I told you once that women do strange things that often they cannot explain, even to themselves. We are prone to weird fantasies, especially when plagued by guilt. I wanted desperately for the child to be alive as an excuse for my actions and continued existence."

She was confusing me. "What guilt . . . what excuse did you need for what action?"

"I should not have left your father's side," she said simply. "I should have died with him in the blazing pavilion."

"But," I protested, "that makes no sense. Your staying with him would have altered nothing. It would have been as senseless a sacrifice as it is with the Cham wives who throw themselves on the funeral pyres of their husbands. It is only natural, with a mother's instinct, that you should leave my father to seek out your child."

"Perhaps you are right. I cannot say. I felt guilt then . . . and I still do. I shall feel that guilt to the day I die. There is nothing that you or anyone else can say that will alter that. It is why, in my weakness, I invented the fiction that I believed the child still lived. Had I rescued the baby, it might have mitigated my sin of deserting your father in his hour of trial. Old Chang humored me in the fantasy. I inflicted it on you, and I regretted having done so immediately."

I do not pretend to understand Apricot Blossom's reasoning; I did not then, and after all these years I still do not. To her the guilt was real. I believe she even thought her disfigurement was a fitting punishment for what she considered as infidelity to my father.

"You spoke of other matters," I said to change the subject.

"Yes. I must leave your house," she said flatly.

"What! Why? You are of my family. My home is yours."

"That is kind of you, Tartar," she said gently, "but it is not strictly true. I am of your father's house. I have been happy under your roof, happier than I deserve to be, but I can no longer stay. Your duty now is to your wife. She is responsible for the household. It is not right that I should be here. My presence is an affront to her. Surely you must see that."

I did see it. It had been brought sharply to my attention that morning. Perhaps I was not being fair to Linh. Yet I was not inclined to see Apricot Blossom leave just so that my wife would be appeased. I pondered this new situation, and then I hit upon what I thought to be a happy solution.

"If you feel you must leave this house, I shall arrange for you to stay in my Lopburi residence. Linh refuses to accompany me there. It is too rustic for her tastes."

"There or here," she said, "I would still be of your household. It is no solution. It would only lead to friction between you and your wife. No, I have decided I must return to Lin-an."

"But you said you would not return to my father's house and that you had no living relatives."

"I will not return to your father's house. What I said was that I had *few* relatives. I have a brother and a sister in Lin-an. Your father, I believe, left me well provided for. I shall not be a burden on anyone."

I had not told her of Horse-master Chang's unfortunate experience with my family. My father most certainly must have provided for Apricot Blossom, but I doubted that she would find the legacy intact. It didn't matter. If she *must* leave, I would ensure that both she and her maidservant lacked for nothing.

"It will take time to arrange your passage," I said. "I must leave for Lopburi in a few days. I will have to attend to finding you a suitable vessel on my return."

"Thank you. In the meantime, I would appreciate it if I could be moved to the servants' quarters."

"You are no servant."

She laughed. "Am I not?" she said. "Whatever my status, I would feel more comfortable there than in these quarters."

"If that is your wish," I said rather stiffly.

"It is my wish."

That night Linh came to my bed. She displayed all the fervor of the early weeks of our marriage. I was soon too exhausted to dwell on the situation concerning Apricot Blossom.

The next morning, Linh was bright and cheerful. Sexual gratification, I had noticed, had this salutary effect on her disposition. She laughingly chided me on my ardor of the previous night, then switched to other topics.

Our house, she contended, was too small. We must do some entertaining, and we needed grander quarters.

As a general, I was entitled to a more spacious pavilion within the military compound. None was available at the moment. I had been allocated one that was now under construction. I told Linh of this. She wrinkled her nose in disdain.

"Military men are too dull," she said. "All they can talk about are blood and battles. I have a friend who is highly placed. He has told me he could procure us a residence in the royal compound. *That* would be much better. We *should* circulate in court circles if you wish to advance to a higher station."

I did not see fit to remind Linh that I was one of the dull military men she held in such contempt. Court circles, as far as I had experienced, dealt with topics of less interest than battles, at least battles on the field of combat. As for my station, I felt that I had already risen high, considering my age and experience. I felt disposed to humor her.

"As soon as I have attended to some details involving the high command, I must return to Lopburi. I will not have time to do any entertaining between now and then. I shall give you advance warning of my expected date of return so that you can arrange a number of functions. As for the royal compound, you may petition your friend on our behalf if you so wish."

My deferring to her wishes put her in excellent spirits. She had, I thought, never looked more lovely or been more vivacious than during the days prior to my departure.

I had sent my elephant back to Lopburi. I intended to ride Ching Chui on the return journey. Before taking my leave, I attended to another matter.

I commissioned carpenters and cabinetmakers to build a small pavilion close to the grape arbor to temporarily house Apricot Blossom and her handmaiden. I gave the workers detailed instructions concerning the heavy drapes and curtains that would be required in the sleeping chamber. I was assured by the workmen that the pavilion would be ready for occupancy within a few weeks.

I had been in Lopburi little more than a month when I received a message from Vidya that our objectives for the forthcoming seasonal campaign were to be the Siamese kingdom of Phayao, the princedom known as Yonok, and the fortified city-state of Chiang Saen. I recalled with foreboding General Dom's speculations concerning probable objectives. Any one of the three objectives could tax the Army of the West to its capacity. All three were a challenge that dismayed me.

I had Ching Chui saddled up and then I set out for Angkor that same afternoon.

When I arrived unannounced in Angkor Thom, Linh greeted me coldly. I had, she reminded me, promised to give her advance notice so that she could arrange for social functions. I told her curtly that I had left Lopburi on short notice and would be in Angkor no more than two or three days to confer with the high command and Prince Vidyanandana on matters of some urgency. She did not ask me what these matters were, nor did I enlighten her.

The next morning Vidya received me with every evidence of displeasure.

"Tartar," he said unpleasantly, "what brings you here? How can you tear yourself away from administrative problems and the pleasures of Lopburi?"

I had no time to indulge in an acrimonious exchange.

I launched directly into the business that had brought me here.

"Have you given thought to the next campaign?"

"No. Why should I? You are the military genius selected to guide the army's destiny. It would seem to be your problem, not mine."

"It will become your problem if we fail in this mission."

Vidya laughed. "Why should we fail? We never have, at least not under the tactical direction of General Dom."

I was becoming angry and controlled myself with difficulty. I would have liked to take him by the shoulders and shake him until his teeth rattled.

"You once said that the Army of the West had proved itself invincible. The reason is that it has been opposed by nothing but inferior forces for a good many years. On this mission, that is not likely to be the case.

"Our farthest objective is almost five hundred miles north of Lopburi. There are rugged mountain ranges between us and our objectives. The Siamese, I am told, are aggressive and excellent fighters. They are very different from the scared rabbits we have fought over the last few years. Due to the length of our march, they will know of our approach well in advance and will have time to build a sizable force to oppose us.

"I am also informed that our objectives are heavily defended. This will undoubtedly mean siege tactics. We will have to take siege engines with us. This will slow us down even more in the mountain passes. I fully expect that this campaign will involve our sitting out the next rainy season somewhere in the north, with our supply lines stretched to the breaking point."

"Then I suggest," Vidya said coldly, "that you make adequate preparations to ensure success."

"I came here," I said, "to suggest that you return with me to Lopburi. This will be no easy campaign. I feel you should be familiar with every phase of the planning. Then, too, to give ourselves as much time as possible, we will have to be on the march before the end of the wet season."

"The planning and preparation are not my concern. They are entirely your province. I have affairs to attend to here, and I don't want to be bothered with the tiresome details you propose. Go back to Lopburi and advise me when you consider the army ready to march."

"You are a fool," I snapped angrily. "Did it ever occur to you that you are a Cham and I a Chinese? If the Army of the West suffers defeats, or even setbacks, under our joint leadership, consider the consequences. We would be sacrificed without any qualms. Both our heads would roll in the dust of the ceremonial square—if we don't suffer an even more humiliating fate. Have you never thought it odd that two men of foreign birth hold the top command positions in the strongest Khmer army in he field? If you have, then you might have wondered if we have been placed in these positions deliberately—that there could be those who want us to fail and face humiliation. You may hold little love for me, but I would strongly advise you to consider your own unenviable position."

My shafts struck home. Vidya's eyes widened in shocked disbelief. Evidently, thoughts of this nature had never crossed his mind. They would, I hoped, shock him into compliance with my wishes. I was only partially successful. Before I left, Vidya promised to arrive in Lopburi a month before the end of the rainy season.

As I left his residence, I cursed myself for being a fool. I had seen no other presence in the anteroom where our conversation had taken place, but I was sure that an eavesdropper had not been far away. My exchange with Vidya would, without doubt, reach the king's ears.

I reflected on this as I rode to the military compound. I concluded that it might not be as injurious as I had thought initially. It might not hurt for the king to know that I was not quite the idiot he evidently took me for. And, fortunately, I had exercised enough caution not to name the king as the author of the dilemma facing both myself and Vidya.

chapter 26

MY BUSINESS WITH THE HIGH COMMAND WAS CONCLUDED rapidly. It was concerned with a requisition for siege equipment and a request for additional recruits. I was assured these matters would be given due consideration. After lunching with a number of staff officers, I returned to my residence.

I rested for about an hour before going to visit Apricot Blossom. The pavilion beside the pergola was smaller than I had visualized. It smelled, not unpleasantly, of freshly dressed timber. I waited for a few moments on the narrow porch, gazing down on the well and the vine-shrouded arbor, until the maidservant ushered me into Apricot Blossom's chamber.

The screening was not as heavy as I had ordered. Apricot Blossom was clearer in outline than the dim shape she had always been when in her curtained quarters in the residence. I noted that, even in this darkened room, she wore the head covering and veil she affected on our nocturnal walks. Perhaps she always had been veiled in the residence. It had been too dark to determine whether she had been or not.

"You should not have come here," she said in lieu of her customary greeting.

"It is a short visit. I had urgent business to conduct. I rode in late yesterday evening and will leave early on the morrow."

"I did not mean that," she said impatiently. "You should not have come to visit me here."

"Why not?"

"Because your wife believes I exert an undue influence on you . . . to her detriment."

"That is nonsense. You have only spoken in her defense. Did you not tell her the purpose of these temporary quarters?"

"Did not you?"

I realized guiltily that I had not. I should have told Linh that I was having the small pavilion constructed, and why, but I had considered it was not her concern. "No," I answered, "I'm afraid not."

"She has requested that I not set foot in her house again . . . and that I not receive you here."

"*Her* house!" I said angrily. "Did she tell you this herself?"

"No. She sent one of her trusted Annamite servants to relay the message. But she is within her rights. The residence is her domain."

"Don't defend her actions," I snapped. "They are beyond reason . . . unforgivable."

"No, Tartar," Apricot Blossom said softly, "she has reason. She believes this to be a trysting place. She thinks you to be my lover."

"What! Surely the Annamite servant didn't tell you this!"

"It is spoken of in the residence. It came to my ears through Mai-ling."

"Ridiculous!" I snorted.

"Yes," she said, with a catch in her voice, "isn't it?"

Before I knew what was happening, Apricot Blossom had removed her head covering, dropped the veil, and drawn back the curtain. The light slanting through the louvered shutters was not bright, but it was more than enough to illuminate the ghastly spectacle that met my gaze.

The memory of that dreadful moment haunts me still. Had I been given warning, I might not have recoiled. I might have been able to suppress the shudder of revulsion that seized me. I do not know whether I could have controlled my shocked reaction or not. I had known her to be disfigured, but over the years I had grown accustomed to seeing her as a faceless wraith. I had come to know her only through the inflections of her voice and the warmth of her personality. On those few occasions when I pictured her in my mind, the image had been of the lovely young woman I had known in my youth. In my wildest imaginings, I could not have pictured what was exposed to me.

The left side of her face was badly scarred, but the right side was a horror to behold. The flesh had been so consumed by the flames that the charred remnants barely covered the bone structure of her skull. On that side of her face, her teeth gleamed through a lipless slit. A portion of her nose was missing. A twisted blob of flesh was all that remained of her ear. Her right eye was a gaping hole. Her hair, combed thinly over from the left, could not conceal the scarred and barren skin beneath.

Her voice was grating, little more than a croak. "Could any man bring himself to love *this?*"

Tears welled from her left eye and coursed down her scarred cheek as she mercifully drew the curtain and replaced the veil and head covering. In the darkness, she sat hunched forward, sobbing brokenly.

Compassion overcame my shocked revulsion. I sat beside her, cradling her in my arms. She clung to me, her head against my chest.

Gradually, her sobbing subsided. "Tartar," she said brokenly, "I should not have exposed this apparition to your eyes . . . or maybe I should have shown myself to you long ago. In my vanity, I wanted you to remember me as I was."

There was nothing I could say to comfort her. I swallowed, then said hoarsely, "You shall not suffer further the indignity of my wife's suspicious jealousy. I will see to that."

"Do not berate her. She does not know she has nothing to fear from my presence. My only wish is to be out of Angkor as soon as possible."

"I cannot stay to see to your passage. I am sorry that it has not already been secured. On my return to Lopburi, I will send Chang to take care of it . . . and to shield you from further insults."

Pleading a headache, Linh had not shared my bed on the night of my arrival. This real, or contrived, indisposition kept her in her quarters the next day. She did not visit my bedchamber that night, as well. I made no issue of this, not really wishing to see her until I was more composed. The next morning, however, I delayed my departure and summoned her to my presence.

"Madam," I said, "you have seen fit to disregard my wishes with respect to my father's concubine."

"She usurps my role as wife," Linh said defiantly. "She makes a mockery of me in my own home."

"You are wrong," I said reprovingly, "but the blame is mine, not yours. It was at her request that I had her moved from the residence to the pavilion I ordered constructed for that purpose. It is a purely temporary arrangement. She felt she was no longer welcome under my roof . . . that her presence disturbed you. She has requested to be returned to China. This will be done as soon as ship passage can be arranged. All this I should have told you."

"She has poisoned your mind against me," Linh said sulkily.

"On the contrary," I said gently, "she has yet to meet you, but she has never spoken ill of you. There is not, nor has there ever been, anything improper between us, as you seem to suspect. I respect and admire the unfortunate creature, but it would be unthinkable for me to consort with a concubine of my father's house.

"I intend to send my sergeant at arms from Lopburi to attend to the matter of her sea passage. Between now and the time she leaves, I do not request you, I command you, to leave the woman in peace."

"I may have been unjust to her," Linh said contritely, one of the few times I ever heard her admit to making an error.

"You have been."

"It may be because I am unwell. I am again with child," she said sullenly.

Her disclosure did not bring me the happiness it should have.

I instructed Chang carefully concerning Apricot Blossom. He understood that he was to arrange not only her passage, but to protect her from insult or injury. He also was to see to it that the small teak chest in my bedchamber at Angkor Thom went with the two women on their voyage. I had taken it for granted that Mai-ling would accompany her mistress, but I also charged Chang with the responsibility of obtaining her merchant father's consent. I didn't anticipate any difficulties in that regard.

It was a peculiar thing about the mute girl, I thought. In my mind, she had become so closely associated with Apricot Blossom that I had thought of them almost as one. I had not, until recent months, even known she had a name.

As I watched Chang solemnly nod in acknowledgment of my instructions, my thoughts turned to him. His wrinkled visage was nut-brown from exposure to the elements. His unruly hair was now snow-white. I knew him to have been a few years senior to my father. It struck me that Chang must now be well into his seventies. It was, I thought, not proper that he continue to be exposed to the rigors of campaigning.

On an impulse, I said, "If you like, you can return to China with the women. There is more than enough in the small chest to take care of all your wants and needs."

Chang glared at me ferociously. "Siao Hu," he spat out, "my place is here."

It had been a long time since he had called me "Young Tartar," I thought, grinning. "Then, Old Stallion, you had better not waste time in idle chatter. We march to the north in less than two months."

As I watched Horse-master Chang ride out on his mottled steed, my thoughts sped ahead of him to Angkor Thom. Though I tried not to think of it, the image of Apricot Blossom's skull-like face came into my mind. Although I would never have admitted it to Linh, nor anyone else, the concubine *had* sometimes entered my thoughts in a most improper fashion. On those rare occasions when she appeared unbidden in my sexual fantasies, her image had been as I had first known her. I had always guiltily pushed her from my thoughts, replacing her with a surrogate in deference to my father's memory. I doubted now that she would ever return to such fantasies.

As I turned to reenter my quarters, another uncomfortable thought struck me. This was the Year of the Horse. In the Chinese twelve-year cycle of lunar years, the return of the year of one's birth is supposed to portend a lucky twelvemonth. With our easy victory in Haripoonchai

early in the year, I had been confident fate smiled on
me. In the last few weeks, that confidence had evaporated.

Vidya did not arrive in Lopburi as he had promised.
Instead, he sent a message that he had been detained
and would join us later on the march. We left Lopburi two
weeks ahead of the change of season. Horse-master Chang
had not returned by the time of our departure. I assumed
he had encountered unexpected difficulties with the ship
passage and would join us later.

The roadway leading north from Lopburi was now
stone-paved for some seventy miles and thereafter topped
with crushed rock as far as Sukhothai.

By the time the army made camp at Sukhothai, the rains
had stopped. I called a halt of a few days to allow the
sun to steam the marshy plain to the north of us into some
semblance of dryness before we resumed the march.

It was at Sukhothai that Vidya joined us. He made no
excuse for his tardiness. I asked for none. I had expected
Chang to be with Vidya's escort and was more concerned
that the Old Stallion had not put in an appearance than
I was with any delinquency on the part of Vidya. With
an army on the march, however, I had other matters
making demands on my waking hours. I was confident
that Chang could handle any situation that might have
arisen, and I put him from my mind.

During our previous campaign, the cavalry strike force
had reported the presence of a Siamese princedom in a
valley they had crossed on their way to the kingdom of
Haripoonchai. This small princely state was called
Lampang. It was my initial objective, intended as a prelude
to the battles that lay ahead.

From Sukhothai we struck north, following the valley
of the Yom River to a point where it curved eastward.
At this point, we crossed a range of scrub-jungled mountains gashed by deep, treacherous gorges. The cavalry
strike force had been deployed several days ahead of the
main body. They were to encircle the princely seat of
the small state and overrun it if resistance proved not too
stiff.

When we emerged into the valley, a dispatch rider arrived to advise me that Lampang had been taken. The
Year of the Horse still had some two months to go before

being overtaken by the Year of the Ram. I was mildly worried about Chang, but my year was starting to look a bit brighter.

There was one thing that puzzled me about the Lampang action. The strike force had met with only token resistance. The prince had not been in residence, and there seemed to be very few able-bodied men among the captives taken. As we continued our northern march, I fully anticipated an ambush and deployed cavalry units in advance of our line of march and well out on our flanks.

We entered a region heavily forested with giant teak trees, and then we were slowed by jungle-matted mountains strewn with huge boulders. As I had expected, the siege engines, catapults, and rams slowed our progress even more in this rough terrain. It was country suited to harassment tactics and ambush, but we advanced unmolested.

There was nothing to indicate in the closing weeks of the Year of the Horse that it would be more than a year, that the Year of the Monkey would be well advanced, before I would again see Horse-master Chang.

chapter 27

WE REMAINED ENCAMPED IN THE VERDANT VALLEY FOR three days. Mountain ranges lay to the east and west. To our rear were the mountains and heavily forested region through which we recently had passed with some difficulty, but without incident. We were within territory nominally under the dominion of the kingdom of Phayao.

A few miles ahead of us lay a line of low hills. On the other side of the ridge was a bowl-shaped valley, one third of which was a large lake extending to the foot of the mountains to the west. The fortified capital of the kingdom was situated about midway up the valley on the eastern shore of the lake.

There were a number of sound reasons for calling a halt here. The mountain crossing had been arduous, and both men and mounts were tired. I wanted them rested for the ordeal I was positive lay before us. I considered as ominous signs the facts that we had encountered no harassment and that the villages along our path had been almost deserted. I had dispatched cavalry patrols to scout Phayao and the Lao River valley beyond. They had been instructed to return with a few captives. On the basis of the reconnaissance, and what information we could elicit from the captives, I would be in a position to plan our next moves. There was something about the situation as it was developing that I found unsettling.

It was mid-afternoon when Commander Imre stalked into my command tent. He was scowling darkly. Spreading out a large square of silk, he used charcoal to sketch in the salient details while he briefed me tersely on the conditions as reported by our returning reconnaissance patrols.

The situation Imre outlined was much as I had suspected. The difference, however, was one of degree. The forces waiting in the valley ahead to bar our advance were greater, much greater, than I had anticipated. From Imre's description, they were well equipped and in a state of readiness. With a sinking feeling, I recognized the extent of our betrayal.

An army of the size and caliber Imre was describing could not have been assembled overnight. It would take months to gather such a force. It must be comprised of forces recruited from all the Siamese states in our path—including Lampang, to our rear. This called for a degree of organization and coordination that could be achieved only if predicated on accurate information received well in advance of our coming. Clearly, the Siamese had known the size and composition of our force from the moment we marched forth from Lopburi. It would not surprise me if they had known our objectives even before the orders were transmitted to the Army of the West.

Our orders had not mentioned annexing our Siamese objectives. I had considered this realistic in view of the distances involved that would impose severe restrictions on the garrisoning and governing of the conquered states. I now perceived another reason. It had not been anticipated in Angkor that we *would* emerge victorious. It was expected that we would either retreat from the formidable force facing us or suffer a humiliating defeat. I was determined that we would do neither.

I questioned Imre closely on a number of points, requested that he prepare a large-scale terrain map, and instructed him to assemble the staff officers and unit commanders in the command tent within the hour.

I should have been dismayed by the magnitude of our task. Unaccountably, I was not. It is the unknown that spawns fear and uncertainty. Now that I knew what confronted us, I felt my spirits lifting. As I walked toward Vidya's silken pavilion, with Imre's rough map under my arm, I experienced a strange exhilaration.

I brushed past the guard unceremoniously. Vidya lay naked on a bed of cushions. Two young Siamese, a boy and a girl, were massaging perfumed oil onto his supine form.

"Go," I snapped at the startled slaves.

Vidya turned his face toward me. "Tartar," he snarled angrily, "how dare you enter without my leave!"

"A matter of urgency." I waited until the slaves left, then said bluntly, "An army is massed in the valley beyond the ridge. It outnumbers our force by about three to one. It is well equipped. Its cavalry numbers more than ours. It has twice as many elephants, and its infantry is almost four times ours in number."

Groping for his *sampot*, Vidya sat up. His face betrayed uncertainty and bewilderment. "Then we dare not face them. We must retreat. We . . ."

I interrupted him. "That is what they expect us to do. That is what they *want* us to do. This is their country, not ours. They would follow. At their leisure, they would cut us to pieces in the teak forests and mountain passes. We will not retreat. Tomorrow at dawn we will be drawn up in battle formation on the other side of the ridge and oblige them with the battle they seem so confident they can win."

I unrolled Imre's crude map. Illustrating my briefing with charcoal lines, I outlined for Vidya's benefit my plan of battle and exactly the part he was expected to play in it. For once, I felt I had Vidya's undivided attention.

At the staff briefing, I made no attempt to minimize the gravity of our situation. I emphasized the advantages we enjoyed. We had, I pointed out, seasoned troops as opposed to the untrained recruits facing us. Our horses and elephants were battle-tested veterans. Theirs were not, or at least not to the extent of ours. I was confident, I stated, that we could win the day despite the odds that appeared to favor the enemy.

I then outlined my battle plan in minute detail, with the exception of the parts that the cavalry and the forces under my personal command would play in the action.

We would strike camp as soon as darkness overtook the valley. Leaving the siege engines and supply train where they now were, the remainder of the army must be prepared to move out soon after midnight. Our force would be divided into two groups. The larger force, composed of approximately three-quarters of the army under the command of the commanding general, Prince Vidyanandana, would cross the ridge and be drawn up in a line of battle at first light on the morrow. The smaller force, commanded by myself, would act independently of the main body and would move out about an hour earlier. Then I detailed the units that would comprise the two formations.

Since the moon was just past the full, I was assuming that the enemy would be aware that we had crossed the ridge and would be drawn up in battle formation by dawn. If so, our main force was to sound the advance at dawn. If not, they were to wait until satisfied that the enemy had formed its line before sounding the advance.

On the conch shell signal to advance, our battle line would move forward, but at slow speed. The center of the line would move at a somewhat faster pace than the wings. Gradually, the line would form itself into the shape of a wedge. Our slow speed of advance, I explained, was to draw the enemy into the southern end of the valley, where the confining hills would tend to compress their line and nullify to some extent their numerical advantage. The wedge shape of our line would mean that the enemy wings would have to move a greater distance to make contact and would thus be separated from their command center.

When the battle was joined, the center of our line was to stop its advance and hold firm. The left-hand wing was to continue its advance. The right-hand wing was to fall back slowly. The wedge formation would then be pivoting in a clockwise direction, forcing the action toward the eastern portion of the valley. I did not explain the purpose of the maneuver. I noted some worried frowns, but there were no questions.

With the briefing at an end, I dismissed the officers, detaining only Commander Imre.

"Long Ax," I said soberly, "the success or failure of my strategy hinges on two crucial factors. One is that the center of our line, the spearhead of the wedge formation, holds firm. The other is the performance of your cavalry."

I drew Imre closer to the battle map. "The ground at this end of the valley is stubbled paddy fields and barren soil. It is, as you have advised me, dry and dusty. I want you to detail six troopers to cut down large bushes, which they will suspend from their saddles by lengths of rope. Before the battle, they are to be in position here, and here . . . three on each flank. When the signal to advance is given, they will sweep across our line of advance from opposite directions. At that early hour, there should be no breeze. The dust they stir up should hang like a curtain in the air for some minutes. They will make a second sweep about fifty yards ahead of the first, cut loose the brush, and rejoin their units."

Imre grasped part of my intention immediately. "You want to hide the slow speed of advance and disguise the fact that our line is forming into a wedge."

"I hope to . . . and to obscure the fact that our force is reduced in size. They have known the composition of our force for some time, but in the early light I don't think they will notice that it has been reduced by about one-quarter. Once the wedge is formed, it becomes all the more difficult to determine the actual size of the force. But the dust screen has another function."

"Which is?"

"One troop of your mounted archers is to fan out ahead of the center of our advancing line. When the second sweep is completed, the troop will ride through the dust toward the advancing enemy. Its targets will be the mahouts of the enemy elephants. The troop is to pick off as many as possible in a sweep to the left down the enemy line, then join up with your units on the left flank."

Imre nodded in agreement. "Seeing cavalry riding out of the dust should startle them," he said with a grin.

"And confuse them by throwing their line into disarray," I added. "Now, here is your most vital task. All your troops of bowmen are to be on our left flank. Their job is to take out the enemy cavalry on that flank. Once the pivoting motion starts, we must not be in a position to be outflanked by their cavalry on our left. When you are satisfied that you have removed that threat, your bowmen are to disengage and race behind our lines to our right flank. When I see them in motion, it will be my signal to attack."

"From where?"

"From here," I said, pointing to a line of hills on the eastern side of his map. "We will be drawn up behind the crest of this ridge. If the rotating wedge works as I hope, the action will have been forced in this direction. I will bear down on their most extended flank and slightly to their rear. I believe their staff officers will think they have been misled—that our force is larger than they had been advised, or that we have received reinforcements without their knowledge. If my evaluation is correct, at this point they will break ranks in confusion and your cavalry can move in for the kill."

"I can see only one flaw," Imre said thoughtfully. "What if the Siamese commander does not commit all his forces to his battle line? What if he holds about one-third of his force in reserve as a second wave?"

"I have considered that. A skilled tactical commander would do just that. It is a chance I have to take. I am gambling on the fact that there are kings and princes from at least four Siamese realms involved. They must believe that through sheer weight of numbers victory must be theirs, and none, therefore, will want to be left out of the action. I have based my strategy and tactics on that assumption. If I am wrong, we will know soon enough."

The sky in the east was flushed with the green-gold of dawn. Below me, the battle lines faced each other at a distance of a little over two miles. Our line started slowly forward before the wail of the conch signal reached my ears. I watched the enemy formation anxiously and breathed a sigh of relief when the entire force moved ponderously forward, gaining momentum as it advanced.

At the base of the hill on which I stood, a cloud of dust rose. A similar puff mushroomed on the far side of the valley. As the troopers, trailing brush behind them, raced toward each other, the curtain of dust drew together and hung in the still air as I had hoped it would. With satisfaction, I noted that Imre had spaced the troop of mounted bowmen at intervals along our line. Behind the screening dust, they moved forward at a trot.

The wings of our formation lagged and the line started to take up the wedge-shaped pattern I had visualized. Vidya's command elephant, I noted wryly, was in the spearhead of the wedge, but well back from the leading edge.

A second billowing veil of dust rose in front of the first, which was by now thinning. The cavalry troopers burst through the dusty curtain at a full gallop, closed the distance to the enemy line, wheeled in unison, and swept along the front at an angle compensating for the enemy's speed of advance. It was beautiful to watch; it was executed like a precision drill. The only difference was that two troopers sagged and toppled from their saddles as a hail of arrows came from the enemy formation.

The troopers had done their job well. I nodded approvingly as a number of enemy war elephants veered drunkenly, bereft of their handlers' guidance. The front of the enemy advance buckled and swayed, but it lost little of its forward momentum.

It was a peculiar feeling, watching the battle lines closing below me. It had about it an unreal quality. Even the noise—the drumbeats, the clashing of cymbals, the thudding hoofbeats, and the shrill trumpeting of elephants—seemed strangely muted. But it was real enough for the actors staging this drama for my benefit. The sky grew thick with arrows. Within a few minutes the centers of the battle lines would clash.

As I rose from my haunches and moved down from the crest to my waiting forces, an old proverb crossed my mind: "It is better to sit on the mountain and watch the tigers fight below than it is to descend and join the fray." It is too bad, I thought as I donned my cuirass and climbed onto my hulking steed, that we are in no position to follow that sage advice.

With a signaler trotting along beside my elephant, I moved uphill toward a small clump of trees at the top. Even before I reached the crest, the swelling din heralded that the battle had been joined. This would be the test, I thought. Could our seasoned regulars withstand an onslaught of hordes of undisciplined peasant recruits in such numbers? It would not be too long before I would have the answer.

Our center seemed to be holding. The lines swayed back and forth and merged beneath clouds of dust, but our left wing, strengthened with most of our war elephants, seemed to be inching forward. The right wing was falling back in an orderly fashion. It seemed to be working. The action was slowly wheeling in my direction.

On the far flank, I could not discern how the mounted archers were making out in their vital role. I caught only glimpses of the confused action through the swirling dust.

It was, I knew, far too early in the battle for Imre to have achieved his assigned goal, but that didn't lessen my anxiety. The minutes seemed to stretch into eternity.

I tensed. Something was wrong. It was a few minutes before I fully comprehended what was happening. Our center, which should have been a rock-like pivot point, was falling back. Vidya's command elephant seemed to be much farther to the rear than it should have been. Then, to my consternation, the conch shell signal to fall back floated up to me through the din of battle. It couldn't be happening. It couldn't be, but it was.

We had better move down from our mountain and join the fray, and fast—or the wrong tiger would win.

I barked an order to the signalman. My elephant was in motion down the slope before the conch shell blast rang out.

As my elephant swayed down the hill, gathering speed with each lumbering step, I was in an agony of suspense. My signal to charge was to have been Vidya's cue to sound the advance in order to halt the wheeling motion of our formation. No signal came. I was on the floor of the valley and moving to engage an oncoming war elephant when, to my vast relief, I heard Vidya's signal. I breathed a prayer of thanks to my ancestors. The sight of my force streaming down the hill must have brought Vidya to his senses.

The entry of my force achieved what I had hoped. The left wing of the enemy formation panicked and collapsed into a milling mob. With Imre at their head, swinging his long-handled ax like a flail, our cavalrymen thundered around the flank and into the panic-stricken mass. The right wing of our battle line, relieved of pressure, advanced slowly until our former wedge became more like a wide-mouthed "V."

The battle raged on for another five hours. Slowly, very slowly, the Siamese were pushed back. The final stages of the fighting took place on the shore of the lake, and, in some cases, within the shallows of the lake itself.

There came a point when I realized the fighting was slackening. Imre rode up at a gallop. He reined in till his steed reared and then swung his ax in a wide arc above his head. He shouted something, but I couldn't make out the words.

It was then that I knew we'd done it. Against almost impossible odds, we'd won the day.

The Army of the West could look back on this day with justifiable pride. It had passed this supreme test with flying colors. There was but one sour note. To all the other flaws in his character, I could credit Vidya with one more I had not suspected. He was a coward.

Our casualties were heavy, but those of the Siamese were almost beyond belief. We had slain almost two-thirds of their forces. Their dead littered the southern end of the valley, were strewn along the lakeshore, and bobbed among the water hyacinths that choked the eastern shalows.

Very few of the defeated Siamese had managed to flee our relentless cavalry. The stunned captives we took very nearly equaled in number our surviving force.

It would be a long time before the Siamese states involved would forget their crushing defeat. It would be many years before they would pose much of a threat to neighboring states.

chapter 28

VIDYA BLUFFED IT OUT. HE CLAIMED HE HAD FEIGNED retreat as a ruse to inspire overconfidence in the enemy. With his capacity for self-deception, he may have come to believe this fabrication himself. If so, he was one of the very few who did. I neither confirmed nor denied his story.

Not without logic, Vidya maintained that the magnitude of our victory made it unnecessary to continue the campaign. After the pillaging and razing of the royal seat at Phayao, he was in favor of our returning to Lopburi. Unfortunately, I was not in a mood to accept suggestions or direction from Vidya. I insisted that we fulfill our mission as directed. King Jayavarman had seen fit to issue the challenge. I was determined he be given full measure.

Under heavy guard, our captives were embarked on their journey to Angkor. The remainder of our force continued northward.

Our second objective was the princedom of Yonok. Its administrative capital, the walled city of Chiang Rai, was less than six days' march to the north. Our final objective, the city-state of Chiang Saen, hugged the southern bank of the Mekong River some two days' march farther north.

We marched north through wide, fertile valleys. The low ranges of flanking mountains drew near, then faded into the middle distance. The villages along our route yielded tribute without demur.

Chiang Rai presented no problems. The city gates were thrown open wide at our approach. The townsfolk could do little else, with no forces to defend the city.

It all seemed too easy. It was. Those few who had escaped the slaughter at Phayao, together with all the able-bodied men available throughout the region, awaited us at Chiang Saen.

Chiang Saen was even bigger than I had been led to believe from stories heard during the northern campaign of Prince In and from our present informants. The city's defenses were every bit as strong as they had been described.

On three sides, the city was enclosed by high brick walls. There were, in fact, an outer wall and an inner wall, between which was a wide moat filled with half-starved crocodiles. The gate at the southeastern extremity was ringed with strong bastions. The northern side of the city needed no defenses since it faced directly on the river, where, during the dry season, the banks dropped precipitously more than thirty feet to the water below.

We set up camp to the south of the city gates, well beyond the range of bowmen manning the bastions and the outer wall. Some two miles to the west, about midway along the walled perimeter, stood a high hill topped with a temple. The temple terrace afforded a commanding view of the city and the river beyond. Seated at the top of broad steps leading from that terrace toward the city spread beneath me, I moodily pondered the problem.

While we could not climb the steep riverbank, it afforded the city dwellers with an easy means of exit and entry. Unless the far bank of the Mekong could be occupied and adequately patrolled, and the river blockaded above and below the city, the inhabitants could neither be sealed off nor starved into submission. With the forces at my disposal, such a course was out of the question.

The city gates were too heavily defended to be stormed without sustaining losses I could not afford. Scaling the outer walls would only land us in the moat, with yet more walls to scale. Unless I knew the depth of the moat, which no one seemed to know with certainty, tunneling beneath the walls had to be ruled out. All that was left was to breach the outer wall, bridge the moat, and breach the inner wall. Judging from the thickness of the walls, it was a task that could take months.

It was now the Year of the Ram, with less than four months remaining in the dry season. If I intended to breach the walls, the action woud have to be initiated without delay if we hoped to be within the city before the rains overtook us. I wondered if King Jayavarman had known about these formidable defenses when he had assigned us Chiang Saen as one of our mission objectives. I concluded ruefully that he had, even if he had not expected us to reach this target.

My gaze swung to the right. I looked down on our elephants and those we had captured at Phayao, grazing contentedly in a heavily wooded area between the hill and our sprawling encampment. Reflectively, I stroked my drooping moustache. The idea came to me at that moment. I smiled at the thought that the big brutes we'd captured could be made to earn their keep in the undignified role of working elephants.

A twenty-foot teak log of some eight feet in diameter was trimmed to a point at its butt end. The point was capped with sheet iron. The huge log was suspended horizontally from the top beam of a braced, log framework by means of chains. Near the top of the fifteen-foot-high frame, a timbered platform was constructed to extend well out on both sides.

Working beneath the protection of the wooden platform, elephants skidded the frame to a position where the iron-sheathed point of the projecting log was within a few feet of the brick wall. The frame was firmly staked in place.

Long lines led back from the log. An elephant strained to pull the log back. The lines were slipped. The log swung forward to crash against the brickwork with a ringing clang. Pulverized brick sprayed out from the point of impact.

Catapults were positioned so that their rock projectiles thudded into the wall above the point where the log ram hammered away at the base.

In a matter of days, instead of weeks, we managed to punch a hole in the outer wall. Behind wooden shields to protect them from the archers manning the inner wall, our foot soldiers cleared and secured a quarter-mile section of the outer wall.

We went to work then to widen the breach and clear away the rubble. Next, a pre-constructed bridge of teak logs was hauled into position, up-ended, and dropped across the moat. When this was done, the teak ram was relocated close to the inner wall, the catapults were adjusted to the new angle, and we started to repeat our coordinated demolition of the inner defenses.

In just under a month, at a cost of four elephants and twenty-three men, we had breached the defenses and were ready to storm the city. I did not anticipate much opposition. During the time when we had been chewing our way through the brickwork, many had fled the city by way of the river escape route.

The honor of first to enter the city went to the cavalry. Two troops of mounted bowmen thundered over the log bridge and rode through the ragged hole in the inner wall. Close behind them streamed a company of infantrymen. I followed close on their heels on my command elephant.

The resistance within the city was much stiffer than I had expected. I moved to one side to leave a clear path for our soldiers pouring through the breached wall. Absorbed in assessing the situation, I did not notice the approach of the charging war elephant. My first intimation of the threat was the shrill trumpeting behind me.

My mahout goaded my mount and it turned ponderously to meet the charge. To my astonishment, the elephant bearing down on me carried the white parasol of royalty. My worthy antagonist was none other than the Siamese monarch of Chiang Saen.

We had not gained much speed before the king's mount crashed head-on into my elephant. My mahout was very nearly unseated. I crashed into the forward railing of my howdah and my cavalry spear went flying from my grasp. The king was armed with a long-shafted halberd. The blade came down in a flashing arc. It was deflected by my cuirass and sliced down my right thigh.

With tusks locked, the elephants swayed in fierce struggle. My mount was the stronger, but he had been forced to his knees by the greater momentum carried by the king's charging bull. As my mount struggled to gain firmer footing, my platform tilted perilously. My leg gushed blood. As I reached out for a bow, I lost my balance, slipped on the planking slicked with blood, and sprawled face-down on the blood-wet platform.

The fall undoubtedly saved my life. The king's halberd whistled in a slanting trajectory scant inches above my head.

The bow was in my hand now. I was already fitting an arrow to the bowstring as I reached a kneeling position. It must have been at that moment that my mahout toppled the handler from the king's elephant. My bull had regained his balance, but the king's steed broke clear and the howdah lurched as my mount plunged forward. I was again thrown off balance.

The king's mount, with no mahout to goad it, veered off like a rudderless ship. The king, his face a mask of fury and frustration, could no longer reach me with his halberd thrusts. Braced on one knee, I tilted the bow and drew back the bowstring.

I did not let fly the shaft. I found I did not wish to kill this man. He could have fled the doomed city. He had not, choosing instead to make a suicidal stand with those fighting men who had remained loyal to him. It was a noble gesture that would cost him his life, but I didn't want it to be by my hand.

Had I sped the arrow to its mark, I would have done the monarch a favor.

I checked the bleeding with a crude tourniquet fashioned from a quiver sling, and I bound the deep wound with a strip torn from my *sampot*. Two hours later, when those defending the city finally surrendered, I was so weak from loss of blood that I had to be carried from my mount.

The halberd blade had sliced to the bone. Hot pitch was poured into the wound. The edges were drawn together and my thigh was bound tightly. I knew nothing of this as it took place. Unconsciousness had claimed me.

The leg became infected. Fever raged in me. For a week, most of the time delirious, I hovered between life and death.

Had I known what was going on, and been in command of my faculties, I would have intervened to stay Vidya's sadism. The Siamese king faced death if he survived the battle, but he did not deserve the fate Vidya devised for him.

Two large hemispheres of bamboo were fabricated to Vidya's specifications. They were of open weave. Iron spikes were affixed pointing inward. At Vidya's command, the hemispheres were taken to a grassy square in front of the city's largest temple.

The captive king was brought to the spectator-lined square. He was fitted into one hemisphere. The second was securely lashed on top of the one holding the king. The monarch was then within a spherical bamboo cage. By twisting his body and arranging his limbs with care, the king could avoid the spikes protruding inward—but not for long.

Six elephants were herded into the square. They paid little heed to the bamboo ball until one bull nudged it with his trunk and the ball rolled a few feet from him. Intrigued by this behavior, the bull nudged the ball again, this time much harder. The king screamed in anguish as spikes tore his flesh.

The other elephants soon joined in the diverting sport. Trumpeting and jostling each other, they flailed the ball with their trunks, kicked it, and tried to toss it aloft with their tusks. Long before the grisly game was ended by the handlers, it would have been impossible to identify the bloody pulp within the sphere as once having been a man, let alone the monarch.

The sphere was left standing in the square until its contents were reduced to nothing but broken, whitening bones.

The captured city was to provide us with quarters for the duration of the rainy season. It escaped, at least temporarily, the fate of Phayao and Chiang Rai.

The poison drained from my system. My leg mended slowly. The months dragged by, with my not noticing much improvement. By the time we made ready to leave the city, however, I could hobble unaided, but the muscles and tendons ripped by the slicing blade were far from restored. A livid scar running from just below my hipbone to a point near my kneecap was to be a permanent memento of the Chiang Saen action. I never did recover fully the use of my right leg, and I walked with a limp from that time onward.

Before leaving Chiang Saen, the city was stripped of its valuables and produce, and most of its inhabitants were taken as captives. It differed from Phayao and Chiang Rai in that we did not burn the city. It escaped the torch on my orders. Vidya, who had avoided me since Phayao, raised no objection.

My reasons for this departure from our standard practice with cities we did not intend to occupy and govern were threefold. The city had served us well as temporary quarters. Its people, through their stubborn resistance to our siege tactics, had earned my grudging admiration. But the most important reason was one I did not discuss. The city remained intact as a tribute to a courageous monarch as partial atonement for his ignominious execution.

The return march to Lopburi took four months. From the former site of Lampang, we turned to the west, crossed a low range of mountains, and entered the vassal kingdom of Haripoonchai. Our purpose was to relieve the garrisons and extract our annual tribute of produce and manpower. By the time we entered Lopburi, we were into the second month of the Year of the Monkey.

I found Horse-master Chang awaiting me at my quarters. His wrinkled face wore an expression of concern plus something else I could not define. We greeted each other affectionately, but administrative matters kept me from questioning him until we shared our evening meal.

My first question concerned my wife and the child she had borne. I wanted to know if she had presented me with a son.

Chang pursed his lips. "She lost the child in her third month of pregnancy. I am told it would have been a son."

I hid my keen disappointment. "Has she recovered satisfactorily?"

"She is well. She leads an active social life. You will

find on your return that you now reside in the royal compound."

I did not welcome this news, but I did not comment on it. I switched to another subject.

"When you didn't return, or join us at Sukhotai, I assumed you'd encountered difficulties in obtaining passage for Apricot Blossom and Mai-ling. Is that what detained you?"

Chang gnawed his lip before answering. "The season of favorable winds was drawing to a close. The few merchantmen remaining in the Great Lake were fully booked with cargo. None would take passengers. Even bribes were to no avail."

I had not imagined there would be such difficulties. I cursed myself for not having arranged the passage when Apricot Blossom first voiced her wish to return to China. "I didn't think of that," I said. "I should not have let the arrangement go until so late. Then you had to wait more than six months until the prevailing winds changed again."

"Your father's concubine didn't want to wait that long. She was anxious to leave. I pursuaded one ship's master to call at Angkor on his return voyage and take the two women a few months later. It meant a long voyage . . . to the island kingdoms in the west before setting course for China . . . a journey of more than six months. Your father's concubine preferred that to remaining in Angkor."

"When did they finally leave?"

Chang shifted uncomfortably. "They didn't," he said bleakly. "They are both dead."

I was stunned by this blunt disclosure. I did not believe I had heard him correctly. I stared at Chang, unable to speak.

"Dead," he repeated.

"When? How?" I asked, completely dumbfounded.

"I was not there when it happened. The servants told me when I returned late in the evening on the day of their death."

I realized that Chang blamed himself for their deaths but in what way I did not know. "How . . . how did it happen?"

"Your father's concubine sent for me. She was agitated, but she would not tell me why. She had been ill for several days, but she insisted that she wanted to leave the pavilion. She sent me to the lakeshore village to arrange with Mai-ling's father that both she and Mai-ling stay with him until the ship came from China.

"When I got back that night, they were dead. An Annamite physician had attended your father's concubine. He told me her illness had worsened suddenly and that she had died of convulsions."

"Mai-ling, she was not ill, was she? How came she to die, as well?"

"The servants told me the child was beside herself with grief when her mistress died. She must have stumbled and fallen into the well. She could not cry out. They found her there . . . drowned. It was suggested that she may have committed suicide."

I tried to visualize the scene but failed. I felt that there was more to it than Chang had told me. I recognized as well that it pained him to talk of the dreadful incidents. I had charged him to see to it that no harm came to Apricot Blossom. He must think that, in some way, he was indirectly responsible for her death, that he had failed both me and her.

"Had you been there when it happened," I said, "you could have done no more for Apricot Blossom than the attending physician. As for Mai-ling, I doubt if your presence would have altered anything."

Chang did not answer. His chin rested on one clenched fist. He stared moodily at the mat, lost in his own reflections.

"Come," I said gently, "I'm tired. My leg pains me. We will talk of this another time."

Apricot Blossom's death was a tragedy, but in one sense it was a blessing. She had been constantly tortured by the thought of her disfigurement and her imagined guilt concerning my father's death. That pain could touch her no longer. I grieved for her, and for her unfortunate maidservant, but it was a grief tempered by the knowledge that death had been a kindness.

I was, I think, sorrier for myself than I was for the dead women. I had not fully realized until she was gone how much Apricot Blossom had come to mean to me. She had become a part of my life, a steadying influence and a source of strength and inspiration. Through her I had gained new knowledge and insight. She had given me wise counsel and unstinting affection. When I most needed it, she had brought meaning to my life. I knew I would long mourn her passing.

chapter 29

I REGRETTED HAVING ALLOWED LINH TO NEGOTIATE FOR quarters within the royal compound. At the time, I had thought her chances of succeeding in such a petition negligible. Her royal lineage, in my estimation, was of questionable merit. My distant claim to royal blood, while legitimate, had no meaning to the Khmer. My rank did not warrant royal quarters. I had considered she would be wasting her time, but I had underestimated her powers of persuasion. Now I was faced with social obligations for which I had no desire.

I wanted no part in Vidya's staged march of triumph to the capital. For some weeks I delayed my departure from Lopburi on one thin excuse after another. I could not blame Linh for having lost our son, but the thought of our reunion held little appeal for me.

The months preceding the rainy season are the hottest of the year. I had grown accustomed to the heat, but that year it caused me more discomfort than it normally did. I grew irritable and short-tempered. My leg, which still pained me, didn't help to improve my mood, nor did the fact that Horse-master Chang seemed unable to shake off his burden of guilt. Administrative details did not absorb much of my time. Finally, I accepted the fact that much of my ill temper stemmed from sheer boredom. As banal and artificial as I found life in court circles, it might at least provide distraction and lift me from my depression. I sent word to Linh that I would arrive within the week.

I expected Chang to be cheered by the news of our return to Angkor. He was not. He protested that the new shipment of horses needed his attention and that he had promised to assist Commander Imre with the training of a batch of raw recruits. I knew nothing of these commitments, but I accepted them at face value. If Chang was reluctant to return to Angkor, I would not press the issue.

Linh's welcome was not what I would call effusive. For her, the happiest aspect of my homecoming revolved around a social function she was planning in honor of the event. She did not question me concerning the northern campaign, nor what had detained me in Lopburi. Not once did she make any reference to the miscarriage that had deprived me of a son.

After the evening meal, our daughter was presented for inspection. She was a pretty child. It was fortunate, I thought, that she favored her mother in appearance. Linh fussed over the child with a show of affection, but she did not seem particularly interested in her. Even before she curtly told the nursemaid to take the child away, Linh's chatter had returned to the gowns she had ordered from Annam.

That night Linh came to my bedchamber. There, for the first time, she saw the ragged scar on my right thigh. Her nose wrinkled in evident distaste, but she said nothing. Apparently, she was not sufficiently concerned to want to know how I had received the wound.

In her lovemaking, Linh lacked something of her old ardor. I was glad of her preference for her mounted position, since my stiff leg precluded most other variations.

The next morning I questioned Linh concerning Apricot Blossom's death. Linh was vague, claiming that she had been suffering from one of her periodic headaches at the time. She had, she said, left the cremation details to the physician who had attended the concubine. Since Linh made no reference to Apricot Blossom's disfigurement, I concluded that she had never seen the poor woman's face. For some strange reason, I was glad that

Linh had not gazed upon the skull-like visage. It was not a desire to spare my wife the shock of that spectacle; it was a sort of mark of respect for Apricot Blossom—a desire to shield her from humiliation, even in death.

I asked Linh where I could locate the physician to question him concerning the details and to obtain from him the funerary urn. He was not, Linh stated, a practitioner in the city. He was a physician who had attended her family and only been visiting Angkor Wat. It had been fortunate that he had been a guest in our residence and had volunteered his services in that time of crisis. He had, she said, returned to Annam soon after the cremation. He had made no mention of a funerary jar.

I questioned Linh on one further point—the disposition of Mai-ling's remains. Linh wrinkled her nose in disgust. She knew nothing about the girl. She understood the servant had relatives who had taken care of whatever needed to be done.

The subject of Apricot Blossom's unfortunate death was dropped. It would not be raised again between Linh and myself for several years.

I had been in Angkor Thom only three days when I received word that I was expected at a royal audience on the morrow.

The next morning I ascended the stone steps leading to the royal terrace, pausing from time to time to rest my stiff leg. I noted the stone lions and seven-headed *nagas* flanking the stairway; these were adornments added since my last visit. Stone-carvers were working on decorative balustrades and on the terrace facing. The air rang with the sounds of chisels on sandstone—a discordant symphony I had come to associate with the city.

As I approached the royal palace, I recalled General Dom's speculation concerning the king's reaction in the event that I met his challenges successfully. I smiled thinly. I was about to find out. Of one thing I was sure—the king would never admit to an error of judgment.

I was escorted to an anteroom where a number of people awaited the king's pleasure. It was about half an hour before I was ushered into the audience hall. My leg throbbed from the exertion of climbing the many steps and from standing in the anteroom. As I approached the throne, at the far end of the long chamber, I was annoyed that my limp seemed more pronounced than usual.

The king sat on a gilded throne heavily encrusted with precious stones. On his head was a golden diadem. A rope of large pearls hung around his thick neck and looped onto his chest. His right hand rested on the hilt of his sword of state. An immense cat's-eye picked up the sunlight from the tall window and winked at me from a ring on his right hand. Behind the king crowded a throng of yellow-robed priests and gowned dignitaries.

As I neared the king, I examined him for signs of aging. The wrinkles around his heavy-lidded eyes seemed deeper, there was a puffiness around his jowls, and I detected, here and there, a glint of silver in his hair. Otherwise, he looked much the same as at our last meeting almost two years earlier.

I attempted to bow before the king, silently cursing my awkwardness.

"We have heard of your injury," the king said. "We can dispense with formalities. We have brought you here to express our pleasure and gratitude for the spectacular victories you have achieved in our name. We are told that the army you defeated at Phayao was of considerable size."

It was not prudent, but I could not resist the thrust. "And well prepared, sire. I believe the Siamese had advance knowledge of our coming and the strength of our force."

"Then," the king said blandly, "your victory is all the more noteworthy. You have earned an enviable reputation as a tactical commander. There are few under your command, Barbarian, who speak of you with other than the highest praise. If the welcome you received on your return to the city a few days ago is any indication, your fame is spreading well beyond the army you command."

There was something in the inflection of the king's voice in his closing remark that did not indicate pleasure, but his expression had not changed.

"Thank you, sire," I said respectfully.

"It was our intention," the king continued evenly, "to reduce the size and activities of the Army of the West in

the interests of economy. Its recent performance has caused
us to reconsider. It would not have a salutary effect on our
armed forces if we were to reduce your victorious army
in its hour of triumph. For the time being, it will continue
at its present strength. We hope that meets with your
approval."

The king didn't care whether I approved or not. He was
merely indicating that the army would enjoy a stay of
execution. Why he had even bothered to tell me this was
a mystery to me.

"The army has served you well, sire," I said in under-
stated praise.

"And it will continue to serve us well under your command. Effective immediately, you are promoted to general
of the first rank and placed in full command of our Army
of the West."

The king seemed to derive enjoyment from catching me
off balance. If I had been made the army's commanding
general, what had become of Vidya? Who would replace
me as tactical commander? Why had I been singled out
for this high honor?

As though he had read my thoughts, the king continued: "No turnover of command is required. Prince
Vidyanandana has been dispatched by us on a mission
to which we hope he is better suited than he is to field
command. Ambition, without sound judgment, is doomed
to failure." Then, abruptly changing the subject, the king
addressed a question to me: "Who would you recommend
to assume tactical command?"

"Commander Imre," I answered without hesitation.

The king's smile broadened slightly. "An excellent suggestion. We understand he is a convert to your cavalry
tactics. We will consider him for the post."

The king shifted his position to discuss something with
a priest on his left. The priest nodded and made a brief
reply. Turning his attention back to me, the king said,
"Desirable as the union is, we may have done you a dis-
service in our choice of a wife. Beauty does not always
compensate for other undesirable qualities. The Annamite
has yet to give you sons. We have chosen a second wife
to grace your household. She is of our own blood, a princess of our house. You will, we trust, find her well suited
to your needs. We are advised that the third day of the
week of the next full moon is an auspicious date. The

wedding will take place on that day in the temple of Neak Pean."

I was embarrassed by the king's criticism of Linh and his public disclosure of her inadequacy in childbearing. I was equally embarrassed by the honor he had bestowed on me by this second arranged marriage. I said nothing. I bowed my head in acceptance of his wishes.

I considered the audience at an end and started to back away from the king's presence. But he was not yet finished with me. He beckoned me close to the throne.

The king lowered his voice to a confidential tone. He smiled up at me affably, and this time the smile seemed to reach his eyes. "Had you failed to achieve our objectives, your heads would not have rolled in the dust. Prince Vidyanandana has yet to fulfill the role for which we have groomed him. You, had tactical command proved beyond your capacity, would have been sent on a mission of trust . . . a mission you may undertake yet."

We Chinese enjoy dissembling. We favor an oblique approach in negotiations and conversational exchanges. To penetrate the verbal disguise and discern the true meaning is a challenge to the wits and adds spice to an exchange. The Cham and Khmer, I had learned, were more direct in approach, less devious in thought processes. This can be disconcerting when one searches for hidden meanings where none exist.

King Jayavarman was an exception. His thinking seemed closer to Chinese than Khmer. What he left unsaid was often more important than his spoken words. Nothing he said was by chance. His speech had to be carefully followed to find the key to its true meaning. I believed the king chose this approach with me *because* I was Chinese. He seemed to enjoy the one-sided verbal sparring. I found it a challenging exercise in deductive reasoning. I would have enjoyed it more had I not suspected a mistake could be fatal. From experience, I knew that correct interpretation often led to startling conclusions.

I would have liked to review my latest conversation with the king with Apricot Blossom. She was quick to grasp the significance of various shades of meaning. To my sorrow, I would never more be favored with her counsel, nor was Chang available to lend me the wisdom of his years. Unaided, I would have to place interpretation on the king's remarks.

I had come to expect the unexpected from the monarch. He had not disappointed me on this occasion.

My promotion to general of the first rank, with my twenty-seventh birthday still some two months off, possibly should have dismayed me more than it did. It would, without a shadow of a doubt, earn me more enemies. I had coped with this problem in my previous promotion. I could, I believed, do so again.

Whatever plans the king had for the Army of the West would be revealed to me as its commanding general before the next seasonal campaign. The king's comments on the subject had been more for the benefit of the assembled gathering than for my edification. For the moment, I shelved that topic.

Vidya had been sent on a mission and had some future role to play. This was of no immediate concern to me. The significant points were that the king had chosen publicly to voice displeasure concerning Vidya's behavior, and the king's application of "ambition" with reference to the prince. As far as I could make out, Vidya's sole ambition was the pursuit of pleasure. But perhaps the king was more discerning than myself.

It was, I was sure, a matter of supreme indifference to the king whether or not my household was blessed with sons. In publicly parading my personal affairs, the king must have had some purpose other than to express concern regarding my lack of male heirs. He had made it clear that he did not approve of Linh's conduct. This would undoubtedly result in social stigma for her. On the other hand, by pledging a princess of the Khmer royal house to me, the king was indicating that I still stood high in his favor. It meant, as well, that it had not been Linh's importuning that led to the acquisition of quarters within the royal compound. It had been because of my pending nuptial arrangement. It remained to be seen if the Khmer princess was as "well suited" to my needs as the king claimed.

In touching on my marriage with Ngo Thi Linh, the king had said: "Desirable as the union is . . ." To me, that confirmed there had been some royal purpose to be served by the marriage—and that the purpose still existed.

I wondered if it could be connected in any way with the mission the king had in mind for me.

The most revealing part of the audience had come in the king's confidential disclosures at the end. By quoting my own words, he had simply confirmed what I already suspected—that Vidya's residence was as well stocked with informants as was my own. But the king had gone well beyond revealing that he was privy to our conversation and my suspicions concerning his motives. He had not suggested that he had had plans for Vidya and myself *if* we survived the campaign. He had made it abundantly clear that we *would* survive to serve his purpose. He could only have had that assurance by striking a bargain with the Siamese. The king had admitted his complicity. Why he had done so was beyond me.

Her name was Sita. She was the same age as Linh, but there any similarity ceased. Sita was not beautiful, but she had an attractive face. She was of about average height, full-breasted, and inclined toward plumpness. On the appointed day, we were wedded in the still-incomplete temple of Neak Pean. The king indicated his approval of the match by attending both the ceremony and the wedding feast.

Sita came to the nuptial couch already deflowered. This, knowing Khmer custom, I had expected. She was gentle, reasonably adept at lovemaking, and undemanding. Her passivity was a relief after Linh's exacting performances.

Sita was even-tempered and possessed of infectious good humor. She was inclined to be placid and accepted her role as second wife without complaint.

I had expected Linh to resent the intrusion of a Khmer princess in what had been her sole domain for three years. I was wrong. Linh seemed to enjoy her position of ascendancy as primary wife. She treated Sita with thinly veiled contempt. She was careful, however, not to openly antagonize Sita. It was by now common knowledge in court circles that Linh had fallen from the king's favor. Linh was acutely aware of this and avoided any provocation that might worsen her situation.

As a wedding trip, I took Sita with me when I returned to Lopburi. She fitted easily into the informal life-style of the western capital. The slaves and servants worked well under her casual direction. She was well liked by the officers and their wives, with whom she associated freely without a trace of condescension. Horse-master Chang, who seemed to have recovered some of his former good spirits, warmed to the princess and approved of the match.

Harmony reigned within my Lopburi quarters. Sita should have been returned to Angkor by palanquin after a week or two of staying in the western capital. I kept her with me for several months.

Soon after my return to Lopburi, I rode out to visit General Dom. The old warrior greeted me warmly.

"General of the first rank," he said with wry good humor. "At your age I was still a captain. To be honest with you, your promotion didn't surprise me. When I learned of your decisive victory at Phayao, and the ingenious siege tactics you employed at Chiang Saen, I felt the king would be obliged to honor you."

"The king," I retorted dryly, "is under obligation to no one."

"Except himself. From what you say, he as much as admitted having conspired to have the Army of the West suffer defeat . . . and to have you and the prince discredited. Your victories changed that, and his views along with it. He now sees in you an instrument to serve a larger purpose."

"If so, he has not disclosed it."

"Nor will he until he considers the time ripe. But, with your promotion, he is setting the stage."

"Maybe, or he could merely have shelved me. The position of commanding general is largely a matter of prestige—an exalted figurehead."

"I don't think so in your case. You have proven your capacity for leadership. It is a quality the king might fear, but it is one he will not waste lightly."

"What worries me is that he made no mention of a forthcoming campaign."

Dom rubbed his chin reflectively. "I don't think there will be one, at least not in the coming dry season."

This assumption surprised me. I had not even considered the possibility. "Why not?" I queried.

"I have heard that the Army of the South is withdrawing from the lower bulge of the peninsula to a line at the southern part of the isthmus. Prince Vidya-nandana's mission, I have been told, is to negotiate a peace with the kingdom of Shrivijaya. No campaign is intended there, and I don't think the king plans one in the west. You saw to it that there isn't much left to oppose us in the northwest."

"Then," I said, "the source of captive labor dries up."

Dom smiled. "Temporarily. You have dumped enough Mon and Siamese slaves on Angkor during your last two campaigns to keep the king's projects humming along for at least two years. I think he is about ready for his move."

"Which is?"

Dom pursed his lips. "I have thought for some years," he said meditatively, "that the king's real objective is the conquest of Champa."

"Then why has it taken him so long? Why would he wait until his source of recruitment is all but exhausted? That Champa might have been an objective crossed my mind several years ago, but when he made no move in that direction when recruitment was at its peak, I ruled it out."

"You shouldn't have. The king is a cautious man. As I see it, he was faced with three obstacles.

"First, the Cham's sacking of Angkor was more than a military disaster. It was a psychological blow of staggering proportion. We Khmer had not been defeated in any major battle for almost four hundred years prior to that time, and we had considered both the kingdom and the capital secure. To overcome the resulting defeatism, Jayavarman needed not one, but a series of victories.

"Second, he considered the Army of the West a threat to his sovereignty, yet he needed the army to achieve his goals of conquest. He moved cautiously to nullify the threat, as you and I have seen first-hand.

"Third, he needed to build a seasoned force second to none, yet with the assurance it would not turn against him. We have seen how he has achieved this aim through the creation of two new standing armies. He undoubtedly intends to integrate all, or part, of his existing armies into a force with the certain capability of dealing a death blow to the kingdom of Champa.

"All this has taken time—time that I am sure he begrudges. He is not a young man.

"The conquests served a number of purposes. They provided him with slave labor and permitted recruitment into his standing forces. What is probably of more importance from his point of view is that they yielded disciplined, battle-tested units.

"He embarked on a number of huge projects, again to serve several purposes. Through them, he is replacing the Brahman hierarchy with a Buddhist elite loyal to his person. The labor inputs required justify his conquests and disguise the true purpose of our incessant campaigning. My only fear is that the building of temples to glorify his person may become an end in itself.

"The king, as you have observed, is a devious man. But I don't think he has ever been swayed from his major objective—Champa. I think that action is not far off. And I think you will play a major part in it."

It was a well-presented, logical summation. If a conquest of Champa succeeded, the king would have at his disposal a well of manpower that would not run dry for decades, even centuries.

I could not dispute Dom's hypothesis. He knew and understood his people and their monarch better than I. The only point I might have questioned was the role he had assigned me in the drama.

chapter 30

I WAS RECALLED FROM LOPBURI BY THE KING IN THE Month of the Dog, a month before the rains were due to stop. I assumed the purpose was to brief me on the campaign objective for the coming dry season.

Sita, who was still with me in Lopburi, accompanied me. During the journey, she happily confided in me that she was pregnant.

I was escorted directly to the audience hall. No one waited in the anteroom. The king was alone in the audience chamber.

He sat slumped on his ornate throne. His chin sank almost to his chest. As I neared the throne, I thought him asleep, but as I drew closer I noted that his eyes were open, staring fixedly at the floor. A muscle twitched in his right cheek. He did not seem to be aware of my presence.

I coughed discreetly. The king started. His head swung slowly in my direction. "Barbarian!" he said thickly.

He straightened on the throne, composed his features, and addressed me in a more normal tone. "We do not make a practice of private audience. What we have to say is for your ears alone." He lapsed into silence.

"Sire," I prompted.

"You will relinquish your command on the morrow. Prince Indra will assume command."

I was stunned. What had brought about this sudden

switch? Had my enemies poisoned the king's mind against me?

The king continued: "At the end of this month, you will be appointed to the high command. Your official title will be Tactical Commander of the Armies. Your task will be to select the finest units from each command and assemble an army representing the cream of our fighting forces. You have two years to put together and train this force. It will be commanded by us. You will be its tactical commander."

"How large is this force to be, sire?" I questioned.

"That you will determine on the basis of its mission."

"Which is, sire?" I knew the answer before I asked the question. Dom had guessed correctly, down to and including the fact that I had been earmarked for a major role in the conquest of Champa.

"Come," the king said brusquely as he got to his feet.

I followed the monarch's stocky figure over to a silk-draped wall. The king seized the silk and drew the drapes apart to reveal an immense map of the entire region.

"There," he said, stabbing with his finger at the map. "The cursed Cham shall feel our wrath. They shall feel the kiss of the sword. They shall grovel in the dust at our feet. They . . . they . . . "

As the king spoke, his voice became more and more shrill. He trembled violently. His eyes bulged and a thin trickle of saliva descended from one corner of his mouth.

Dom, I thought, was right. The king had not been swayed from his purpose. How could he be? The conquest of Champa had become an obsession to the monarch.

The king clenched his fists and turned his back to me. Slowly, the trembling subsided. When he spoke, it was once again in his normal voice. "No one, Barbarian, absolutely no one, is to know that Champa is our objective."

"Sire," I said, "there is already speculation that Champa is to be your next target for conquest."

The kind turned slowly to face me. His countenance once more wore the benign expression that was depicted in the stone of the entrance to the temple of Ta Som and which smiled outward from the towers above the city gates.

"Speculation without confirmation," he said evenly, "is nothing more than rumor. We two alone shall know where and when nemesis will strike the Cham."

I lingered a few days in Angkor before returning to Lopburi. It was Linh herself who told me of her second miscarriage. It had occurred, she said, some weeks earlier during my absence.

"Was the fetus that of a boy or a girl?" I asked.

"I do not know. It was too early in the pregnancy to tell."

I looked at her closely. She was wan. There were dark circles around her eyes. "We must," I said gently, "have a physician attend you."

"I have had one attend me," she snapped.

"We must seek advice from a competent practitioner. If pregnancy endangers your health, we must know what can be done to right the condition."

"That's easy," she said, a sneer on her lips. "Let your Khmer sow drop your litters."

I requested that General Dom be recalled to temporary active duty to assist me. The request was granted promptly. My next request, that General Imre be seconded to my staff, met with strong resistance from Prince Indra, who had relieved me as commanding general of the Army of the West. The prince considered himself above directives from the high command.

Imre, with an intimate knowledge of the composition and capabilities of the Army of the South, was essential to my operation. I had a stormy session with Prince Indra in Lopburi, but I was unable to persuade him to part with his tactical commander despite the fact that no campaigns were scheduled for the Army of the West. Reluctantly, I took the matter to the king.

General Imre joined my staff. I learned that Prince Indra was severely reprimanded by his father. From that day forward, the prince's dislike for me deepened into bitter hatred. It didn't hamper my assigned task, but many years later I had cause to regret the prince's implacable enmity.

We got down to the task at hand in the Month of the Boar. In the closing month of the next year, the Month of the Bull in the Year of the Cock, fifteen months from the time we'd started, the job was done. The armies of the South, West, and Angkor had been reduced to approximately one-third their original size. An integrated force, more than twice the size of the Army of the West I had so briefly commanded, was encamped north of Angkor Thom. It had been dubbed the Army of the Azure Banner. It was nominally commanded by the king himself. Prince In had been appointed as second-in-command. I was in overall tactical command. General Imre was second-in-command of tactical operations.

The king's leadership was symbolic. He would actually lead the army on its departure, but he would return to Angkor Thom with his royal escort after two days of marching. Thereafter, command would be vested in a surrogate appointed by the king. I assumed the honor would pass to Prince In. I did not discover I was mistaken until the day of our departure.

During the months of preparation, I met often with the king to brief him on our progress and to discuss various aspects of the strategy I was formulating. These meetings took place in his private chambers. The Jayavarman I came to know during these sessions was somewhat different from the monarch as I had known him previously.

The king was a man of many moods. He could be exuberant, or sometimes he sank into deep depression. He could be jocular, or scathingly contemptuous. For the most part, he was coldly aloof, but sometimes he treated me with fatherly affection. I never knew in what mood I would find him, nor when that mood might change. I learned one telltale sign of approaching anger. When the fingers of his left hand twitched, I exercised extreme caution. The calm countenance he presented to the court and the kingdom was a carefully contrived facade. Behind that mask was a violent man, held in check by an iron will.

The king, I learned, was a gifted military tactician. The tactics I had employed at Haripoonchai, Phayao, and Chiang Saen had earned his sincere admiration. He agreed with most of the proposals I put forward for the coming conquest. Where political considerations shaped the strategy, I deferred to the king. He not only had sound and up-to-date information concerning Champa's political and military structure, but he displayed shrewd insight in its interpretation.

He was a lonely man. There is room for but one on the pedestal of a god-king. I do not know if he believed in this spiritual and temporal duality at the time of his ascension to the throne, but I can attest to the fact that he firmly believed himself a divinity by the time of our close association.

It was a peculiar situation. The king's obsessive compulsion to subjugate the Cham certainly had been fanned by the 1177 fall of Angkor, but it went back much further. It was a deep-seated monomania that seemed to have been implanted in his youth. Now that I had been chosen by him to translate the dream into reality, I was permitted an occasional glimpse of his innermost thoughts. He was a strange and tortured man. I probably knew him better than any but his immediate family, but I did not pretend to understand him.

The news came to me by messenger when General Imre and I were returning from an inspection of the Army of the South. Sita had presented me with not one son, but two. The twins had been born on the twelfth day of the second month of the Year of the Cock. The news filled me with joy. Sita had proven even better suited to my needs than the king had imagined.

On my homecoming, I was met by a beaming Sita and was presented to my infant sons. They were beautiful babies. I thought I could detect the likeness to myself that both Sita and the nurse assured me was self-evident.

I was surprised to find that Linh was delighted that Sita had borne me twin sons. The event seemed to have drawn the two women closer together.

The pattern that developed, when I was on one of my frequent field trips during those months, was that Linh and Sita alternated in my bedchamber. Linh had regained her feral instincts and Sita had grown more responsive.

A few months after the birth of the twins, Sita again announced her pregnancy. She gave birth to a baby girl on the eve of the departure of the Army of the Azure Banner.

It was 1190. By the Chinese lunar calendar, it was the Year of the Dog in its second month, the Month of the Snake. Our departure, led by the royal procession, was an awesome spectacle.

The king and his entourage issued from the royal gate in the city's eastern wall. Majestically, the royal procession passed down the broad avenue between the ranks of the army that were drawn up on both sides of the roadway. First came two companies of foot soldiers of the palace guard. Behind these were the standard bearers and royal musicians. Following the waving flags and banners was a column of about four hundred maidens of the royal court wearing flowers in their hair and carrying lighted candles. Next came more girls carrying the royal trophies and insignia. Following these was a company of girls of the royal ceremonial guard armed with shields and spears. Then, their howdahs topped with vermilion parasols, came a long line of elephants bearing ministers, princes, and state dignitaries. Behind these, most of them on palanquins shielded from the sun by gilded parasols, came the king's wives and concubines. The principal wives, including his chief wife, Queen Jayarajadevi, rode elephants. Then, his elephant flanked by mounted troops of his personal guard, came the king himself.

The king's elephant was richly caparisoned, its tusks sheathed in gold. The king stood proudly erect. He wore his golden diadem and his rope of pearls, and carried his sword of state. The cat's-eye ring flashed on his finger. Above his head was the white parasol of state, around which were clustered ten more white parasols once the property of proud kings now dead or captive.

To the rear of the king's elephant marched two companies of the palace guard. Between the companies, again flanked by mounted troops, was the elephant bearing the surrogate designated by the king to assume command upon the king's return to Angkor. I could not at first believe my eyes. The man selected to nominally command the Army of the Azure Banner was Prince Vidyanandana. I had not been advised that he had returned from his mission to the island kingdoms.

On the evening of the second day of our march, I was summoned to the king's pavilion. On my arrival the king dismissed his servitors, guards, and attending dignitaries.

When we were alone, the king looked at me coldly. His face did not wear its customary smile.

"Barbarian," he said solemnly, "it has taken us nine years to build an impregnable city and raise an invincible army. If our throne were inviolable, we would lead this force to its hour of triumph. This cannot be. On the morrow, we part company. The fate of the army . . . of Champa . . . rests in your hands."

The king paused; I said nothing. I knew he imagined he had enemies within his court, within his very house. He trusted no one. He may have had cause, but I had yet to find direct evidence of the disloyalty he suspected.

He continued in crisper tones. "When the Cham are brought to their knees, the kingdom is to be divided into two subject states. The northern portion, including Vijaya and Indrapura, will be ruled in our name by Prince In. He will assume the honorific title of Suryajayavarman for this purpose. The southern section, consisting of Panduranga, will be under the vassal overlordship of Prince Vidyanandana. You will then assume sole command of our army and return with it to Angkor Thom. You will bring with you the Cham king and no fewer than one hundred thousand of his subjects as slave labor. Although he deserves to die for his perfidy, the Cham king is not to be harmed. You will be held responsible for his safety."

I found the condition concerning the Cham king unusual. Defeated monarchs were not normally accorded such favor. I nodded gravely. "It shall be as you wish, sire."

The king leaned slightly forward and regarded me intently. "Some years ago, Barbarian, you correctly surmised why we had placed a Cham and a Chinese in command of one of our most powerful armies. You will have noted, we are sure, that that condition prevails once more. In the first instance, you enjoyed a guarantee of safety, although you knew it not. In this undertaking, there is no such immunity. Should you fail us, your head, and that of Prince Vidyanandana, will surely roll."

chapter 31

I HAD TIMED OUR DEPARTURE SUCH THAT OUR MARCH would bring us to the eastern highlands well before the shift of wind brought the monsoon rains to Kambuja. When those rains did come, we would be nearing our objectives, which would by then be starting their dry season. In the coastal plains of Champa, the Army of the Azure Banner would have six months or more of weather suitable for military operations.

We proceeded southeast from Angkor to Kampong Thom and from thence due east until we reached the Mekong River. When we had crossed the river, the army was divided into two forces of approximately equal strength.

One force, with Vidya commanding and General Imre in tactical command, headed on a southeasterly course. It would cross a wide plateau, thread its way through a mountain range, and descend into the fertile plains and valleys of Panduranga.

The second force, with Prince In nominally commanding and myself in tactical command, veered to the northeast to negotiate the mountains, cross the central highlands, and emerge from a mountain pass onto the coastal plain at Vijaya.

I had timed it so that the two forces would arrive at their target destinations simultaneously. Placing the two cities under siege, the uncommitted forces would converge on each other from the south and north like a giant pincer, sweeping everything in their paths before them until the forces met to pulverize the remnants of the Cham defending forces.

For some months before our departure from Angkor, rumors had circulated that the Cham were raising an army to invade Kambuja. I had not considered the story to be based on fact. It had, I thought, been a fabrication instigated by the Khmer king to justify the assembling of his own force and its launching against Champa. I learned, however, that the rumor was not false. When we arrived at Vijaya, it was to find a large Cham force being mustered some miles to the south of the capital.

We clashed with the Cham Army, which proved no match for us. It broke off the engagement and retreated southward with some of our units in hot pursuit.

By rights, the retreating Cham Army should have run into the arms of Vidya's advancing force and been ground to pieces. That didn't happen. Vidya's force had not advanced far enough north to make contact with the retreating army before it reached a large bay where most of the Cham force were embarked on Cham naval vessels.

The Cham fleet sailed north from the bay and managed to slip through the Khmer warships I had dispatched from Angkor in support of our land operations. The Cham ships arrived at Vijaya, their aim to disembark the soldiers to reinforce the city's defenses. They were too late. By the time they arrived, King Jaya Indravarman had surrendered both his capital and his kingdom.

Had the Cham forces arrived in Vijaya sooner, it might have delayed, but it would not have prevented, the fall of the capital. Had Cham forces in the far north been shifted from Indrapura to Vijaya to further reinforce the capital, it might have made our task more difficult, but, again, it would not have tipped the scales in favor of the Cham. Our forces were overwhelmingly superior to the peasant army the Cham had thrown against us. The one exception was in the caliber of the Cham naval units. They, operating in waters they knew well, had put the Khmer fleet to shame.

The Cham admiral's bold but futile dash up the coast had been made *against* the prevailing wind. He had slipped through the Khmer ships blockading the entrance to the lagoon at night, making use of oarsmen. I was informed that the admiral had been second-in-command of the Cham fleet that had invaded Kambuja nine years earlier. I resolved to meet this enterprising officer. His name, I learned, was Mohammed bin Abdullah. I smiled when advised of his name. It was no more unusual, I thought, to find an Arab commanding Cham naval forces than it was to have a Chinese in tactical command of the Khmer land forces. He had my grudging admiration. It was unfortunate that I would have to condemn him to death.

The kingdom was divided. I had the Cham king placed under heavy guard, advising him that he would not be harmed. Prince In was proclaimed Suryajayavarman and installed in the palace as ruler of the northern vassal state.

There were details to be attended to. The captives had to be assembled from the capital and the surrounding countryside. The units that would remain behind as a garrison force serving the newly installed Khmer ruler had to be selected. My force had to be provisioned. The senior Cham officers had to be sentenced and imprisoned or executed. I was kept occupied in Vijaya for several weeks before I was ready to depart for Panduranga. One of my final acts was to order Admiral Mohammed brought before me.

I was not at my best that morning. The night before I had taken my pleasure with one of the Cham king's daughters. It had been an unrewarding experience. The frightened girl had not responded to my lovemaking. I had sent her back to her quarters and had slept badly. Now, as I sat irritably going over lists of stores and provisions, a task I detested, my stiff leg ached dully.

The admiral was brought before me in chains. I did not immediately look up.

"Well, well," a deep voice spoke in amused tones, "so the cockerel has become a full-grown fighting cock. So *you* are the one they call the Tartar."

I looked up sharply into a face I remembered well. Standing before me was the pirate captain I had vowed to kill. My astonishment must have shown on my face. The admiral laughed.

"Come now," he said, "I am not yet a ghost come to haunt you."

"I thought you to be Arab," I said. "Your name . . ."

"Is Arabic," he said, completing the sentence for me. "My father was a shipmaster who plied these waters; my mother was a Cham princess. My father bequeathed me my name, my Islamic faith, and a natural bent for nautical pursuits."

Now that I examined his features closely, I could detect facial characteristics betraying foreign blood. His height, which I had noted in my boyhood, was greater than that of the average Cham. I had grown a good deal in the intervening years, but I concluded the admiral was not much shorter than myself.

"Strange are the ways of the One God," the admiral observed. "Had I known when ordered to pluck your father from the sea that his son would one day be my executioner, I would have had your head parted from your torso on the spot."

I realized that this conversation would not make much sense to the soldiers guarding the admiral. I dismissed them. When they were gone I stood up, massaging my stiff thigh as I did so. I had been right. The Cham admiral was not much more than an inch shorter than myself

So, I thought, my father had surmised correctly. Our ship had not been set upon by chance, and not by pirates —but by naval units. "Why," I asked, "were you ordered to capture my father and his diplomatic party?"

"There were two reasons. I would have thought that one of them, at least, should have been obvious after our naval invasion of Kambuja."

It had not occurred to me. I had not given it much thought up to this moment. But, as the admiral had stated, it should have been obvious. "You needed an excuse to reconnoiter the river approaches to Angkor," I said thoughtfully.

"Exactly. The ship that transported you and the Cham naval escorts were manned by the officers, ship's captains, and pilots of the invasion fleet then being assembled."

"I would have thought that our arrival during the season when the delta is flooded was poorly timed to suit your purpose," I observed dryly.

The admiral chuckled. "It was not what we intended. You were not to have sailed from Vijaya until the change of season. The arrival of your Sung naval escort advanced that date by about two months. But, as our victory attests, we were able to gather the necessary data in spite of the flood conditions."

"You mentioned a second reason for our abduction."

"As events transpired, it is a reason less obvious than the one we have just discussed. A prince of the royal house was to be insinuated into your party. When it came time for your departure, it would then not seem strange if he accompanied you on your onward journey under the pretext of being sent to further his religious education. A prince such as the one I have been told now reigns in Panduranga under Khmer patronage."

Vidya was not attracted to me by my warmth of personality, I thought wryly. He sought out my company on his father's command. At the time, I had been completely fooled, even though the relationship had puzzled Apricot Blossom and my father. I wondered bleakly if White Lotus had been instructed to provide me with diversion, as well. At any rate, I was glad to learn of the deception. It explained Vidya's subsequent attitude. As far as he was concerned, no friendship had ever existed.

I perceived a reason for the elaborate pretense. The Khmer would not be suspicious of a Cham prince who arrived in their midst as Vidya had done. "Was it intended that this prince ascend the Khmer throne if your invasion succeeded?" I queried.

"He was placed there for that purpose. He was tucked away safely in some remote monastery when the invasion took place. I know not why the king did not follow through on the plan."

I resolved to question the Cham king on that point. King Jayavarman must have known all this, I thought. He knew that Vidya felt himself cheated of a throne by his father's actions. The Khmer king had played skillfully on Vidya's bitterness, using it to serve Khmer ends.

I paced the room slowly, deep in thought. I was glad that impulse had made me order the presence of the Cham admiral. Many things that had mystified me, many things that my father had discerned dimly, were now made clear. There was one more question to be answered.

"For this strategy to be worked out, you had to have advance knowledge of our coming."

"Just so. We knew when your father was assigned his

mission by your emperor. We knew of his preparations for the voyage, and we knew the date and time of your departure from Canton. In the guise of pirates, we made preparations to intercept you. What we hadn't counted on was the storm. When the typhoon blew itself out and we put to sea on a search pattern, we had little hope that either you or your escorting vessels had survived the tempest. We were amazed to find that your ship weathered the storm. Her master was an excellent seaman. Rather a pity he had to be killed."

I stopped pacing and turned to regard the admiral thoughtfully. He returned my stare unwaveringly.

"Why," he asked. "if you knew not who I was did you have me brought here?"

"Your use of your ships during the recent engagement impressed me. I wanted to commend you personally on the performance of your fleet."

"Before sentencing me to death," he added dryly.

"Before sentencing you to death," I agreed obligingly. He shrugged. "Insha Allah."

"When I first met you," I said, "I vowed to kill you one day with my own hands. I do not feel inclined to let our executioners rob me of that pleasure. I have decided that you shall live. Your sentence will be imprisonment."

"I would," he said, "prefer execution."

"Hear me out," I said impatiently. "If you agree to what I propose, you shall be free of your shackles in less than two months."

His eyebrows lifted in surprise. "What do you propose?"

"That we establish a secret and secure means of communciation and that you keep me advised of military and political developments in Champa."

"You are asking me to act as a spy in my own country?" he said indignantly.

"It is no longer *your* country," I reminded him. "I have just handed it to the Khmer. There are some aspects of the conquest that trouble me. I must return to Angkor within a few weeks. I want to be kept informed of events here as they transpire. Besides, you are in no position to bargain. If you do not agree to provide me with reliable information, you can rot in prison until you die."

He looked at me searchingly for a moment, then threw

back his head and laughed. "You have," he said, his teeth flashing in a smile, "bought yourself an informer."

As we journeyed southward along the coast, I questioned the Cham king on a number of points. He readily admitted the plot to hold my father and his party for the purposes described by Admiral Mohammed, and he boasted of the plan's effectiveness. That my seduction by White Lotus had not been on his direction was some consolation. The king described her as a "willful child, much like her mother."

The reasons he gave for not having installed Vidya on the Khmer throne were twofold. The defeat inflicted on the Khmer had been of such proportions that he had considered the kingdom destroyed to a point where the empire would disintegrate of its own accord. Under those conditions, he had not thought it worthwhile to perpetuate the monarchy, deeming military occupation sufficient to keep the Khmer in thrall. His second reason was that he had received discouraging reports from Vidya's Brahman tutors and did not consider that his son could be depended on to govern in the Cham king's name. He implied that he had felt that Vidya would plot against him and bitterly resented the confirmation of that fear now that Vidya had indeed turned against his father.

To my surprise, the Cham king disclosed his reason for yielding his throne after a siege of such relatively short duration. He had been dismayed by the strength of our forces, but that alone had not prompted his action. Had he felt his life would be forfeited, he would have held out longer. He had, however, received assurance through a reliable source that his family would be spared and that he would be given safe conduct to Angkor if and when the Khmer forces conquered his kingdom. Under those circumstances, he had chosen not to prolong a war he could not hope to win.

I marveled anew at King Jayavarman's guile.

We arrived at Panduranga to find Prince Vidyanandana firmly in control of the city and the surrounding countryside. In his role as viceroy of the southern kingdom, Vidya had taken it upon himself to assume an honorific title. He was, I was informed, to be known henceforth as Suryavarman.

From General Imre, I learned why the force under Vidya had not adhered to my timetable in its northern advance. The prince had overridden my orders and used the forces under his command to ruthlessly suppress any opposition to his authority within the region before ordering the northward advance. He had callously slaughtered any of the regional nobility he thought might oppose his overlordship.

I was furious. I seriously considered placing Vidya under arrest and returning him to Angkor. I might have done so had there been anyone with whom he could be replaced.

Vidya received me in the palace with all the haughtiness of a reigning monarch. I was not disposed to accept this treatment. In cold anger, I accused him of disobeying my orders and advised him of the action I had contemplated. I reminded him bluntly that we were both representatives of the Khmer king, and while he was to govern as a figurehead, I now was in sole command of the greatest army ever fielded by the Khmer in their long history of conquest. I told him that if I didn't receive his full support and cooperation in the gathering up of the regional captives and the provisioning of the army for its return march, I would carry out my threat and take him back to Angkor in chains. It was a badly shaken prince whom I left behind me when I stalked out.

I commandeered quarters for myself within the palace compound. It would take a week or so to prepare the army for its homeward march. I was anxious to be gone. The garrison I allocated to Vidya was the barest minimum I considered necessary to perform its function.

I was seated on a low couch, a slave massaging my stiff leg, when a guard announced that two women sought an audience with me. I dismissed the slave, adjusted my *sampot*, and told the guard to escort the visitors to my chambers.

They were a woman of about my own age, or a bit older, and a young girl. The girl stood shyly in the shadow of an archway. The woman advanced boldly toward me. From her rich dress and jewelry, I judged her to be of the local nobility. She stopped a few feet from me, subjected me to an appraising scrutiny, and smiled. There was something about the smile that tugged at my memory.

"Tartar," the woman said, "you haven't changed too much."

Recognition dawned on me slowly. "White Lotus!" I exclaimed in astonishment. She had changed so greatly that I was hard put to visualize her as the young girl I had known so intimately. She had grown fat. Her once firm breasts were large and flabby. Only her voice remained the same.

She laughed. "Oh," she said, "I have changed. Bearing children ages women rather quickly. I have had eight since last we met in our little pavilion."

The memory of our last night together flooded back to me. I felt my face flush in embarrassment. "Your husband?" I asked to mask my confusion. "He was a prince of this southern region, was he not?"

"Ah, you remember," she said teasingly. "He was, and still is, a prince of the realm. He has been graciously allowed to retain his head and his title, thanks to my dear brother, whom Siva has seen fit to return to us after a long absence."

At her reference to Vidya, I frowned. "That was kind of him," I said sarcastically.

"Yes, wasn't it? But I do not visit you to discuss my brother. I have brought someone I think you should meet, my oldest child, Golden Dawn." She turned toward the girl by the doorway. "Come," White Lotus said, "and be presented to an old and dear friend of mine, the general commanding the victorious army encamped outside our city."

The girl advanced slowly, her eyes downcast. Her face was still partially in shadow. From what I could see of her figure, she had the lithe, pert-breasted appearance her mother had once boasted.

"How old is the girl?" I asked.

"Fifteen. She was born after my marriage . . . seven months from the date of your departure."

White Lotus, I knew, was telling me that this was my daughter. I didn't know what to think. The girl could well be of my flesh. Recalling what Apricot Blossom had told me, I could not see how White Lotus could be so positive in the matter of paternity.

"You have risen high, Tartar. My brother tells me that two princesses share your bed in Angkor Thom and that you reside in the royal compound. Perhaps you would like a third wife of royal blood. Golden Dawn is not yet betrothed. The mother may have been beyond your reach. The daughter is not."

I looked at White Lotus sharply. Surely she must be joking. From her expression, I could not tell if she spoke in jest or not.

"I think," I said gently, "we should let the girl speak for herself. You wouldn't want to be wedded to a scarred old warhorse like myself, would you, child?"

She looked up. She had the loveliest face I have ever seen. Her dark eyes were widely spaced. They were like deep pools that beckoned me. A smile trembled on her lips. I do not know why, but I felt slightly dizzy. I could find nothing in her features to remind me of my own. The only thing that could possibly link her to my blood was her height. Now that she stood closer to her mother, I noted the girl was several inches taller than White Lotus.

"Well," White Lotus said testily, "the general asked you a question."

Golden Dawn stepped forward to stand in front of me. "I would be honored," she said softly.

I was taken aback by her response. From White Lotus' look of shocked surprise, I knew she had not anticipated the answer, either.

"We shall discuss the matter when next I return," I said gruffly.

Golden Dawn reached forward. For a moment, her delicate fingers rested on my sun-blackened forearm. "I shall await your return," she said with simple dignity.

It is preposterous, I thought. The girl could not make up her mind on a matter as important as her marriage in a single meeting. Besides, she may be my daughter. I tried to put her from my mind. But as I drifted into sleep, her face floated before me in the darkness—and my arm tingled where her touch had lingered.

chapter 32

KING JAYAVARMAN JOINED HIS TRIUMPHANT ARMY OF
the Azure Banner when it was two days' march from
Angkor Thom. We would return to the capital as we had
left it, led by the royal procession. It was the last month of
the Year of the Dog. The campaign had lasted almost
eleven months. The major difference between the army
that had streamed forth from Angkor and the army now
returning was that on the westward march columns of
captives stretched out for miles in its rear.

The king received me privately. He was in an ebullient
mood.

"Barbarian, we are pleased. You have more than justified the trust we placed in you. You have brought
honor to our house and realm. We shall publicly bestow
honors upon you on our return to the capital."

"Thank you, sire."

"We wanted a few words with you in private. It came
to our attention that you had occasion to publicly re-
buke our viceroy, Prince Vidyanandana, who calls himself Suryavarman."

"That is so, sire." I wondered if I was about to be
taken to task for exceeding my authority.

The king gave a throaty laugh. "You did not believe
him an ambitious man. What think you now?"

"I knew not then that the prince considered himself to
have been robbed of a throne promised him by his father.
Yes, sire, he is ambitious."

"His father is an ambitious schemer. If there is one man the prince fears above all others, it is his father. There is no love between them. It is for that reason that we have given his father sanctuary.

"The prince is arrogant, vain, and aspires to greatness. He is also a fool. He does not appreciate that whatever successes he has enjoyed have been earned for him by others—or simply handed to him as gifts. Without you to back him up in Panduranga, he is nothing."

I did not think Vidya to be the fool the king seemed to believe him to be. We had stripped Champa of much of its manpower. I had left Vidya with a very limited Khmer force at his disposal. But he was, after all, a Cham. He was of the royal house, and in his own country. That was a combination that I would not discount too readily. I voiced none of these thoughts to the king, confining myself to nodded assent.

"On your return to Angkor Thom," the king said, changing the subject, "the Army of the Azure Banner will be disbanded, its units returned to the armies from which they were borrowed. That will leave you without a command. We do not feel that a staff assignment in the high command would be much to your liking. We have given this a good deal of thought. We considered the mission we once had in mind for you—to send you to Annam as our envoy. We feel this, too, does not offer you sufficient scope. What we have decided is that you will undertake a mission of trust for us in Annam . . . and then proceed to the court of your emperor as our ambassador."

My heart sang. This was not only a high honor, but it meant I would return to my native land. It was a hope I had cherished, but one that had grown dimmer the higher I rose in the king's service.

"Thank you, sire," I said sincerely. "May I inquire concerning the nature of these missions?"

"You will be fully briefed in good time. You are to be ready to depart with a suitable retinue five months hence when the winds are favorable for sea passage to Annam."

Horse-master Chang was delighted when advised of our good fortune. He admitted to me that he, too, had almost given up hope of seeing our beloved homeland again.

There was much to do. My diplomatic missions, particularly that to the Sung court, would involve trade negotiations. In my party I included merchants, clerks, and interpreters. My military escort was made up of a company of spearmen from the Army of the West. My personal guard was my former command, the Sixth Cavalry Troop of the Cavalry of the Golden Banner.

Linh was also delighted with the thought that she would visit Annam, although the prospect of journeying to China held no appeal for her. With Sita doing her bidding, Linh took charge of selecting the slaves and servants we would need to look after ourselves and the children.

How strange are the ways of life, I thought. My father had considered first a naval career for me. In the Khmer forces, I had risen to high rank in the army. Then my father had petitioned the emperor to have me trained for diplomatic service. In a sense, my father's wishes had been fulfilled—but I would be an envoy to, not from, the Sung court.

It was during this time of preparation that I received my first communication from Mohammed bin Abdullah. It came by way of a shipmaster of a Chinese merchantman. The message was written in the code we had devised for this purpose. Its contents were thought-provoking.

In the northern portion of the divided realm, Prince In's governorship was irresolute and capricious. There was much dissatisfaction throughout the region, particularly in and around the old capital of Indrapura, where Cham forces remained more or less intact.

In Panduranga, Vidya ruled with an iron grip. He was slowly strengthening his military base. What was of particular interest was that he had commandeered a number of naval vessels that were being fitted out to carry livestock. It was rumored that the purpose of these ships was to obtain as many Chinese horses as the holds would carry.

The message closed with the information that Mohammed had been offered command of the naval forces, the bulk of which were within the region of Vidya's jurisdiction. Mohammed, his former rank restored, had accepted the offer.

When I had struck my bargain with Mohammed, it had been on the assumption that I would be attached to the

high command and could put his evaluations to good use.
Now the situation was changed. I would soon be far removed from the scene. I appreciated that my selection for
these diplomatic missions was not based on my negotiating skills, nor was it a reward for services rendered. I had
served my purpose in the conquest of Champa, and the
king now wanted to put as much distance between Vidya
and myself as possible. In the king's estimation, Vidya,
without my military skills to prop him up, was harmless.

I should not have been concerned with Champa. I was
tired of warfare, happy to see an end to my military
career. Nonetheless, I could not help dwelling on the
implications of Mohammed's message.

I foresaw a troubled situation developing in the region governed by Prince In. The prince was not a man
of sufficient strength to hold the land under subjugation.

With Vidya, I felt the king had been guilty of under-
estimation. Vidya was by no means the fool the king
thought him to be. The prince may have shirked his
responsibilities of military command, but the principles
of warfare had not escaped him. Now he was selecting
the ablest officers available from the remnants of the
Cham forces to build a new force. His exposure to the
Cavalry of the Scarlet Banner appeared to have left an
impression. If the rumor concerning the Chinese horses
was correct, he intended to build his cavalry along the
same lines. Vidya would not be without a power base
for long. How he intended to use it was another matter.

I put these thoughts from me. Let others worry about
them. I had no intention of jeopardizing my diplomatic
status by voicing my suspicions concerning Champa.

Alhough it would be some months before it would
reach him, I coded a short message to Mohammed. In
it I thanked him for his information, advised him of my
diplomatic assignment, and released him from any further
obligation.

The only other purpose served by Mohammed's message was that I was reminded of Golden Dawn. I put
those thoughts from my mind, as well. Under my changed
circumstances, it was unlikely that I would ever see her
again.

On a Khmer merchant vessel, with four warships acting as an escort, we set sail from the head of the Great

Lake in 1191, the Year of the Boar, in the Month of the Ram.

Another chapter in my life had closed. I looked forward to new experiences and to my return to China with keen pleasure. Had I been granted a glimpse of what lay in store for me, I might have embarked on the adventure with considerably less enthusiasm.

chapter 33

WE DISEMBARKED AT THE PORT OF HAIPHONG IN THE Month of the Monkey and traveled inland some eighty miles to the capital, Hanoi. It was not an arduous journey, although the weather was exceedingly hot at this time of year. On our arrival, we were met with ceremonial pomp and taken to spacious quarters on the shore of a lake they call The Lake of the Restored Sword.

Hanoi reminded me somewhat of my boyhood home. Like Changsha, it was a river port. The junks that plied this river were similar in construction to those I had known as a boy. The Chinese influence in architecture and civic administration was much in evidence in the Annamite capital, as well it should have been, since Annam had once been a southern province of the Middle Kingdom. It had been so from the early days of the Han dynasty, becoming a protectorate during the T'ang dynasty. It had been under Chinese domination for about one thousand years before becoming an independent state when the T'ang dynasty collapsed some three hundred years ago. It is only natural that the Annamites should mirror Chinese custom and practice, even though they are markedly different in many ways.

Annam is what we Chinese call this land. The name derives from a Chinese general of the Han dynasty who was called "The Pacifier of the South." The name became applied to the country and means "Pacified South."

It is not the name by which it is known to its inhabitants. They call it Nam Viet; the kingdom, Dai Viet; and themselves, Vietnamese.

Yueh is what we call the race from which the Annamites stem. Their early history is confused. It is thought they originated somewhere in the lower Yangtze basin, from whence they migrated some two thousand years ago to the southern coastal regions of China, then down the Red River to this deltaic region. They were a backward people. In the coastal regions of China, they were conquered and absorbed by the Ch'u tribes of South China. Here, in this remote southern region of the Red River and its delta, the Yueh were exposed to the benefits of Chinese culture but stubbornly resisted integration. To call this land the "Pacified South" was either a deliberate irony or wishful thinking.

The Annamites adopted our calligraphy, religious beliefs, and Confucian hierarchical structure, but they clung tenaciously to their ethnic individuality. It is hard to credit, but they actually believe themselves superior to the Chinese.

In my dealings with the Annamites, I found them singularly unattractive. They were arrogant, bellicose, sadistic, and deceitful. Their high-born women were, like Linh, appealing in face and form, but they exhibited many of the traits I found so disagreeable in my wife. I found them to be aggressive, avaricious, and totally lacking in scruples. I came to agree with the Khmer interpretation of the Annamite character. The Khmer refer to Annamites as "people with a black heart."

The selection of myself, a Chinese, to act as an envoy to the Annamite court did not assist my petition. The Annamites bitterly resent the Chinese, considering us their traditional enemy. Since they had been overrun by Khmer forces during the reign of King Jayavarman's grandfather, the Annamites bore no love for the Khmer, which made my task doubly difficult. I could see now why the king had arranged a marriage for me to an Annamite princess. Had it not been for the intercession of influential members of Linh's family, I might not have been received by the Annamite emperor at all. As it was, I was left waiting for some weeks before being permitted to present my credentials.

I was coolly received by Emperor Li Cao-Ton, then

turned over to his minister of state. My mission was to obtain a nonaggression pact between Kambuja and Annam. Incorporated in my submitted draft treaty were a number of clauses guaranteeing that neither state would encroach upon or intervene in the territories, dominions, or spheres of influence of the other. As an inducement toward acceptance of the pact, I also offered trade concessions.

The Annamites equivocated endlessly, finding one excuse after another to prolong the negotiations. Then, unaccountably, I was summoned to the ministry and advised that the emperor had consented to ratification if we were prepared to delete the term "spheres of influence." I could have done so. The term was ambiguous and had little meaning where our territorial claims were ill defined. But the sudden Annamite about-face made me suspicious. On the pretense that I would have to consult with Angkor, it was my turn to employ stalling tactics. It is just as well that I did.

A few days later a courier arrived from Angkor to advise me that what I had anticipated in Champa had taken place. A Cham military leader had driven Prince In from Vijaya and had taken over the throne, proclaiming himself King Jaya Indravarman V. This the Annamites must have known. They must have known, as well, the rest of my communication from Angkor. The Army of the Azure Banner had been reassembled. In nominal command was none other than the recently deposed Cham king, Jaya Indravarman IV. Its tactical commander was General Imre, who had been elevated to general of the first rank. As soon as the weather permitted, the army would march on Champa to retake the throne from the usurper and install Jaya Indravarman IV as a subject monarch.

On one pretext or another, at one point even feigning illness, I strung out the treaty negotiations over many months. A season of drizzly rain, followed by cold, dry winds from the northeast, came and passed. The weather grew warmer. The spring planting was under way before I received word that Imre, with the assistance of forces from Panduranga commanded by Prince Vidyanandana, had carried the day and retaken the Cham capital.

I do not think word of this had reached the Annamites. I agreed to the deletion of the offending term, and the pact was sanctioned by the emperor.

My task was completed. We had been in Annam al-

most a year. It was with a light heart that I sent word to
horse-master Chang to make ready for our onward journey to Lin-an.

Fate decreed that the Old Stallion would not see China
again in this life. A distraught cavalry trooper brought me
the news that Chang had been kicked in the chest by a
skittish mare and lay near death in his quarters.

By the time I arrived on the scene, Chang was dead.
The gnarled old man had fought valiantly, but to no
avail. The mare's kick had caved in his chest. Broken ribs
had punctured his lungs. He had drowned in his own
blood. Troopers gathered around his deathbed sobbed
openly. I fought back the tears that stung my own eyes.
Old Chang would not want his passing marked by a wom-
anish display of grief.

One of the troopers handed me a scroll. Horse-master
Chang had entrusted it to the trooper just before he died,
instructing the soldier that it was to reach no other hands
but mine.

I did not untie the scroll until I was by myself. For
some reason I was reluctant to examine its contents. I sat
beneath a flame tree by the lakeshore for some time, the
scroll in my lap, before I could bring myself to unroll it.
Chang, I knew, could neither read nor write. The scroll,
which I assumed to be his last will and testament, must
have been prepared for him by someone of scholarly bent.
At last I unrolled it. As I did so, a square of silk that had
been within it fluttered to the ground. I placed a stone
upon the silk square, then addressed myself to the scroll.

It was the most astounding document, the most damning indictment, I have ever read. I have it still. It began
with a familiar salutation:

Siao Hu,

Your father's concubine made me swear on the
heads of my ancestors that I would never reveal to
you anything concerning your primary wife that
would cause you grief or pain. It was the firm conviction of your father's concubine that the Annamite
princess was wed to you to serve some purpose of
the king. Were you to know what your father's concubine had learned, she feared that in your anger

you would harm the Annamite and bring upon your
head the wrath of the king. I could not but agree;
still, the oath of silence sits ill with me. I believe you
should know what has transpired beneath your roof.
When you read what I am about to divulge, I will
have joined my ancestors and am no longer bound
by the vows.

Before I relate the events that took place during
your absence on the campaign against the Siamese,
I feel there is something else you should know. It,
too, was told me in confidence, but it may help you
to better understand your father's concubine and her
actions. She loved you deeply, not with the sisterly
affection you imagined, but as a woman loves a man.
This did not come about until long after your father's
death. It does him no dishonor. Slowly, she transferred the love she held for your father to you, his
son. She would gladly have died to protect you. In
fact, she did, but not by her own hand. Her maidservant, as well, Mai-ling, died in the service of her
mistress and yourself. Do not let the fact that the
concubine loved you bring you shame. She knew you
could give her only your pity, perhaps your affection,
but never your love. She respected the memory of
your father. She would never have told you of her
love.

Mai-ling kept your father's concubine informed of
all that happened in your house. People talked freely
in the presence of the mute girl, thinking their secrets
safe. None knew the girl could write. It was through
Mai-ling that the concubine learned of your wife's
jealousy, the reason she gave for wishing to leave
your house and return to China. That was not the
real reason. She also knew what was common knowledge in your household. In your absence, the Annamite took many lovers to her bed. Of those that were
named to me, I recall only two, Prince Vidyanandana and Prince Indra of the royal house. The
concubine did not wish you to hear of this infidelity
from her lips, yet she feared her love for you and
hatred of your unfaithful wife would one day betray
her into disclosing what she knew of the Annamite.
The concubine told me of this when she directed me
to accept passage on the long voyage.

The Annamite lost her child while preparations were under way to move your household to the royal compound. She was attended by an Annamite physician and a Khmer midwife. Your father's concubine learned something at that time that distressed her greatly. She would not tell me what distressed her, but she beseeched me to have her moved to the home of Mai-ling's father without delay. Had I not gone to the trading community to do her bidding, she might still live.

On my return to Angkor, both the concubine and Mai-ling were dead. I was told the story I related to you in Lopburi. I was suspicious, but I could not prove their deaths had come about in any other manner. I did not see the bodies, which had already been removed on the orders of the Annamite physician.

The next morning, I found the piece of silk enclosed here beneath the teapot in my quarters. I had it read to me by a friend, the same man who has prepared this testament. He has been sworn to secrecy. Mai-ling's message speaks for itself. I still lack proof, but I knew that both women were murdered on orders from your wife.

I know well that my words will bring you pain and anger, yet I feel you should not remain in ignorance concerning the adulteress and the evil she has wrought within your household. Let not the bitterness in your heart lead you into rash action.

I join my ancestors in sorrow at our parting, my son. My life at your side has been rich and rewarding. My spirit will watch over you. May happiness, good fortune, and longevity attend you until our spirits meet again before the Emperor of Jade.

The scroll bore no signature characters. It needed none. I rolled it up slowly and tied it carefully before turning to the square of silk at my side. The characters it bore were cramped and uneven. It had been written in haste and obviously by a trembling hand. It was with some difficulty that I deciphered its message:

Horse-master Chang,

I should not have told my mistress of the conversation between the physician and the midwife. Had I not, she would not have known that the miscarriage was brought about by herbs and instruments and not from natural causes. As you know, this information so distressed my mistress that she became ill and has been confined to her bed.

The wife learned of your mission to my father and of its purpose. She was furious. She screamed at the midwife, accusing her of a breach of trust. She must suspect that we have learned of the abortion. She has sent her physician to attend my mistress, whose condition grows worse hourly under his ministrations.

I pray for your speedy return. I fear they intend to do us harm.

Wu Mai-ling

My heart was leaden within my breast. Horse-master Chang, Apricot Blossom, Mai-ling—I had once considered them all the family I needed. The last of them was gone. What had I now? A shamelessly adulterous wife who had killed the unborn children in her womb—for I was sure now in my mind that her second miscarriage was no more natural than the first—a woman who had killed without compunction to conceal her shame and guilt. I had a second wife, a plump and placid woman of whom I was fond, but for whom I bore no love. I had two daughters and two sons, and Sita bore another life within her womb.

I sat for a long time beneath the tree, deep in thought. The rays of the evening sun slanted long shadows before I stood up and rubbed my thigh to ease the stiffness.

I called Linh to my presence. The scroll and square of silk were on a cushion at my side.

"Be seated," I said curtly. "We have some things to discuss."

She seated herself primly. "Please be brief," she said. "We have important guests coming to dine with us this evening."

"They will find no table here this night. Tell me, how many of your lovers' bastards has your family physician relieved you of?"

Linh's eyes grew round in astonishment and fear. "I . . . what! . . ."

I pointed to the scroll and piece of silk on the cushion. "These documents have just come into my possession.

They damn you from beyond the grave. One is the testament of Horse-master Chang. The other was written to him some years ago by the maidservant of my father's concubine. You knew not that she could write."

Her gaze fixed itself on the scroll in horrified fascination. Her finger trembled at her throat.

"Look on them well," I said coldly. "They tell of your infidelity. They name your lovers. In them is an account of how you aborted your second baby . . . and how you arranged the murders of two women who had done you no harm. Have you anything to say in your defense?"

Her lips trembled, but she said nothing.

"In my country," I continued, "the punishment for any one of the crimes you have committed against me and against my house is a slow and painful death. Were we in my homeland, you would suffer that fate. In my heart there is nothing but loathing for you. It is not mercy that prompts me to spare you that fate."

"What . . . what are you going to do?" she questioned in a quavering voice.

"You will leave my house within the hour. You will not return. Your daughter stays with me. You have forfeited your right to be her mother."

"What am I to do? Where am I to go?"

"I neither know nor care. But this I can promise you. If I ever see your face again, or hear that you have set foot in Kambuja, your neck will feel the kiss of the executioner's silken scarf."

My party and I embarked on a Khmer warship at the port of Haiphong in the sixth month of the Year of the Rat. Sita didn't question me concerning the absence of Linh. Although it was never mentioned between us, I believe she knew of the Annamite's adultery.

chapter 34

By sea the distance from Haiphong to Lin-an is approximately sixteen hundred miles. Even with the winds favoring us, the voyage took three weeks. We arrived at our destination in the seventh month of the year, the Month of the Monkey. It is the hottest, muggiest, and wettest time of the year in South China.

As we had been during our stay in Annam, the dignitaries of my party and I were dressed in ceremonial robes for our arrival in the Sung capital. During the sea voyage, we had favored the more practical Khmer *sampot*. I was perspiring freely, and I silently cursed my garb as we disembarked from the Khmer warship into barges that were to conduct us through canals to the heart of the city. Sita, in the flowing gown dictated by Chinese fashion, looked every bit as uncomfortable as I felt. She snapped irritably at the nurses tending the children, a thing she rarely did.

I don't know what I had expected Lin-an to be, but it was different from anything I had imagined. It had been described to me by my father, Apricot Blossom, and merchants who had visited it in recent years, but it had to be seen to be believed.

Lin-an is a seaport at the western end of Hangchow Bay. It is built on marshy ground. Its chief means of communication, for transporting both goods and passengers, is a network of canals and waterways that lace the urban area and surrounding countryside. At the time when it was reluctantly selected by High Ancestor as his temporary dynastic seat, Lin-an was not an overly large city. In the fifty-five years since it had become the royal capital, it had grown by leaps and bounds. It was now the richest and most populous city in the world. I was told that in 1192, the year of my introduction to Lin-an, its population numbered well over a million.

My initial impressions of the city, as our barges threaded through its waterways, were of overwhelming congestion and ear-shattering din. Houses of wooden and bamboo construction, some of them rising to an unheard-of height of three stories, crowded against each other along the banks of the canals. Washing, hung on bamboo poles projecting from the dwellings, formed a colorful archway above the narrower canals. From the houses came the smell of smoke from cooking fires, the odor of cooking food, and a number of less pleasant smells. The incessant noise was compounded of shouts, laughter, singing, a babble of voices, the twanging of musical instruments, and the clatter of pots, pans, and gaming tiles.

The surface of the canals was scummed with offal and, now and then, the bloated bodies of dead pigs, dogs, and cats. I was told it was not uncommon for human corpses to be found bobbing in the littered waterways. The teeming city abounded in thieves and cutthroats. I was told it was unwise to venture forth without an armed escort, even by day in some of the more crowded quarters of the city.

There were, of course, more sedate sections in the city. We were met at a boat landing by a large party of court and civic officials and taken to the Imperial Way. On this broad avenue were carts, men on horseback, and women being borne in sedan chairs. Imposing edifices, temples, and palaces lined the thoroughfare. The quarters assigned to us were well along the Imperial Way in the western part of the city. They consisted of a large residence flanked by outbuildings, formal gardens, and flagged courtyards, all of which were enclosed by a high tile-topped wall.

I was advised that the emperor was ill and would not be able to receive me for a week or two. This did not displease me. It would give us time to settle into our quarters and adjust to life in the capital. It would give me time to test the political climate before embarking on my official duties.

It was good to be back in my homeland, to hear my own tongue spoken by every resident of the city. It was equally good that on my return I enjoyed high rank and position, as well as considerable wealth. Still, I could not help but find Lin-an somewhat overpowering.

I had been little more than a boy when I had left China's shores. I was now thirty-one. Much had happened to me during my seventeen years in the barbaric lands to the southwest—and this bustling city was a far cry from the Changsha of my boyhood or the Khmer, Cham, and Annamite capitals I had come to know. Home I might be, but it was almost like being plunged into a different world.

High Ancestor had abdicated his throne the year I was born. His son, Hsiao Tsung, Filial Ancestor, had ascended the Dragon Throne that same year. It had been Filial Ancestor who had appointed my father envoy to the Khmer court at Angkor. Had he still reigned, my name would be known to him and my diplomatic tasks made easier. Unfortunately, that was not the case. Filial Ancestor had abdicated at the age of sixty-one, three years ago—at the time when I was preparing the Army of the Azure Banner for its conquest of Champa. His forty-six-year-old son, Kuang Tsung, Luminous Ancestor, now reigned as emperor in his father's stead. This gave me added complications with which to contend.

Luminous Ancestor had not been a well man at the time of his ascension to the Dragon Throne. He became increasingly dominated by his empress, a strong-willed and vindictive woman. The empress had cordially detested her father-in-law, Filial Ancestor. She had slowly poisoned her husband's mind against his father. Shortly before my arrival in Lin-an, she had succeeded in effecting an open break between the ailing emperor and the ex-emperor. This rift was reflected in court circles. The riven court was rife with intrigue. What I badly needed to know before venturing into this arena was which dignitaries and eunuchs had the ear of the empress, which of these could be relied upon to further my cause, and which ministers remained loyal to Filial Ancestor and could, by their endorsement, jeopardize my mission.

I needed wise counsel. Fortunately, I knew where to seek such advice.

My father's longtime friend, the Confucian philosopher Chu Hsi, still resided in the capital. Chu had exercised a good deal of influence on Filial Ancestor and still enjoyed a position of prestige. It had been Chu, in fact, who had sponsored my father's petition for an ambassadorial posting. No one knew the political ins and outs of the Sung court better than Chu. No one but Chu was in a better position to assist me.

I sought out the venerable patriarch and presented myself at his modest dwelling. I was brought immediately into his presence. The white-bearded philosopher, now in his mid-sixties, was seated on a low stool in his study. He motioned me to a stool at his side.

"Hsü Yung," he said cordially, "it is good to see you after all these years, although I must confess I would not have recognized you. You do not favor your honorable father . . . may his spirit rest in peace."

"I am told I resemble my mother; in fact, I so rarely hear my name that I scarcely recognized it. Due to my Khitan blood, I am known only as Siac Hu."

"The Young Tartar," the old man chuckled. "It is apt. It suits your fierce visage. We have heard of the Tartar and his exploits in remote lands. You have come to Lin-an, I understand, as an envoy of a barbaric king who calls himself Jayavarman. It is kind of you to come here to pay your respects to an old friend of your father, a man I admired greatly."

"I have come," I said, "not only to pay my respects but to trespass on that friendship."

Chu's eyes twinkled. "In what way may I serve the son as I would have the father?"

I outlined the tasks assigned to me in detail, explaining that my lack of familiarity with court rivalries and the political structure could hamper, if not forestall, my success in the mission. Chu listened intently, from time to time interjecting penetrating questions.

When I had concluded, he said, "I can be of little assistance to you personally. I have some influence with the emperor, but none with the empress. She equates me with Filial Ancestor, for whom she bears nothing but hatred. Unfortunately, as you have suspected, the emperor has become little more than a puppet. Like the Empress Wu of the T'ang dynasty, the empress dominates her husband and wields great power. Like the Empress Wu as well, she aspires to even greater power and might, if not checked, attempt to usurp the throne. I, for one, would bitterly oppose any such attempt on her part. For a woman to hold supreme power is against the tenets of my faith and philosophy. But, for the moment, she governs in her husband's name. Your petitions must be favorably presented to her if you are to have success. There are some men of character in whom she places trust. I shall see to it that you are presented to them with my highest recommendations."

"Thank you."

"Now," he continued, "let us address ourselves to your individual projects. With respect to the expansion of trade with Kambuja, you should encounter few difficulties. The trade routes to the western world have long been closed to us by the Chin in the north and the Hsi Hsia in the northwest. The Dragon Throne seeks the expansion of maritime trade by any means possible. I would caution the merchants in your retinue, however, that they should not seek barter agreements. The Sung treasury has been depleted sadly by tribute payments to the Chin and through heavy military demands. Your proposals should be couched in terms of Khmer payment in gold and silver. Another point that your trade mission will discover for itself, I mention only so that you can give them direction. Advise them to concentrate on manufactured goods rather than raw materials. There has been a decided shift in our economy during my lifetime. Urban growth has encouraged industrial development. Have your merchants seek brushes rather than bristles; cordage, not fibers; tools and implements instead of metals; and brocades rather than plainer yardgoods. An excellent example is in glazed stoneware. The imperial ware of your youth is no longer produced by the royal kilns here in the capital. This kuan ware now comes from the *chiao-t'an,* suburban factories. I understand that porcelains from your own Changsha are much in demand and should not escape your attention.

"The nonaggression pact you seek should give you no trouble. It has been the policy of our dynasty to avoid foreign entanglements and expansion through conquest. As far as I can see, that policy is likely to continue. A treaty such as you suggest would be a mere formality for the Sung court, although you may find that the negotiations are lengthy.

"Personally, I do not agree with the uses to which the explosive black powder is being put. Since it is the Khmer king's wish that you explore its military potential, I shall arrange for you to visit our military installations, armories, and arsenals. You need not mention this to the emperor. It might be misconstrued and act as an impediment to your pact negotiations. The powder itself, I understand, is made up of ingredients that should be available in Kambuja.

"As for your visit to the Chin, it would not receive official sanction and is best left unvoiced at court. I think it can be arranged, but you could not go in an official capacity. I will see what can be done."

"It is not an important matter," I said. "The visit is to satisfy my own curiosity. It was not suggested by the king. If it causes any problems, I can forget it."

"I don't think it will cause problems. We shall see. But in the most important negotiation facing you, there *are* problems. I do not think the court can help you in any way. The kingdom of Nan Chao has not been a tributary state since the waning days of the T'ang dynasty. The Sung court has little, if any, influence on its ruler. It lies in a remote, almost inaccessible, region in the southwest. To expect the emperor to exert influence to stem the southern migration of its people, who call themselves T'ai, I believe, is to request of him something that he could not grant even if he wished to. But he would not agree to your proposal. It runs counter to our policy of nonintervention in the domestic affairs of neighboring states. There, I am afraid, you will fail."

I was sorry to hear this. The Siamese were aggressive, as were the Lao tribes. Both peoples called themselves T'ai. They hailed originally from the remote kingdom of Nan Chao. King Jayavarman anticipated further clashes with the Siamese, even though they had been soundly beaten by the Army of the West. It had been his hope that China could exert a restraining influence through Nan Chao. This did not seem feasible, but I was not yet prepared to admit to failure.

The conversation turned to other matters: my father's

death, my life since then, and the highlights of my military career.

"Conflict seems to suit you," Chu observed. "Your father lamented your preference for physical activities . . . but we would be in a sorry state if the world was composed of nothing but scholars."

"At the time of his death, he had in mind a diplomatic career for me. I undoubtedly made a better soldier than I will a diplomat."

"There are similarities in both callings."

I laughed. "I prefer swordplay to the parry and thrust of words."

"Tell me," Chu asked, changing the subject, "do you find China much changed?"

"I can't say. I knew only Changsha . . . and a bit about Canton. I've yet to visit either. This is my first time in Lin-an. It's not quite what I expected."

Chu Hsi's face registered disgust. "It is a cesspool," he said bitterly. "It breeds crime and corruption as a swamp breeds noxious gases. I have devoted my life to advocating moral regeneration—a return to the high ideals of Confucianism. As far as this loathsome city is concerned, I have wasted both brush and breath. It is given over to naught but the seeking and gratification of carnal pleasures. If its capital represents the kingdom, China is in a sad way."

I recalled Apricot Blossom's contention that male prostitution was practiced openly in Lin-an. It did not seem appropriate to question Chu Hsi on this subject. There were some aspects of life in the capital I would have to explore for myself.

I waited more than a month before I was allowed to present my diplomatic credentials to Luminous Ancestor. It was but a foretaste of the procrastination and vacillation I was to encounter at the Sung court.

It was during that time of awaiting official acknowledgment of my presence that I received my second message from Mohammed bin Abdullah. As before, the courier was a Chinese shipmaster.

Admiral Mohammed started his account of recent events in Champa by saying that he still considered himself bound by our bargain. While it was true that I was no longer directly involved with the affairs of his country, that situation might change one day. He would continue to report, from time to time, on events he considered of major importance. Firsthand knowledge of this nature, he suggested, might assist me in the discharge of my diplomatic duties. He stated that there were several Cham residing in Lin-an who had his confidence and could be trusted. He named three of these.

The Cham navy had played only a minor and insignificant role in the retaking of Vijaya. General Imre's Khmer army had arrived at Panduranga and been joined by Vidya's forces. Vidya was referred to throughout the admiral's communication as Suryavarman, which I at first found confusing until I remembered it had been the honorific title Vidya had assumed.

Imre's and Vidya's combined forces, with Vidya's father, Jaya Indravarman, in nominal command, had marched on Vijaya. The usurper had not put up a fight. He had fled to the north, and it was rumored he had taken refuge in Annam.

The Cham throne was restored to King Jaya Indravarman IV, and through him the kingdom was once more in Khmer thralldom. It did not remain so for long.

No sooner had General Imre withdrawn on his return march to Angkor than did Vidya turn on his father, killing both the garrison left behind by Imre and the Cham king. The story circulated by Vidya was that the Khmer garrison had killed the king and that he, Vidya, had avenged his father's murder. To lend substance to this fabrication, the king's body was cremated with full funerary honors. According to Mohammed's account, eighteen of the king's surviving wives had dutifully thrown themselves upon the blazing pyre. Throughout this macabre charade, Vidya had played the part of a grief-stricken son.

Vidya, as Suryavarman, ascended the Cham throne and declared the kingdom a reunited entity. Within a month, he had concluded a nonaggression treaty with the Annamites and had brought the Cham army defending the northern frontier to Vijaya to reinforce his forces defending the capital. Having done this, Vidya foreswore allegiance to the Khmer king.

By that time the rains had started in Champa. The Army of the Azure Banner, well on its way to Angkor, had not been turned back toward Vijaya. In any event, it had lost its commander. General Imre had been stabbed to death in his tent by an unknown assassin while the withdrawing army was still in the central highlands.

My first reaction to Mohammed's disclosures was anger. Imre had no reason to doubt Vidya's loyalty to the Khmer king. Had he known of Vidya'a ambitions, Imre would not have requested the prince's assistance. Had he known of the hatred between Vidya and his father, Imre would have left a stronger garrison with the Cham king. If Imre had been briefed more fully by the Khmer king, none of this would have happened. Or would it? Could I have done any better?

Unlike Imre, I would have marched directly on Vijaya. I would have left a much stronger garrison with the Cham king. But my orders still would have been to withdraw my army before the advent of rain in Champa. And, once I had withdrawn, Vidya would have moved against his father. The results for Champa would have been the same, and it would have been my blood, not Imre's, that soaked into a sleeping mat.

Imre's ignorance certainly had worked to Vidya's advantage, but it was clear that Vidya had been planning the takeover of the throne for some time. I had known because of Mohammed that Vidya had been building an effective army. But had the Khmer king known this? The speed with which Vidya's pact with Annam had been concluded meant that he had been secretly negotiating with them for many months. He must have had assurance from Hanoi that the pact would be ratified if he succeeded in taking the throne. He could not have defied Angkor without sure knowledge that he could strengthen his defenses at Vijaya with the Cham forces normally employed in the north to stem Annamite incursions. It occurred to me that the usurper who chased Prince In from Vijaya might also have been acting on directions from Vidya and would have quietly stepped aside when Vidya was ready to ascend the throne, unify the country, and defy King Jayavarman. I had not the slightest doubt that Imre had been assassinated on Vidya's orders.

It was ironic, I thought wryly. Vidya must have been engaged in secret negotiations with Hanoi at the same time that I was openly negotiating in the name of the Khmer king. The Annamite emperor must have been amused.

King Jayavarman, I knew, would be beside himself with rage at the loss of Champa. He would, I was positive, field an army against Champa as soon as the weather permitted the campaign. I wondered if I would be recalled to command that force.

chapter 35

A DISPATCH ARRIVED FROM ANGKOR THOM. I WAS IN-structed by the minister of state to progress negotiations as rapidly as possible. No mention was made of the situation in Champa. I was not recalled to military service.

The rains stopped in the Month of the Dog. I could expect no more communications from Angkor for at least seven months. I settled down to progressing my negotiations "as rapidly as possible." The speed of advance was that of a paralyzed snail. The trade negotiations were going forward well, but I took no direct part in them. My particular concerns were the non-aggression treaty and the petition concerning Nan Chao. Of these, the first was cordially received, but, as Chu Hsi had predicted, its ratification looked to be a long way off. Month after month, I was casually advised that the document was under consideration. The second petition was politely, but firmly, rejected—again as Chu Hsi had rightly surmised.

I considered the Nan Chao situation carefully. Even if the Sung court had been able to exert political pressure on that remote kingdom, how could a southern migratory flow from within its borders be stemmed or stopped? I did not see how the movement of families seeking more fertile land, or seeking to escape oppression, could be halted. The kingdoms of Chiang Saen and Phayao, and the prince-doms of Lampang and Yonok, had been wholly independent states. The Siamese, as far as I could determine, had migrated to that region centuries earlier and had no connection whatsoever with the ancient kingdom of Nan Chao. King Jayavarman did not seem aware of this.

By petitioning Nan Chao to stem a flow of migration that either did not exist, or was the merest trickle, the Khmer king could produce the reverse effect and encourage migration. If the lands occupied by the Siamese and the Lao were considered so desirable by the Khmer king, wouldn't this spark interest in the king of Nan Chao?

I really knew next to nothing about Nan Chao, nor could I find anyone in Lin-an who knew much about the remote kingdom. Chu Hsi, when I questioned him, said that the kingdom had come under Chinese domination during the expansions of the Han and T'ang dynasties. If this was the case, the migratory flood Jayavarman feared had taken place many centuries ago in response to Chinese military pressures.

I wrote a carefully worded report on the subject to the minister of state in Angkor Thom. I suggested that, until we had more knowledge concerning the kingdom and its aims and aspirations, the petition should not be pressed, but shelved. I dispatched this communication via a south-bound Chinese merchantman, and I promptly put the matter from my mind.

The months of the Dog, Boar, and Rat are the loveliest time of the year in Lin-an. These autumn months are sunny and bright by day and pleasantly cool at night. I took advantage of the season to explore the capital and its environs. I took Sita, who was heavy with child by the middle of the Month of the Boar, on boating excursions on the West Lake until her time grew close.

West Lake was a haven of tranquility that provided an escape from the bustle of the city. Outside the capital, the lake nestled in a parkland of low hills mantled with trees and flowering shrubs and carpeted with grassy slopes. The lakeshore was studded with temples, pagodas, and pavilions; their flaring, tiled roofs and the bright red, gold, and green of their decoration contrasted charmingly with the darker green of shrubs and evergreens. Brilliantly painted, ornately carved sampans plied the lake, affording sight-seeing. Some of these craft offered diversions such as singing girls and meals prepared and served on board. Soldiers policed the area to keep it free of refuse.

I had ample time to explore Lin-an. My diplomatic duties could not have been described as arduous. As far as I could ascertain, the social obligations of diplomacy are its most demanding aspect. While I could not altogether avoid the ceaseless round of social functions, I attended only those I considered absolutely necessary and entertained sparingly at my own residence. This might not have endeared me to the diplomatic community, but it gave me time to become acquainted with the capital.

Apricot Blossom had discoursed on the iniquities of the city. Since her knowledge derived from hearsay rather than experience, I had discounted much she said and frankly had disbelieved her in many instances. I learned that her father, far from exaggerating the evils of the metropolis, had exercised restraint. In many facets of life in the capital, Chu Hsi's scathing condemnation was warranted.

Apricot Blossom had deplored the fact that women were held in such low esteem that it had been the practice to kill, or abandon, girl babies. A tub of water was placed at the bedside of expectant mothers. If the newborn was a girl, it was promptly drowned. This barbarous custom was of such prevalence in Lin-an at the time High Ancestor had established his court that he had issued an imperial decree against the practice. I found out the decree was no longer necessary. Urban growth had created such a demand for courtesans and prostitutes that a girl-child was a valuable commodity. For many of the poorer families, the income provided by the sale of their little "flowers" to brothels or bathhouses was a means of survival. Apricot Blossom, had she known of this new status accorded womanhood due to the insatiable appetites of the male population, would probably have preferred infanticide.

The hypocrisy deplored by Apricot Blossom's father, and bitterly decried by Chu Hsi, not only prevailed but was a strong contributing factor to vice in Lin-an. The daughters, wives, and concubines of upper-class families were sheltered and strictly secluded. The men of the family, while projecting an image of Confucian probity at home, gave free rein to their licentiousness in the city's many brothels, bathhouses, and teahouses offering the companionship of singing girls. I was informed that there were three thousand bathhouses in the city, each with a capacity of approximately one hundred customers. Some of these featured nothing but blind, or deformed, girls. Prostitutes were estimated to number upward of twenty thousand and came in all shapes and sizes, from the drabs who serviced seamen and garrison troops in sleazy dives to beautiful courtesans who maintained lavish apartments.

I had disbelieved Apricot Blossom with respect to male prostitution in the capital. In this, as well, she had not exaggerated. Male prostitutes not only existed, but they had banded together in a society for mutual protection. Chu Hsi had been so outraged by the affront of male prostitution that he had persuaded Filial Ancestor to decree the practice illegal. The punishment for male prostitution was arrest and one hundred strokes of the rod. A reward of fifty strings of cash was established for those who denounced a male prostitute. Still, in spite of this interdiction, the perversion continued to flourish clandestinely. I was myself accosted on several occasions. My reaction was not as violent as it had been when I had first been exposed to homosexuality in the cavalry. I contented myself by coldly rebuffing the advances.

I was not able to confirm Apricot Blossom's contention that there were men who bound their feet and paraded themselves in female guise, but I was assured this was not uncommon. I questioned Chu Hsi on this. He confirmed that it was indeed true and that it was not confined to eunuchs, as I had imagined.

What most repelled me about the prevalence of vice and perversion in the capital was not the licentiousness and restless search for variety in sexual acts, but the clandestine nature of their fulfillment. My exposure to the Cham and Khmer societies had made me look upon sexual gratification as a natural and healthy part of life. The native costume of those lands exposed the female form in all its beauty, while communal bathing left nothing to the imagination. Infidelity, which I soon discovered was fairly common though not openly discussed in Lin-an, I could not tolerate. I had a deep aversion to perversion, but I was no longer as outraged by such practices as I once had been. What I cannot abide is hypocrisy. When the mood struck me, I visited openly many of the better-class brothels and bathhouses. I made no secret of this, nor the fact that I supported a lovely and talented courtesan. Sita, who considered this conduct natural, did not disapprove of my actions. They were frowned upon by dignitaries of my acquaintance not because of my acts, but because I freely discussed them. It amused me to learn that I was considered in court circles as lacking in taste and refinement.

A corrupt, vice-ridden cesspool Lin-an may have been, but it was certainly a lively one. Shops in the city displayed luxury goods from all parts of China and from the rest of the world, as well. Antiques commanded high prices, as did the contemporary works of artists and artisans. Poetry and drama were much in fashion. In the market squares, entertainment was provided by theatrical performances, jugglers, acrobats, and magicians. Whatever else could be said of Lin-an, it was vibrantly alive.

I had great admiration and respect for Chu Hsi, but I did not share his missionary zeal. I had no desire to impose rectitude on this brawling, boisterous city. Had it not been for its diversions, I would have found life in the diplomatic community intolerable.

Sita presented me with a lusty, bawling son early in the Month of the Boar. I was delighted and hosted a large banquet in honor of the event.

My brood was growing. My daughter by Linh was seven, the twin boys were going on five, and my youngest daughter would be four in the space of a few months. I was mindful of Apricot Blossom's liberal education, and on my arrival in Lin-an I had employed tutors not only for my sons, but for my daughters, as well. They were being instructed in reading, calligraphy, mathematics, history, and the Confucian Classics. I made it a practice to gather them around me each evening to question them on the day's instruction and to spin them tales of the glories of their ancestors. I told them not only of my father's line, but of their Khitan heritage, as well. We spoke in Khmer, their native tongue. For the benefit of my sons, I also included stories of the glories of their royal Khmer forebears. I must admit that my youngest daughter was too young to gain much from these sessions, and the boys did not display any great interest, either. They had inherited Sita's placid temperament and were not, I fear, overly intelligent. My eldest daughter, on the other hand, was keenly attentive and hung on my every word.

In the Month of the Rat, the weather grew cooler. By the Month of the Bull, a cold, dry wind blew from the north and it was bitterly cold. I had grown accustomed to the warmth of southern climes and found it difficult to adjust to this weather. I wore thick, felt shoes, quilted jackets, and heavy outer garments, yet still the chill penetrated to my bones. My lips cracked in the dry cold. Within the residence, charcoal braziers burned by night and day, but they only dispersed the chill in their immediate vicinity. I was forcibly reminded of the winters of my youth. Winter was a season I had all but forgotten.

Midnight of the last day of the Month of the Bull ushered in the new lunar year, the Year of the Bull. In ceremonial robes, I honored my ancestors in the Confucian shrine of my residence. As I placed joss sticks in the sand-filled pewter urn, the din of firecrackers from my doorstep and those of neighboring residences assailed my ears. The noise served not only to frighten away any evil spirits that might attempt entry with the returning Spirit of the Hearth and the spirits of my ancestors, but it reminded me that I must look into the uses to which the Sung military forces were putting the black powder.

Two of my half brothers and one half sister and their families resided in the capital. My brothers were both minor officials. My sister's husband was a member of the judiciary. There had been polite exchanges between us shortly after my arrival in Lin-an. Now, in the days allocated to visiting during the New Year's celebrations, they came to my home and I and my family returned their visits for feasting and exchanging gifts. Although they attempted to hide the fact, my kinfolk were envious of my high station. They looked upon Sita and the children as curiosities, treating them with exaggerated politeness. My brothers dutifully pressed me for details concerning my father's death and pretended great interest in my adventures, but they were more concerned about their own petty affairs. I had had little in common with them when I was a child. I had even less in common now and resolved to have as little to do with them as possible. I was a stranger in their midst, an alien being. I am sure they were as uncomfortable as myself. No mention was made of my patrimony, nor did I raise the subject.

I had considered visiting Changsha, where three brothers, one sister, and my father's surviving wife still lived. After my exposure to my relatives in Lin-an, I abandoned the idea.

The cold weather persisted through the first month of the year, the Month of the Tiger. In the next month, when the weather moderated, I embarked on my investigations with respect to the explosive powder and its military uses.

As Chu Hsi had stated, the ingredients of the explosive mixture were readily available in Kambuja. The powder consisted of a mixture of saltpeter, sulfur, and charcoal. Its preparation into black powder was a simple process.

Chu Hsi was as good as his word. I had free entry into military establishments and arsenals. I watched demonstrations of various types of bombs, bombards, and rockets with keen interest. Their construction and manufacture were explained to me in detail and I took voluminous notes.

I found two inventions to be of particular interest. One was a metal box, open at both ends and compartmentalized to hold sixteen rockets. The box was mounted on a base with two upright, supporting arms so that the box was free to pivot between them. An angled arm at the rear of the side of the box allowed the launcher to be fixed at five different angles of elevation. The rockets could be fired by lighting all the fuses simultaneously or in any desired series. By means of holes in the angled arm and wooden pegs, the angle of the launcher's tilt could be altered in a matter of seconds.

The second engine of destruction was an urn-like object of cast bronze. It was about three feet in depth and one and a half feet across at the mouth. It was mounted on a bronze base in a somewhat similar fashion to the rocket launcher so that the mouth was angled about forty-five degrees from the horizontal. This angle could be altered to bring the open end closer to the horizontal by placing a bronze bar in one of three different step positions at the rear of the base to pivot the urn on the base uprights.

A quantity of black powder was poured into the urn. A cloth was placed over the powder. A heavy ball of iron, slightly smaller in diameter than the open mouth, was heaved into position and rolled down the straight-sided urn onto the powder. A thin trickle of powder was poured into a small hole in the upper side of the urn's bottom end. This device, I was told, was called a mortar.

A glowing joss stick was touched to the small hole. There was a thunderous roar and a great cloud of smoke. The heavy, bronze mortar bucked backward as the iron ball was hurled from its mouth with terrific force.

Had I had one or more such mortars at Chiang Saen, the brick walls could have been pounded to pieces in hours instead of weeks. In my mind's eye, I visualized what explosive-headed rockets shot from the launcher and iron balls hurled from mortars would do to an advancing battle line. It was a devastating picture. The destructive power of these two devices was awesome to contemplate. They would, I was convinced, revolutionize warfare in the not-too-distant future.

I obtained scale drawings of the various devices. Later, as I recorded my impressions in the form of a report, I wondered idly why it had taken so long to adapt black powder to military use. A bomb was nothing more than a giant firecracker encased in metal instead of paper. Explosive-headed rockets had been used in fireworks displays on festive occasions for centuries.

The warm spring merged into a hot, humid summer. It was the season when the winds favored maritime traffic from the southwest. I waited for news from Angkor Thom—and possibly from Admiral Mohammed, as well. The only communication to reach me that summer was from the Khmer ministry of finance. It dealt with trade negotiations. I received no word concerning any campaign in Champa, nor any acknowledgment to my report on the kingdom of Nan Chao.

The season of harvest came. I could expect no communication from Angkor until next year. I dispatched a report by a southbound merchant ship. In it, among other matters, I indicated my intention of visiting North China in the spring.

Winter gripped Lin-an. The Year of the Bull gave way to the Year of the Tiger. My non-aggression pact was still "under consideration."

chapter 36

SITA RARELY VOICED COMPLAINT, BUT I KNEW HER TO BE unhappy. She had not enjoyed the year we had spent in Annam. She liked China even less. She found it difficult to adjust to the seasonal changes. The winters she found particularly trying. She had made a halfhearted attempt to learn the language, then had given up a task that seemed beyond her. She had made no friends. The only people she could talk to were myself, the Khmer of my staff, and our Khmer servants. Thoroughly miserable, she found solace in food and grew fatter by the month.

I reluctantly concluded that she could not adapt to life in China. My only course of action seemed to be to return her to her own country. Although I had practically made up my mind to do so by the second month of the year, I delayed my final decision. I was planning to visit northern China of the Chin dynasty, a journey of some months. On my return, if there seemed to be no improvement in the domestic situation, I would make arrangements for her passage to Angkor.

Although the Sung and Chin remained politically opposed to each other, a lively two-way trade existed between them. It was for this reason that Chu Hsi had foreseen little difficulty in my visiting the northern realm in a private capacity. Provided with identification as a wealthy merchant, and armed with the names of a number of northern commercial contacts, I set forth on my journey in the early part of the third month.

The first leg of my journey was by sea from Lin-an to the northern river port of Tientsin, a distance of about one thousand miles. Except for a storm we encountered in the Yellow Sea, off the Shantung peninsula, the voyage was uneventful.

At Tientsin, I purchased a sturdy stallion and continued my journey northward to the Chin capital of Peking. After resting several days in the capital, I rode northwest to see the Great Wall, of which I'd heard much.

I gazed on this monumental work in awe and wonder. The crenellated battlements snaked along the mountain ridges as far as the eye could see. I stood on the carriageway atop the wall gazing northward to where, beyond the mountains that restricted my vision, the grasslands stretched for countless miles. The wall, fourteen hundred miles in length, had been constructed to hold back the nomadic barbarians who peopled those steppes. In height, the Great Wall equaled the twenty-foot height of the walls of Angkor Thom, but in length the Great Wall staggered the imagination.

The wall was a mirror of China's history. Credit for its construction was given to the first emperor of the militant Ch'in dynasty, the short-lived precursor of the mighty dynasty of the Han. That dated the wall fourteen hundred years in the past from the time I now stood upon its broad ramparts. But there were parts of the wall that were much older. The first emperor had linked up ancient fortifications that had shielded states such as Yen and Chao from northern incursions.

It was said that more than a million laborers lost their lives in this inhospitable region while working on the Ch'in emperor's gigantic project. I could well believe it. But the laborers, and the wall's Chinese defenders, had died in vain. The bastioned gates in the mountain passes had been forced open and the wall scaled many times. For centuries descendants of nomadic Tartars had ruled in northern China—the Jürched horsemen, who called their dynasty Chin, (Golden Tartars), being the latest.

It was while I was in this region, in Peking, I believe, that I first heard of a fierce warrior whose name was to become familiar to me—and to the rest of the world. His name was Temujin. He was chieftain of a tribe that called themselves Mongols. The tribe ranged the steppes on the shores of a far-northern lake named Baykal. Nominally, the Mongols were vassals of a Kerait prince who was himself a vassal of the Chin. Using tactics remarkably similar to those I'd employed with my cavalry strike forces, Temujin was conquering and uniting under one banner the nomadic tribes of his region. Appropriately, he had been born in the Year of the Horse. He was the same age as myself.

From the Great Wall, I turned my stallion's head southward. In leisurely stages, stopping at inns along my route, I followed the Imperial Courier road. The road threaded through a chain of fertile basins on a southwesterly course. Leaving the road, I crossed the Huang-ho, Yellow River, at a point near Loyang.

In olden times, some two thousand years ago, Loyang had been the royal seat of kings of the Chou dynasty. More recently, a mere fifty-four years ago, it had been the scene of an action Apricot Blossom had mentioned. The Sung general Yüeh Fei had driven the Chin back to Loyang and Chengchou—to the very gates of the former Sung capital of Kaifeng. Then, heeding the counsel of an adviser, Ch'in Kuei, High Ancestor had chosen to buy off the Chin rather than continue fighting. The price of peace was an annual payment of two hundred fifty thousand ounces of silver and two hundred fifty thousand bolts of silk. General Yüeh Fei's reward for his service to the emperor was imprisonment and strangulation in his prison cell. Two generals who had commanded under the victorious Yüeh Fei were publicly executed to appease the Chin.

The peace bought by High Ancestor lasted twenty years, until the year before my birth. When I was four years of age Filial Ancestor, following his father's advice, again purchased peace through tribute. This uneasy truce had lasted almost thirty years.

On my southward journey through North China, I had seen much military activity—signs pointing to a large-scale buildup of forces. The Chin, I learned, were in financial difficulties due to this military burden. In South

China, the coffers of the Sung emperor were almost empty due to military expenditures. From my experience, burgeoning forces were a prelude to but one thing—war. In my estimation, peace between the Chin and Sung would not endure much longer. War did erupt at the instigation of the Chin, but not for some years. It was delayed by a natural calamity that overtook North China a few months after my visit.

The Yellow River is known as "China's Sorrow," and with good cause. Unlike the more southerly of China's great rivers, which flow through well-defined valleys, the Yellow River meanders aimlessly over the northern plains. Down through the centuries, it has surged over its banks to flood and devastate huge tracts of land. In the process, it often changes its course by many hundreds of miles. It did so again in the Year of the Tiger, bringing great suffering and economic woes to North China.

From Loyang, my path lay to the southeast. I traversed the mountain ranges and fertile valleys of South China, crossed the mighty Yangtze Kiang at Anch'ing, and arrived at Lin-an late in the fifth month, the Month of the Horse.

The impressions I formed during my journey were of a vast and varied land—and I had covered but a fraction of it. The plains of the north, with their wind-deposited loamy soil, contrasted sharply with the mountains, lakes, and valleys of South China, where the soil was chiefly alluvial. The northern uplands were suited to coarse grains, the southern valleys and deltas to rice culture. But between the people of the north and south, there was not as much difference as I had anticipated.

During their three generations of suzerainty in North China, the Chin had adopted Chinese customs, practice, calligraphy, dress, and spoken dialect to a point where they were almost indistinguishable from their southern neighbors. Only in their capital, Peking, had I noticed remnants of their traditional Jürched garb. In this process of integration, the Chin seemed to have lost much of their former vigor. They were, I concluded, a dynasty in decline—an opinion I had already formed of the Sung dynasty.

On my return to Lin-an, I recorded my impressions of North China and the Chin dynasty in the form of a report. I did this to justify both the execution and expense of the journey. I had defrayed its cost not from personal but from embassy funds, even though the trip had not been authorized.

Shortly before my return to Lin-an, the former emperor, Filial Ancestor, had died. Luminous Ancestor, on the urging of his empress, refused to perform the traditional mourning rites. This breach of filial duty was widely condemned. Chu Hsi, and many staunch Confucians, were calling for the ouster of the emperor. I took no part in this controversy, although I thoroughly agreed with Chu Hsi's outraged attitude.

In the sixth month, the Month of the Ram, Luminous Ancestor yielded to the mounting pressure and abdicated. He was succeeded by his son, Ning Tsung, Tranquil Ancestor, a young man eight years my junior.

One of Tranquil Ancestor's first actions on ascending the Dragon Throne was to instruct his prime minister to clear the substantial backlog of court business. Within less than a month, the non-aggression pact between Kambuja and China was signed and sealed.

In the latter part of that same month, the Month of the Monkey, I received two communications. One was from the Khmer minister of state. He acknowledged my report on the kingdom of Nan Chao, instructing me to withhold further action for the time being. He requested information concerning my progress with the non-aggression pact. By his dispatch I was instructed to compile a report on the commercial seaports of southeastern China. Again, there was not a word about Champa. The second communication, a coded message from Admiral Mohammed, brought me up to date on the latter score.

During the early part of the dry season of the previous year, the Army of the Azure Banner had appeared near Vijaya. No attempt had been made by the Cham army to meet the Khmer on the field of combat. A Khmer fleet had put in an appearance to blockade Vijaya. The Cham capital had been placed under siege.

Admiral Mohammed's naval forces had engaged the Khmer units and soundly defeated them. Throughout the siege, the capital was freely supplied with produce and reinforcements by the Cham navy.

Vijaya withstood the siege. Shortly before the rainy season, a frustrated Army of the Azure Banner had withdrawn to the west.

This year, at about the time I had been returning to Lin-an, another Khmer army had marched on Vijaya. This time the Cham army met them on a plain to the northwest of the capital. The battle raged for two days, with heavy casualties on both sides. It was the Cham who emerged the victors. A badly mauled Khmer army had retreated into the central highlands, pursued and harassed by Cham forces. No Khmer naval units had taken part in this second campaign.

Mohammed did not sound entirely pleased with the situation in the kingdom. He exulted, naturally enough, over the military triumphs of the Cham, but the cost of the victories troubled him. Champa, he stated, was groaning under heavy taxation and manpower levies to support the army Vidya had built up to defy and defeat the Khmer forces. Vidya's reign was becoming tyrannical. He ruthlessly suppressed any opposition. Even the mildest criticism met with imprisonment or public execution. Several nobles and high-ranking officers with loyalties to the former regime had been tried on trumped-up charges in recent months, sentenced to death, and executed. Although he didn't say so, I gathered that Mohammed did not feel secure in his own rank and position.

What I could not understand was why I received none of this information concerning the situation in Champa from Angkor Thom. I was also in total ignorance with respect to affairs within Kambuja and the empire. Granted that for long periods of the year no communications could reach me, and when they did the news was outdated, but it made no sense to me that an ambassador on foreign soil was not kept informed on political and military matters pertaining to the country he represented.

I could only conclude that this information was being withheld deliberately. Perhaps the Khmer king wished to keep the news of his military reverses from myself and my staff in case we would inadvertently pass it on to the Sung court to the prejudice of his and our position. Had I known the real reason I was being kept in the dark, I would have been much more concerned.

The rout of the Khmer army at Vijaya was a serious setback for Kambuja. Had I been in tactical command of the army, the outcome might have been different. That I had not been recalled to active duty I put down to face-saving. Neither the high command nor the king would look with favor on placing a Chinese in command of their recently defeated forces. To do so would be an admission of Khmer ineptitude.

My assessment of the high command's attitude proved to be reasonably on target. With King Jayavarman, I was wide of the mark. I should have known better. Gods, since they are incapable of error, are not concerned with loss of face.

When I broached the subject of her return to Angkor to Sita, she raised halfhearted objections. It was not a very difficult task to persuade her to my point of view.

I was sending her children with her, together with the Chinese scholars who were their tutors. Since they were products of mixed cultures, I felt the children should be given the benefit of education in both Khmer and Chinese traditions. To be truthful, I was not too optimistic. It was a bit early to judge with respect to my youngest daughter and her baby brother, but the twins seemed to me rather dull-witted.

Trac, as Linh had named our daughter, in honor of an Annamite queen who had driven the Chinese from her realm, albeit briefly, I decided would remain with me in Lin-an for the time being. She was a lively, intelligent child. She did not get on too well with her half brothers and half sister. I felt she would be better off with me. She, at least, showed promise in her studies. She was of an age when her isolation from the male members of the family should start and when her feet should be bound. I expanded her tutelage to include cooking, singing, and embroidery, but I would not permit foot binding. For this departure from accepted custom I was widely criticized.

On a warm, clear day in the Month of the Boar, Trac and I stood on the deck of a barge and waved good-bye to a high-sterned junk that bore Sita and her brood on their southbound journey.

The departure of Sita and the children wrought changes in the domestic scene that I had not fully anticipated.

Sita, despite her self-indulgence and indolence, had run the household with reasonable efficiency. True, she had had at her disposal an ample household staff of both Khmer and Chinese servants under the able stewardship of a Chinese factotum, but hers had been the deciding voice in the planning of menus, arrangements for social functions, squabbles among the servants, and disputes with tradespeople. Now, with no woman to run my house, these duties fell to me. They were not particularly onerous, but they were nonetheless little to my liking. Thanks to Apricot Blossom, then Linh and Sita, I had had little exposure to the petty annoyances and day-to-day problems of domestic management. I had, I am afraid, taken the smooth functioning of my household for granted. Sita had not been gone a week before I found myself fervently wishing for a woman to remove this domestic burden from my shoulders.

Since the advent of our last son, I had summoned Sita to my bedchamber but rarely. Her growing obesity had made her considerably less attractive in my eyes. I had derived my sexual gratification from the courtesan I maintained, and, when the mood struck me, from various accommodating young ladies of bathhouses and the more fashionable brothels. I continued this practice following Sita's departure and did not miss her in that capacity. Unaccountably, however, the very fact that there was now no wife to summon to my bed, should I desire her presence and services, I found intensely irritating.

I toyed with the idea of moving my courtesan from her apartments to the residence. There was another avenue open to me if I craved female companionship. The Sung court made it a practice to supply courtesans to foreign embassies for any desired length of stay. I could have availed myself of this privilege. It was an impersonal arrangement well suited to my present needs. I rejected both of those passing thoughts for two reasons. The first was that I didn't feel it proper that a courtesan should assume the role of mistress of my house. The second, and more compelling, reason was my daughter. Trac was at an impressionable age, and I did not feel that the presence of a courtesan would prove a desirable influence.

I could, of course, take another wife. It had been suggested that it would not be difficult to arrange a suitable marriage. In court and commercial circles, I had been introduced to a number of young ladies of marriageable age. By reason of my exalted position, I was considered a most desirable match. I was, however, reluctant to embark upon another contract of that nature due to my unsatisfactory experiences with two arranged marriages. I decided that, for the time being, at least, my house could do without a mistress. That I changed my thinking in this regard before many months had passed was due to Trac.

Trac was nine. In the spring of the coming year she would be ten. Already she showed promise of being a great beauty. I had feared that she would miss her half brothers and half sister, but this did not appear to be the case. She did not lack for companionship since there were many children her age belonging to the resident household staff with whom she played. Now, in our evening sessions wherein I questioned her on her studies and spun yarns for her benefit, I allowed Trac to include two or three of her favorite companions. In truth, I expanded the gathering as much to have an audience as to give her companionship. I found, somewhat to my amazement, that even though the twins and their younger sister had not been an attentive group, I missed their presence more than I cared to admit.

I should not have been unduly concerned with respect to Trac. She not only had young friends to divert her; she had, as well, her nurse, a governess, several body servants, and a number of tutors. Hers was a full day. Nonetheless, perhaps as much for my own enjoyment as for hers, I adopted the practice of taking her with me on excursions to West Lake and to various eating establishments, where I delighted in introducing Trac to cuisines from the far corners of the realm and foreign lands. On these outings, she skipped along at my side chatting animatedly on all manner of subjects and bombarding me with questions.

Two incidents involving Trac took place in the Month of the Rat. The combined effect of these events served to channel my thinking concerning the introduction of a permanent mistress to my household.

The first incident, which I found most disturbing, occurred in mid-month. I had taken Trac on a sight-seeing boat ride on West Lake on a bright, crisp afternoon. Throughout the trip, she had been unusually quiet. I appreciated that she had something on her mind, but I refrained from questioning her, confident that she would reveal whatever it was that troubled her before the day was done. I was not mistaken.

Late in the afternoon, we stopped at a lakeside pavilion for tea and cakes. Trac paused in mid-bite, looked at me solemnly, and queried with disconcerting directness, "When is Mummy coming back?"

I misunderstood her question. "She did not like the climate. She has taken the children back home and won't be coming back. We may be joining her next year."

"I didn't mean *her*," Trac said impatiently. "I meant my *real* mother."

It came as a distinct shock. I had all but put Linh completely from my mind. Now, as I looked at the earnest little face across the table, memory swept back painfully. I was stricken with dire misgivings. I wondered what Trac had heard from the servants who had been with us in Hanoi, or from their children, that had prompted her question.

"Your mother," I said, choosing my words with care, "cannot return to us. I am afraid she has gone away for good."

"Why? Is she dead?"

What had the child been told? "Did someone tell you she died?" I questioned.

"No, not exactly . . . but if she isn't dead, she could come back, couldn't she?"

I deliberated a moment before answering. I did not want to lie to Trac; on the other hand, I could hardly tell her the truth and expect her to comprehend why I had banished her mother from under my roof. I chose the course of dissimulation.

"She has gone from our lives. There is no way that she can come back in my lifetime. Would you say then that she's dead?"

Trac munched on a sweet cake, a frown of concentration on her face. "Yes," she said gravely. "If she *can't* come back, she *has* to be dead." Licking her fingers, she looked at me questioningly. "Did you love her very much?"

"You would not be here had we not loved each other," I answered ambiguously.

"Was she very beautiful . . . as beautiful as they say?"

"Yes," I answered truthfully, "she was beautiful . . . almost as beautiful as you will be one day."

"Then," Trac said brightly, "I hope I am just like her when I grow up." Then, with the disconcerting swiftness with which her mood could change, she jumped from her stool and ran to the ornamental railing. "Look, Papa," she laughed excitedly, "come and look."

I joined her at the railing to watch a mother duck, trailed by tumbling ducklings, waddle sedately to the water's edge.

We returned home by sedan chair. Trac made no further mention of her mother. She was her normal self, chatting away brightly on a variety of topics. My answers concerning her mother seemed to have satisfied her curiosity, whatever had prompted it. I, I must admit, was far from satisfied. Her questions had shaken me.

When we arrived at the residence, I kissed Trac fondly and sent her off to the women's quarters for her evening meal. I sat down to a solitary repast with a troubled mind.

I prayed to the gods and my ancestors that the child's wish to be like her mother would not come true. I believed that Linh had no real affection for her daughter and was not, in my estimation, a fit mother for the child. But now, for the first time, I had cause to doubt the wisdom of my action in depriving the child of her rightful mother. And the incident set in motion another train of thought. Within a few years Trac would make the transition to womanhood. She would need guidance—instruction in matters pertaining to sex and female deportment that were beyond my competence. I resolved to talk seriously with Trac's *amah* and governess concerning these aspects of the child's education. The problem, I recognized, would have been solved automatically had I not allowed Sita to return to her homeland.

Disturbing as was my conversation with the child concerning her mother, it was a second incident involving Trac that crystallized my thinking and galvanized me into action. To discharge my social obligations, it was my practice to·host a large reception at the end of the eleventh month—the Month of the Rat. To this end, I had conducted several conferences with my steward and chief cook with respect to decoration, floral arrangements, staff duties, and the food and drink to be served my guests. As I recall, Trac was present at at least one of those discussions.

On the evening before the function was to take place, I went to the main kitchen to satisfy myself that everything was proceeding smoothly. I paused on the threshold, witness to an unlikely scene. Trac, her back to me, was addressing the assembled kitchen staff. In a piping voice, she was imperiously issuing detailed instructions concerning the preparation and presentation of the food and beverages for the morrow's function. The staff, their bearing respectful but their twinkling eyes betraying suppressed amusement, listened attentively to Trac's instructions. The chief cook noticed my presence in the doorway and favored me with a broad wink. Without making my presence known, I withdrew, chuckling to myself.

A short time later, after some reflection, the incident did not appear so amusing. My close association with the child over the past weeks had caused her to adopt a proprietary attitude not only to myself, but to my household. Obviously, she considered it her right, her duty, to assume the role of lady of the house. The authoritarian attitude the child had displayed toward the kitchen staff, ludicrous though it might appear at first glance, was a disconcerting mirror image of her mother's approach to the servants. This must not be allowed to continue. My house *must* have a mistress other than a nine-year-old child.

I was not prepared to consider another marriage. I decided, as my father had before me, to take unto myself one of the lovely young ladies of Lin-an in the capacity of a concubine.

By the time the winds of winter struck the capital in full force in the Month of the Bull, Jade Ring was installed in the women's quarters as chatelaine of my establishment and as a decorative and welcome addition to my bedchamber. She was the demure daughter of a minor court official who was delighted with the honor I had bestowed

upon his house. Trac appeared to accept her reversion to
the status of elder daughter with good grace.

As I paid homage to my ancestors on the advent of the
Year of the Hare, I could not help thinking that 1194, the
Year of the Tiger, had been an eventful year.

chapter 37

WHILE MY DILEMMA WITH TRAC CERTAINLY PRECIPITATED my action, it should not be concluded that I rushed heedlessly into my contractual arrangement with Jade Ring. I believe that I subconsciously sought to emulate my father's felicitous selection of a concubine from the first moment I set foot in Lin-an.

In the closing months of Sita's last pregnancy, and when she presented me with our youngest son, I gave no heed to my subliminal desire. Over the next two years, as Sita grew fatter and fatter and correspondingly less appealing, I found myself seeking out more attractive company. My setting up a courtesan in her own establishment was an indirect result of my growing disaffection at home. I gave no conscious direction to the selection of a suitable concubine to grace my establishment, but the thought must have been there, even if submerged. For, when the decision to seek a concubine was forced upon me, I found that I had already categorized many of the young ladies who had been presented to me and mentally winnowed them down to a mere handful.

Why did I select nineteen-year-old Jade Ring from those I considered to have suitable qualifications? A number of factors influenced my decision. While not literate, Jade Ring had at least a smattering of education in calligraphy, which was more than could be said for her competitors. She was adept at the arts of embroidery and music, and she had a captivating singing voice. What was even more important, from my point of view, was that she was well schooled in cooking and household management. Through her family association, she seemed well versed in the political structure of the realm. While her knowledge of history and geography was cursory, extending little beyond the confines of the capital and not at all to the barbarous realms beyond the borders of the Middle Kingdom, she was an avid listener and, I believed, intelligent. In time, I felt she could become my confidante as well as my consort. Her performance in the bedchamber had yet to be put to the test, but I found her lovely in face and form, provocative, and highly desirable. But I suppose the feature that most attracted me to her was that her delicate beauty put me in mind of Apricot Blossom as she had been when my father had brought her to Changsha twenty years earlier.

As I had fully anticipated, Jade Ring came to me a virgin. I was gentle in my initial lovemaking. Jade Ring was responsive and increasingly amorous. I soon found that I had no desire for pleasures outside my own bedchamber. I continued my visits to my courtesan's establishment out of a sense of duty, but they became infrequent and perfunctory. My visits to brothels and bathhouses ceased entirely. Finally, in the first month of the new year, I came to a financial arrangement with the courtesan, released her from any continuing obligations, and stopped visiting her altogether.

In the "flowery battle," as we conducted it in those early weeks of our association, I must say that I was more than pleased with Jade Ring's performance. Under my tutelage, she learned quickly how best to arouse and sustain my passion. She was, in turn, coquettish, smolderingly seductive, and wildly passionate. She derived as much pleasure as I did from our prolonged and frequent sessions of copulation. She acted upon me like a heady drug. I found myself hopelessly infatuated with this new and captivating mistress of my domicile.

If I may be forgiven, I would like at this point to digress and touch once more upon the practice of foot binding. It must be borne in mind that I left my homeland at the age of fourteen and had given little thought to the subject other than the fact that my mother's unbound feet had set her apart from my father's older wives. From that point, until my return to China eighteen years later, all but one of the women to whom I had been exposed, and all those with whom I'd had intimate relations, had unbound feet. The one exception, of course, was Apricot Blossom.

In an earlier portion of my chronicle, I gave Apricot Blossom's views on the custom as it was discussed between us. Her opinion, that the practice was a demeaning imposition on her sex, more or less reinforced whatever vague thoughts I had previously held and formed the basis for my preconceived convictions on my homecoming. I looked upon bound feet with aversion, considering the deforming practice an iniquitous aberration.

Once in Lin-an, however, where I was exposed to the tiny lotus feet of ladies of quality and their less fortunate sisters who emulated the fashionable practice, my thinking underwent a gradual change. For the first time in my life, I saw bound feet without their gauze wrappings. While they were pitifully malformed, I did not find the tender lotus buds as repelling as I had anticipated. I did not find them attractive, nor did they stimulate me as they appeared to do to men of my acquaintance, but I grew accustomed to them. I was able to ascertain answers to those questions Apricot Blossom had not considered herself competent to answer.

I recalled that Apricot Blossom had observed dryly that the custom could not have prevailed for centuries without the willing compliance of the fair sex. Unquestionably, bound feet were a symbol of status—the status being that of high station, or of ladies who devoted their talents to sexual gratification for monetary gain as favored courtesans or prostitutes. In either category, the women considered their lotus feet as objects of beauty and marks of distinction. I found that many women were inordinately proud of their tiny feet. Jade Ring was one who was of that persuasion.

One aspect of foot binding had been overlooked in my discussion with Apricot Blossom—or it may have been that she was not aware of its prevalence in Lin-an. Many women believed that bathing the feet caused them to grow larger. The first time I was exposed to the overpowering odor of unwashed feet I gagged and curtly ordered the prostitute to rebind the offending appendages. She was highly incensed and informed me that most men were excited by the smell of unwashed feet, which acted on them like an aphrodisiac. On another occasion, I caught a whiff of the ripe odor before the girl had completely unwrapped her tiny feet. I lost all desire. I upbraided her for her lack of cleanliness, placed some money on the mat, and left. As I descended the steps from the upper story to the floor beneath, with as much dignity as I could muster, I was followed by a stream of shrill obscenities.

Although Apricot Blossom claimed she derived no enjoyment from the fondling of her lotus feet, I can attest to the fact that she was the exception rather than the rule. The tiny, constantly protected feet were excessively sensitive, and, with most women, definitely erogenous. On Jade Ring's direction, I fondled, pinched, and squeezed her tender lotus feet during our extended foreplay. The nibbling, biting, and fondling of lotus feet is supposed to have an erotic appeal for men. This was not so in my case, but I became aroused by Jade Ring's moans of pleasure as I caressed her sensitive feet.

I came to the conclusion that Chinese women were not to be pitied for their deforming aberration. Women, I have discovered, will quite happily undergo almost any distress to conform to the dictates of fashion. I had confirmation of this from an unexpected source in the late summer of the Year of the Hare. But I have digressed enough and am getting ahead of my story.

Jade Ring was all that I had hoped for as a chatelaine. The household ran effortlessly and smoothly. I undertook more entertaining at the residence than had formerly been my wont. Unfortunately, my infatuation blinded me to, or caused me to overlook, certain negative aspects in our relationship.

Her knowledge of the politics of the capital, I soon discovered, was superficial. She was shrewd rather than intelligent. She was a good listener only because she had little to contribute to any conversation that went beyond her limited sphere of knowledge. If I had thought I had acquired a second Apricot Blossom, I was sadly mistaken. Jade Ring bore a striking resemblance to my father's late concubine in her youth, but there any similarity ended. I was disappointed, but I was sufficiently enamored of Jade Ring to accept her imperfections.

In a way, Jade Ring reminded me somewhat of Linh. Although she did not carry it to the narcissistic extremes Linh had exhibited, Jade Ring was vain. She spent a good deal of her time selecting silks and brocades, being fitted for new gowns, being coiffed by her hairdresser, and being bathed, scented, and having cosmetics skillfully applied by her handmaidens. In clothing and jewelry, Jade Ring had expensive tastes. Since I derived a good deal of pleasure from her beauty, I did not begrudge Jade Ring the time she devoted to her toilette. These were, after all, womanly pursuits, refinements in which I hoped she would instruct Trac.

It was in her relationship with Trac that I was keenly disappointed in Jade Ring, although, in all fairness, the fault was not all on Jade Ring's side. I had hoped that Jade Ring could exert the maternal influence I felt Trac badly needed. What I had not counted on was the antipathy that developed between the child and the concubine.

I was slow in appreciating the situation. The signs were all too evident, yet in my early infatuation with the concubine I chose to ignore the mounting tensions. Trac, while she was still often gay and affectionate during my evening sessions with her and her young companions, grew increasingly moody and withdrawn. At the same time, Jade Ring was often unaccountably irritable. One evening, late in the third month, matters were brought sharply into focus and could no longer be ignored.

That evening Trac came to my study. Her little face was puffy from recent crying. Gently, I questioned her to determine what troubled her. She burst into tears. Through her sobs, she blurted out that Jade Ring had slapped her for no reason.

I was angry that Jade Ring would have the temerity to strike the child, yet I reasoned that the concubine could not have done so without *some* justification. Later that evening I questioned Jade Ring concerning the incident. She immediately flared up.

"She is a deceitful, spiteful child," Jade Ring said defiantly. "She has tried my patience to its limit. I will not tolerate her insolence and lack of respect for my position as mistress of your house."

I was astonished by this uncharacteristic outburst. "She has been impertinent to you?" I asked incredulously.

"She is *always* impertinent. How can I discharge the

duty you have placed upon me if the girl will not accept my advice or do my bidding? How can I run your household efficiently if she sets the servants against me?"

"How could she influence the servants? She is but a child."

"She has spread gossip and vicious lies about me through her *amah* and through her companions among the children. To you I am sure she will deny this, but it is true. She is almost ten and will soon be a woman . . . but what kind of a woman I dare not contemplate. I can do nothing with her . . . nothing. You have sons to carry on your line. I hope to present you with more sons in time. Why do you feel it necessary to rear this girl as though she were a son?"

"She is being instructed in the womanly arts," I countered defensively. I did not consider it wise to add that I had known a woman educated in a similar manner to that which I had devised for Trac. She had been a woman who was sensitive, loyal, loving, and the essence of femininity.

"Yes, and in calligraphy, sciences, and the classics. I am surprised you have not included horsemanship and the martial arts in her curriculum. Do you want her to become a civil administrator?" Jade Ring retorted scathingly. Then she added, "Such schooling is not seemly for ladies of breeding. It would be unheard of in my father's house."

I felt a twinge of guilt. I *had* contemplated having the stable master instruct Trac in horsemanship. Perhaps I *was* being too liberal and unconventional in the matter of Trac's schooling.

"This," I said curtly, "is not your father's house. Nonetheless, I shall consider your position and point of view. Until I have had time to reflect on it, we will consider the matter closed."

It is much easier, I have found, to maintain discipline and morale in a military force than it is to promote harmony in a household where emotional elements cloud the issues. As I saw it, the best way to reduce the friction between Trac and Jade Ring was to keep them as widely separated as possible until I could effect a reconciliation between them. To this end, I relieved Jade Ring of direct responsibility with respect to Trac's instruction in matters pertaining to her sex and station. Instead, Jade Ring would supervise such instruction through the girl's nurse and governess.

I then summoned Trac's *amah* and governess to my presence. I admonished them for spreading false stories concerning Jade Ring and cautioned them against such a practice on fear of instant dismissal. They both protested vehemently that they had not been guilty of gossip. From their shamefaced countenances, I suspected that there was a good deal of truth to Jade Ring's assertion. I appreciated, however, that mine was a useless dictum. To stop rumors and gossip in a household of many servants is like trying to command the wind to stop blowing. I then told them sternly that they must discipline Trac severely if they found she was fabricating or spreading falsehoods. Next, I advised them that henceforth they would be responsible for Trac's instructions in deportment and matters pertaining to her sexual education. In this area, unless I directed otherwise, they were to be guided and directed solely by the mistress of the house.

Lastly, I had a long, serious discussion with Trac. I pointed out to her that she owed the same deference to Jade Ring as mistress of the house as she would owe Sita or her own mother. I demanded of Trac that she accord Jade Ring the same respect as she would myself. I sternly commanded the child not to antagonize Jade Ring in any way. If I were to learn that she had disobeyed me, I would not only be very disappointed, but, I intimated, there would be dire and instant reprisals at my hand. Trac listened to me solemnly, then dutifully agreed to comply with my directives.

Peace, albeit an uneasy one, descended on my household. It was the best I could do for the moment, since my duties called for my absence from the capital for the better part of the summer.

Late in the fourth month I and the staff I had selected to conduct a survey of the more important ports of southeastern China embarked on a Sung warship that had been placed at my disposal. We sailed first to the Pearl River estuary and the port of Canton.

The busy river port had changed but little since I had first become acquainted with it two decades earlier. I was reminded of the inexorable passage of time only by the fact that my father's friend any my erstwhile benefactor, the former governor of the city and prefecture of Kwantung, had joined his ancestors two years before my return to China. I had repaid the sum advanced to Horse-master Chang on my behalf many years ago, yet I would be indebted eternally for his generosity. I took advantage of my brief sojourn in the city to pay my respects to the surviving members of the ex-governor's family.

The survey consisted of the assembling of data on harbor depths and approaches, port facilities, the types of cargo available, lists of the more important commercial establishments, and prevailing economic and political conditions. In addition, as an emissary of the Khmer court, I was called upon to entertain local officials and prominent businessmen. It was not a particularly difficult task, but it was time-consuming.

From Canton we sailed to the northeast, calling at the ports of Swatow, Amoy, Ch'uanchou, Fuchou, Wenchou, Nant'ung, and Nanking, the latter two being the major ports in the Yangtze estuary.

My staff and I disembarked from the warship at Nanking and returned to Lin-an by an overland route. It was now the first week of the seventh month—the Month of the Monkey. I had had ample opportunity to sample the delights of the various ports of call, but I had exercised considerable restraint. I was anxious to receive the tender ministrations of Jade Ring and looked forward to my homecoming. It was my hope that nothing had happened during my absence to disturb the tranquility of my household.

I arrived home to be greeted by an unpleasant situation. A month earlier, Jade Ring had been stricken with a fever and a severe chest infection. She was being attended by a physician and had installed one of her sisters in the women's quarters to see to the running of the establishment. The physician assured me that Jade Ring was on the way to recovery but that she would need care and rest for several weeks to come.

Jade Ring imparted some sad news. She had discovered herself to be pregnant shortly after my departure, but, due to the fever, she had lost the baby. I consoled her, stating that we would have more than enough time to conceive other children once she had regained her health.

At least on the surface, Trac seemed to have regained her former good spirits. I noted, however, that she did not mention Jade Ring, nor did she inquire after the concubine's condition.

I busied myself with the survey report, although, quite frankly, I could not see what purpose it would serve. Most of the data contained in the report was well known to Khmer traders and seafarers.

During the Month of the Monkey, Jade Ring made excellent progress. By the last week of the month, she was well enough to visit my bedchamber.

As though Jade Ring's return to my bed was a signal, Trac became once more of contrary and unpredictable temper. One evening toward the end of the month, she treated me to a totally unexpected outburst.

"Why," the child said angrily, "must I be like a servant or peasant of the fields?"

I didn't at first follow her reasoning. "You are of high station," I retorted lamely. "I am descended from emperors of the realm. Your mother was of Annamite royal blood. What do you mean?"

She stamped her foot and pointed to the toe of her felt slipper. "My feet," she said petulantly, "are those of a servant. Why did you forbid the *amah* to bind my feet so that I could be attractive . . . like her . . . like other ladies of the court?"

I was taken aback. I had thought that Trac would be grateful that the painful and crippling deformity had not been inflicted on her. The "her," I appreciated, did not refer to the *amah,* whose feet were unbound, but to Jade Ring. It came as a shock to me that any child would actually *want* to have her feet bound to conform to the dictates of fashion.

As patiently as I could, I explained to Trac that foot binding was a purely Chinese custom. Even in China, I stated, there were women of exalted station who did not have bound feet. I quoted my own mother as an example. I pointed out that Trac's mother's feet had not been bound, nor had Sita's. I also stated that no woman in the land where Trac had been born—and where in all likelihood she would one day return—followed the practice of restricting growth of the feet. It was only in China, I stated in closing, that bound feet were considered things of beauty, and even here not everyone felt that way. I emphasized that I, personally, did not find bound feet to be the least bit attractive.

Trac listened to me in sullen silence. I do not believe my arguments satisfied or convinced her, but she seemed somewhat mollified.

In the Month of the Cock, I received an official communication from Angkor. In the dispatch, the minister of state congratulated me fulsomely on my having secured the non-aggression pact. As I had by now come to expect, there was no mention of Champa or of the political situation in Kambuja. What did come as a surprise was a new assignment. I was directed to proceed, as soon as my duties permitted, to the kingdom of Nan Chao as an emissary of the Khmer court. My mission was to obtain a non-aggression pact similar to the one I'd concluded between Kambuja and the Sung court, to study firsthand the economic, political, and military posture of Nan Chao, and to prepare a full report on my findings upon my return to Lin-an.

My duties, such as they were now that the coastal survey was completed and the report ready for submission, permitted my immediate departure, but there were other considerations. The most practical route, as far as I could ascertain, was to follow the Yangtze upriver through its tortuous gorges to the "Red Basin" of Szechwan. From Szechwan, the route continued upstream to where the Yangtze turned eastward after forcing its way through the rugged mountains that encircled the Szechwan basin. Somewhere in the region to the southwest of the Yangtze's western reaches lay the kingdom of Nan Chao and its capital, Tali. In Lin-an I could locate no one who was quite sure what lay beyond the marches of Szechwan, but I was assured I could obtain guides in Chungking or farther upstream at Luchou. By any estimate, I calculated the return journey to be somewhere between three and four thousand miles.

With winter only a few months off, it would have been madness to embark on such a journey in this season. I must confess, however, that I was tempted to strike out without delay to escape the unpleasant atmosphere in my household. Sanity prevailed and I decided to start the journey in the early spring, taking with me four cavalry troopers as a mounted escort. That left me five to six months with little to look forward to but diplomatic social functions . . . and setting my house in order.

By the latter part of the Month of the Cock, it was painfully apparent that what I had assumed to be a negotiated peace on my domestic front was nothing but a fragile truce that showed ominous signs of collapse. Jade Ring complained almost constantly of real or imagined affronts she claimed had been instigated by Trac. On her part, Trac heatedly denied the accusations, but it was obvious that she was fighting a childish, yet effective, war of subversive attrition against "her," as she referred to Jade Ring. The conflict was causing divided loyalties among the servants, giving rise to an increasing spate of petty disputes. My house was anything but the haven of tranquility I expected it to be. The situation was becoming intolerable.

The most frustrating aspect of the situation was that it defied every effort on my part toward resolution. As best I could, I consoled Jade Ring. To placate her, I allowed her sister to remain installed in the residence, against my better judgment. With Trac, reason, cajoling, and threats seemed to be of no avail. In the Month of the Dog, I reached the conclusion that the differences between the girl and the concubine were irreconcilable as long as both were under the same roof.

As I had many times since coming to Lin-an, I sought the advice of Chu Hsi.

chapter 38

DURING MY ACCOUNT, CHU HSI INTERJECTED QUESTIONS. When I had concluded, he pulled his white beard thoughtfully.

"It is of your making," he said reprovingly. "Your daughter loves you not only as a father, but as a man. She is jealous of the concubine as a rival for your affections. Your concubine is aware of this. She begrudges the time you spend with Trac and the affection you bestow upon the girl. As you know, the written character for trouble depicts two women under one roof. In your ignorance you have created this unenviable condition in your own home."

"But," I said protestingly, "Trac is merely a child. She is only ten. What does a ten-year-old know of physical love?"

Chu smiled thinly. "With a girl, ten years is but a few short paces from womanhood. All daughters have romantic attachments for their fathers. In the normal course, where the girl matures under the influence of the women of the house, the husband becomes a father figure. In Trac's case, her upbringing has been anything but normal."

Again I protested. "She had been raised under the influence of her mother, Sita, her nurse, and her governess. Is that not normal?"

"Is it?" Chu said chidingly. "Ask yourself the question

341

and answer it honestly. From what you tell me, the child received little affection from her mother. Sita, admirable wife though she undoubtedly is, could not be blamed for favoring her own offspring to the exclusion of Trac. The girl turned more and more toward you for emotional sustenance.

"By your own admission, you favored Trac over your children by Sita. You encouraged the girl in fields of schooling of which I do not approve . . . at least not for women. And, while I do not wholly approve of foot binding, it has distinct advantages of female immobility and dependency. These advantages you precluded by your adamant refusal to permit foot binding."

"I have an aversion to foot binding," I said defensively. "It does not apply to Trac alone. I would forbid the deforming custom with respect to all my daughters."

"Even if Jade Ring should present you with a daughter?" Chu questioned seriously.

I hesitated. I had not considered such an eventuality. "Yes," I said thoughtfully, "even in that case."

"Be that as it may. In any event, at Trac's present age it would be an excessively painful process. The chief reason she expressed a desire to have her feet bound was in order to compete for your favor with the concubine.

"But where you committed your cardinal error was in sending Sita and her children back to Kambuja and keeping Trac with you in Lin-an. At her impressionable age, she construed this as an indication that she was the focal point of your affection. You reinforced this conception by devoting more time to her than you had formerly. She reacted instinctively and predictably. She sought you out more than she previously had, she became more intimate and affectionate, and she grew possessive. She thought herself, in fact, to be the mistress of your house. Without doubt, she also fantasized herself as eventually sharing your bed.

"Then you shattered her dreams by introducing a concubine to your house and bed. At first, Trac seemed to accept this new state of domestic affairs . . . but only because she knew not how to combat it. Under the surface, she felt herself betrayed and seethed with hate and jealousy. It was not long before this manifested itself in rebellious conduct. As, by trial and error, Trac formulated a plan of attack, she has become virtually unmanageable, and life in your establishment has become more and more unbearable."

I spread my hands in a gesture of helplessness. "With Jade Ring," I said bitterly, "I hoped to normalize conditions . . . to restore a balance to the household."

Chu looked at me searchingly. "Do not delude yourself on that score," he said curtly. "From what you have told me in the past, I have long suspected that you have been seeking to duplicate your father's good fortune with Apricot Blossom. I am told that Jade Ring is a close facsimile of Apricot Blossom—at least in appearance. No, you were motivated by self-interest. Trac provided the excuse for taking a concubine . . . but she was not the reason."

What Chu said was all truth. I had dimly perceived much of it, suspected some of it, but I had not admitted it to myself. That the error had been mine from the beginning, and that I had unwittingly compounded the error, I now grudgingly conceded. But an admission of culpability did not resolve the dilemma.

"What am I to do?" I asked bleakly.

"That," Chu said in warmer tones than he had employed up to this point in our discussion, "is what we are here to determine. As you have correctly suspected, there can be no peace under your roof under the conditions that now prevail. One of them, Trac or Jade Ring, must leave your roof . . . at least for an extended period until Trac discovers outside interests that divert her from her present course. The question is, which one should go?

"Sending Jade Ring back to her father's house would involve considerable, if not unconscionable, loss of face for herself and her family. But that is not the issue. Banishing Jade Ring would be conceding victory to Trac. What is now an unhealthy situation could become a disaster. Unless you exercised extreme caution, it could evolve into an incestuous relationship."

"That's unthinkable!"

Chu looked at me quizzically. "Is it?" he queried. "You must have heard of such cases. I have known of several. It is, unfortunately, not as uncommon as you might think. Where there is a strong attraction of daughter to father, the reverse, or a mutual attraction, it can happen despite strong resolve to the contrary. One night, or day, when defenses are down through drink or for other reasons, the father yields to temptation and violates the daughter who may willingly, or unwillingly, accept the advance. From that point, there is no turning back. Even if the illicit affair remains cloaked in secrecy, the moral foundations of the household have been destroyed.

"I am not saying it would happen in your case . . . but the danger is there. In my estimation, you have no choice. It is Trac who must be sent from your house."

Although I could not visualize any conceivable circumstances under which I would be tempted to violate Trac, I could not dispute Chu's logic. "I have considered sending her to Angkor," I admitted, "but I feel she is too young to make the trip and to readjust to life in Kambuja."

"In the long run, that may be the only solution," Chu said flatly. "But, fortunately, an interim solution presents itself. Your forthcoming journey and the unconventional schooling you have imposed upon Trac present us with, if not the answer, at least the excuse. You can announce that, in the interests of Trac's education during your extended absence, she must be placed in a suitable environment where such liberal views on schooling are accepted and practiced. You then dictate that she be introduced to this environment as soon as possible to assist her in making a proper adjustment.

"On your return, which you feel could be as much as a year hence, time may have worked its healing miracle and Trac will accept the presence of your concubine without rancor. If not, nothing has been lost and you can then consider returning Trac to Angkor."

"It sounds like an admirable solution," I said skeptically, "but just where do I find the suitable environment your mention?"

Chu shook his head. "I am not yet sure. Among my friends and acquaintances, there are some who hold views on female education almost as liberal as yours. For the most part, the heads of such households are also opposed to foot binding. I will make inquiries. I am confident I can find a household suited to your needs that will accept Trac . . . but it may take some time. You will have to be patient and, in the meantime, keep peace in your household as best you may."

It became my practice, as much to escape the constant tensions in my residence as for any other reason, to take long, solitary walks through the parkland at West Lake. One afternoon in late autumn, I strolled through the wooded glades, lost in melancholy musing.

What had made me consider that a diplomatic career would be preferable to military life? I was a man of action, not of words. I had spent five years now as an envoy. I had achieved nothing of any importance other than to become acquainted with portions of the land of my birth. I derived no pleasure from this useless existence and, with few exceptions, I had been bored to tears most of the time. I was thirty-four. Did I want to spend the rest of my days in such a meaningless occupation?

The answer was that I did not. I had reached a decision. Once my forthcoming mission to Nan Chao was completed, I would quit the Khmer diplomatic service. But this decision gave rise to other questions. What would I do? Where would I go?

I had spent my entire adult life in the service of the Khmer king. I was more familiar with Kambuja and its empire than I was with my homeland. Since my return to China, I had found myself in the uncomfortable position of being an alien in my own land. I had made few friends in Lin-an. The only real skills I had were in waging war. Could I employ those skills to their best advantage in China? I believed I could. If I had placed the correct interpretation on my observations of the previous year, war with the Chin—once they had recovered from the ravages of the Yellow River floods of last year —was inevitable. If I offered my services to the Sung emperor, I was almost sure to be accepted. But did I really want that?

I was accustomed to warmer climes and found I had little liking for China's harsh winters. Why not return to Angkor? If I resigned from the Khmer diplomatic service, I was almost certain I would not be made welcome in Kambuja. I could offer my services as a soldier of fortune to the island kingdoms in the southern archipelago. Or I could turn my eyes to the west and wander through strange and far-off lands. One fortunate aspect was that I would not want for money, whatever course I chose.

I had amassed a considerable fortune in gold and silver from my campaigns. Shortly after my arrival in Lin-an, I had been persuaded to purchase a large tract of marshy land on the outskirts of the city. Many of my acquaintances had scoffed at my acquisition as folly, but I had seen its possibilities. I had had the land drained by means of the construction of waterways broad and deep enough to accommodate large barges. I had then had constructed to my specifications a series of large warehouses protected by deep moats. I had hired armed guards to patrol the premises night and day. I had correctly assessed the need for storage space, particularly storage facilities safe from thievery. It had been a profitable venture. In less than three years my original capital investment had been repaid and my fortune had more than quadrupled. The scoffers were silenced. At thirty-four, I was a wealthy man, a very wealthy man, indeed.

What of my obligations to my family? Even though my twin sons were a disappointment to me, I had a responsibility to them. Their younger sister showed little promise. I did not know my infant son, but if he took after his mother and the rest of her children, he was not likely to amount to much. Sita, while I still harbored affection for her, bored me to distraction. I had given Sita a large sum of money, sufficient to keep her and the children in comfort for the remainder of her life, and I had endowed the children with ample patrimonies. Although I felt somewhat guilty about it, I had no inclination to resume my status as head of that household.

Trac, who had caused me so much concern and torment over the past year, was now, oddly enough, the least of my worries. A week earlier, Chu Hsi had located a family he thought suitable, a well-to-do merchant with four wives, a concubine, thirteen children, of whom eight were girls. Chu assured me the merchant's views were remarkably similar to my own. I had visited this worthy gentleman and had found him all that Chu had indicated. He was a man eight years my senior. As a young man, he had traveled extensively at home and abroad and adopted views concerning liberal education that were almost identical to mine. Like myself, he had developed an aversion to foot binding. His youngest wife, his concubine, and his daughters had unbound feet. His sprawling residence could accommodate Trac and her entourage without any inconvenience. He would be happy to add Trac's tutors to his own instructional staff. We settled on an equitable fee. To seal the bargain, I offered him warehousing facilities at an attractively reduced rental. This he accepted with delight and alacrity.

The day after my visit with the merchant I apprised Trac of the arrangement. I expected her to object. She did not, but she was strangely quiet. Obediently, she came with me the next day to visit the merchant's residence and to meet his children—or at least those that still lived at home, of whom two girls and a boy were close to Trac's age. Trac was reserved, but I felt she found the children to her liking. I believe that she had accepted the fact that I would be absent for a long period and had no wish to remain under the same roof as Jade Ring during the extended separation. She accepted this alternative arrangement without demur. Even as I trod the gravel pathways of the park, she was at my residence supervising her packing. Her move to the merchant's ménage would take place on the morrow.

Jade Ring? I had accepted the fact by now that, despite a striking similarity of features, she was not, nor could she ever be, another Apricot Blossom. My initial infatuation had gradually dissipated and was replaced by amused tolerance of her vanity and shallowness. She still had the ability to arouse me sexually. If I stayed in China, she would retain her position as favored concubine. If I returned to Angkor, she would accompany me. If I chose to wander farther afield, I doubted very much that I would take her with me. However, should she present me with children, that might alter my thinking. At any rate, there would be time enough to consider her position on my return from Nan Chao.

So absorbed was I in my thoughts that I didn't notice the old monk sitting with his back to the outer wall of a small pagoda. His long staff protruded into the footpath. I didn't notice it, either, tripped over it, and went sprawling onto the gravel of the path.

Thinking I had been set upon by footpads, I scrambled to my feet as quickly as my stiff leg permitted and whirled to face my attackers. All I saw was a saffron-robed oldster groping for the staff my clumsiness had knocked from his grasp. As he patted the grass at his side and in front of himself, I realized he was blind. I stepped forward, picked up the staff, and placed it in his hand.

"Forgive me, Father," I said. "It was clumsy of me. I was deep in thought and didn't see your staff."

The old monk chuckled. "We are all blind in one way or another, my son. What brings you here?"

"Whim, Father. I was walking to assist my thinking. I'm afraid I don't recognize this pagoda or this particular region of the park. I must have taken a wrong turn."

"You did not come seeking me?"

"No," I answered, somewhat puzzled by his question. "I know you not."

"Then fate has interceded. Come, help me to my feet. I have warmed these old bones enough in the afternoon sun. There will be those who await me in the shrine."

As I assisted him to his feet, he added, "You see, my son, having been robbed of my vision, I have been granted an inner sight. There are many who visit me to learn the meaning of their lives, through my gift. I thought you to be one of them."

"No," I said with a rueful laugh, "but I was pondering what turn my life might take when your staff tripped me."

"Stand before me," the monk commanded.

I knew not what he wanted, but I obeyed him. When I stood in front of him, he seemed to know where I was positioned. He reached up and touched my face. The fingers of his right hand, as light as feathers, traced the contours of my face and neck. Once his tactile inventory of my features was completed to his satisfaction, he groped for my hand and grasped it in a grip of surprising strength.

"You are a man of strong beliefs, my son," he said solemnly, "a man of great spiritual and physical reserves . . . yet you attract violence and are a man of violence."

"No, Father, I am an envoy from a distant land . . . a man of peace."

He ignored my remark. His voice deepened as he intoned slowly and distinctly, "You have been a warrior. You will be one again and command a great army. But before that day you will make a long journey . . . a journey into sadness, where some will die, but you will not. You will govern a mighty kingdom and find much happiness . . . but in the midst of happiness you will be betrayed by one of your own house. You will attain greater years than did your father before you . . . and you will die with honor."

While he spoke to me thusly, the old monk seemed to straighten and grow in stature. Now his shoulders sagged and he released my hand. Tapping his staff in front of him, he shuffled through a gate and into the courtyard of the pagoda. With my mouth agape, I watched his retreating back.

While the winter that saw the end of the Year of the Hare and heralded the Year of the Dragon was the coldest I have ever experienced, it was the happiest I spent in the capital. Peace and tranquility reigned in my house. Jade Ring, now that the tensions were removed, was gay, vivacious, and attentive to my wants. Trac, whom I visited several times each week, remained aloof from most of the children, but she had formed a close friendship with Kai-ying, a daughter of the merchant's house who was close to her own age. Trac and I spoke of her studies, her new friend, and other things, but not once did she mention Jade Ring directly or by inference.

We entertained more that winter than we had previously, and I actually found myself enjoying some of the season's social gatherings. As spring approached, I busied myself with preparations for my journey to Nan Chao. The strange words of the blind monk had fled my mind.

chapter 39

MY ESCORT AND I LEFT LIN-AN AS SOON AS THE WEATHER permitted in the second month of the Year of the Dragon. It was the fifth month of the year before we reached our destination.

For the most part, our journey was by river craft. During the four months of our upriver passage and overland trek, I marveled anew at the vastness and diversity of my homeland. The steep-sided gorges of the Yangtze were awe-inspiring and explained for me why the marches of Szechwan were relatively isolated. The Szechwan basin, fertile, red-soiled, mountain-cradled, and pleasantly mild of climate, was a revelation to me. It was not difficult for me to visualize why the mighty, militant Ch'in state, protected on its flanks and rear by high mountains, had evolved and flourished in this temperate region some fifteen hundred years ago. What was more difficult for me to understand was why the kings of this fair and favored land had forsaken the pacifistic teachings of the Taoist philosopher Chuantzu and had adopted the harsh tenets of the School of the Law. But then, I reasoned wryly, the ambitions of kings and the convolutions of statecraft are often difficult to comprehend. Had it not been for the ruthless militancy of the first emperor, China might never have become a unified realm.

We obtained the services of a guide at Luchou. Not far from that outpost of civilization, the river became compressed between confining hills, and, in consequence, more turbulent. Its course upstream now lay to the west. Where it swung sharply northward, we left the river and struck out into heavily forested and largely uninhabited mountainous terrain.

Our horses were panting from the exertion of the climb, their necks streaked with sweat. Our guide pointed. There, at long last, was our goal, Tali, a small community nestling on the shores of a lake far below us on the valley floor. Dwarfed by a backdrop of soaring peaks, it looked like a toy town.

We picked our way down a treacherous descent toward the lower slopes, terraced with clinging paddy fields, and toward the flatlands of the valley beyond. It was little wonder that this isolated realm of deep valleys, high tableland, ridges of contorted limestone karsts, and towering mountain ranges had attracted only the most determined of Chinese conquerors.

As we neared the capital, we were met by a large military patrol of heavily armed foot soldiers. They conducted us to a barracks just north of the town. Here an officer solemnly examined my documents. Through our guide, who acted as our interpreter, we were requested to wait.

An hour later a senior officer appeared. He looked at my official papers, scrutinized me and my escorting troopers, and smiled affably. Unfortunately, as he advised us through the interpreter, the king was absent on affairs of state. On his return, undoubtedly he would be honored to receive such a distinguished visitor. In the meantime, we were to consider ourselves honored guests of the kingdom.

We were taken to an inn on the outskirts of town. Our horses were tended to and stabled. We were treated to a sumptuous repast and gallons of a heady rice wine. Sometime later, I retired to a chamber that was not large, but which was clean and comfortable.

I awoke with a start, instinctively aware I was not alone. As I sat up, strong arms seized me and I received a hard blow on the temple.

I was stripped of everything but my breechclout. Trussed like a hog for market, I was dragged from the inn and dumped into the bed of a bullock cart. The cart bumped along over an uneven roadbed, the motion compounding my misery. My head still rang from the blow I had received. I tasted blood in my mouth.

We stopped before buildings I recognized as part of the barracks to which I'd been escorted earlier in the day. I was dragged from the cart. The ropes binding my ankles were removed, but not those pinioning my arms behind me. I was pushed through the entranceway of a stone building and half-dragged, half-shoved, along a corridor until we came to an open-doored, low orifice. Once inside in a low squatting position, leg irons secured to the stone walls by heavy chains were affixed to my ankles. The bonds that trussed my arms were removed. The iron grille of the cell door clanged shut behind my departing abductors.

I surveyed my surroundings in the dim light. The cell was about eight feet long by four feet in depth. The overhead stone ceiling was so low that the best I could achieve was a sitting position. The fetid rice straw on which I lay stank of excrement and stale urine. And, as I very soon discovered, I shared this bed of stinking straw with lice, ticks, and rodents.

Those who had seized me and brought me to this prison had spoken little, and what they said had been in a tongue I could not understand. This, however, was some sort of military prison, which implied that my abductors had had official sanction. It made no sense. As an envoy of the Khmer court, my person and the persons of my official party were, or should be, sacrosanct. My head ached. I could not think clearly. It must be, I concluded, a terrible mistake. In the morning, when I was released, I would lodge a strong complaint concerning the invasion of my privacy, the injury I had sustained, and the indignities I had suffered.

I was not released in the morning. The filthy hole in which I was chained remained my home for a considerable period of time.

Periodically a guard peered in at me. He did not respond to my questions or demands to see his superior. In fact, in all the time I was chained in the cell, he did not utter a single word.

Once a day I was brought a cup of tepid water and a

bowl of watery soup. This was suplemented every third or fourth day by a small bowl of unseasoned rice.

There were no sanitary facilities. I lay in my own filth. To the best of my recollection, only twice during my incarceration was the straw removed, myself and the cell sluiced down with water, and fresh straw dumped into the cell.

By the third or fourth day I had to accept the fact that my imprisonment was no mistake. I was being deliberately and cruelly detained, treated like a dangerous criminal. I racked my brain for some answer, but I could conceive of no reason why imprisonment had been visited upon me.

I kept track of time by watching a small square of sunlight creep across the stone flooring outside my cell. About the fifth day of my incarceration the sun must have been hidden behind clouds. It occurred to me that I should keep track of the days. I did so by clearing a patch of the stone floor and placing on it pieces of straw, adding one piece each day. In my third week, when the cell was cleaned and the straw renewed, my makeshift calendar was washed away. I painfully reconstructed it, but after a few more days I could not be sure whether I had added a straw, or perhaps added one or two too many. I abandoned the project as futile. Time became meaningless.

Early in my imprisonment I was plagued by visions of food. The thought caused the saliva to gather in my mouth and the juices to rumble in my shrunken gut. It was an agony and a self-inflicted torture. I learned, with difficulty, to suppress such visions the moment they appeared.

There were other visions that caused mental rather than physical agonies. They were not as amenable to control. I tried to impose disciplines by giving myself mental exercises, but my mind rebelled against the dictates of reason and my thoughts strayed unbidden into strange channels. I was given to fancies and weird hallucinations.

I thought, one by one, of the women who had played significant roles in my life. I thought of my mother, then of my initiation into esoteric sexual practices by White Lotus. I dwelt wistfully on the memory of Morning Mist and our children and on the uncomplicated life we'd shared in the Jarai village. I thought of Linh and her in-

satiable sexual demands. I found myself wishing I had not
been swayed by Horse-master Chang's testament and had
had Linh put to death for her perfidy.

I thought of my children, chiefly of Trac. I wondered
what would become of her. Now that it seemed too late
to remedy the oversight, I wished I had given more of
my time and affection to the twin boys and my daughter
and youngest son. When I thought of their mother, I saw
her not as she had been when she left Lin-an two years
ago, but as the plump and amiable bride of many years
earlier.

The images of Jade Ring that came to mind were confused; they were distorted and out of focus. In my feverish eye of the mind, she would one minute be herself and
the next minute Apricot Blossom. It was as though the
two women were one and the same—as though it were
Apricot Blossom, not Jade Ring, who was my concubine.
So strong was this delusion that at one point I imagined
Jade Ring with the horrible disfigurement that had been
visited on my father's concubine.

Another face, one that did not properly belong with
the others, intruded into my thoughts. It was the haunt-
ingly beautiful face of Golden Dawn. What brought her
to mind was the foolish pledge she had made to await my
return. She may have kept that childish vow for some
months, or even a year or two, but by now she would be
twenty-one. By this time she must be married and probable had several children. She was, I thought bitterly, a
good deal luckier than those who did, in fact, await my
return—Sita, Jade Ring, and the children. They were not
likely to see me again in this world.

Muscle slowly wasted away from my vermin-infested
body. My hearing deteriorated. My vision grew blurred.
As I grew weaker and weaker, I realized I was being
killed, slowly but surely. In my more lucid moments, I
prayed for the release of death.

I cannot say with certitude how long I rotted in that
wretched hole. It seemed an eternity, but it could not
have been more than a few months, or I could not have survived.

The details of my release and transfer to a Buddhist
monastery are hazy. I recall the shackles being struck
from my ankles. I was taken from the cell. Unable to

stand, let alone walk, I had to be carried from the prison and placed in a horse-drawn cart. At that point, I lost consciousness.

My next recollection was a day or so later. I lay on a pallet of clean straw. My head had been shaved. I had been deloused and my festering sores had been treated with soothing salves. I was tended by a saffron-robed monk who fed me rich, steaming broth and sweetened tea—although it was some days before I could manage more than a single mouthful without gagging.

My new abode was a Buddhist monk's monastic cell. Yet, even though my position had improved a thousandfold, I was still a prisoner. Although I couldn't have crawled even a few feet in my weakened condition, soldiers guarded my cell night and day.

It was several days before I recovered sufficient strength to take interest in my surroundings. The monk who tended me, as did some others in the monastery, spoke Mandarin. Questions put to those who could understand me were answered readily enough, but they brought me very little enlightenment. None could tell me why I had been thrown into military prison, how long I was to be detained here in the monastery, or what had befallen the small party that had accompanied me to Nan Chao. All that I was told by the monks was that they had orders to make me comfortable and nurse me back to health. Those charged with tending me and the guard detachment were to ensure that I neither escaped nor communicated with anyone outside the monastery. Should I manage to escape or communicate beyond the confines of the monastery, the monks assured me that both they and the entire guard detachment would be put to death. From what little I had learned about this kingdom, I did not deem the threat of execution an idle one, even though for the life of me I couldn't think of a reason I should be held incommunicado.

I thought I perceived a reason for my detention, but that did not strike me for some months, when I had regained much of my strength and powers of concentration. I still could not understand what had prompted the T'ai officials to chain me in a cell in which I had nearly perished from starvation. Now that I was being accorded reasonable treatment, I concluded I was being held for ransom and would be released unharmed once King Jayavarman was apprised of the plight of his envoy and had negotiated my deliverance.

It was some time before I mastered the spoken language well enough to converse with other than the Chinese-speaking monks. It was then, from the officer who came to inspect the guard detachment each week, that I at last learned what had become of my cavalry escort and the Chinese guide who had brought us to Tali. On the same night that I had been chained in a cramped cell in the military prison, the five members of my official party had been seized, taken to an isolated gully some distance from the town, put to death, and buried in a common, unmarked grave. The officer who told me this did not know why the execution had taken place. He only knew that it had occurred because the officer in charge of the execution squad was a friend of his.

The news shocked and sobered me. I wondered just what sort of maniac I had to contend with in the person of the king of Nan Chao. I was to learn something of his character, but that day was a good deal away when I first speculated on the king's sanity.

Winter came to Nan Chao before I was fully recovered. And with winter came a new year, the Year of the Snake. Spring came to the valley. It melted into summer, then summer gave way to autumn, and it was winter again before I realized it. It was the Year of the Horse.

To occupy my time, I studied not only the language, but I learned as much as I could from the abbot and his monks concerning their faith, the country, and its structure. As my strength returned, I spent a good deal of time indulging in rigorous exercise and in practicing the martial arts with the monks and soldiers.

They were followers of Theravada Buddhism, the gentle sect I had encountered in the Mon and Siamese kingdoms. While it was too submissive a doctrine to appeal to me, I studied their creed and philosophy and noted the points of difference between the Mahayana Buddhism of the China of my childhood, that of Kambuja's religion of state, and this Theravada form, which stressed personal attainment of salvation through one's own efforts and comportment. To me, it seemed too weak and debilitating a faith to sustain a fighting man like myself.

The kingdom of Nan Chao, I was told, was very ancient. The present capital, Tali, had been founded sixteen generations ago. By my reckoning, that placed its founding about four hundred years ago in the early T'ang dynasty. I didn't consider the city ancient, nor did I consider it much more than an overgrown town.

The inaccessibility of the kingdom exposed it to few outside influences. I was told that only twice during the history of the realm had it faced marauders and been overrun, both times by Chinese armies from the east.

Fleeing from those invading forces, many T'ai crossed the mountains and rivers in the west and settled in the plateaus and valleys as independent princedoms. Others had followed the Turbulent River and its tributaries farther south to settle in remote and sheltered valleys. As I had suspected, there was today little or no contact between the descendants of those early migrants and their former homeland, Nan Chao. The king of Nan Chao exercised no authority over those independent states. Unless the kingdom of Nan Chao was subjected to yet another invasion, there wasn't much likelihood of further migrations and King Jayavarman's fears were groundless.

There were pockets of T'ai in the Annam highlands. We Chinese referred to those who had settled in the mountainous country west of Annam as Lao. Those who had fled to the western plateaus now called themselves Shan, which is where, I suspect, the Khmer derived the names Siam and Siamese.

The social structure of Nan Chao was rigidly feudal. At the apex was the king. Next came the nobility, who governed the numerous small fiefdoms scattered throughout the larger valleys of the realm. Beneath this aristocracy, in descending order of importance, were the priesthood, military leaders, artisans, and farmers. The entire structure was hereditary, with station, position, and calling being passed down from father to son.

The economy was essentially agrarian, but mining played an important secondary role. The limited arable ground of the valleys augmented by terrace farming of the lower mountain slopes met the requirements of the relatively small population of the realm. Because of the difficult terrain, there was virtually no commerce with China. What trade there was—the movement of tin, lead-zinc, and copper ores south from Nan Chao through Annam and the return flow of manufactured trade goods —was directed naturally along north-south lines by the mountain ranges that connected Nan Chao with the south.

The martial arts practiced by the monks and soldiers of Nan Chao differed from the arts as taught to me in my youth. The monks were particularly adept at a form of unarmed combat involving the extensive use of kicking. Although my stiff leg was a handicap, they taught me how to get great force into a kick with my left leg. My usage of the extended hand and stiffened fingers was superior to theirs. In balance, despite their footwork, there was no one who could beat me once my full strength returned. The officer who inspected my guards, noting my superiority, doubled my guards from two to four whenever I was allowed onto the monastery grounds or into the courtyards for exercise or martial arts practice. Such precautions, at least until the Year of the Ram, were unnecessary since I had no intention of trying to escape.

I was treated with kindness and consideration by the monks. I ate the same food they ate, wore the same simple garments, and adhered fairly closely to their daily routine. Nonetheless, there was no time that I was not acutely aware that I was a prisoner. My cell, while similar in size and content to the other monastic cells, differed in that it was fitted with a heavy iron door. From dusk to dawn, I was locked into my cell. Again, during periods of meditation, I would be locked in. And, at all times, guards were at my door when I was in my cell, whether the door was secured or not. Whenever I left the cell, for whatever reason, I was accompanied by guards who kept me under constant scrutiny.

From the time I had concluded that I was being held for ransom, I had given no thought to escape. But, as the Year of the Horse drew to a close, I changed my thinking. I did not abandon the idea that I was being held for ransom, but I was no longer so confident that negotiations for my release were just a matter of time. It had been more than two years since I had been brought to the monastery —even if I was vague about the exact date, it had still been before winter struck in the late months of the Year of the Dragon. Even considering the remoteness of Nan Chao and the difficulties involved in overland or river travel between Tali and Angkor, there should have been something concluded by now. I could do little at this time of year, but it was beginning to look as though my only avenue to freedom was escape. During the winter months, as the Year of the Horse gave way to the Year of the Ram, I thought of little but making good my escape once spring returned to the valley.

It is one thing to talk blithely about escaping; it is quite another to make good an escape. Consider my situation.

If the monastery had been a fortress, a better site could not have been selected. The monastery perched on a sundered pinnacle of rock to the north of, and overlooking, the city. The top of the pinnacle where the monastery was located was separated from the promontory from which it had split away by a yawning chasm. This abyss was spanned by a narrow stone bridge that was the only means of exit or entry for the monastery. Prior to my imprisonment in the monastery, the bridge had been unguarded. For the past two years, guards had been mounted at both ends of the bridge.

The western wall of the monastery was an upward extension of the cliff face. From the window of my cell, it was a sheer drop of almost seven hundred feet to the jagged rocks at the base of the pinnacle. They hadn't considered it necessary to put bars on the window.

My guards were changed regularly in order to prevent any possible fraternization with me and a consequent relaxation of their vigilance. Since their lives would be forfeited should I escape, their surveillance was anything but lax.

To win freedom, all I had to do was elude my eagle-eyed guards, escape not only from the confines of the monastery, but from the pinnacle, as well, and put enough distance between myself and the pursuit that was bound to follow to forestall my being retaken. If I could reach the forested hills, even though I was unfamiliar with the terrain, I felt I could avoid recapture and, eventually, reach the Yangtze River. My chances of succeeding were slim, if not nonexistent.

By the Month of the Dragon in the Year of the Ram,

when the spring sun warmed the valley and was melting
the snow from the surrounding peaks, I was ready but for
two things. To embark on my desperate bid for freedom,
I needed a stout staff of about five feet in length—and a
moonless night.

chapter 40

I COULD NOT HOPE TO PROCURE ANYTHING WITH WHICH I could lower myself from my cell to the pinnacle's base. I conceived of a makeshift rope long enough to suspend myself far enough beneath my cell window to achieve my purpose. Using my feet against the cliff face and the monastery wall, I could induce a pendulum-like motion, increasing the arc of swing until I could grasp the southwestern corner of the building. From there, I should be able to ease myself onto the low wall enclosing the southern courtyard.

During the winter months and early spring, a number of the monks' gowns mysteriously disappeared from the courtyard drying racks. One of my garments was lost in this manner, about which I complained loudly.

In my cell at night, I removed the stitching that made the robes into cylindrical sheaths, thus acquiring straight lengths of cloth. These lengths I wrapped around my waist. One of the few places in the monastery where my guards relaxed their vigilance was the lavatory and ablution chamber, which had a single entrance-exit and where the windows were high and could all be watched from a central vantage point. In the end lavatory cubicle was a pile of stone and bricks that was to be used for additional construction in the spring. Behind the stacks of brick was hidden my garment-fabricated rope, which grew longer each time I tied on a new length of cloth.

When I considered the makeshift rope long enough to serve my purpose, the rash of garment thefts ceased as mysteriously as it had started.

Until needed—that is, until I considered the weather warm enough to make my escape feasible—the rope stayed hidden in the lavatory cubicle underneath a pile of loose bricks. Now, as the weather had warmed and the moon was waning in the Month of the Dragon, the fateful night was almost upon me. I went ahead with the last item of preparation.

My cell contained nothing to which the rope could be anchored. What I needed was a bench, iron bar, or strong staff to act as a crossbar against the inner stones framing the window. I obtained a stout staff without arousing suspicion by a simple subterfuge.

At martial arts practice, I pretended to stumble and sprain the knee of my stiff leg. The monks found a strong staff to assist me as I hobbled about in feigned pain. In another day or two, when the dark of the moon was firmly established, the staff would serve another purpose.

My plan was to retrieve the rope from its hiding place and, with it wound around me underneath my loose robes, bring it to my cell on the evening of my night of escape. When my cell door had been barred for the night, I would add my blanket and spare garments to the rope. I would wait until the monastery settled down for the night before making my next move.

With one end of the rope secured beneath my armpits and the other tied to the center of the staff, I would brace the staff firmly and lower myself to the full extent of the rope. This would suspend me about sixty feet beneath my windowsill and some twenty feet down the cliff below the monastery's foundation. Then, keeping a steady weight on the rope to prevent the staff above from shifting its position, I would push against the rock face to set the arcing swing in motion.

There were a good many "if's" in my plan. *If* the rope didn't break, *if* the anchoring staff held, *if* I could generate enough momentum to swing me to the level of the courtyard wall, *if* I could reach and hang onto the wall, I should be able to reach my first objective, the courtyard facing south. If not, I was faced with a plunge of more than six hundred feet, an alternative I did not care to contemplate.

If I could reach the southern courtyard and *then* shake the staff loose and retrieve my rope, I would then go to the northern courtyard under cover of darkness. There, I could anchor the staff beneath a stone bench and lower myself down the northern cliff face to a ledge I judged to be about fifty feet from the top. I had noticed goats grazing on the ledge, and, although part of the ledge was hidden from view from above by an overhang, I assumed there must be some way to reach the valley floor at the bottom of the pinnacle. Trying to grope my way down from the ledge with nothing to light my path but the stars would be a highly dangerous undertaking, but it was infinitely superior to the alternative.

If, when I reached the southern courtyard, I could not dislodge the anchoring staff, then I would have lost the rope and could not lower myself to the northern ledge. In that event, the only thing left would be to take out the soldiers guarding the bridge and make good my escape by that route. Just how I, unarmed, was going to accomplish these killings without raising any alarm, I was not quite sure.

That was my escape plan. How it would have worked in practice I shall never know.

I was summoned by the abbot shortly after the afternoon meditation period. Flanked by two guards, I was escorted to the abbot's private quarters. In my two and a half years of imprisonment in the monastery, I had seen the abbot, but I had never been summoned to his presence. My heart was leaden in my breast. I was sure that my makeshift rope had been discovered and its purpose guessed. Why, I thought bleakly, couldn't it have remained hidden for just two or three more days?

A monk directed the guards and myself to the abbot's antechamber. There we found not only the abbot, but a rickly dressed man seated in a blackwood chair that was heavily inlaid with mother-of-pearl. When the guards saw the man, they dropped to their knees and prostrated themselves full-length at his feet. Even before the abbot gravely introduced him, I knew I was in the presence of the king of Nan Chao. Anger seethed within me. This smiling, handsome nobleman had callously decreed the deaths of my cavalry troopers and the innocent guide. He was, as well, the author of all my misery and misfortune over the past three years.

"I trust you have enjoyed your stay with us," the king said amiably. "I regret that I was absent in the extreme south of my kingdom when you first arrived and that the accommodation provided you was rather . . . shall we say . . . uncomfortable. I hope it has been more to your liking since I had you moved here."

I could barely trust myself to speak. "I hope," I rasped, "that my ransom has adequately compensated you for any expense entailed."

The king's smile broadened. "I have turned a substantial profit, but it is not quite as you think. You were not held for ransom. I was advised in advance of your coming and was paid to detain you in total isolation . . . until advised otherwise. The arrangement, unfortunately, did not extend to your retinue."

"So they . . ." I started to retort hotly, then stopped as what the king had just disclosed sank in. I was speechless. Three years! Almost three years of deprivation and imprisonment by *arrangement* from outside Nan Chao. Who? Why? I stared stupidly at the king in disbelief.

"So they were put to death," the king said, obligingly finishing my sentence for me. "They had no market value and could have proved embarrassments."

I found my voice. "It did not occur to you," I said gratingly, "that as a foreign envoy I should have been immune from such harm as you have inflicted on me . . . and that immunity should have extended to my entire party."

The king chuckled. "You are an audacious man to stand before me as a prisoner and lecture me on the niceties of protocol. It might interest you to know that I was assured that you would be relieved in your diplomatic post to the Sung court well before your arrival in Nan Chao. You did not know it, of course, but you arrived here with no diplomatic status; therefore, you had no rights, privileges, or immunity."

I frowned as I absorbed what the king was telling me. Unless he was lying to excuse his unlawful actions, he was telling me that, without my knowledge, I had been dismissed as envoy of the court at Angkor sometime between my departure from Lin-an and my arrival at Tali. I supposed it *was* possible, but I could see no reason and had never heard of such an action. No, I concluded, this was a fabrication to cloak the king's guilt.

The king must have read the disbelief written on my face, but he continued blandly: "You have profited from your visit. You speak our tongue. You have learned much about my domain. You look to be in excellent health apart from a recent slight injury the good abbot tells me you sustained practicing martial arts. We shall be sorry to lose you. I shall be even sorrier to lose the revenue from your keep."

"Lose me? . . ." Was the king joking?

"Yes. You will be happy to know that you are now free to leave. Tomorrow, the possessions taken from you a few years ago will be returned to you and a horse and guide will be placed at your disposal. I apologize for any inconvenience our hospitality has caused you . . . and wish you a safe journey."

I had difficulty getting to sleep that night. My mind was in a whirl.

If what the T'ai king said was true, there was only one man who could have arranged for my dismissal from his service and negotiated my incarceration in Nan Chao. That man was King Jayavarman, although why he should have treated me so cruelly escaped me. By the same token, it was only the Khmer king who could have lifted the sanction he had imposed. I was now free because he had need of me in some capacity.

I fervently thanked my ancestors for their timely intervention. I would not have to embark now on my escape plan. Frankly, even though I had been committed to the plan, I had not given it much chance of success.

I decided I would not mention or do anything about the rope hidden in the lavatory cubicle. It would be discovered when the postponed construction got under way in a few weeks' time. By then I would be far away. The rope would explain the mystery of the purloined garments. The monks would know that I had planned an escape. They could offer prayers of thanks to the Enlightened One that I had not carried through my plan, for, had I succeeded in making good an escape before my banishment had been lifted, many monks and an entire guard detachment of soldiers would have been executed. The T'ai king on Nan Chao did not strike me as a man given to empty threats.

I thought about Jade Ring, Trac, Sita, the children, Chu Hsi, and the many people I had thought I probably would never see again. It was while these happy thoughts churned in my brain that suddenly, with startling clarity, an image sprang to mind. I saw him vividly, as I had seen him that autumn afternoon almost four years earlier —the blind monk.

I heard his strange prediction ring in my mind: *". . . but before that day you will make a long journey . . . a journey into sadness, where some will die but you will not. . . ."*

It was uncanny. I had not died, and it didn't look as though I was going to. Was it possible that the blind monk had some kind of special powers and the ability to foretell future events? Or had the oldster's choice of words been no more than a happy coincidence? On the other hand, if the sightless soothsayer did possess the gift of inner sight he claimed, there had been a good deal more to his prediction than his reference to a journey that seemed to describe my experience in Nan Chao. The old monk had opened his predictions by stating that I had been a soldier and would be again in command of a mighty army. Those may not have been his exact words, but that was close enough to what he had said.

If, in all these years, King Jayavarman had been unable to wrest Champa from Prince Vidya, then he might be turning to me now in desperation. That would explain this lifting of an edict of banishment. It would also explain this elaborate exile by imprisonment, for, if the Khmer king had wanted me permanently removed from the scene, he could have had me assassinated.

On that cheerful thought, I drifted into sleep.

The downriver journey did not take as long as my upriver journey had taken. I arrived unannounced at the capital in the early part of the Month of the Ram, a few days short of my thirty-eighth birthday. I had been away almost three and a half years. I wouldn't say my homecoming was marked by a tumultuous welcome.

I went directly to my residence—only to find it was no longer my residence and had not been for more than three years. The king of Nan Chao had not lied. I had been relieved of all diplomatic duties by royal edict three months after my departure for Nan Chao. A replacement had arrived from Angkor a month and a half later. The new envoy had taken over the residence and most of my former staff. Jade Ring, I was advised, had set herself up in a residence in a fashionable district not too far distant.

The envoy's reaction to my appearance without warning beggars description. He was, to put it mildly, dumbfounded. He had been of the belief that I had been killed. I assured him wryly that I was no ghost. The story I gave the new Khmer envoy was the one I was to give in most circles—that I had been kidnapped by bandits and that my ransom had been paid by the Khmer King.

Not wishing to cause the consternation I had generated at the embassy residence, I sent advance word of my arrival to Jade Ring. She met me at the entrance of a sumptuous establishment. Her effusive show of affection masked a nervousness I considered only natural. When she had received word of my being relieved of diplomatic duties, she had thought me either dead, or, if not, that I would never return to Lin-an.

The residence was big, far bigger than I would have considered necessary. Jade Ring had spent lavishly to make the establishment what she considered a fitting setting for her beauty. The hanging silks, carpets, carved and silk screens, bronzes, porcelains, stoneware, and jade and ivory pieces must have cost a small fortune. It was as well that I was a wealthy man.

There seemed to be a large number of people living in the residence. In fact, as I soon learned, in addition to the unmarried sister who had been living with us at the time of my departure, two of Jade Ring's married sisters and their husbands had apartments in the residence, as did Jade Ring's mother. There were a number of children, in the nursery and women's quarters, belonging to Jade Ring's married sisters. There was one exception, Jade Ring told me hesitantly. Three-year-old K'uo, named in honor of the reigning emperor, she said was my son. She had not known herself pregnant when I left. Little K'uo had been born in the late autumn of the year of my departure. She introduced me to the child shyly, watching to see what my reaction would be.

The boy did not look much like me and seemed small for his age, but he was sound and sturdy. I kissed him and patted him affectionately on the head, which pleased Jade Ring.

Jade Ring had hurriedly vacated the master bed-chamber. It was far too feminine in its appointments to suit me, but that could be rectified later.

I will not pretend that our lovemaking on my return from Nan Chao was satisfactory. It was anything but satisfactory. During the first few weeks after my return, Jade Ring was tense and nervous. That was to be expected. Her reaction to my presence wasn't helpful, but it was my performance that was the problem.

On several occasions, I could muster only partial erections. At other times, I became aroused quickly and ejaculated much too soon. I seemed to have lost the ability to control my passions. This caused me considerable anxiety. It was my fear that my months of starvation and years of imprisonment might have robbed me of my virility. That I knew Jade Ring to be shamming orgasms did nothing to help my depressed state of mind and fear that my enforced abstinence had induced impotence.

One of my first actions on my return was to visit Trac. Sobbing for joy, she ran into my outstretched arms. She assured me that she had never believed me dead. She claimed that, had I died, she would have known of it in some intuitive fashion.

Trac's early promise of beauty was being fulfilled. At fourteen, she was little short of ravishing. Unlike her mother, Trac seemed oblivious of this happy accident of face and form. Trac was gay, vivacious, and unaffected. Obviously, she had adjusted to and been accepted fully by the merchant's family. The wholesome environment had produced the desired effect. If her constant reference to Hsien, an eighteen-year-old son of the house, was any criterion, she had made a successful transference of affection from myself to the fortunate lad. I found, to my wry amusement, I experienced a twinge of jealousy.

Shortly after my return, I went to pay my respects to Chu Hsi. He was ailing and bedridden. I told him what had befallen me in Nan Chao—the true, not my fabricated, version. Chu Hsi was shocked.

"How can you serve such a tyrant? He is devoid of

honor. He repays your loyalty with treachery and deceit," Chu Hsi observed indignantly.

"He believed himself a god," I explained. "Gods have no concepts of such things as honor . . . they are above such emotionalism. The king doesn't think in terms of treachery or deceit . . . only expediency. I have suffered at his hands, but when it suited him he heaped honors upon me and elevated me to a high station."

Chu Hsi nodded and grunted his acceptance of my explanation. He then questioned me concerning the changes I had found on my return to Lin-an, Trac, and Jade Ring. I expressed my delight concerning the transformation in Trac. Then because I knew he placed much store in filial piety, I expressed keen joy over K'uo, the son Jade Ring had presented me with in my absence.

I was about to continue with a description of my latest residence, but I noticed that the old man's face was pale and drawn against his pillows. His eyes were closed. I had no wish to tire him further.

As I rose to take my leave, the old philosopher's eyes opened. "Forgive me, Hsü Yung," he said, "I am very tired. Promise me you will come again before the week is out."

I gave him my word, then left.

chapter 41

I HAD EXPECTED THAT THERE WOULD BE SOME COMMUNICA-
tion from Angkor waiting for me at the embassy on my return from Tali. That had not been the case. There had
been only a coded message, which I knew to be from Mohammed. It had come, the envoy told me, more than a
year ago.

Mohammed's message was a surprise. It came not from
Champa, but from Annam, where Mohammed had sought
sanctuary. How he came to be in this predicament was explained in the message.

Three years after the humiliating defeat of the Khmer
Army by the Cham forces in the Year of the Tiger, King
Jayavarman launched a third attack against the Cham
capital. The Khmer forces met with no more success in
this attempt than they had in the previous two campaigns.

When the siege of the Cham capital was lifted and the
Khmer forces withdrew westward, Vidya had expressed
anger that the province and city of Panduranga had not
supported the capital city as fully as it should have. He
had commanded the Cham Navy to assault a coastal town
in the south of Panduranga province as a punitive expression of his displeasure. Mohammed had refused to carry
out the order. Knowing his rebellious act would cost him
his life, he slipped aboard a northbound Arab merchantman.

Mohammed's message closed with the advice that

Vidya—whom Mohammed referred to as "Suryavarman"
—had entered into negotiations with the Annamite emperor, Li Cao-Ton, for the latter's recognition of the Cham
regime. Should this come about, Mohammed noted, Haiphong would no longer provide him with sanctuary.

I learned that earlier this very year the Annamite emperor had issued an edict of investiture bestowing official
recognition on Vidya's regime. I inquired of Mohammed's
Cham friends in Lin-an concerning his present whereabouts. I was told that he had had to flee from Haiphong
and was now in self-exile in, of all places, Canton.

I had been back in Lin-an not yet a month when two
communications addressed to me arrived at the embassy.
One message, which did not surprise me, was from the
high command. It restored my former rank of general and
ordered me back to active duty. As soon as the monsoon
winds favored my passage, I was to return to Angkor.

The second communication, from the ministry of state,
requested that my report on the kingdom of Nan Chao be
forwarded as soon as possible. It was a ridiculous directive.
Who in Angkor, I wondered, wanted such a report? Certainly not King Jayavarman. He had well-established communication links with the T'ai king and undoubtedly knew
more about the kingdom of Nan Chao than I did. Jayavarman had never been concerned about migration from
Nan Chao. He had never expected my petition to the
Sung court to receive serious consideration. Nan Chao had
been a trap baited for me from the outset. That seemed
to have been its sole purpose. Why, I wondered, had King
Jayavarman chosen the Year of the Dragon to spring the
trap. I ignored the directive. After all, I had not been
attached to that ministry for more than three years.

Although my reinstatement to general of the first rank
had not indicated a posting, I was positive I knew what
assignment awaited my return—the conquest of Champa.
To that end, there was much I could do here before the
winter months and my departure.

Among other matters I attended to, I passed a message
through Mohammed's friends requesting that he visit me
in Lin-an.

Chu Hsi received me in his bedchamber. He was
propped up in bed and looked wan and frail, but he

seemed somewhat stronger than he had been on my first visit. He motioned me to sit beside the bed and told me to help myself to tea.

Chu Hai cleared his throat. "My son," he said uncomfortably, "I have some disturbing information to impart."

I looked at him questioningly. He did not meet my eyes. "It is not my practice to meddle in the domestic affairs of others," he said in a low voice. "Had she not practiced an unforgivable deceit upon you, I would have held my peace. In time, you would have discovered for yourself the profligate nature of your concubine and would have taken appropriate actions to curb her excesses."

"I know she is extravagant," I said defensively. "The household accounts are in a mess. She has squandered money in my absence, but I don't think she is evil . . . just weak and easily led."

Chu looked directly at me, his seamed face mirroring acute discomfort. "She told you K'uo was your son. It is untrue."

"What? . . ." I asked stupidly. "How . . . how know you this?"

"Three years ago, as you had instructed him to do in financial matters, your steward, Hung, came to me seeking advice. It was then about five months after you had left for Nan Chao. Notification of your dismissal had been received. Your Khmer replacement had arrived and was installed in the embassy residence. Your concubine had moved your household to its present premises. Rumor had it that you were dead.

"Hung's concern was for what he considered excessive spending and conduct. From the time of your departure, your concubine had entertained lavishly. Once installed in the new residence and, on the assumption that you were dead, joined by members of her family, Jade Ring's expenditures on entertainment became astronomical. According to Hung, her parties, attended mostly by courtiers and courtesans, were nothing but drunken orgies. Since your concubine was some months pregnant at the time, Hung did not consider her behavior seemly or prudent. He wanted me to exert a restraining influence.

"With the fiscal discretionary powers you had vested in me prior to your embarking on your journey, I could have restricted Jade Ring's spending. I was reluctant to interfere. I was of the opinion that, as her pregnancy advanced, her entertaining would lessen. And, like Trac, I did not believe you dead. My counsel to Hung was to maintain his accounts as accurately as possible and do everything he could to prevent your concubine from being preyed upon by either her relatives or tradespeople. He was to keep me advised concerning what went on beneath your roof. If I thought matters were getting out of hand, I would reconsider intervening on your behalf.

"It was as I had anticipated. In the latter months of her pregnancy. Jade Ring's party-giving subsided. After she gave birth to K'uo, her entertaining again increased, but never to the previous levels, and it has gradually moderated over the last two years."

The recounting tired Chu. He sank back on his pillows and closed his eyes.

"Hung?" I queried.

"He had a dispute with Jade Ring. He was dismissed about a year ago. I secured him an excellent position with some friends," Chu answered without opening his eyes.

"And the boy . . . K'uo?"

"He was born in the Month of the Hare in the Year of the Snake."

I rubbed my eyes wearily. It was a twelvemonth from the date of my departure. The boy couldn't possibly be my son. "His father?" I questioned.

Chu still didn't open his eyes. "I do not know. Hung didn't know. If your concubine knows, she has told few, if any, the father's name." Chu turned his head toward me and opened his eyes. "Believing you dead," he said solemnly, "for her to seek solace in the arms of a lover may not be honorable, but it is at least understandable. Had she concealed from you the existence of the child, I might have tolerated the deception. Had she admitted the child and explained to you the circumstances of his conception, I would have applauded her honesty and supported her cause. But to try and foist off the fruits of her infidelity as a child of your loins in order to ingratiate herself with you . . . that I cannot condone."

No more could I condone her action. My problem was that I did not know yet how I would dispose of the matter.

I walked for some time, steeped in melancholy reflections. I noticed neither my fellow pedestrians nor the passing traffic of sedan chairs and horsemen. When I came to an intersecting waterway, I slumped dejectedly onto a wooden bench. Gazing moodily down at the slime-slicked water, I was oblivious to the activity around me.

Was I cursed in some way? Were all my associations with women doomed to failure? It certainly looked that way from the record. I had found happiness briefly in my youth, only to have Morning Mist and the children snatched from me. Apricot Blossom had become my trusted friend and confidante—and been murdered for her loyalty and affection. Linh, the Annamite nympho-maniac I had married, had lied, cheated, been unfaithful to me without compunction, and killed out of spite and fear. Sita . . . placid, cow-like Sita was loyal to me, but probably out of lethargy rather than inclination. Even my mother, I thought glumly, had not survived my entry into the world.

Now, I had returned to find that my concubine had mothered a child by another man. It did not anger me as much as it saddened me. It was a blow to my pride. Jade Ring had barely waited for my bed to grow cold before taking a lover. Believing me to be dead did not excuse her action, at least not in my eyes. I recognized her for what she was—vain, sensuous, self-indulgent, easily led, and, above all, foolish. Had she known I was not dead but merely imprisoned, I believed she would have been unfaithful. There was, I felt, a weakness in her character that would have led inevitably to infidelity if the oppor-tunity presented itself.

What would I have done had she told me the truth con-cerning K'uo's conception? I was not sure, but I did not believe I would have adopted the lenient response Chu Hsi had suggested. The point was purely academic. The fact was that she had attempted to deceive me and had not succeeded. For that, she would pay. She must be pun-ished for the cupidity that had led to the deception and the stupidity of her thoughtless actions. Yet, I did not feel toward her the animosity her infidelity warranted. I had to accept the fact that I had chosen her of my own free will and that my infatuation had blinded me to faults that should have been self-evident. She would be pun-ished, but I sought no harsh retaliation.

When she stood before me, my resolve nearly wavered. Her hair was piled high in an elaborate coiffure. Her makeup had been delicately and expertly applied. There was about her a faint scent of jasmine. Her inner gown was of pale yellow silk and blended pleasingly with the light green brocade of her outer robe. Even knowing her faults and her guilt, I still found myself responding to her allure.

She seated herself primly and smiled up at me coquettishly. "You wished to see me?"

There was nothing to be gained by prolonging the unpleasant confrontation. Nothing would alter the situation. Even though I still found her physically attractive, nothing could restore our relationship to its former intimacy.

"I have learned today that K'uo is not my son," I said without preamble.

Her features seemed to melt. Her cosmetics stood out vividly against the sudden pallor of her cheeks and brow. "He . . . he is . . ." she stammered, but she was unable to continue.

"You have betrayed my trust . . . brought dishonor on my house," I said harshly.

Tears welled from her eyes and coursed down her cheeks, streaking her makeup. She clenched her hands tightly together in her lap. "I was told . . . you . . . were . . . dead," she managed to say through the sobs.

"Had you honored my memory, you would have mourned for me for at least a decent interval before succumbing to your lust."

Her shoulders shook with sobbing. She did not answer.

"Why," I asked more gently, "did you seek to deceive me with the boy?"

"They . . . they said . . ." Her sobs choked off the rest of her words. She had said enough, however, to confirm something I had suspected.

"They? Your sisters? Did they suggest this deception?"

Jade Ring nodded affirmation.

"It was stupid of them, or their husbands, or both, to think that if I were obligated to you for having given me a son that that obligation would extend to keeping them in idle luxury. I have no responsibility toward them and no intention of continuing their support. It was my intention that they leave this house by the end of this month. You will now inform them that they must leave this house by midday tomorrow. Your mother, if she wishes, may stay until the end of the month."

I took a pace forward and stood so close that the hem of my robe brushed her garment. Looking down at her, I said deliberately, "In determining the punishment to mete out to you, I have taken three things into consideration. The first is that if you believed me deceased, you may not have considered yourself under further moral obligation. The second is that I think your rapacious sisters have preyed on your vanity and encouraged your libidinous nature. And, lastly, I shall be leaving China within a few months."

Her sobs had subsided to sniffles. I had her undivided attention.

"Banishing you from my roof would parade your shame for all to see and subject us both to humiliation. In a few days, when I have located suitable quarters, it is I, not you, who will leave this house. For the remainder of my time in Lin-an, I shall continue to meet the day-to-day expenses of this establishment. When I leave China, it and its contents will be yours to dispose of as you will ... but there will be no further financial support."

She looked up at me, her expression betraying her bewilderment. I don't know what she had expected, but it could not have been the leniency I had just exhibited. I *was* being lenient, even generous, but not for the reasons I had given her. It was because the determining factor in my taking her to my bed as a concubine had been her close resemblance to Apricot Blossom—and for that she could not be blamed.

"There is, madam," I continued, "one final condition. Until I leave this house, you and the boy will confine yourselves to your quarters. I do not wish to see either of you again. Is that clearly understood and agreed upon?"

Jade Ring nodded her assent dumbly.

I had grown accustomed to celibacy. I neither missed Jade Ring's ministrations as much as I thought I would, nor did I feel obliged to partake of the pleasures of the city. In truth, in the four months prior to my departure, I was kept busy almost continuously.

I visited once again a number of Sung military establishments and conferred with senior officers and state officials. I procured from them some military equipment and arms I felt would be needed in Kambuja. In the name of the Khmer Embassy, I negotiated a number of contracts with military suppliers.

During this time, Mohammed bin Abdullah visited me in Lin-an. He stayed the better part of a week. We had several serious discussions at the conclusion of which Mohammed agreed to cooperate with me fully if and when the situation in Kabuja developed, as I was sure it would. It was strange indeed that this man whom I had once sworn to kill saw eye to eye with me on many matters. Once my sworn enemy, he was rapidly becoming a close friend.

The blind monk and his predictions often came to my mind. What he had foretold—at least the opening predictions—had been disquietingly accurate. I would have liked to address some questions to him concerning his latter predictions. His references to happiness, betrayal, and an honorable death I found disturbingly cryptic.

In the Month of the Boar, almost four years to the day since my chance encounter with the blind soothsayer, I went to West Lake to search him out and question him. Although I searched diligently that day and on several subsequent days, I could not remember the footpaths and turnings I had taken on that previous encounter. I could not find the pagoda—or the blind prophet.

chapter 42

I EMBARKED ON A MERCHANTMAN FOR THE VOYAGE TO
Angkor late in the first month of the Year of the Monkey.
The northerly winds were still bitterly cold. We clung to
the coast on a southwesterly course to Canton. The seas
were gray and storm-tossed.

When we left Canton, we set a south-southwesterly
course. Soon we found favorable winds, clearer skies,
and warmer weather.

During the voyage, when my thoughts winged back to
Lin-an, they did not concern themselves with Jade Ring
and that closed chapter of my life, but with Chu Hsi and
Trac.

In the closing months of the Year of the Ram and the
first two weeks of this year, 1200—the Year of the Monkey
—I had often visited the ailing Chu Hsi. The white-
bearded philosopher who had such a profound effect on
the manners and morals of his time passed away quietly
in his sleep in the third week of the first month at the age
of seventy-one. He was mourned in Lin-an and throughout China. During my time in Lin-an, he had been my
friend and mentor, giving freely of his time and wise counsel. None mourned his passing more than I.

Prior to my departure, I had spent as much time with
Trac as tasks permitted. She could have come with me
to Angkor, the city of her birth, but she preferred to
remain in Lin-an. I could not blame her for this decision.

She was deeply in love with Hsien. When he completed his classical examinations, they planned to get married. It was a match of which both Hsien's father and I heartily approved and to which I had gladly given my blessing and consent.

Our parting on the quayside was tender. As the merchant junk slipped her lines and drifted clear of the wharf, Trac stood at Hsien's side and waved. I wondered when I would next see my lovely daughter—and the beautiful grandchildren the couple no doubt would bestow upon me.

We arrived at the confluence of the Mekong and Tonle Sap rivers during the third month. The water levels were at their seasonal low. I boarded a shallow-draft river craft for the onward journey to the head of the Great Lake.

Before leaving the merchant junk, I stowed my Chinese garments in my chest. Clad once more in a familiar *sampot*, with the hot morning sun beating down on my bare back and shoulders, I stood in the bow of the craft as it nosed in toward the lakeshore.

The shoreline sloped from the lake level to a rim some thirty-five feet above. A stone ramp, caked with sun-baked mud, led upward toward the rim. The upper part of the slope was matted with shrubs and low trees. It was the abundance of this lake and the phenomenal fertility of its shores that had made it possible for the Khmer to embark on the conquest of their neighboring states. Kambuja owed its empire to this natural catch basin for the Mekong overflow.

When I had described the Great Lake to the people in Lin-an, they had laughed in polite disbelief. A lake that covered an area of one thousand miles in the dry season, then rose to cover more than twice that area in the rainy season—a likely story. A lake with depths as shallow as three feet in the dry season, and as much as forty feet in the wet season—patently a fabrication. Rice strains that grew taller than a man, and which were harvested from sampans—amusing nonsense.

If they had not believed those facts, they would have thought me a raving lunatic had I told them of the fish that were baked solidly into mud that was dried brick-hard by the sun in the hot season, yet revived to wriggle into the

lake when the rains softened the mud. Had I told them
that the water rose to drown small trees and that, when the
level receded, men with handcarts descended the mud-
slicked stone ramps and plucked live fish from the
branches of the trees that emerged as the water receded,
they would have locked me away as a madman.

Behind me, I heard the sail rings rattle down the mast.
We slid alongside a floating platform at the bottom of a
ramp. I breathed deeply of the steamy air and smiled
broadly. I was back in a land more suited to my tempera-
ment than my homeland.

I was met at the lakeshore by a troop of cavalrymen
and escorted directly to the walled city. In the decade of
my absence, the walls had weathered, and inside the
rammed-earth galleries had acquired carpets of grass; otherwise, Angkor Thom looked little changed.

One exception was the Bayon in the city center. The
temple was a scene of frenetic activity. The stone terraces
of the pyramidal base were finished. An army of artisans
and stonemasons swarmed over the towers rearing upward
from the different levels. In the galleries, stone-carvers
followed charcoaled outlines and chipped away at bas-
reliefs. It was a familiar scene—to the same ringing accom-
paniment I remembered.

While my residence in the royal compound was much
as I recalled it, there were other changes. A fire had destroyed the royal palace and a number of other buildings
on the northern terrace. The palace was being rebuilt.
Until its completion, the king was residing temporarily in
the temple of Preah Khan.

Sita seemed pleased to see me. Once more back in her
own land, she had regained her sunny disposition, but she
had lost none of the weight she had acquired before her
return to Angkor; in fact, she appeared to have put on
even more weight.

She regaled me with court gossip. I learned that the
king's chief wife, Jayarajadevi, had perished in the palace
fire. The king had elevated her older sister, Indradevi, to
the exalted station of chief wife. Indradevi, Sita informed
me, had been a renowned teacher of Buddhist doctrine.
Due to her influence, Sita claimed, the king was involved
in a project to build a series of hospitals throughout the

realm. And Indradevi, as a project of her own, was composing a biography of the king, which was being inscribed
in the gallery of the temple within the royal compound,
Phimeanakas. Prince Surya, the heir apparent, had recently been married to his fifth wife, a Mon princess. It
had been a gala affair, Sita assured me, and it was a
pity I had missed the festivities.

On my homecoming to Angkor, I summoned Sita to my
bedchamber several times, but, thereafter, I did so infrequently. I was fond of her and, taken in small doses,
her chatter amused me. The trouble was that as her girth
had increased, the limited appeal she had held for me
diminished. For her part, she seemed perfectly happy sub-
limating her sexual drive through the nobler activity of
gluttony.

To atone for my former lack of interest, I tried to spend
as much time as possible with the children. By so doing, I
learned that my earlier instincts had been reasonably accurate. With the possible exception of the youngest son,
eight-year-old Imre, my children by Sita were neither inspired nor inspiring. The twins, Dom and Yasod, were
now twelve years of age. They were a stocky pair of lads
with amiable but vacant expressions. Their sister Sita,
named after her mother, was a chubby replica of her
mother. The child was maturing early and, at eleven, had
already been deflowered by Brahman courtesy.

I reinstituted the practice of evening sessions to review
their daily lessons and to discuss topics of mutual interest.
Dom and Yasod did not appear to have retentive memories and didn't display much interest in anything. Young
Sita seemed to have but one subject in mind—boys. Only
little Imre, sturdy and almost as tall as his older brothers,
showed interest in sporting activities. I talked with the
Chinese tutors I'd sent to Angkor and the Khmer tutors
who had been employed locally. They reported that the
children were not too scholastically inclined. This, I discovered, was a masterpiece of understatement.

King Jayavarman did not keep me long in suspense. A
few days after my return to Angkor, I was summoned to
attend the king at Preah Khan. It was an illuminating
private audience.

I don't know why I expected to find Jayavarman unchanged. He was, after all, in his mid-seventies and, despite his self-appointed status as a god, a mere mortal. I think I had come to consider Jayavarman as indestructible. The changes wrought in him during the decade since our last meeting came as a shock to me. His hair was iron-gray. His face was puffy and a muscle in his right cheek twitched almost incessantly. There was loose flesh at his jowls, neck, and biceps. His chest sagged and he bulged at the midriff. Yet, even with the toll time had taken, he conveyed an impression of regal dignity and immense power.

The audience started on an unexpected note. The king coldly accused me of disloyalty. The accusation stunned me and I wondered what vicious lies had been spread by my enemies during my lengthy absence.

The king amplified his opening thrust by stating my treachery came as no surprise. He had come to expect disloyalty. He was beset by plots and intrigues on every hand. There were none, absolutely none, within his realm to be trusted. Knowing what to expect of me, he had taken the precaution of putting as much distance as possible between myself and the traitorous Prince Vidyanandana. But I had been more cunning than the king had expected. I had managed to reach across even that great distance to treacherous purpose.

There was no point in trying to defend myself against such accusations without knowledge of what he believed me to have done. "In what way have I offended you, sire?"

The king's voice rose shrilly. "Did you not spare the life of a Cham admiral? Did you not communicate with him by secret code both here and when in China? Did not that same Cham admiral play a large part in thwarting our attempts to dislodge the usurping prince? Could the admiral have done so without the knowledge of our military capabilities given him by you? With the Cham acting as an intermediary, you have conspired with Prince Vidyanandana against us. Deny it, Barbarian. Deny it if you can."

The diatribe was too absurd to dignify with denial. The king knew my feelings with respect to Vidya. If his agents knew of Mohammed, the king knew of the admiral's defection and that Mohammed as well bore nothing but hatred for Vidya. Jayavarman might not believe the accusations now, but he had, in whole or in part, not so long ago. I understood now why information concerning Champa had been withheld from me in Lin-an. I now knew why I had been imprisoned in Nan Chao.

"If you believed me a traitor, why was I not killed, sire?"

The king seemed genuinely surprised by my question. "We may have had need of you," he said impatiently.

"And had you not, sire . . . what then?"

"Our payments to the T'ai king would have ceased. If they stopped without an explanatory directive, you were to be disposed of," Jayavarman said matter-of-factly.

At least, I thought wryly, it was an admission that the king now needed my services.

The king seemed to withdraw. It was as though he had forgotten my presence. He stared fixedly at a point somewhere beyond me. He began to mumble. As his voice gradually rose in pitch, his words became more distinct.

It was *his* Champa. *He* had conquered it, only to have it snatched from *his* hands by base betrayal. Those who had betrayed him would pay. They would pay dearly. Champa would be, *must* be, his.

As the king railed against those who plotted against him, the ineptness of his military commanders, and the perfidy of Prince Vidyanandana, he became more and more agitated. He trembled uncontrollably. His voice rose almost to a scream. His eyes bulged. Spittle sprayed from his lips.

The fit of fury passed. Jayavarman slumped forward, his tirade reduced to incoherent muttering. His trembling gradually subsided. For some moments, he remained hunched slightly forward. Then, he shook his head, straightened, and fixed me with a baleful glare. His face hardened.

"You have been recalled to active service for one purpose, Barbarian—the taking of Champa. To achieve that end, you will form an army of which you will be sole commander. You have, as of this moment, full powers to requisition anything you need and to recruit anyone you may require. You will assemble this force with all possible speed. When you have worked out your strategy and are ready to move against Champa, you will confer with us."

King Jayavarman's thought processes astounded me. His reasoning often escaped me. I, who had handed him Champa as a vassal state ten years ago, stood accused of plotting to wrest Champa from Khmer control and frustrate the king's every effort to recapture the prize. I was supposed to have allied myself with a patricidal, unscrupulous opportunist I loathed. I had demonstrated that I was not to be trusted. I had been removed from harm's way by imprisonment. Had the king not felt I might be useful at some future date, I would have been "disposed of." Now, when he felt that I, and I alone, could give substance to his dream, he had completely reversed his stand. I, a man not to be trusted, had been vested with such sweeping powers that I held the kingdom and its empire in the palm of my hand. If my ambitions so dictated, Kambuja was mine for the taking.

The king was deranged. I had recognized years earlier that the conquest of Champa was for him an all-consuming passion that defied reason. He had demonstrated anew that this obsession held him in an unrelenting grip. But what is madness in mortals if inspired eccentricity in a god-king.

I addressed myself to the task of shaping an army.

I had foreseen difficulties, but the situation was worse than I'd anticipated. Repeated defeats in Champa had all but destroyed the morale of the Khmer forces. A spirit of defeatism prevailed not only in the forces, but throughout the realm.

For a decade, the entire military thrust had been directed toward the three abortive campaigns in Champa. The demoralized armies of the West and South, reduced in strength to provide manpower for the eastern campaigns, had been unable to hold their former gains. In the northwest, the kingdom of Haripoonchai had ridded itself of the Khmer garrison forces and regained its independence. The Army of the South had fallen back to a line across the narrowest part of the southern isthmus.

The plunder and captives that had once flowed toward Angkor had dried up. The flood from Champa that was to compensate for this loss had failed to materialize. Recruitment for both military and labor forces was from within a realm squeezed dry of manpower.

As General Dom had suspected might happen, temple-building seemed to have become an end in itself. The completion of Ta Prohm, Preah Khan, Neak Pean, and Ta Som had not resulted in any saving of labor, since the work force simply had been diverted to the as yet unfinished Banteay Kdei and the monolithic Bayon.

The temples, as they were completed, imposed a burden on an already strained economy in yet another way. Thousands of villages were assigned the honor of supplying with produce, and supporting through a steady stream of acolytes and novice priests, one or another of the temples.

In only one area was there a conspicuous reduction of effort. It was an area where the realm could least afford a slackening of work—the irrigation and flood-control projects. But here, again, no saving of labor was effected since the labor force was fully employed in Queen Indradevi's humanitarian project. Throughout the realm, one hundred twenty hospitals were in varying stages of construction.

While the pattern of life in Angkor Thom had not changed much, dissension was rife in the countryside. The realm smoldered just short of the flash point of open revolt.

It was against this political and economic background that I was expected to shape a new army—and to inject into it the will to win.

My enemies were many. They prowled around me like hungry predators. One false step on my part would bring them in for the kill, yet I had no time to exercise caution. I traveled much and worked long hours. I drove the staff I assembled as hard as I drove myself. It was demanding and exhausting work.

chapter 43

THE REMAINDER OF THE YEAR OF THE MONKEY AND THE first four months of the Year of the Cock were devoted to a program of intensive training, with much of the effort concentrated in two specialized fields. The first of these was to convert the major part of the cavalry units to troops made up exclusively of mounted archers. The second involved training in a new form of weaponry and warfare.

With the cavalry training, I shuttled between the armies. Diehard traditionalists who opposed me were summarily discharged or transferred to other duties.

On my return to Angkor from China, I had brought with me some military hardware of a specialized nature together with a number of Chinese military personnel skilled in the fabrication and usage of such weapons. Cloaking the project in utmost secrecy, I set up a training center ninety miles east of Angkor near the ancient, abandoned capital, Sambor Prei Kuk. A foundry was established at the site to duplicate the Chinese weapons. A factory went into operation in which black powder was processed and stored in wooden casks. I fear that the ruins of Sambor, already some five centuries old, sustained a good deal more damage during the siege-training practice sessions.

By the time the rains came in the Year of the Cock, all the cavalry units had been remounted on Chinese steeds that I had procured before leaving Lin-an and that had been shipped to me in the season of favorable winds. The units of bowmen, crossbowmen, and infantrymen had been brought to full strength and had been drilled to a high degree of readiness.

During the rainy season, I gradually denuded the capital of its Army of Angkor. Its personnel were divided equally between the armies of the South and West. Had a Cham or Annamite army appeared it could have overrun Angkor Thom unopposed by other than the palace guard.

As the rainy season drew to a close, the armies of the South and West went on the offensive. The Army of the South swept down the isthmus and the peninsula in a series of brilliant victories against superior forces. The Army of the West, to which were attached cavalry units from the Silver Banner and the Golden Banner in addition to its Cavalry of the Scarlet Banner, overran Lampang. The combined cavalry units were then formed into an independent strike force that swept with lightning swiftness into the kingdom of Haripoonchai. The tactics employed were the two-column advance and swift encirclement I had used so effectively some years earlier in this same terrain. They were the cavalry tactics employed by Temujin's Mongols in the faraway steppes. They proved their worth. Haripoonchai capitulated, the first state in this region to fall to a force composed exclusively of cavalry.

The victories achieved all that I had hoped for. Morale ran high in the forces. When the plunder and prisoners taken in the campaigns converged on Angkor Thom in the rear of the triumphant processions of the victorious army commanders, the mood in the countryside underwent a dramatic change for the better.

Before embarking on my final phase of preparation, I dispatched a coded message to Canton. Mohammed had advised me he would need about a year to lay the groundwork for the part I intended him to play in the forthcoming action.

It was now time to assemble the army that, until now, had existed only in my head. I called it the Army of the Jade Banner.

Observers from my staff had accompanied the armies on their dry-season campaigns. They now reported to me on which were the most effective units and which officers had demonstrated leadership qualities, administrative abilities, and daring.

Gradually, throughout the rainy season of the Year of the Dog, the Army of the Jade Banner took shape. It was by no means as large a force as the army I'd assembled twelve years earlier for the conquest of Champa, but it had compensating features that the Army of the Azure Banner had lacked. The officers of this army were all hand-picked, and they, in turn, had selected the men who would serve under them. There were three other features to this point, known only by myself, which set the Army of the Jade Banner apart from any other fighting force ever fielded by Kambuja.

The army I was now assembling at an encampment north of Angkor Thom appeared to have in its composition only a token cavalry force. It ultimately would have, in fact, the largest cavalry force ever to accompany a Khmer army—only the army wouldn't know that for many months to come. The Cavalry of the Jade Banner would be formed slowly and in secret. It would be quartered and trained at a separate location. Throughout the better part of the campaign, it would act entirely independently of the main body.

Another thing not yet known to the officers and rank and file of the army was that special units trained in the use of special weapons waited at Sambor Prei Kuk to join the Army of the Jade Banner on its eastward march.

The third factor calculated to ensure victory for the Army of the Jade Banner was known to no one in the entire Khmer empire but myself. He was an ex-admiral of the Cham Navy, Mohammed bin Abdullah.

The pennants and banners of the new army were jade-green, trimmed with gold edging. The jerkins of the soldiers were dyed green. The trappings of cavalry horses and war elephants attached to the force were gold-trimmed green. The officers and men appreciated that they were part of an elite force. An espirit de corps developed that bordered on arrogance.

The rainy season of the Year of the Dog gave way to the cool, dry months at the close of the year. The Army of the Jade Banner drilled and trained at Angkor. The Cavalry of the Jade Banner, secretly assembled over many months, was encamped on the west bank of the Mekong at a point where, long ago, Morning Mist and I had crossed the much-divided river. The cavalry was commanded by an eager, quick-witted officer who had served under General Imre. I had promoted this officer, Chun, to general of the second rank and coached him carefully in what I expected of him.

King Jayavarman was as good as his word. I was in sole command of the new army and no one questioned that authority, even though there were many in the high command and elsewhere who bitterly resented me. Throughout the training program, the campaigns in the south and northwest and the assembling of the Army of the Jade Banner, neither the king nor any of his ministers had interfered in any way. Without doubt the king's agents were keeping him abreast of developments, but there were some aspects his spies could not know. The king might have been advised of the Cavalry of the Jade Banner now encamped and undergoing training in an uninhabited region some one hundred forty miles northeast of Angkor. I had slowly siphoned off the cavalry units composing the Cavalry of the Jade Banner from the armies to which they'd been attached and routed them to the mustering point by various and devious ways; nonetheless, it was difficult to cloak an operation of that size and scope in total secrecy. From its inception, the Sambor Prei Kuk project had been under tight security. There was a good chance that the king did not know of the special units and engines of war at Sambor. Of my campaign strategy, my tactical employment of Mohammed bin Abdullah, and my plans for military governorship once victory was ours, the king had no knowledge. Within a few months the Army of the Jade Banner would be ready to move out. It was time King Jayavarman was fully briefed.

The private audience I requested was granted. The king received me in his chambers at Preah Khan. It was over two years since I had seen him last. He was not much changed.

In detail, I outlined my overall strategy, my intended use of the cavalry and special units, my battle tactics, and my siege tactics. From his questions, I recognized that the king knew of the Cavalry of the Jade Banner and, despite my security clamp, a good deal more than I had expected about Sambor Prei Kuk. The part I intended

Mohammed to play in the action both surprised and pleased the king. He gave a throaty chuckle and nodded approvingly.

From past experience I knew that while the king might give me considerable latitude in military planning, he considered political strategy his own province. I approached my post-battle plans with caution.

"I have found it much easier," I said, "to win the day on the field of battle than it is to govern and pacify a conquered realm." The king looked at me sharply, but he said nothing. I continued evenly: "With your approval, sire, I intend to keep the Army of the Jade Banner in Champa for a minimum period of three years as an army of occupation."

"It is our wish that your army remain as an army of occupation until ordered by us to withdraw," the king rasped.

"Thank you, sire. It is my intention to impose martial law and military governorship on Champa. To make this more acceptable to the vanquished Cham, and to promote cooperation, I believe a Cham, not a Khmer, should occupy the position of chief civil administrator. After careful consideration, I suggest that Ong Dhamapatigrama, a Cham of proven administrative ability here in Angkor Thom, fill this position in Vijaya."

"It is our intention that Prince Indra ascend the Cham throne," the king said gratingly.

"Sire," I said reasonably, "no nobleman of your court should occupy that seat until victory is consolidated and authority extended over the conquered state. I consider that will take a minimum of three years. To have a Khmer nobleman ascend the Cham throne before that will invite friction between the military command and the governing clique. It would lead inevitably to palace intrigue and weaken the entire structure."

Even as I spoke, I realized I was overstepping my bounds. I had had the temerity to challenge the king. The fingers of the king's left hand were twitching. His face was expressionless. The danger signals were all there, but my words could not be retracted.

"You dare to dispute my judgment?" the king questioned softly.

I abandoned caution. If I backed down now, my position could never be retrieved. "Sire, you have seen fit to place me in sole command of this undertaking. I am confident I can take Champa in your name. I am equally confident that it cannot be held in your name unless my authority extends to consolidating your victory. If it is to be otherwise, I will resign my command."

I have never seen anything quite like the expression that came over the king's face. He paled. The muscle in his cheek twitched uncontrollably. His face registered more than shocked disbelief; it was something akin to horror. His eyes seemed to go out of focus. He started to say something, but he was seized with a violent fit of coughing. He gripped the arms of his chair with such force that his knuckles were white.

As his coughing subsided, the king slowly relaxed his grip on the chair arms. I noted that the fingers of his left hand no longer twitched. When at last he looked at me, his face was again expressionless.

"Barbarian," he said harshly, "you shall have your Cham administrator . . . but purely as a figurehead. It is you who will govern, in fact, as you intended. You will bear full responsibility for your actions and those of the Cham figurehead." He seemed about to add something, but he thought better of it and dismissed me with a curt nod.

As I left his presence, I expelled my breath in a long sigh of relief. I had never, on the battlefield or elsewhere, been closer to death than I had been a few moments earlier.

The departure of the Army of the Jade Banner in the predawn hours in the second month of the Year of the Boar, 1203, was without pomp or ceremony. It was a far cry from the ceremonial exit from the capital of its precursor of thirteen years earlier, the Army of the Azure Banner.

There were other differences. When I had exercised tactical command of the Army of the Azure Banner, I had been a brash and confident twenty-eight going on twenty-nine. Now, in sole command of a much smaller army, I was nearing my forty-second year and had grown less impulsive and considerably more cynical with each passing year. But the most ironical difference between that earlier army of conquest and the present force was that the Army of the Azure Banner had had as its nominal commander Prince Vidyanandana, while the Army of the Jade Banner had been specifically enjoined to return Prince Vidyanandana in chains to Angkor Thom.

At Kompong Thom, the special units from Sambor Prei Kuk joined us with a long line of creaking wagons, their contents hidden beneath heavy canvas. The Cavalry of the Jade Banner, still encamped on the banks of the Mekong some one hundred twenty-five miles north of our present position at Kompong Thom, was poised to cross the river and follow the path into the mountains that Morning Mist and I had taken twenty-six years ago, but it would not move out for some weeks to come.

With the added refinement of the role I hoped Mohammed to play, my strategy was based on a Chinese proverb: "When the tiger threatens your front door, do not forget the wolf at the back." My main force was the "tiger" marching boldly to the attack. The Cavalry of the Jade Banner was my "wolf at the back."

My main force was the visible army. It was not of sufficient strength to mount a two-pronged offensive. Vidyanandana would expect me to attack the capital, Vijaya. My line of march would appear to indicate Vijaya as my objective. Then I would suddenly alter my direction and, at a forced-march pace, strike for the coastal plain and Panduranga. Once Panduranga fell, I would march to the north.

I had purposely kept the size of the Army of the Jade Banner relatively small. The siege of Panduranga would confirm the limited number of my forces to Vidya's spies. When I turned to the north, I fully expected the seasoned, confident Cham army based on Vijaya to sally forth and march south to challenge my advancing force. That was exactly what I wanted the Cham to do. I could conceive of no reason why they would not—they outnumbered my army by more than two to one.

There was, of course, always the chance that Vidya so

feared me that he would not risk a pitched battle no matter how attractive the odds appeared. In that case, I
would continue my march to the north and place the capital under siege. At that point, the formidable siege engines
I would not use at Panduranga, the bronze mortars and
the rocket launchers, would be unveiled and put to use.

What of the "wolf at the back," the cavalry strike force
that was an army in itself? When it reached the interior
plateau, it would race across the highlands and descend
on Vijaya without warning. Its arrival was timed to coin-
cide with the main force's northward march on Vijaya. If,
as I anticipated, the Cham army was marching south to
meet me, the Cavalry of the Jade Banner would leave a
token containing force at Vijaya while the bulk of the
strike force would ride in pursuit of the Cham Army. They
were to avoid contact with the Cham force, staying no less
than an hour's ride from its rear. Once my Army of the
Jade Banner was locked in combat with the Cham force,
the Cavalry of the Jade Banner would race to join the fray
—the wolf would join the tiger.

In the event that the Cham Army had not marched to
intercept me, the cavalry strike force was to seal off the
landward approaches to the capital. They would maintain a tight perimeter patrol until my main force joined
them to mount the siege in earnest.

What part did I hope Mohammed would play in this
scenario? In the past, attempts to besiege Vijaya had
been protracted efforts, or had been frustrated altogether,
by the Cham Navy's ability to reinforce the defending
garrison and resupply the beleaguered city. If it could be
prevented, I didn't intend the navy to succor Vijaya this
time. For more than a year, working from Canton through
trusted colleagues in Champa, Mohammed had been sow-
ing the seeds of dissension in the naval force. For the
past three months, having returned to Champa clandestinely, Mohammed had personally directed the sedition.
By coded message he had assured me that the navy would
mutiny and rally to my cause at the propitious moment.
The signal for this event would be the fall of Panduranga.
If Mohammed was right, instead of being the besieged
capital's salvation, the navy would be Vijaya's nemesis by
sealing off its harbor and steward approaches.

Panduranga fell without a fight. The city had known of our approach only two days before we descended from the mountains to the valley and marched on the city. The city had not had time to muster its defenses. Its gates were thrown open to us.

The governor of Panduranga was a Cham named Ong Ansaraja. I knew him to be the son of King Jaya Harshavarman II, from whom Vidyanandana's father had usurped the throne. Ong Ansaraja, therefore, was the rightful heir to the throne upon which Vidya now sat. Frankly, I couldn't understand why the man held a position of such authority—why, if he posed a threat to Vidya, he had not been killed years ago. But he hadn't been, and his station and lineage may have had some bearing on why he surrendered Panduranga—the city and the province—without a struggle.

I sent Ong Dhamapatigrama, as chief administrator designate, together with three of my senior commanders, into the city to receive Ong Ansaraja's formal surrender. At this stage, I had few demands. The city and the province were to lay down their arms, my troops were to be supplied with fresh provisions, and women, preferably willingly, but by force if necessary, were to be sent to our encampment outside the city gates. The questions of manpower levies and confiscated goods and valuables could be pursued later.

Ong Dhamapatigrama returned about an hour later to advise me that the regional governor had accepted my terms and would await my pleasure to discuss additional matters pertaining to the surrender. Before leaving my command tent, Ong Dhamapatigrama hesitated, then turned to face me with a broad smile.

"It almost slipped my mind," he said. "The governor asked me to convey a personal message."

"Which is?"

"That, at your convenience, one of his daughters awaits your pleasure."

"Interesting," I observed sardonically. "Since, by right of conquest, I can take my pleasure with any, or all, of his daughters, wives, and concubines, why should this particular daughter slake my thirst? What response did you make to his generous offer?"

"That the girl should be escorted to your tent this evening. If she doesn't appeal to you, you can always return her unused. I thought it might be a diversion on a campaign of conquest to have a bed partner who comes willingly to your couch on the first encounter."

"It is a novelty," I admitted, "but not unheard of."

chapter 44

THERE WAS MUCH TO BE DONE. THE GARRISON TROOPS and troop commander had to be selected. There were edicts and proclamations to prepare for the civilian population and orders to be given my troops to govern their conduct in the conquered city. I worked on these matters through the afternoon, had a simple meal of rice, fish, and fruit brought to my command tent, and worked into the early evening.

A sound caught my attention. I looked up to find Mohammed bin Abdullah standing just within the tent. In the lamplight, his face looked grave. I could read neither success nor failure into his expression.

With my leg cramped from having been seated too long, I rose awkwardly from the cushions. Mohammed strode forward. He grasped my right forearm with both his hands. His teeth flashed white in a triumphant smile.

"Tartar, the navy is yours to command."

When Mohammed was comfortably seated, with a cup of wine in his hand, we reviewed the situation. Mohammed advised me that the bulk of the navy based in the south had mutinied and installed him as reinstated commander-in-chief. He anticipated that those naval units farther north at Vijaya and Indrapura, which had not yet learned of the mutiny, would join his cause when the news reached them. In response to my question, he indicated it would take at least a week for word of the mutiny to reach the capital.

I explained the position in which I found myself. The ease with which we'd taken Panduranga had upset my timetable. In my calculations I'd allowed a week for the siege of the city and three more days of marching to the north before the Cavalry of the Jade Banner was due to encircle Vijaya. Prematurely sealing off the seaward approaches of the city by naval blockade might alter the situation adversely. It might persuade Vidya to keep his army within the city walls.

My instructions to Mohammed were to put out to sea with the fleet but stand well off the coast and not impose the blockade for ten days. He nodded in agreement, indicating the delay of a few days posed no problems.

Our conversation drifted into other channels.

"Are you happy to be home once more?" I queried.

Mohammed breathed deeply of the warm night air. "Yes," he said with feeling. "Your land was a haven and your people were hospitable, but I had difficulty adapting to both climate and custom."

"Custom?"

"Customs and attitudes," Mohammed explained. "On the surface, the Chinese I met were unctuously puritanical. Behind that facade, I found them decadently corrupt. I grew used to the pious front that masked hypocrisy and deceit, but I did not grow to like it. I find the Chinese too devious, too oblique, for my tastes."

In Mohammed's appraisal, I heard echoes of Chu Hai's views. "Tranquil Ancestor is young, but he shows signs of being a good emperor," I said thoughtfully. "But in my estimation it is too late for moral reform from within. The Sung dynasty has grown tired. The administrative structure is flabby and tottering. It is strange, but the views you have just expressed are remarkably similar to those held by a philosopher I knew well. But in your candid appraisal, perhaps you forget that I am Chinese."

Mohammed laughed. "No, I had not forgotten. But you are of mixed blood and mixed cultures. You have lived among us so long that you think more like a Khmer —or a Cham—than you do like a Chinese. I find your approach to life . . . and death . . . refreshingly uncomplicated."

"I'm glad," I said dryly, "that they appeal to you."

Then I added teasingly, "But surely you must have found the dainty-footed damsels of Canton appealing."

"They were most obliging, most accommodating, and not lacking in beauty or skills. But my tastes run to the more robust charms of Cham women . . . and to the esoteric aptitudes they have acquired from early childhood. I'm afraid I find the frank and open Cham approach to sexual gratification preferable to the secluded practices of China. The flush of beauty has faded from my wives, but they know my habits and my wants . . . they are comfortable, not contrived."

Mohammed had to return to the large bay twenty miles to the north where the Cham fleet lay at anchor. We cut short our conversation so that he could ride north to join his flagship and set sail on the morrow.

When he had gone, my thoughts were still on him. In our conspiratorial relationship, we seemed to have grown close. He was a decade older than myself, yet I felt completely at ease with Mohammed and not at all conscious of the discrepancy in our ages. How awesome to contemplate are the anomalies of life. Who would have thought, witnessing a scene that was played out twenty-eight years in the past, how time could alter the script? Who, seeing a boy sprawling on the deck of a dismasted junk glaring up in hate at a laughing pirate, would have imagined that the man and boy one day would become friends and colleagues?

As I got ready to bed myself for the night, my errant thoughts touched on various portions of my conversation with Mohammed. He had suggested that I was closer in attitude to the Khmer and Cham than I was to the Chinese. There could be little doubt that my many years in Kambuja had shaped my thinking and superimposed foreign attitudes upon me. On my return to my homeland, I had even felt uncomfortably alien upon occasion. Even as had Mohammed, I had been critical of the manners, morals, and conditions as I found them in Lin-an. But the point that Mohammed had missed, the point missed by most barbarians from foreign lands, is that Chinese culture is a product of some three thousand years of civilizing influence, from the Shang Yin kingdoms to the Sung dynasty of today. Where other realms measure their life-spans in centuries, we Chinese think in terms of millennia. I may voice dissatisfaction with some aspects of life in China and certain Chinese customs I consider out-moded, but I am always conscious of and take pride in my Chinese blood and heritage.

I smiled at the response Mohammed had given to my question concerning Chinese women. "Comfortable" was the adjective he had applied to his wives. I supposed that the term could have been applied to Sita—in the sense that a stack of straw or a sackful of rice chaff can be associated with both bulk and comfort. Yet, even though most of my sexual relations had been confined to women of this geographical region, in my fantasies the mental image was most often a Chinese. As I now recognized, my taking Jade Ring as a concubine had been an attempt on my part to live out a sexual fantasy. Still, if the women of my dreams were chiefly Chinese, it would indicate that my preference lay in that direction, just as it was natural that Mohammed should prefer Cham women.

In my case, there was one notable exception. Although she had not entered my thoughts for some time, my fantasies in my youth had revolved around the child-woman who had initiated me into sex—White Lotus.

I do not consider myself a superstitious man. I have found that most phenomena that appear at first glance to be of supernatural origin yield to logical explanation upon closer examination. Still, there are visions, manifestations, and experiences that can be ascribed only to authorship from the spirit world. That White Lotus should have intruded into my thoughts after long absence and at that particular moment defies logic and can have been nothing but a projection from the spirit realm. For, at the very moment that the image of White Lotus sprang vividly to mind, the guard announced that a young woman had arrived, escorted by an unarmed detail of Cham guards.

In the press of work during the afternoon, and with Mohammed's visit, the fact that the governor's daughter was to join me this evening had completely flown from my mind. I was weary. The intrusion did not please me. I was almost of a mind to order the girl escorted back to her dwelling, but curiosity overrode fatigue. I told the guard to usher the visitor in and rose to pour myself a cup of wine.

With the wine cup almost to my lips, I froze in stunned disbelief. The girl stood just within the tent flap. I could have sworn I was gazing on the White Lotus of my erotic imaginings. It was not until she moved gracefully toward me, and into the brighter light of the oil lamps, that the illusion was dispelled and the reason apparent. She was infinitely more beautiful, but there was much about her to remind me of her mother. The woman before me was Golden Dawn.

She stood a few feet in front of me and said simply, "I have waited."

I could find no words. I set the bronze cup on my map table. Turning to Golden Dawn, I folded her in my arms.

She stood proudly before me in the flawless perfection of her nakedness. I was suddenly and unaccountably shy. My fingers trembled as I undid the knot and let my *sampot* drop to my feet. At that moment, she did a strange and moving thing. She dropped to her knees before me, embraced my legs, and tenderly kissed the jagged scar on my right thigh.

She was not a virgin; I had not expected her to be. But, even though she responded eagerly to my thrusts, penetration was difficult. I eased into her inch by inch until her lubricating juices allowed me to fully sheathe myself in her warm, tight scabbard. As my tempo quickened, she matched the rhythm of my strokes and moaned with pleasure. As our climax neared, she clutched me frantically to her breast. Then her hand slid down until her fingers dug themselves into my buttocks. I groaned in ecstasy as I exploded deep within her, my spurting juices mingling with hers. She arched to meet me, quivered convulsively, and cried out.

In all my lovemaking, I had never experienced anything to match the fulfillment of that coupling. It was a wonderful and wondrous thing how we had responded to each other, how closely matched had been our appetites and responses. Now, as our bodies cooled, she lay beside me, one leg across my thighs and her head upon my chest.

"It is how I dreamed it would be," she said softly.

"But you are not a virgin," I said. "You have been schooled in the art of love. Have you never before reached a climax in lovemaking?"

She raised herself and looked solemnly down at me. "Since the ceremony initiating me to womanhood, no man

has shared my bed. I have waited long to give my body
to you. It was worth the waiting."

I knew she spoke the truth. I accepted her tribute humbly and drew her tenderly to my chest. "How," I asked
wonderingly, "could you choose me above all others on
the basis of a single meeting?"

She laughed softly. "I saw you several times in the palace before the night my mother brought me to your chamber at my request. I watched you unobserved and listened
to you speak with the officers and men of your command.
I fell in love with you and have loved you to the exclusion
of all others since then."

"What if I had not returned to Champa . . . to Panduranga?"

"In my heart I knew you would return to me. I hoped
and prayed it would be while I was still young and attractive. But, had my heart deceived me, had you not returned to claim me, I would have given myself to no
other."

Before dawn streaked the eastern sky, Golden Dawn
and I made love a second time. It was a repetition of,
and equally as satisfying as, our first lovemaking.

It was not until she left to return to her father's house
that several disquieting thoughts struck me. She had not
made mention of her mother, nor had I. When White
Lotus came to mind, so did the disturbing thought that it
well could be that I had made love to my daughter. Angrily, I put the thought from me.

There was no question in my mind that I would take
Golden Dawn in marriage. But, to overcome my scruples
and the lingering suspicion that she could be of my blood,
I convinced myself that my reasons for the union were
political. On her mother's side, she was a princess of the
ruling house. The prince who acknowledged her as his
daughter was descended from the tenth dynasty of Cham
monarchies. Linkage by marriage to the present and
former ruling houses was a sound and eminently practical
course of action for one who would have to govern the
conquered realm.

Although I went to her father's palace with all the pomp
of a conquering general, I was, in fact, a nervous and
humble petitioner for his daughter's hand.

Ong Ansaraja received me in an anteroom. The prince

was tall for a Cham, only a few inches shorter than myself. He was a handsome man of dignified bearing. I judged him to be in his late fifties. He welcomed me formally.

"I have come," I said stiffly, "to seek your approval of my marriage to your daughter."

Ong Ansaraja scrutinized me for some moments before speaking. He smiled faintly. "I have heard much of you," he said. "For some years, my daughter has spoken of no man but you. Even if I disapproved of you as a suitable match, I could not deny her in this matter. You have my approval."

"I trust her mother has no objections," I said.

"Her mother was taken from us by a wasting ailment seven years ago."

"I'm sorry," I said, but in truth I was not. My heart lifted at the news of White Lotus' death. I had been dreading confronting her and had feared that she would prove awkward and might well try to prevent the union.

"When I have taken Vijaya," I continued, "I will send for Golden Dawn and have her properly escorted to the capital, where the ceremony will take place on an auspicious day."

"You seem confident that the capital will fall to you. Unlike Panduranga, Vijaya is heavily defended and will have ample time to prepare for your coming. I believe the army that can be fielded against yours outnumbers you almost three to one."

"I am aware of that," I said evenly. "Nonetheless, I am still confident the capital will fall to me in less than a month. But, since war is an unpredictable business, there is no guarantee that I will survive the battle to come. It is for that reason that I propose the marriage ceremony not take place until the campaign is at an end."

I heard a slight sound behind me. I turned to find Golden Dawn standing in the doorway. How long she had been within earshot I do not know, but she left no doubt that she had overheard my last statement.

"Have I no say in this?" she questioned.

Ong Ansaraja looked at her reprovingly. I was perplexed. No Chinese woman of breeding would have intruded into such a conversation or, outside the confines of the bedchamber, ventured to dispute a man's decisions. That Cham and Khmer women enjoyed more latitude and freedom of expression I was well aware, but I felt that in this matter the decision must be mine.

"Your father has given his consent to our union," I stated reasonably. "It is now for me to determine when it is best for this event to take place."

Golden Dawn advanced to my side. She placed one hand lightly on my forearm and looked into my eyes. "The ceremony that binds us can take place today, tomorrow, or at any time before you leave Panduranga. It does not matter. I would prefer to accompany you as your wife, but, if need be, I will go as your concubine, courtesan, or body servant. Whatever fate has in store for us from this day forward, I intend to be at your side."

I glanced at Ong Ansaraja, whose face wore a puzzled frown, and back to Golden Dawn's determined countenance. I took her hand in mine and smiled down at her. "It shall be as you wish. I will marry you as soon as your priests can arrange the ceremony."

And so it was, three days before the Army of the Jade Banner resumed its march, that Golden Dawn and I were joined as man and wife in accordance with Brahman rites.

When the army moved northward, Golden Dawn, with a single handmaiden as her companion, rode with the supply column. At the end of the day's march, she shared my pavilion and at night my sleeping mat. The only thing that marred my happiness was the thought of the fighting to come. I wished that she could be spared the spectacle of death and suffering. My only consolation was that the supply train would be reasonably safe and well to the rear of the scene of conflict.

chapter 45

As I HAD HOPED, THE CHAM ARMY HAD ADVANCED TO intercept me. They had formed on a broad, grassy plain some sixty miles south of Vijaya. Bordered on the east by sand dunes and the sea, and to the west by undulating hills, the plain was ideal for large-scale maneuvering and calculated to favor the Cham superiority of numbers.

We arrived at the southern extremity of the plain after a week's march north from Panduranga. We broke camp in the predawn hours, leaving the supply train in the security of the hills, and we moved down onto the plain. As a cinnabar sun rose from the sea on our right, the battle lines were drawn up facing one another. I scanned the enemy ranks. Their numbers were indeed formidable. Nowhere could I see a white parasol. Vidya, I concluded, had not seen fit to honor me with his presence.

The enemy formation started to move ponderously forward. A moment later, the wail of their conch shells and the booming of drums and gongs were borne to me in the still morning air. I stood atop my war elephant, legs apart, holding my sword above my head. I brought the blade down in a gleaming arc.

On this signal the ranks of my forward crossbowmen to the right and left of my position in the center of the battle line parted in a number of places to reveal flat-bedded wagons that until now had been screened from the enemy's view. The wagons, mobile platforms for six rocket launchers and two bronze siege mortars spaced at intervals along each wing of my formation, were pushed forward and their wheels braced. When I was satisfied they were all in position, I raised my sword.

There was a sustained roar as one hundred ninety-two explosive-headed rockets sped toward the advancing ranks of the enemy. Even before the smoke cleared, the special-unit troops were reloading the launchers, adjusting the elevation, and repositioning the wagons. I counted out the reload time interval, then described a circle above my head with my flashing blade. A second wave of rockets, this time fired in series, swooshed toward the enemy. When the noise of the rocket firings started to decrease in volume, I dropped my sword blade. There was a thunderous roar as the siege mortars hurled their iron missiles into the wavering battle line facing us.

Now, on my barked command, our conch shells blared the signal to advance. Our line started forward at a measured pace, and my elephant, clearly marked by the gold-fringed, jade-green parasol above my head, was in the van at the center of the line. On our flanks, my cavalry fanned out. The wings advanced at a slower pace than the center to form the wedge I favored against a superior force. Bowstrings twanged and a cloud of arrows arched toward the enemy formation.

I had visualized what rockets and mortar projectiles would do to an advancing battle line, but I scarcely could credit the havoc they had created. The first wave of rockets had been directed toward the enemy cavalry formations and had made a shambles of screaming men and horses on the enemy flanks. The second wave of rockets had fanned inward from the wings with the heaviest concentration on the center of the enemy formation. The enemy line had wavered, then buckled. War elephants, trumpeting in terror, had turned and fled, trampling the Cham foot soldiers to their rear. What had been a disciplined fighting force a few moments earlier had become a milling, confused mass of panic-stricken officers, soldiers, and animals. Then the iron projectiles had plowed into the formation, mowing down everything in their path and leaving wide gaps in the ranks. The Cham advance had been halted.

Even though we had been carefully briefed by our special-unit officers on what to expect, it was obvious that my officers and men were stunned by the destructive power of the explosive onslaught. It had been with difficulty that we had kept our trembling horses and elephants calmed during the deafening din of the war-engine barrage. Now, with the wagons withdrawing to the rear, our ranks closed and on the advance, I am sure there were many like myself who breathed a prayer of thanks that we had not been on the receiving end of such unleashed fury.

The Cham battle line had wavered, buckled, and been brought to a halt. There were ragged gaps in their formation. But they had not broken and fled the field of combat. They were a battle-tested force, and now, faced with an advancing formation of traditional pattern, they started to rally and close the gaps in their ranks. Weight of numbers still favored them, but they were stunned and shaken by the holocaust that had been visited on them. Hours of desperate combat still faced us, yet before the hand-to-hand combat had even started, we had achieved a psychological advantage which, if properly exploited, should win the day.

Slowly, our wedge advanced into the enemy ranks. My elephant was like a rock in a stormy sea. All about me elephants swayed in titanic struggle, foot soldiers were locked in combat, and mounted men swept in and out of my range of vision. For some reason, no war elephant advanced to challenge mine. On my swaying platform, my feet spread wide and my bow in hand, I sent shaft after shaft into the fray with deadly accuracy. I was forty-two, but my eye had not lost its keenness, nor my arm its strength. Nor had the spirits of my ancestors deserted me. Arrows and crossbow quarrels clanged off my helmet and cuirass, a thrown spear laid open my left forearm, and an arrow creased my neck, but they were trifling wounds that slowed me not at all.

The battle had been swaying back and forth for more than an hour when the balance tipped dramatically in our favor. Through a thin curtain of dust, I saw green pennants trimmed with gold. With General Chun leading the seaward column at full gallop, the Cavalry of the Jade Banner thundered in on the enemy's rear flanks.

I threw back my head and laughed. Raising my bow triumphantly above my head, I shouted into the din of battle, "Match *this* day's victory, Temujin!"

Temujin not only matched my feat, but he piled victory upon victory to surpass my conquest a thousandfold—but those victories were, as yet, some years in the future.

It was a victory of staggering proportions. The dead and dying littered the plain. Relentlessly pursued by the Cavalry of the Jade Banner, the remnants of the once-mighty Cham Army were in full flight.

I gave orders that our surgeons tend the Cham wounded along with our own and that funeral pyres were to be raised to honor not only our dead, but the fallen Cham, as well. Demoralized though they had been by my revolutionary battle tactics, the Cham had fought valiantly.

The capital, four days' march to the north, had yet to capitulate, but from this day's battle Champa ceased to be an independent kingdom and became once again a vassal state of the Khmer empire.

When my neck wound was cauterized and my left arm bound, I left my war elephant with its handler and swung into the saddle of a riderless steed. I was anxious to share my moment of triumph with Golden Dawn.

Golden Dawn welcomed me with a trembling smile and tears in her eyes. They were tears of joy—and tears of sadness, as well. She had known I would triumph; she had told me she knew this even as I left my pavilion that morning well before dawn. As her husband and lover, she exulted in my victory—but it had been achieved by inflicting a crushing defeat on an army of her people. From the hills where the supply train was encamped, she could have seen the distant battle only as a confused swirl of dust and muted sounds. She could now see the black smoke rising from the many funeral pyres and assumed, correctly, that the casualties had been heavy. She mourned her country's dead.

We did not speak. We did not have to. I knew without her telling me that she was torn between conflicting emotions. I held her close to comfort her. There, looking down on the top of her head, I made a solemn vow. I was, and had been for most of my adult life, a warrior, a creature dedicated to death and destruction. Now, if only for a few years, while still a soldier, I would be in a position to build rather than destroy. I resolved that I would construct wisely on the wreckage of my conquest—that

Golden Dawn's land would not be stripped by King Jayavarman of its wealth and human resources.

The capital had been sealed off from supplies and reinforcements by my cavalry in the landward approaches and Admiral Mohammed's naval forces from seaward. Vidya knew he could expect no mercy from me. I expected that, once he found no relief in sight and no escape open to him, Vidya, as Suryavarman, would defend his capital to the bitter end. With the highly effective siege engines in my train, I did not think the breaching of its walls and the taking of the city would require many weeks. It came as a surprise, however, when the city surrendered within three days of the arrival of my main force on the scene.

To my chagrin, Vidya was not in the captured city. After ordering his army to intercept me, he and his family had embarked on a warship and sailed north to the city of Indrapura. I dispatched General Chun and a strong force to effect Vidya's capture and return to Vijaya.

General Chun returned empty-handed. On hearing of the defeat of his army, Vidya had set sail for Annam. I dispatched a courier to Hanoi. My message to the Annamite emperor was that King Jayavarman VII would look upon the granting of Annamite asylum to Suryavarman as a hostile act. I suggested that the former Cham despot be arrested and extradited to Vijaya.

Emperor Li Cao-Ton, with a powerful Khmer army occupying the territory south of the Gates of Annam, prudently chose not to risk the wrath of King Jayavarman. He acted to place Suryavarman under arrest, but he did not succeed. Vidya, alerted to the fact that the emperor was going to have him arrested and deported, set sail for an unknown destination. I did not learn of this until the return of my courier some months after the fact. I was furious that Vidya had eluded me, as was Admiral Mohammed, who had his own score to settle with the fleeing tyrant. Mohammed's anger was further fueled by the fact that Vidya was making good his escapes by means of the Cham warship he had commandeered. It was Mohammed's sworn oath that he would never give up pursuit and would find the elusive vessel wherever it sailed.

There was an element of poetic justice in Vidya's escape from Annam. The circumstances did not reach my ears for almost a year after the event. Vidya had been warned of his pending apprehension by one who bore me no love—his onetime paramour, my estranged wife, Princess Ngo Thi Linh. Evidently Linh had expected to accompany the fleeing Vidya in some capacity, such as minor wife or concubine. Vidya had sailed in the dead of night, abandoning Princess Linh in Haiphong. For her complicity in Vidya's escape, Linh was arrested and, some weeks later, executed. Of all the acts committed by Linh meriting her execution, her warning of her ex-lover of his danger was the least deserving of a death sentence. Yet it was for this act, which could be considered as charity by some, that Linh finally paid the penalty for her past sins.

I found that Linh's death left me not elated but indifferent. It was Golden Dawn, when news of the execution reached her, who expressed satisfaction. By that time, Golden Dawn had had from my lips most of the details of my romances and marriages. She firmly believed that Linh deserved to die.

Before Golden Dawn entered my life as my wife, I had come to the conclusion that conjugal happiness would always elude me. I very quickly revised my thinking. I recalled Apricot Blossom's words concerning love. She had said that I was fortunate in having found the meaning of love in its fullest measure with Morning Mist—that I would recognize it when it again entered my life. At the time, I had thought it impossible to recapture the love Morning Mist and I had shared. Since then, I had found passion, infatuation, and sexual gratification—but not love. Now, as Apricot Blossom in her wisdom had predicted, love and true companionship had reentered my life, and I recognized this as such.

That my relationship with Golden Dawn was a deeper, more mature and more meaningful association than that which I had shared with Morning Mist also gradually impressed itself on me. Golden Dawn combined in her person the attributes that had endeared me to the women who had meant the most to me. She had the tenderness and warmth coupled with the independence and resourcefulness that had so much been parts of Morning Mist's character. She gave to me the wisdom, understanding, and loyalty Apricot Blossom had extended to me. Without the flaws of vanity and selfishness, she embodied the compelling sexual attraction of Jade Ring.

With Golden Dawn, my ardor did not cool as it had so often in the past with other women. On the contrary, throughout our married life we never ceased to find ecstasy and shared fulfillment in our lovemaking. In time, as our shared experiences grew in and out of the bedchamber, we became ever closer to each other. A touch, glance, or word between us was sufficient to bring us both a flood of memory of the joy, or pain, we had experienced together.

What I had no way of knowing at the time of our nuptial ceremony, and what I found out to my delight as our marriage progressed through its first months, was that Golden Dawn was highly intelligent and had acquired background knowledge far beyond the scope of most, if not all, Cham women. What is even more remarkable was that she had absorbed this knowledge on her own initiative. From the age of fifteen, when she had decided she would one day be my wife, she had prepared herself to be the woman she felt I would both need and want. She had not confined herself to learning the techniques of lovemaking. From Brahman and Buddhist priests, and from scholars and statesmen, she had set about gaining a depth of understanding of religions, cultures, philosophies, histories, and geographical features not only of her own realm, but of its neighboring states. She became well versed in the political, economic, and social structures of Champa, Annam, and Kambuja. In the process, she had learned to read and write Sanskrit, speak the regional tongues fluently, and even speak some Chinese of Mandarin dialect. Calligraphy she had not mastered, but she was taking instruction in that, as well.

As the ties of our marriage bound us ever closer, Golden Dawn came to be not only my wife, but my companion, confidante, helpmeet, and beloved paramour. It should not be inferred from this, however, that our life together was unruffled and free from friction. Golden Dawn was not a submissive creature. Like myself, she was a person of strong will, quick temper, and hot passions. It was inevitable that we would clash where our views differed. We had many arguments, some of them of a violent nature, but rarely did our differences endure beyond the bedchamber.

It did not come about at once, but over our months and years together our marriage became a living entity. We were the combined product of our complementary parts—the Yin and the Yang, heaven and earth, male and female, positive and negative principles of nature that together made the indivisible whole. In Golden Dawn I had at last found happiness. I guarded it jealously.

What I have recorded concerning Golden Dawn and myself took place, as I have noted, over the course of some years. Where Golden Dawn intuitively recognized what could be between us as a young girl, with me the appreciation came by a much slower process. I had been moved by a declaration of love by a fifteen-year-old girl, and the vision of that moment had sometimes returned to haunt me for many years, but I had not taken it seriously. It was only from the moment that she had given herself to me as a woman in my command tent at Panduranga that a dream took on substance—for both of us.

The months that followed my conquest of Champa were busy ones. There was much to be done to subjugate the conquered realm. The state had to be garrisoned. The administration had to be restructured and brought under firm control. Pockets of resistance had to be subdued. Tribute, in the forms of produce and booty, had to be extracted. Manpower levies of slave labor for Kambuja had to be imposed. Not only had opposition to the new regime to be promptly and firmly dealt with, but concomitant adjustments had to be made to ensure that the economy of the realm continued to function.

I had given a good deal of thought to the captive labor that had to be sent to Angkor. It was not my intention to have the burden fall too heavily on the hamlets and villages of the realm to the detriment of its agrarian economy.

One of my first acts was to have Ong Dhamapatigrama, as titular viceroy, issue an edict banning work of any kind on religious edifices. This provided me with artisans and craftsmen I could divert to Angkor, categories of labor best suited to please the Khmer king. The edict raised a storm of protest from the Cham priesthood. Had the ecclesiastical fraternity known what else I had in mind for them, they would have been outraged to an even greater extent. Had *I* known the storm this issue would precipitate between Golden Dawn and myself, I might have approached the matter with more caution.

Upon our entry into the fallen capital, I took over the recently vacated royal compound. I installed Ong Dhamapatigrama, as nominal head of state, in the grand palace. Golden Dawn and I occupied the palace formerly reserved for the Cham king's chief wife. Other royal pavilions reserved for lesser dignitaries were allocated to General Chun, now my second-in-command of the army of occupation in addition to being commander of the Cavalry of the Jade Banner, to others of my military and administrative staff, and to Admiral Mohammed. The pavilion and outbuildings occupied by Mohammed were. in fact, those that once had housed my father and his ambassadorial retinue during our period as hostages in the Cham capital.

The council through which I governed the vassal state consisted of Ong Dhamapatigrama as figurehead chief of state, myself as commanding general of the occupying forces, General Chun as my second-in-command, Admiral Mohammed as military adviser, the military governors I had assigned to the three provinces, and their Cham administrative counterparts. Ably guided and assisted by Mohammed and Ong Dhamapatigrama, and by Golden Dawn in a non-official capacity, the actual decisions for the governing of the realm were made by me. It was a grave responsibility of which I was ever mindful. No matter what facade I structured to assist me, it was I, and I alone, who was responsible to the Khmer king for the subjugation and governing of the state.

The position Admiral Mohammed occupied in this structure was something of an anomaly. Champa was an occupied state under martial law and military governorship. As such, it had no armed forces of its own. Nonetheless, I permitted the Cham Navy to function as an autonomous force and had every intention of rebuilding the Cham Army as units subservient to my Khmer forces. Mohammed, who had given me his undivided loyalty, had earned my confidence, respect, and friendship. He had given me his friendship in return and the benefit of wise counsel and sound advice. I looked upon him as my minister of war.

Before fleeing the country five years earlier, Mohammed had seen to it that his wives and children had been widely dispersed and safely hidden throughout the realm. It was to take some months for his family to be reunited. But, despite his precautions, two of his oldest sons had been apprehended by Vidya and summarily executed as a reprisal for their father's defection. Mohammed had good reason to nurse a bitter hatred for Prince Vidyanandana.

chapter 46

OUR FIRST MONTHS IN THE ROYAL COMPOUND AT VIJAYA saw a good deal of feverish activity. Not only were the daily affairs of state making heavy demands on my time, but the routine was constantly disrupted by matters pertaining to our various households. Ong Dhamapatigrama had sent for his wives and children. On their arrival by Khmer warship, together with the wives and children of other members of my staff, the days were filled with interruptions as domestic problems took precedence over the daily order of business. In my house, even though I had not sent for Sita and the children, there was also much activity.

Golden Dawn had sent to Panduranga for the slaves and servants who would comprise our household staff. I installed my sergeant at arms in the residential pavilion in the dual capacity as my personal secretary and major-domo. The household guard, grooms, and my personal military escort had to be properly quartered. There seemed no end to the details that had to be attended to. Gradually, however, under Golden Dawn's competent direction, order emerged from chaos and I was able to devote more time to the governing of the realm.

I stole as much time as possible from my official duties to spend with Golden Dawn. This was a time when we were learning to know, understand, and appreciate each other. But I was not, in fact, being delinquent in my administrative function. From the beginning, I made it a practice to discuss with Golden Dawn the measures I intended to adopt in governing the realm. The influence she had on many of my decisions made itself felt throughout the country.

We were not, for example, made welcome as deliverers from oppression. Our imposition of Khmer authority met with a good deal of resistance. My normal answer to such opposition would have been harsh reprisals. It was Golden Dawn who stayed my hand by arguing persuasively that repressive measures would only breed more resistance—that words were more effective than the sword.

Through the intervention of Golden Dawn's relatives and family connections, many factions opposed to my regime were persuaded to air their grievances publicly. In a surprising number of cases, the differences were reconciled with relative ease. The instances wherein I used force in recalcitrant trouble spots decreased each month. The practice of settling diputes by open forum became the cornerstone of my policy. The sword was still there, but it was seldom unsheathed.

I was not always swayed by Golden Dawn's arguments. One such instance gave rise to an incident that was my first indication that I had not acquired a passively submissive wife. It began the afternoon I disclosed to Golden Dawn my plans for the Brahman priesthood.

"You *can't* do that!" she cried, flaring up at me. "You cannot strip the temples of their junior priesthood and send them as forced labor to Kambuja!"

"You forget yourself, madam," I said sharply. "It is not your place to tell me what I can and cannot do. It is I, not you, who govern this realm."

"I agreed with your decision," she continued with less asperity, "to halt the construction of new temples. With less enthusiasm, I accepted your decree that no major repairs be effected in the existing temples. But this plan of yours I cannot accept."

"Why not?" I questioned. "You agree that the cult of Siva is a state-imposed religion. Have you not yourself remarked on the religious tolerance of your realm, where Brahmanism of various cults, Buddhism, and even the faith of Islam are allowed to flourish unmolested? You have also agreed that, regardless of which cult or faith is in the ascendancy by royal decree, at the village level it matters little since the religious practices are mere super-impositions on age-old animistic customs and practices. Your religious freedom has resulted in a profligate, pro-liferating priesthood that is a burden to your people and your economy. I merely propose to thin those ranks. In so doing, I not only ease the economic yoke, but I save a good many villagers from labor conscription."

"You do not understand," she retorted angrily. "The priesthood may well be a burden . . . but it is a burden that is accepted without rancor. The ceremonies of which-ever faith is practiced are a part of daily life and are welcomed as a relief from the tedium of everyday chores. Tamper with the priesthood, and you do so at your peril. You could well provoke revolt among the very people you seek to assist. You *must* not do this!"

"Nonetheless, it is what I intend to do," I said coldly, and, turning on my heel, I stalked from the room.

That night Golden Dawn sent word that she was indis-posed and would not join me in my chambers. When the next night I received a similar message, I went angrily to her quarters.

When I stormed into her chamber, Golden Dawn was with several handmaidens. They were engaged in hand-looming silken fabrics.

"Come," I said curtly.

Without a word, Golden Dawn rose and followed me to my chambers. Once within my bedchamber, she gasped as I rudely ripped the *sampot* from her body.

"You deny me your love?" I questioned angrily.

"That I could never do, my lord. But, if you persist in flying in the face of reason, I can deny you my body."

"You profess Brahmanism," I said heatedly. "Then you believe in the sacred symbolism of the linga. You cannot deny me your body."

"You forget yourself, sir," she said, stamping her foot in rage, "It is I, not you, who . . . "

In her anger, she looked lovely. The wrath ebbed from me. As she echoed my pompous words of our earlier argu-ment, I could not suppress a smile. Seeing my expression change, she must have realized she was paraphrasing me. Her hand flew to her mouth. Her eyes wrinkled with laughter and she flung herself into my arms. With her face buried in my chest, her shoulders shaking with mirth, she clung to me.

"You are right, my Tartar," she said softly. "I can deny you neither my love . . . nor my body."

The next morning, I modified my stance. The edict that was issued temporarily suspended the induction of novices into the Brahman and Buddhist priesthoods.

During the evenings and nights of those first months, we exchanged confidences. Golden Dawn told me of her childhood in Panduranga and of the hopes and dreams of her youth. She recounted incidents of her family life and of the past glories of her father's family. She admitted that her belief that I would one day return to claim her love had become almost a forlorn hope when ten years had passed and she knew not where I was or whether I was alive or dead. During the first seven years of that decade, she had rejected many suitors. In the latter three years of that period, to the despair of her father, the offers of marriage had dwindled, then ceased altogether. She had discouraged so many hopeful candidates for her hand that she had earned a reputation of being frigid.

In her twenty-fifth year, she had resigned herself to the fact that she was a spinster and had decided to devote the remainder of her life to teaching and scholastic pursuits. Then, in her twenty-sixth year, she had learned that I was once more in Angkor and restored to my former rank. The speculation in Champa, later confirmed by the news that I was raising an army at Angkor, was that I had been charged with the conquest of Champa. She had known then that her years of self-imposed spinsterhood had not been in vain.

When word reached Champa that my army was on the move toward her country, she knew her prayers had been answered. But, like everyone else, she had believed I would strike at the capital. When I had appeared without warning at the gates of Panduranga, to her it had seemed a miracle performed by the gods for her benefit.

She told me that she had come to my command pavilion in an agony of fear that I would reject her. Had I done so, she declared earnestly, she would have taken her own life. When I had not, it had been the fulfillment of the dreams she had cherished since the day she had first seen me. Had I not married her in Panduranga, she stated candidly that she would have followed me, even if it had been as a camp-following prostitute. I was her life, she stated simply, and she would not willingly be parted from me as long as our lives endured.

I was deeply moved by Golden Dawn's disclosures. In truth, I felt a twinge of guilt that, during the years she had remained steadfast in her resolve, I had kept a courtesan, taken a concubine to my bed, and found fleeting pleasures in many another bed.

One point that had puzzled me was clarified in part. I had learned more of Golden Dawn's father, Ong Ansaraja. He was a man of honor and integrity, highly respected in Panduranga. He was the antithesis of Prince Vidyanandana, and in many instances, before and after Vidya's takeover of the monarchy, he had strongly opposed Vidya's policies. That such a man had not been disposed of, that he had retained a position of authority under Vidya, was to me a mystery. I questioned Golden Dawn on this score.

Golden Dawn did not have the complete answer. She knew only that her mother had knowledge of some event or incident in her brother's past that he feared to have disclosed. White Lotus had informed Vidya that she had passed this information to trusted friends, and, should any harm befall her or her husband, the details would be disclosed publicly and in full. Although it must have infuriated Vidya, the threat had been sufficiently compelling to shield Ong Ansaraja from his wrath. Golden Dawn did not know the nature of the secret or to whom it had been disclosed. She did not believe her father knew it, or even that it had been employed to protect him and his house.

In my turn, I told Golden Dawn of my boyhood in Changsha and sketched in details of my homeland. I told her of my family and how I came by the name of the Tartar. In telling her of the adventures and misadventures that had befallen me since leaving China in my youth and following my return to China as an envoy of the Khmer court, I omitted much that I did not consider suited for her ears or that might disturb her. I did not, for example, dwell on my military career, my campaigns of conquest, or my solitary confinement in Nan Chao. In response to her questions, I told her how I came by the scar on my thigh and my stiff right leg. I explained something of the court intrigue in Angkor and of my rather unusual and perplexing relationship with the Khmer monarch.

In describing to Golden Dawn the astonishing Sung

capital of Lin-an and my life within its confines, I told
her of the practice of foot binding and its origins and of
my aversion to the disfiguring custom. I told her of Sita's
intense dislike of the climate and of her return to Angkor
with her children after she had suffered through two winters in the capital. In telling her of Trac, I explained my
views on education for female children—views to which
Golden Dawn heartily subscribed. I told her of Jade Ring
and her attempted deception on my return from Nan
Chao. What I did not tell her at that time, although she
coaxed many of the details from me in the years to come,
was of my courtesan and the delights of the brothels and
bathhouses of Lin-an.

When I talked of Trac, I did not mention the unfortunate attraction the girl had developed for me as a child,
the conflict this had created in my household, or Chu
Hsi's interpretation of its causes. I spoke of Trac's beauty,
her intelligence, and the latest news I had of her. About
a year before I left Angkor with the Army of the Jade
Banner, I had received a scroll from Trac in which she
had told me that Hsien had passed his classical examinations with ease, that she and Hsien had been united in
marriage, that Hsien now held a position as a minor official in Nanking, where the couple was now living, and
that she had been proud to present her husband with a
fine, healthy son—and myself, her honored father, with a
grandson. I teasingly told Golden Dawn that in marrying
a grandfather she had become a step-grandmother before
she herself had become a mother. Her only response to
this sally was a quiet smile.

In my reminiscences, I sometimes mentioned her uncle,
Vidya. She questioned me about him. I did not divulge
his homosexual tendencies, his cowardice, or the fact that
he had cuckolded me, but the picture I presented was not
an appealing one. I told Golden Dawn that I suspected
Vidya of patricide—to me the most unforgivable of
crimes. For that alone, I stated, Vidya deserved to die.
In this, Golden Dawn, who bore no love for her maternal
uncle, agreed.

Of all the topics I discussed, the one that was of most
interest, and which drew from Golden Dawn the most
penetrating questions, was the subject of the women who
had shared my life. I talked with some hesitancy of Morning Mist, our children, and the tragic fate that had over-

taken them. With less reticence, I told her of my arranged marriages to Ngo Thi Linh and Sita. With some bitterness, I told her that Linh had aborted our second child, had been unfaithful to me, and had been responsible for the deaths of my father's concubine and her maidservant. I told Golden Dawn how this knowledge had come to me and how, as a result, I had banished Linh from my roof forever.

Golden Dawn was horrified by my account of Linh. She stated that she could understand Linh's self-love and insatiable sexual appetite, but that the crimes Linh had committed against me were unforgivable. In Golden Dawn's opinion, I should have ordered Linh's death without compunction.

I spoke as well of Sita and my children by that union. I was as charitable as I could be, but I could not hide the fact that Sita held no appeal for me. In talking of the twins, Dom and Yasod, and of their sister Sita, my lack of enthusiasm must have been apparent, although Golden Dawn did not comment upon the fact. Only when I spoke of young Imre did I evidence much affection.

Golden Dawn had known before our marriage that her status would be that of a *ying*, a minor wife. She accepted this, but she advised me that she did not wish to share me, nor would she willingly submit to direction from another woman. If, she now told me, it was my wish to bring Sita and the children to Vijaya, she, Golden Dawn, would prefer to live apart and, if necessary, assume the role of a concubine. Mindful of Chu Hsi's remark that the Chinese ideogram for strife was a pictorial representation of two women beneath a single roof, I could not but agree with Golden Dawn. I told her that Sita seemed perfectly content to remain in Angkor, and, in a few years' time, when we returned to Kambuja with the withdrawing army of occupation, I would see to it that she had separate accommodations in the Khmer capital.

Golden Dawn questioned me concerning Apricot Blossom. Would I, she asked, have returned the concubine's love if she had not been robbed of her beauty? I answered that this could not have been. Had she not been disfigured, while I would have supported her out of deference to my father's memory, she would not have shared my roof. The intimacy that had grown to be would not have taken place, nor would she have transferred the love she held for my father to myself. The disclosure of that love by horse-master Chang's scroll had been totally unexpected, but I conceded that the knowledge of that love may have reinforced an idealized image I had acquired of her since her death. Had that image not haunted me, I ruefully admitted, it was highly unlikely that I would have taken Jade Ring as a concubine.

One thing that I found odd in Golden Dawn's questioning was that she displayed little interest in Jade Ring. Her questions concerning the concubine were perfunctory. On the other hand, she questioned me at considerable length about Morning Mist. One night, in reply to my query, she explained why this was so.

"She was the closest to your heart. She bore your first child and will always live in your memory. She is the only rival for your affections whom I truly fear. The dead do not age. Their imperfections die with them."

There was, I recognized, something I had not told Golden Dawn, in fact, which I had voiced to no one, concerning my union with Morning Mist. "She lives in my memory, as you say, but you need not fear her. Ours was a love that could not have endured outside her Jarai world. It could not have survived mine. I have known that for some years and think I sensed it even then. I believe Morning Mist knew it, as well. Had fate not intervened, sooner or later I would have returned to face the wider challenges of the world I had known before we met. Even then, although it was not discussed between us, I was growing restive, which Morning Mist sensed. Our love was wonderful in many ways, but it was doomed from the start. Our worlds were too far apart . . . and I was too young to resign myself to a lifetime in a mountain village."

"Perhaps," Golden Dawn murmured pensively, "the gods, in their wisdom, were kinder than you suspected in taking her from you as they did."

I found the royal compound had changed but little since the months I had spent there so many years before. The temple where I had received instruction, the royal elephant stockade, the grounds I had roamed with Vidya, and the ornamental lakes where now Golden Dawn and I enjoyed the communal bathing were much as I remembered them.

One afternoon, compelled by curiosity, I sought out the small pavilion that had been a trysting place for White Lotus and myself. It was still there, but the glade was overgrown and the pavilion was in a sad state of disrepair. I gave orders for the pavilion to be restored to its former state.

I said nothing of this to Golden Dawn. When the work was completed to my satisfaction and the pavilion refurbished as I remembered it, I intended to surprise her.

One hot afternoon toward the end of the dry season, I left my work earlier than usual. I took Golden Dawn to the same tree-shaded lake I had bathed in when I first met her mother. When we had refreshed ourselves and dried out in the hot sun, I took her by the hand and led her along the footpath along which I had first been conducted by White Lotus.

When the pavilion came into view, Golden Dawn looked at me questioningly, but she said nothing.

When we had made love, I lay contentedly on the fur-draped couch, letting the perspiration dry on my body. The golden sunlight of the late afternoon slanted through the open window. Insects droned drowsily beyond the window. Golden Dawn sat naked on the edge of the bed at my side.

"Is this where you made love to my mother?" she asked softly, not looking at me.

It took a moment for her question to register. "What . . . how . . . !" I exclaimed in confusion.

She turned and looked at me seriously. "Did you make love just now to me . . . or to her?"

"It is you I love . . . and to whom I made love. How?. . ."

A faint smile played upon her lips. Her fingers lightly traced the scar on my left arm. "You did not know she told me of your youthful affair with her. She described your lovemaking in some detail . . . I think to discourage my love for you. I'm afraid it had the reverse effect. She told me of a pavilion such as this."

In my disclosures about the women in my life, I had purposely made no mention of White Lotus. Not only would it have been in poor taste, but it would have raised a subject I wished to avoid. But now that Golden Dawn had brought the specter into the open, it must be faced.

"Did she . . . did she tell you that you could be my daughter?"

"She told me I was."

My acute misery must have been written on my face. She grasped my hand tightly in both of hers. "Do you believe yourself to be my father?" she asked softly.

"I . . . I do not know."

"Nor did my mother. I think she told me that to discourage my affection for you." She dwelt a pause, then continued. "As a girl, my mother was . . . was given to sexual experimentation. I know this because she told me of her many affairs and urged me to follow a like practice in preparation for my marriage bed. Before her marriage, she took many lovers . . . including my father."

"Do you think yourself of my blood?" I asked dejectedly.

"No," she said reflectively. "No, I do not. I think I would sense it if you were my father. But . . . even if you are, it makes no difference. You are my love . . . the only man I shall ever love."

She swung her legs onto the couch and lowered herself onto me. With her head in the curve of my neck, she whispered softly, "This is an enchanted place. You must bring me here often."

We did visit the pavilion many times. I believe that at least two of our children were conceived there.

chapter 47

THE RAINS CAME TO CHAMPA LATE IN THE NINTH month of the year. In the third month of the rainy season, the Year of the Boar gave way to the Year of the Rat. It was an eventful year.

In the third month of the new year, the Month of the Dragon, Golden Dawn gave birth to our first son. For her, it was a difficult delivery. For me, it put an end to an agony of suspense.

The only thing that marred my happiness during the first year of my marriage to Golden Dawn was the fear that ours was an incestuous relationship. It ceased to haunt me years ago, but I recall vividly how it preyed upon me then. Try as I might, I could not put it from my mind for long. And, when Golden Dawn announced her pregnancy to me in the Year of the Boar, my fears increased a thousandfold.

As a boy, I was taught that incest was a sin that brought disgrace and ruin on one's house. I was told, as well, that children produced through an incestuous coupling were invariably deformed monsters. It is not difficult to imagine how these teachings affected me during Golden Dawn's pregnancy. I suffered the tortures of the damned condemned to the Buddhist purgatory. And my suffering increased as her time drew near. I think I was resigned to the fact that our child would be malformed—a fitting punishment for our crime against nature.

Naturally, I said nothing of these feelings to Golden Dawn. I was sure that no word or action on my part betrayed my inner turmoil.

She was attended in her chamber by a physician, a midwife, and two maidservants. In the hallway outside her door, I paced like a caged tiger, cursing myself for having inflicted this cruel indignity on Golden Dawn. Despite the coolness of the rainy afternoon, I was sweating profusely.

My restless stalking was arrested in mid-stride by a strangled wail within the chamber. I stood transfixed, my eyes upon the closed door and my mind in a whirl. In a few moments, although it seemed an eternity to me, the door opened and the physician emerged. He informed me jovially that I was the father of a fine, healthy boy. He laughed at my expression of stunned disbelief and told me I could visit my wife and son in her chamber—to introduce myself to my new son, was the way I think he put it.

The midwife held the baby out for my inspection. He was red and wrinkled, with a shock of black hair, and his eyes were tightly closed. He seemed a rather large baby, but I could detect no flaws. I expelled my breath in a sigh of relief and silently gave a prayer of heartfelt thanks to the spirits of my ancestors.

Pale and wan, Golden Dawn lay on her couch propped up with silken cushions. I dropped to my knees beside the bed and cradled her in my arms.

"He is a beautiful baby," she said, smiling happily. Then she added in a whisper, "I knew he would be . . . you need not have worried so, my love."

From that day forward, no further mention was ever made between us that Golden Dawn might be my daughter. I put the possibility from my mind, but I must confess I was beset by nagging doubts during each of her four succeeding pregnancies. In the years of the Tiger and Dragon, she presented me with two more lustily bawling, healthy sons. In the Year of the Snake, a daughter was born, and in the Year of the Monkey, the tenth year of our marriage, we were blessed with a fourth son.

We named our firstborn son Mohammed. The admiral was delighted. He came often to visit his namesake and showered the lad with presents.

Admiral Mohammed's one complaint, made in jest, was that the boy would not be raised in the True Faith. My reply was that the boy would be raised to know of and have respect for all creeds. If, in later years, the boy should choose to follow the Islamic faith, so be it—it would be the will of Allah.

The month after the birth of our son, I received a scroll from Trac. She and Hsien were still in Nanking, where Hsien had received a promotion. Trac had presented him with a daughter during the winter.

What she had to say next pleased me immensely. She thanked me from the bottom of her heart for the broad education I had insisted on her having. and for not permitting her feet to be bound. She and Hsien agreed that their infant daughter would benefit from similar schooling. When I read that part of the scroll to Golden Dawn she was as delighted as myself.

I had not as yet informed Trac of my marriage to Golden Dawn. I did so now, and in the scroll I told her of her new half brother Mohammed. On behalf of both Golden Dawn and myself, I congratulated her on Hsien's promotion and on the birth of their daughter I requested that, if time permitted, she tell me of the political and economic picture in South China and how fared the war between the Sung and Chin dynasties. I did, in fact, receive this information on a regular basis from the Khmer Embassy in Lin-an, but I felt it would be beneficial to have Trac keep abreast of affairs.

In the Month of the Horse, the dry season returned to Champa With the change of wind, a vessel bearing important visitors arrived from Angkor. It was an official delegation comprised of the Buddhist patriarch, six senior abbots, and twenty Buddhist officials. The patriarch requested an audience with the viceroy.

Ong Dhamapatigrama received the patriarch in the royal palace The patriarch was accompanied by four of the six abbots. Ong Dhamapatigrama was flanked by myself on his right and Admiral Mohammed on his left.

Without preamble, the patriarch stated his business. He had come. he stated, as an emissary of King Jayavarman. It was the king's wish that Mahayana Buddhism replace the Sivaite cult of Brahmanism as the state religion of

Champa. In addition, ministerial positions in the vassal state's administrative structure were to be handed over to Khmer Buddhist officials. The patriarch, who stated that he would return to Angkor as soon as the winds favored his passage by sea, had brought with him the advance party that would effect the religious takeover. More would follow within a few months.

I was dismayed. Perhaps I should have foreseen such a move to impose religious and administrative controls on the part of Jayavarman, but the fact is that I had not. The king's wishes were, of course, commands. I needed time to consider how best to cope with this unexpected situation. After a hurried conference between Ong Dhamapatigrama, Mohammed, and myself, the viceroy advised the patriarch that the administrative council would consider the most expeditious means to implement the king's wishes. This, he stated, would entail about one week. As an interim measure, the ecclesiastical party would be housed within the royal compound and the council's decisions would be communicated to the patriarch in due course.

Ong Dhamapatigrama voiced his grave concern about a religious switch at this stage of our consolidation of authority the moment the patriarch and his party had departed. He was no more concerned than myself, particularly since the Brahman priesthood had become increasingly cooperative of late. I was not overly concerned with respect to the ministerial positions, but a religious changeover would have a disruptive effect I did not want at this stage—or at any stage. Neither Mohammed nor I was opposed to Buddhism as the religion of state, but neither of us welcomed the divisive effect of a religious imposition of this nature.

"I don't suppose it is an edict we can ignore?" Mohammed questioned gloomily.

"No," I replied, "not without foreswearing allegiance to Jayavarman, a course of action I will not consider."

"Can we stall the takeover . . . at least for another year?" Mohammed asked hopefully.

"We will have to," I stated flatly, "but at the moment I can't see how."

"Should we refer the matter to the council? Do you want the members assembled?" the viceroy queried.

"No," I said thoughtfully. "A matter of this magnitude

must be my sole responsibility. Give me a few days to think it over."

When I told Golden Dawn of the patriarch's demands, she was as dismayed as I had been.

"Buddhism has been the religion of state by royal decree a good many times in the past," she said. "It was so decreed in the reign of my great-grandfather. I have been told that each time there was a major change of religions, it caused great turmoil administratively and brought the country to the verge of revolt Those are conditions you certainly don't want just now."

"Not now, nor at any time during my tenure of governorship."

"Could not the holy men be made to see this? Could you not persuade them to your point of view?"

"It is unlikely. They are motivated by self-interest. They owe their positions to King Jayavarman and would not willingly flout his wishes. Their allegiance is to him . . . not to me."

"Then, if reason won't prevail, you must use guile."

"Exactly. The ministerial positions are no problem. I will create positions with high-sounding titles but with no administrative powers. That is what I think the king expects me to do, anyway."

"Then why has he insisted on this condition?"

"To plant informants in our midst. I certainly don't welcome their presence and I will have to guard against them, but they are an annoyance more than they are a threat It is the imposition of Buddhism as the official religion that is my concern. The king thinks himself a living god, a reincarnation of the Buddha. He will not be swayed from transplanting his faith to Champa's soil."

"Could you not delay the changeover? The king is old. He may die and thus remove the necessity for change."

"Mohammed suggested stalling tactics. I have considered such a solution but find it not the answer. The king is a man of remarkable constitution. He may well live much longer than anyone expects. But you have hit upon the key to my solution."

In detail, I outlined my stratagem to Golden Dawn. She listened closely and made a number of astute suggestions.

I had the patriarch summoned to a private audience. When we had exchanged greetings, I launched into my carefully prepared discourse.

"How is the king's health?" I inquired politely. "It is now more than two years since last I saw him. At that time, he seemed to be suffering from a nervous disorder."

The patriarch looked at me sharply. "The king is well enough for his years."

"Ah, yes . . . he must be almost eighty. I suppose we must accept the fact that he will not be with us too much longer."

The patriarch bowed his head slightly. "Yes, I fear that is the case."

"When he passes from us," I questioned mildly, "what do you think will then be the religion decreed for the empire?"

The patriarch hesitated. "Buddhism, as it is now," he answered, but without conviction. The prelate knew better than I the bitter resentment that the king's excess of temple building had generated in Kambuja, and that the Buddhism espoused by Jayavarman was not popular with either the people or the nobility. I had heard rumors that Kambuja would revert to Brahmanism immediately upon the king's death. I was sure those rumors had reached the patriarch, as well.

"That may be," I said, allowing concern to creep into my tone, "but . . ." I allowed the sentence to trail off unfinished. In a firmer tone, I continued. "It is our wish to implement the king's command as rapidly as possible, but there are some difficulties I should bring to your attention."

"Such as?"

"Due to an acute shortage of labor, I have found it necessary to halt all construction and repair of temples throughout Champa. Your abbots and priests can assume their duties in the Buddhist temples within the realm, but the expansion required to make Buddhism the state religion means that, in many cases, the Brahman priesthood will have to be ejected and your priests will take over their temples. To keep the friction and strife that is bound to ensue to a minimum, I do not think we should proceed with undue haste."

I allowed the patriarch time to digest what I had said before continuing. "Your faith, Your Holiness, has been entrenched in Kambuja for a generation. In a year or so, when my army of occupation is withdrawn—or the king dies—it will be rooted but lightly in Cham soil. If Buddhism does not survive the ascension of a new Khmer monarch . . . or even if it does . . . " I completed the sentence with an expressive sweep of my hand.

It did not take much imagination to envision what would happen under the circumstances I had just outlined. An outraged Brahman priesthood, with no military force to deter them, would sweep the newly transplanted faith from Champa It would be a process that undoubtedly would involve considerable violence and loss of life.

"As you can see," I continued thoughtfully, "it is a delicate situation. It is my hope that you and your abbots can devise a formula that will assist us in making a peaceful transition I would appreciate it if you would confer with them and let me know what is decided."

The aged prelate's face wore an expression of worried concentration. He said nothing.

"This," I added, "has, of course, no bearing on the political appointments you requested. The ministerial positions are now under consideration and will be announced to you in a few days."

When the patriarch left my presence, all arrogance had gone from his bearing. His footsteps dragged.

It took only one day for the patriarch to reach a decision. He requested a private audience. This time, it was I who went to his assigned residence to meet with him.

His solution proved him to be a pragmatist He had, he stated, no wish to put his faith or his priesthood in a position of jeopardy If I would have an edict issued decreeing Buddhism as the state religion of the realm, it need not be publicly promulgated. He would, on his return to Angkor, present the edict to the king as proof that the monarch's wishes had been complied with. The abbots and priests in his party had been assigned only to the Buddhist temples and, by common agreement among themselves, would act in an unobtrusive manner, deferring where necessary to their Cham counterparts. When additional Khmer priests arrived, they, too, should be assigned only to Buddhist temples until they could be returned quietly to Kambuja.

It had worked out as I had hoped. A sense of self-preservation had overridden religious fervor. Had I advanced such a proposal to the prelate, it would have been coldly, arrogantly, rejected. Instead, the patriarch and his party had formulated a practical solution, with which I solemnly guaranteed fullest cooperation.

We parted with the unspoken knowledge that the patriarch and myself were conspiratorially joined in a deception which, if ever discovered by Jayavarman, would cost both of us our lives.

In the second month of the end-year season of rains, Admiral Mohammed strode into my anteroom followed by two seamen carrying a large basket. The sailors deposited the basket at my feet. I looked at Mohammed questioningly.

"Open it," he said.

I did so. Inside, nested on a bed of straw, lay four human heads. The contorted, bloodless faces stared up at me with sightless eyes. I recognized them as once having graced the shoulders of Prince Vidyanandana and his three oldest sons.

"We located the ship bearing the former royal family," Mohammed said.

"So I see," I replied dryly. "Where?" I questioned, closing the lid of the basket.

"Unbeknownst to the Sung authorities, he found refuge on an island off the South China coast. I understand he was planning to sail to the Japanese islands. The captain of his ship was ordered to return to Vijaya with the royal family. He exceeded his authority and has been severely reprimanded."

"And, I hope, promoted," I said.

"And promoted . . . I forget which came first," Mohammed said with a broad grin.

"The remainder of the family?" I queried.

Mohammed's grin grew even wider. "Unfortunately, in the excitement, they were left behind on the island."

For some time after Mohammed and his seamen had left, I sat staring thoughtfully at the closed basket.

It had started here when Vidya had been instructed to court my friendship. Now it had come full circle. I had admired him once and had had affection for him. Had he been of different character, we could have been close friends. Now, it was I—in fact, if not in name—who, by an

irony of fate, occupied the seat of authority to which Vidya
had aspired and had obtained through treachery. In the
basket reposed grim reminders of the price of overweening
ambition.

I ordered that the heads be pickled in brine and dispatched to the Khmer king at Angkor Thom.

chapter 48

I HAD CONSIDERED IT WOULD TAKE AT LEAST THREE YEARS to pacify Champa. It took less time than I had anticipated. I toured the towns and villages of the realm extensively during the Year of the Bull and came to the conclusion that we had achieved enough stability to consider reducing the army of occupation to garrison forces and turning over most administrative functions to the Cham. I delayed advising Angkor of this condition until well into our third year, 1206, the Year of the Tiger. My reason for this was purely selfish. Golden Dawn was again pregnant and I had no wish to return to Kambuja until the baby was born. As it transpired, I need not have concerned myself on that score.

In establishing Khmer suzerainty, I was assisted by a number of factors. Not the least of these was that we were looked upon not so much as conquerors as deliverers. Vidya's regime had been so oppressive that the authority I imposed seemed mild by comparison.

I avoided a major disruption of the economy by employing a number of devices. To retain as much labor as possible, I initiated projects within Champa to which King Jayavarman could have little objection. I started construction on a roadway to link Vijaya with the Khmer network of military roads. I embarked upon the establishment of hospitals, the Khmer queen's favorite project. And I or-

dered the building of towers commemorating the Khmer
king's victory. In this way, I kept the annual levies of
forced labor to a minimum. In addition, I did not force
the pace of these projects. They were seasonal in character
and the laborers returned to their fields and hamlets for
the seasons of planting and harvesting.

Through General Chun, the military commanders were
encouraged to employ their troops in regional activities.
Khmer soldiers assisted with well-digging, bridge repair,
and construction and maintenance of irrigation canals. Our
soldiers became integrated into the communities. We encouraged fraternization, and marriages between Khmer
soldiers and Cham women became a common occurrence.

While the fact that Buddhism was now officially the state
religion was a well-kept secret, the Brahman priesthood
knew that, in some way, they had been protected. Their
initial antipathy to my regime gave way to wholehearted
cooperation. In appreciation of their support, in the Year
of the Tiger I partially relaxed my earlier edicts. Repair
work was permitted in the temples, subject to civil administrative approval, and a limited number of novices was
allowed to enter the priesthood.

While I was the architect of the structure of authority
imposed on the realm, I cannot take all the credit for the
rapidity of its acceptance. Three people deserve to share
that honor with me. They were my beloved wife, Golden
Dawn, Admiral Mohammed, and the titular viceroy, Ong
Dhamapatigrama.

Few know how vital a part Golden Dawn played in the
shaping of the state. Together, late into the night, the two
of us charted the course of action I would adopt. I came to
value her advice highly, and in my moments of doubt her
love and her confidence in me sustained me. Nor was her
assistance confined to herself. Her family was of material
help. Her father, whom I had retained in his position in
Panduranga, was my staunch ally in various projects. Her
kinfolk in the north cooperated with me unstintingly.

Of the few who knew the part Golden Dawn played in
my decision-making, Admiral Mohammed was one. He
should have been. He had become not only my fast friend,
but also a close friend of my family. He was often present
to lend his wit and wisdom to my discussions on matters of
state.

On my journeys throughout the countryside during the

years of the Bull and the Tiger, I was often accompanied by Mohammed. At times, one or more of his older sons came with us, as well. I found that Mohammed, for his defiance of Vidya and the part he had played in the overthrow of the tyrant, was something of a national hero. His popularity among the people, and my association with him in the public mind, helped my cause.

My selection of Ong Dhamapatigrama to act as nominal chief of state was a happier one than I had imagined. A man of probity, devoid of pretensions or vanity, he worked tirelessly to restructure the civil administration and to implement the reforms I proposed. A cautious and methodical man, he provided an excellent counterbalance to Mohammed's impetuosity.

The yoke of thralldom rested lightly on Champa.

In the first month of the Year of the Tiger, our second son, whom we named Jaya, was born to Golden Dawn and myself. Two months later, before the favorable winds of the rainy season changed, I dispatched a request to King Jayavarman. Stating that tranquility now reigned in his conquered domain, I suggested that the army of occupation be withdrawn and the state revert to Cham civil administration.

When the wind changed to the southwest, I expected to receive a response to my petition. None came. I received dispatches concerning affairs of state in Kambuja and the empire, but nothing whatsoever related to my proposed troop withdrawal. I received my answer indirectly, but not until the following year. What happened then, about midway through 1207, the Year of the Hare, was that Ong Dhamapatigrama was granted the honorific title of Yuvaraja by royal decree. In no way did this relieve me of any responsibilities. All it did was confirm what I had suspected. At least for the present, King Jayavarman had no intention of relieving Champa of its military occupancy.

In the twelfth month of the Year of the Hare, I received a communication from Trac. She proudly announced the birth of a second son. Her scroll contained news of another event that had taken place the previous year. Knowing of the interest I had expressed in the Mongol chieftain, Temujin, she wrote that an assembly of nomad chieftains had created a state modeled on military lines. The man selected to be the supreme leader of this unified nation was Temujin. Upon him was conferred the title of Genghis Khan.

In my return communication to Trac in the fifth month of the succeeding year, the Year of the Dragon, I announced the arrival of Anan, my third son by Golden Dawn. I requested that Trac locate tutors in subjects I mentioned and arrange for their passage to Vijaya. I also asked her to keep me advised of the activities of Genghis Khan, for, from what little I knew of the fierce warlord, I suspected he would direct his newly acquired fiefdom on a course of conquest that could involve China.

The years of the Dragon, Snake, Horse, Ram, Monkey, and Cock followed each other in sedate succession. With the exception of the Year of the Horse, they were years of unruffled tranquility in Champa.

In the Year of the Snake, Golden Dawn added a daughter to our growing family. We called her Lavender Jade. Frankly, I was delighted that Golden Dawn had presented me with a daughter. If the child grew up to resemble her mother, she would be a beautiful and remarkable woman.

In 1210, the Year of the Horse, the Annamite emperor, Li Cao-Ton, died and was succeeded by his son, Li Hue-Ton. I had met the new ruler when he was then the heir apparent and had found him to be an arrogant, headstrong, and chauvinistic young man. If his character remained unchanged, I anticipated trouble.

Admiral Mohammed, General Chun, and I held a council of war. As a result of our deliberations, units of the Army of the Jade Banner, together with supporting Cham units and most of the Cavalry of the Jade Banner were quietly moved to the northern province of Amaravati. Cham naval units stood out to sea off the northern coast, bearing reinforcements. Ong Ansaraja, who would command the force if it should be required, and General Chun, who would be its tactical commander, journeyed to the northern city of Indrapura to await developments. Preparedness, as General Dom had taught me long ago, was one of the cardinal rules of warfare.

I had guessed correctly. The new emperor disregarded the non-aggression pact between Annam and Kambuja. In the fifth month, an Annamite army of considerable size spilled southward from the mountain passes at the Gates of Annam. It was three days' march within Champa when it found itself confronted by the Army of the Jade Banner.

The ensuing battle was short and bloody. The Annamites were no match for my seasoned troops. The routed army was chased back across the frontier and many miles within Annam.

My victorious army returned to Vijaya in triumph, bringing the spoils of war and long columns of captives. Li Hue-Ton, I hoped, had been taught a lesson he would not soon forget.

That year, and for the next two years, the labor battalions I dispatched to Angkor consisted almost wholly of Annamite prisoners.

From the Year of the Dragon onward, I made it a practice to visit Indrapura in the north and the southern city of Panduranga annually. When not deterred by advanced pregnancy, Golden Dawn accompanied me.

In the villages along the way, and in the cities, we were accorded a royal welcome. It was as though we were the monarch of the realm and his consort. In a sense, I suppose we were the reigning head of state and his queen. It was by now well known throughout the realm that though I was by title merely the commanding general of the army of occupation, I did, in fact, firmly hold the reins of both military and political power. I was, in my gleaming cuirass backed by green silk and my helmet plumed with green, a commanding figure. Golden Dawn, whose *sampot* of jade-green silk was richly hemmed with gold, colorfully complemented my trappings of rank. I was quietly proud of my wife's beauty, regal bearing, innate dignity. and the magnetic quality she possessed that drew people of every walk of life to her.

On these journeys, I did not flaunt my high station. No elephant; were in my train. Golden Dawn and I, and Mohammed and one or more of his sons, when they accompanied us, went on horseback. We took few servants. My mounted escort was of modest proportions.

In the towns and villages along our route, when we could escape from official functions, Golden Dawn and I roamed the streets and byways unaccompanied. On such occasions, I wore a red- or rust-colored *sampot* of plain cotton. Golden Dawn favored a cotton *sampot* of deep vermilion trimmed with gold embroidery, well suited to her complexion.

We mingled freely with the common people, simple farmers, and tradesmen. We joined in their communal bathing, delighted along with the townsfolk in the performances of jugglers, snake charmers, and acrobats that were presented in the market squares and partook of food and drink in the food stalls lining the squares. We did not enjoy anonymity. I was too imposing of stature, and by now both Golden Dawn and I were well-known figures even in the smallest communities. The people treated me with awed respect. Golden Dawn, on the other hand, with her natural grace and earthy wit, inspired more confidence. Within a short time of meeting us, people found themselves captivated by the magic of her charm and spoke unreservedly in our presence. I learned a good deal more about the realm, its temper, and its problems from these informal encounters than I did from the reports of my military governors, administrators, and the myriad political informants I maintained throughout the state.

I learned, for example, that the crushing defeat I had inflicted on the Cham Army had all but faded from memory. My Khmer soldiers on garrison duty were accepted in most communities. The administrative structure I had imposed was mildly corrupt, but this, since corrupt officials had always been the rule rather than the exception, was tolerated. What rankled, what was an affront to Cham pride, was that after all these years the country was still under martial law backed by force of arms. This resentment, I found, did not abate; it intensified with each passing year. I did not believe I had cause to fear revolt, but the army of occupation, in spite of the protection it afforded against Annamite incursions, was to the Cham like a burr beneath a saddle blanket.

During those years, I derived a good deal of pleasure from my growing family. The boys were lively, mischievous, and of sturdy build. Their tutors reported them to be intelligent, but, as I had been at their age, they were more inclined toward pranks and adventure than toward their studies. Little Lavender Jade was a lovely and vivacious child who showed every promise of taking after her mother.

Almost as soon as they could toddle, the boys were taught to ride—at first on Cham ponies, later graduating to

larger Chinese steeds. I undertook their instruction in bowmanship and the rudiments of the martial arts myself. I
instituted the practice of gathering my children around me
each evening as I had done with Trac and my children by
Sita. The discussions were lively and on a wide range of
topics. In my new family circle, there was another marked
difference. Most evenings we were joined by Golden
Dawn, who contributed much to the conversational exchange and to my enjoyment.

In the Year of the Monkey, Golden Dawn did not come
with me to Panduranga. She was again heavy with child.
In her stead, I took nine-year-old Mohammed. He was
treated throughout the journey as though he were the
crown prince of the realm.

On our return from the southern visit, Golden Dawn
proudly presented our fourth son. In honor of the viceroy,
we named him Dhama.

Through these years I heard much concerning the exploits of Genghis Khan—both from Trac and from Lin-an.

In the Year of the Horse, his mounted marauders swept
out of the steppes behind their horsetail banners, bent on
rape and pillage. The Mongols moved against the Tangut
dynasty of Hsi Hsai to the northwest of the Sung realm,
then directed their attention to the Chin. In fierce campaigns of 1211 and 1212, the years of the Ram and Monkey, the Mongols brought about a palace revolution in
Peking.

In 1213, the Year of the Cock, I had problems of more
immediate concern than the faraway depredations of
Genghis Khan. For some years, the news from Kambuja
had contained references to mounting pressures on the
western, northern, and southern frontiers of the empire.
Now word reached me that the Army of the South had
withdrawn to the defense position it had held more than
twelve years earlier, that the kingdom of Haripoonchai
had again regained its independence, and that Siamese
forces had taken Lampang and were threatening to overrun Sukhothai.

In our eleven years in Champa, the Khmer component
of the Army of the Jade Banner had dwindled to less than
half its original number. As the attrition of retirement had

thinned our ranks, replacements had been for the most part Cham recruits. Still, even discounting the troops that would have to remain in Champa on garrison duty, the Khmer Army was still a considerable force. Had it been in Kambuja, divided among the standing armies. the scales of battle might have been tipped in favor of the Khmer. The Cham units within the vassal state were now, in my estimation, strong enough to withstand attacks from the Annamites. Then, too, withdrawing the Khmer component of the Army of the Jade Banner would serve to ease the political strain within Champa.

I discussed the situation first with Golden Dawn, then with the viceroy, General Chun, and Mohammed. The solution appeared to be for me to make a personal appeal to King Jayavarman that the army of occupation be withdrawn When the clouds gathered in the Month of the Dog, heralding the onset of rain in Champa and the beginning of the dry season in Kambuja, I set out with a small cavalry force as my escort—my destination, Angkor Thom.

chapter 49

MY PRESENCE IN ANGKOR THOM WAS GREETED BY A
marked lack of enthusiasm in official circles and not much
warmth in the household I had neglected for so long. For
several weeks, my petition for an audience with King
Jayavarman was ignored.

I prowled my residence like a caged animal or roamed
the capital disconsolately. There had been a number of
changes in Angkor Thom during the eleven years of my
absence.

The frenzy of construction had all but halted. The
Bayon, the last temple still under construction, was completed, apart from stone carvers still at work on the bas-
reliefs of the stone galleries. The Bayon lacked the
symmetry and size of Angkor Wat, yet it was a structure of
overpowering impact. It differed in design from any Khmer
temple I had seen. Its terraces did not rise as high in pyramidal base and its upper terrace departed from the con-
ceptual presentation of a mythical Mount Meru. The
upper terrace was circular. In its center, a gold-sheathed
tower soared one hundred fifty feet skyward. Around this
central tower were fifty smaller towers, each one graced by
four serene faces of the Bodisattva Avalokitesvara, cast in
the image of Jayavarman. From whatever angle one
viewed the temple, some of the two hundred fifty faces
of the king stared back with heavy-lidded, sightless eyes
and an enigmatic smile. The effect was impressive but

disturbing. It was an astonishing monument to the megalo-maniacal monarch who had inspired its conception and construction.

There were changes as well in my household. Sita, now in her mid-forties, had grown grotesquely fat. Her daughter, now in her mid-twenties, was married to a court official had two vapid children. and was beginning to look much like her mother. The twins. Dom and Yasod, were in their late twenties. Both held uninspired positions in the palace guard in the rank of captain. Both had taken insipid wives. When I visited their households, I was introduced to a number of lackluster children. I am afraid I am not being entirely fair in my descriptions. I had found Sita's brood unprepossessing in earlier years. Now I had a tendency to weigh them and their offspring against my children by Golden Dawn. In the comparison, the former were found sadly lacking.

The exception was young Imre. In his early twenties, he had equaled his older brothers in military rank. He was a captain of cavalry, as yet unmarried. Friends of mine in the high command spoke highly of him and indicated he was being groomed for accelerated promotion. Unfortunately, since he was serving with the Army of the South's Cavalry of the Silver Banner, I had no chance to become acquainted with the lad.

For many years now I had found Sita singularly unattractive. Now she was little short of revolting. Where in the past she had been amiably complacent, she was now moody and querulous. I avoided her as much as possible. With the exception of one particularly unnerving encounter and its unfortunate aftermath. I saw little of her.

One night I awoke with a start. In the moonlight streaming through the opened windows of my bedchamber, I beheld Sita, in amorphous nudity, beside me on the couch.

"I summoned you not," I said coldly.

"Nor have you done so for many years," she retorted. "I, who have been a loyal and dutiful wife . . . who have borne you children and stayed by your side through trial and tribulation, who have followed you uncomplainingly across half the world, am I now banished from your bed forever? I have given my life to you and your children. Is this the reward I get?"

I was startled by her outburst. "I have much on my

mind," I said gruffly but not unkindly. "Leave me in peace unless I bid you to come to me."

Without a doubt she had suffered at Linh's hands. She had not liked traveling since the earliest days of our marriage. She had disliked China and, like myself, had been frustrated in Annam and my homeland, but I could not see how my trials and tribulations had deeply affected her.

"Am I nothing but a servant to stay behind and tend your house in your absence? Have you no thought for me and your children? Do you? . . ." Her voice faltered, then rose to a shrill and quivering pitch. "Did you not take a concubine to your bed the moment I left China? Do you not strut and preen yourself with your Cham slut -oh, yes, I have heard how you romp and revel with that woman— when it is I, not she, who should be mistress of your household in Champa?" She became choked with sobs of self-pity and could not continue her tirade.

"Go from me, woman," I said wearily. "We will discuss this on the morrow, when you are more composed."

She hunched the silken wrapper she had let drop to the mat around her plump shoulders. Her rotund body racked with convulsive sobs, she stumbled from my bedchamber.

For some time, I lay with my hands locked behind my head, my thoughts on Sita's words. Who would have thought that placid, cow-like Sita could be capable of jealousy? Who would have thought that she, in her indolence, would aspire to be my chatelaine in Champa? I did not believe she actually wanted that responsibility. But I had to admit that she had legitimate cause for complaint. I had neglected our children. I had been a husband in name only to Sita for some two-thirds of our married life. Now, in her middle years, with her children gone from our roof and myself many miles distant, she felt rejected. She was at an age when women are prone to strange fancies. She was magnifying her woes out of all proportion. I resolved that, in the days to come, I would comfort her as best I could— but I would not, could not, take her to my bed.

At last, I was granted an audience with the king.

I was ushered into the audience chamber. The king, now an incredible eighty-eight, I found much aged. His hair was snow-white and thinning. Loose skin hung in crepe-like folds at his neck and on his withered arms. He seemed to have shrunken in size and he trembled as though afflicted with palsy.

I scanned the faces of the dignitaries and courtiers forming a backdrop to the enthroned monarch. There were few friendly faces. Only the heir apparent, Prince Surya, nodded a greeting. Prince Indra turned on me a baleful glare of ill-concealed hatred. The assemblage, I could not help thinking, looked like vultures poised to drop in heavy-winged voracity on the seated figure of their god-king.

I stated my case as persuasively as possible. The king's fixed gaze did not leave my face.

When I had presented my verbal petition, the king spoke. His voice, strangely enough, had lost little of its former resonance.

"The army stays where it is to enforce our mandate. Return, Barbarian, to the task with which we have charged you."

In the fading light of evening, I walked slowly along the terrace of the dead kings at the western end of the royal compound. With my mind deep in thought, I paid no attention to the statues of the gods and kings that lined the terrace.

Mine had been a wasted journey. The king's consuming obsession of a Champa in permanent bondage could not be swayed by logic or reason. He would destroy his empire before he would withdraw my army of occupation. As long as the king lived, the Army of the Jade Banner would remain in Champa. My only consolation was that the aging monarch would not reign much longer. But what then? What lay in store for Champa, and Kambuja, when Jayavarman died?

I turned my footsteps toward the southern terrace and my residence. So immersed in troubled thought was I that I had entered the compound and was almost at the top of the stairway leading to the gallery of the main residence before I realized something was wrong. I paused and scanned the compound. The torches had been lit at the entrance to the compound and in the courtyard, but my troopers, who should have been guarding the compound gates and patrolling the courtyard, were nowhere in evidence. I turned my attention to the gallery. The household guards, who should have been at their posts at the entranceway, were missing, as well. Framed in the entrance by lamplight from within the residence was the dumpy figure of Sita.

I strode forward angrily. She took my arm to lead me within the anteroom.

"Where are the guards?" I demanded sharply.

"What? . . ." The words froze on my lips.

Grim-faced soldiers converged upon me. I tried to disengage my arm from Sita's clutch, but she clung to it desperately. Before I could pull free, the soldiers were on me. A heavy blow to my chest knocked the wind from me. My legs buckled. The last thing I remember before a blow to the head sank me into oblivion was Sita's face. Her eyes glittered with malice; her lips were twisted in a malevolent smirk.

I regained consciousness in almost total darkness. Only a small sliver of light about four feet wide broke the Stygian gloom. I tried to move, only to find that although my arms were free, leg irons shackled my ankles. All I could do was hobble at a shuffling gait.

The sliver of light, I discovered, came from beneath a heavy wooden door that was securely locked. I groped along stone walls and determined I was in a windowless cell some seven feet in width and eight feet in length. I stumbled across some object that turned out to be an empty wooden bucket. It was the only furnishing within the confines of the room.

There was no doubt in my mind who had authored my predicament. It could only be the king. Why? This was the second time in my life that I had been roughly thrown into prison on the king's orders. But why? My coming unbidden to Angkor Thom to present a reasonable petition surely couldn't warrant this treatment. Or could it? The king's mind could have been poisoned against me by my enemies in the Khmer court, or . . . a chilling thought struck me. Jayavarman had discovered the deception of the imposition of his faith on Champa. If that was so, what did he intend for me? What was to be my fate?

I had not long to wait for my answer—an answer fantastic beyond belief.

I had been in the darkened cell for two days, maybe three, before I saw anyone other than an uncommunicative guard who brought me drinking water and meals consisting of a watery soup and cold boiled rice. I was rapidly losing all sense of time. Then the cell door was flung open and two soldiers beckoned me to follow them. Matching their strides to my hobbled gait, they conducted me down an enclosed gallery to a room only slightly larger than my cell. They pushed me down upon a wooden bench in front of a low table.

A Brahman priest entered the room carrying some documents. He seated himself at the table facing me. Beneath his headdress, his face was thin, the thinness accentuated by a pointed beard flecked with gray. He regarded me gravely.

"We know of your treason," he said calmly. "Your plot to reinstate the Cham monarchy with yourself as reigning ruler is known . . . as is your plan to overthrow the Khmer monarchy and ascend that throne, as well."

I stared at the priest in disbelief. I could not believe my ears. He let his hand rest briefly on the documents he had placed to one side of the tabletop.

"It is all here," he continued. "We have signed confessions from many of your co-conspirators. All of them implicate you as the ringleader. It is useless for you to deny your criminal acts." From the top of the pile of documents, he took one and placed it in front of himself. "We have prepared your full confession. All that is required is your signature."

"Enough of this farce," I grated angrily. "Who accuses me of such utter nonsense?"

The priest did not reply. He inclined his head in a nod. I had not noticed the guards wrapping their fists with leather thongs. At the priest's nod, they stepped forward and proceeded to beat me unmercifully. I was beaten until I was insensible.

I came to my senses back in the darkened cell. My head was spinning. I ached in every muscle of my face, neck, and torso. What was *this* madness? What purpose would faked confession serve? Why did Jayavarman feel he needed this to justify his actions? I could find no answers. I crawled painfully to the corner and vomited into the bucket that already stank of my filth.

The interrogation was repeated the next day—and again and again until I lost track of their numbers. I lived in a world of excruciating pain bounded mercifully by unconsciousness. The interrogators changed, but the charges remained constant.

To this day, I can hear the words, sometimes softly spoken and sometimes shouted hoarsely: "Admit your guilt." "Confess." "Sign." "Affix your seal and you will be left in peace.'"

There was no fixed pattern to these sessions of interrogation and torture. They would take place in the morning, the afternoon, or at night by torchlight. There were times when I was dragged from my cell twice in the same day. There were other times when I was not molested for days on end.

If the charges stayed the same, that could not be said of the savage beatings inflicted on me. They varied with the guards administering the punishment. I was beated with truncheons, flayed mercilessly with leather strips and bamboo canes, and immersed in troughs of water until I thought myself drowned. No part of my body was spared. I was beaten on the soles of my feet, my thighs, my buttocks, and my scrotum. At times, particularly sadistic torturers revived me again and again when I slipped into unconsciousness to continue with their cruel sport.

I lived in constant pain. My ribs were cracked so that even shallow breathing was an agony. I knew I suffered internal injuries from the blood I coughed up or passed in my urine. Yet, the beatings always stopped short of breaking any bones in my limbs.

The food I was given was sufficient to sustain life, but not strength. It was not the starvation diet I had been subjected to in Nan Chao, but, though slower than on that previous occasion, my muscles gradually wasted away from my frame. Raw, ulcerous sores developed on my buttocks, knees, and elbows. After I had been imprisoned for some weeks—I know not how long, since by then my sense of time was distorted—the shackles were removed from my ankles. They were no longer needed. Even had my dazed brain been capable of conceiving some plan of escape, my weakened body could not have put it into effect.

The human body, I discovered, can absorb terrific punishment. There comes a point when the brain refuses to accept the messages from tortured nerves and takes refuge in oblivion. The tortures of the mind are not so easily remedied. The mind seeks release in hallucination. I was constantly preyed upon by weird fancies and distorted images.

I ceased to care what happened to my body, but I was haunted by the fear that I could not retain my sanity. In fact, looking back, even though my memory of those months is mercifully blurred, I believe I was driven to the brink of madness—and at times beyond.

One particularly harrowing hallucination stands out in my memory. It happened not once, but several times. My spirit seemed to disassociate itself from my body and stand, disembodied, surveying the scene with strange detachment. Could that skeletal figure, bellowing with pain as bamboo splinters were forced beneath his fingernails, be me? Was that wretched, retching wreck that lay sprawled at my feet vomiting bile and blood onto the stone floor in a darkened cell me—or was it some stranger? At those times, I felt my spirit was very close to the netherworld— that it would one day simply shrug and walk away from the wreckage.

If my mind and body cried out so for surcease, why did I not bring the torture to an end by signing the damning document? I believe I came close to doing so, to babbling out a false confession and affixing my name to anything put before me. At the last moment, however, I was stopped by the nagging fear that to sign the document was to sign my death warrant. I forcibly rejected those cowardly impulses. I was determined that, if I must die, I would not give Jayavarman the satisfaction of labeling me a traitor. Now, looking back, I do not like to speculate on how much longer I could have sustained that resolve.

There were two things that above all helped preserve my faltering sanity. The most important was my memory of Golden Dawn and our children. When my mind wandered, I forced it back to a normal process by concentrating on the image of my wife or one of our children.

The other thing was the long-ago prediction of the blind monk. The soothsayer's words came back to haunt me. I had made the long journey into sadness—to Nan Chao— and survived as he said I would. As he had stated, I had governed, in fact, if not in name, a mighty kingdom. With Golden Dawn I had found much happiness—and in the midst of that happiness I had been betrayed by one of my own house, Sita. If all those predictions had come accurately to pass, what of its remaining prescience: ". . . *you*

will attain greater years than did your father before you
. . . and you will die with honor"?

I dwelt on the sightless seer's closing phrase with bitterness. If I were to outlive my father's span of years, it would avail me little as a living corpse. As for an honorable death, there could be no honor in being known as a traitor.

chapter 50

AS I HAVE SAID, MUCH OF MY MEMORY OF THAT FRIGHT-
ful experience, an ordeal that made my solitary confinement in Nan Chao pale into insignificance, is mercifully
masked. I do not, for example, recall with clarity the details of my rescue from imprisonment.

I have a dim recollection of the sounds of struggle outside my cell and of being taken from the cell wrapped in
some sort of robe or shroud. I remember dimly being
carried through the night on a litter and then being transferred to a cart filled with straw. That we traveled quite
some distance I know, because I was aroused from a sleep
of sheer exhaustion a number of times to be fed spoonfuls
or rich, steaming broth. I think there was some sort of
covering over the cart, and I dimly recall the sound of rain,
But, for the life of me, I cannot remember the faces of my
rescuers.

The first thing I remember with certainty was emerging
from a fitful sleep to find a shaven-headed Buddhist monk
sitting cross-legged by the hardwood bed upon which I lay.
The unyielding surface of the low bed had been softened
with an overlay of cushions. My lower limbs were covered
by a cotton sheet.

Seeing my eyes on him, the monk rose. He adjusted a
cushion behind my head.

"You have been delirious," he said. "Do not try to talk

until you are stronger. Monks will come to feed you in a few minutes."

There was something vaguely familiar about the monk, but I could not place him. My eyes closed and I drifted back into sleep.

When next I awoke, I felt somewhat stronger. The monk I noted, still sat cross-legged at my side. I wondered if he had kept a solitary vigil for long and if he was acting as a guard.

The monk smiled softly. "Do you feel strong enough to talk?" he asked solicitously.

I nodded "Where am I?" I croaked.

"A place of safety . . . a monastery near Koh Ker." He paused, then added, "You know me not?"

"I think I should, but I do not."

"Mangra."

No wonder he had looked somehow familiar: Prince Mangra, Sita's brother, and my brother-in-law by that union But there was good reason that I knew him not. He had not attended the ceremony that had joined his sister to me He could not. He had been many hundreds of miles from Angkor at that time.

I had last seen him when he was but a lad, for Mangra was the prince who had accompanied the Army of the West on its campaign against the Mon kingdoms in the west when I had been the newly appointed commander of its Cavalry of the Red Banner. I recalled him from those days, an intense lad with a consuming interest in Theravada Buddhism. Shortly after our return from that campaign, he had journeyed to the Mon kingdom of Thaton to become a novitiate in the Mon faith. As an ordained monk, I had heard that in 1190, the Year of the Dog he had accompanied the proselytizing Mon monk Chapata to establish a chapter of the Sinhalese faith in the Burman kingdom of Pagan. Since then, the only word I had had of him was that, despite the fact that he was one of Jayavarman's favorite sons, he had been disinherited for his defection from his father's Mahayana faith.

"How come you here?" I questioned.

"Some months ago I learned that my father had been stricken with a seizure and lay near death Although we are not on the best of terms, I journeyed to Angkor to be at his bedside should he die. It was a lengthy journey from Pagan, and I fully expected to be told of his death on my

arrival. Instead, I found he had made a miraculous recovery, and apart from a partial paralysis of his right side,
he is well and better than could be expected for a man of
his advanced years."

I had heard nothing of Jayavarman's illness during my
imprisonment—but then no news of the outside world had
filtered through to me. I found myself wishing fervently
that the stricken king had died in agony and had been condemned in death to the hells of his faith.

"Shortly after my arrival in Angkor," Mangra continued, "my sister came to me in tears. In an agony of remorse, she told me what had befallen you and the part she
had played in it by sending your cavalry troopers on a
trumped-up mission, dismissing your household guard,
and allowing access to your abductors. She beseeched me
to rescue you . . . if you still lived."

Mangra paused. He regarded me thoughtfully. "Sita is a
foolish woman," he said sadly, "but she is not an evil one.
She is frightened and confused . . . and nursed some griev-
ance against you that she would not divulge. She regretted
her part in your abduction almost as soon as it had taken
place. She humbly begs for your forgiveness."

"I have forgiven her long before this," I said wearily.
"Had she not been an accomplice, your father's henchmen
would have devised some other means to take me prisoner.
Why does he hate me so to have me tortured for crimes he
knows full well I have not committed?"

"My father does not hate you . . . or, if he does, it is a
hate strangely mixed with love."

I stared for some moments at Mangra, not believing
what I had heard. Finally, I said bitterly, "He has a peculiar way of showing his affection."

"It was not my father who had you abducted. It was, I
regret to say, a number of my power-hungry brothers, of
whom Prince Indra is the chief spokesman. They hate and
fear you. By coming to Angkor as you did, you placed
yourself within their grasp. They had no intention that you
return to your army in Champa."

So convinced had I been that Jayavarman had had me
imprisoned that it took me some time to absorb what
Mangra had disclosed. But it made sense now that I
thought of it. I had no doubts concerning Indra's passionate hatred of me. But why was this hatred shared by
other princes of the royal house?

"Why does your house hate and, as you say, fear one who has done them no harm? Was Prince Surya of that number?" I questioned.

"No. Surya was not among them. There are many of my house who hold you in esteem who, like Surya and myself, believe you will remain loyal to our house . . . at least until my father dies. A clandestine power struggle for my father's throne is well advanced. Surya is a kindly, well-meaning man. I do not think he is strong enough to survive the struggle and attain the throne. which is rightfully his. Those who aspire to the throne, such as Indra and his clique have good cause to fear you."

"Why?"

"They don't believe you intend to *send* the Army of the Jade Banner home to Kambuja. They are convinced you intend to *lead* it to the gates of Angkor Thom and wrest the throne by force of arms for yourself. And they hate and fear you for other reasons of which I doubt you have knowledge."

"Then," I said thoughtfully, "they tried to wring a confession from me to discredit me in your father's eyes."

"No, that was not the reason. My father would not have believed the document. He once may have questioned your loyalty, but he does not now. The confession was to provide the excuse for your execution when my father died."

"Why did they not have me put to death and make an end of it?"

"They feared my father's wrath even more than they feared you."

"Do you mean," I queried incredulously, "that they might have had to produce me alive at some time prior to your father's death . . . even if I was a babbling wreck?"

"Just so . . . and I am sure that Indra would have devised a plausible story to explain your condition at that time."

I would have liked to question Mangra further, but I was tiring and found it difficult to concentrate. I requested that he leave me while I rested.

The next morning, when Mangra came again to sit at my side. I picked up the questioning where I had left off the previous afternoon.

"I have given much thought to your words," I said. "I

believe I understand what has happened and why, but some of your words puzzle me. You stated that your father would not question my loyalty, even if confronted with my signed confession. This, from bitter experience, I find almost impossible to credit. You said as well that some of the royal house hate and fear me for reasons I know not."

Mangra smoothed a fold of his saffron robe. "I will try to satisfy your curiosity. You must bear in mind, however, that what I tell you has been gleaned from Prince Surya and others of the royal house since my return from Pagan.

"You know my father better than many of his own house, certainly far better than I, who have not seen him since my youth. But there are things you cannot know— whims and caprices of his that have not been talked of outside the royal house. It is upon these, as they have been disclosed to me, that I based my statements.

"You know my father to be of unbalanced mind. How long this affliction has been upon him I cannot say, but I know that he has become progressively more deranged as his years have advanced. He deludes himslf, for example, into believing that he is the living Buddha. He truly believes himself to be a god.

"Mortals defy gods at their peril. You have defied my father and are the only one to do so and live to tell of it. Surya believes that if my father fears any man, he fears you.

"Surya does not pretend to understand the workings of my father's twisted mind . . . nor do I . . . nor, that I know of, does anyone. But many have noted a curious change that came over him after your act of defiance.

"When his madness was upon him, my father imagined enemies behind every blade of grass and traitors lurking everywhere. At such times, he cursed and railed against his ministers, his military commanders, and even his own family. You did not escape these ravings, but in your case there was a subtle difference. In his more lucid moments, my father often spoke of you with affection. He spoke as though you were a favorite son.

"After your act of defiance, he never again cursed you even in his madness. He claimed at those times you *were* his son—a reincarnation of a son from a previous existence—and the only one throughout the realm loyal to his person.

"Surya believes my father acceded to your wishes concerning the governing of Champa because he had no choice. My father had come to the conclusion that only you could hand him Champa as a prize that had come to be an obsession with him. But, in so doing, my father had allowed a mortal to defy a god. To reconcile this lapse of godlike conduct, in his mind he endowed you with godlike qualities. I do not know if this is so or not, but I *do* know that my father firmly believes that Champa will remain under Khmer domination only as long as you are there and govern in his name.

"Perhaps you can see now why Indra and the others hate and fear you so. It is not alone that they fear your military prowess; it is that they live in dread that my father, on his deathbed or earlier, will renounce all claimants to the throne and name you his successor."

What Mangra told me gave me a good deal to think about. My head was awhirl. If the king had harbored such affection for me, he had kept it from me admirably. I put these thoughts from me, to be digested at my leisure, and I returned to other questions.

"Where was I held captive?"

"It took me some time to discover that, although it was not far from the capital. You were being held at the temple of Banteay Samre."

"How did you effect my rescue?"

"As soon as I knew where you were . . . and determined the numbers guarding you, I recruited an armed band of sufficient strength to force its way into the temple and bring you out. With the exception of the one who led the band, no one knew who was being rescued.

"When they effected your release, they traveled southeast to a point of rendezvous where they were met by myself and some trusted monks. We came here by a circuitous route. It took us some days. Traveling in this season is not easy. But the rains also assisted us. Prince Indra will without doubt comb the country to find you, but I am sure he knows not who was responsible for your rescue. I am sure we were not followed here."

"Then, if my presence here is a secret, I will have time to regain my strength before I strike out for Champa."

"There are some here who know who you are," Mangra said. "A secret known to more than one is no longer a secret. Indra will eventually discover where you are. For that reason, I have sent word to the viceroy in

456 / THE TARTAR

the Cham capital relating what has befallen you and where
you are. It is my hope that they will send an armed party
to conduct you from here before your presence is discovered by those who wish you harm."

I prayed silently that he was right. "Why," I asked,
"did you not recruit my cavalry troopers to effect my
rescue? Then I would have had an armed escort loyal to
me to discourage my pursuers."

"They were no longer in Angkor Thom. They had been
told that you had been sent on a mission and were then
sent back to Champa."

"Who was it who led my rescuers, the one who knew
my identity?"

"Your son, Captain Imre."

I was fed nourishing foods. I slept a good deal. The
sores on my body healed. the discoloration ebbed from
my bruises and contusions, my scars faded, but my
strength returned slowly. After several weeks in the
monastery. while I was no longer the cadaverous caricature I had been on my arrival, I was still gaunt and weak.
When the sunny periods of the day permitted, I exercised in the monastery courtyard and cursed at the slowness of my muscles to respond. I had also a good deal of
internal pain and a stiffness of my joints, which abated
with agonizing slowness. It could not be helped. I no longer
had the resiliency of youth on my side.

I had been rescued in the Month of the Ram. My
abduction had taken place in the Month of the Bull of
the preceding year. That meant I had been imprisoned,
and almost constantly tortured, for seven months. It also
meant that my fifty-third birthday had passed unnoticed
during my imprisonment. It was not reasonable to expect
my broken body to regain its former strength quickly at
my age, but I fretted constantly at the slowness of its
response to food, rest, and exercise.

I was worried on another score. Koh Ker was not much
more than forty miles from Angkor Thom, while it was
some three hundred twenty-five miles due west of Vijaya.
The rainy season in Kambuja would hamper Indra's
search for me, but it would impede as well the progress
of my rescuers from Champa for well over half their
journey. I had no doubt that such a party had been dispatched as soon as word reached the viceroy of my

predicament. The party should be well on its way by now, but if it didn't arrive soon I would have to consider some other way of extricating myself from this precarious situation. But for whatever I planned, I needed my strength.

With my back to a tamarind tree, I sat half-drowsing in the morning sun, turning over in my mind an alternate plan to get me to Champa undetected. A shadow fell across me. I started, then looked up to find myself gazing into the grinning face of Mohammed bin Abdullah.

"Well, Old Fighting Cock, we thought you were spitted and roasted."

"Had I been, Old Pirate, I would have been spared the sight of your ugly face," I responded with a grin. Of a truth, I was never happier to see his face than I was at that moment.

Mohammed's grin grew wider. "But two days' ride from here is one whose face you will find more appealing." Then a frown chased the smile from his face as he scrutinized me carefully. "Can you ride?" he asked.

"If the pace and distance are not too great."

"We will go at a pace that suits you, but in that case your charming wife and a number of units of your beloved cavalry are three days' ride from here. Come, I suggest we not tarry. The climate of this place suits me ill."

chapter 51

I HAD OVERASSESSED MY CAPABILITIES. IN LESS THAN TWO hours in the saddle, my head ached fiercely, I had abdominal cramps, and my backside was chafed raw. A straw-filled bullock cart was commandeered and became my vehicle of state. It took us the better part of four days to reach the eastern bank of the Mekong, where the main body of the cavalry and an impatient Golden Dawn awaited us.

The journey to Vijaya took well over a month, despite the fact that in the latter weeks I could spend many hours at a time in a well-padded saddle. During the journey, a tender and solicitous Golden Dawn was never far from my side.

I spoke but little of my interrogation and torture to either Mohammed or Golden Dawn. I did not need to. The evidence of my suffering was there before their eyes. I was thankful Golden Dawn had not seen me as I was when I was rescued. I told her with quiet pride that it had been my brother-in-law, Prince Mangra, who had planned my rescue and my son, Imre, who had led the rescue party. To this day, I have not told her of the part Sita played in my abduction.

For me, life soon resumed its normal cadence in Vijaya. Through a rigorous program of exercise, I slowly regained much of my former vigor. I am afraid, however, that I have never recovered fully from the ordeal. Recurring abdominal disorders, a stiffness in my joints, a tendency toward shortness of breath, and the deafness in my left ear I attribute to my sadistic torturers.

If I made a reasonable physical recovery within a relatively short span of time, I cannot say the same for my state of mental health. I was given to moods of black depression. I nursed a consuming hatred for Prince Indra and those who had served me ill. Vengeance would be mine.

Those of the Khmer royal house who hated and feared me would not be disappointed in those sentiments. I would strengthen the Army of the Jade Banner through Cham recruitment and build it into the most formidable fighting force the region had ever seen. When I deemed the army fully prepared, I would declare Champa an independent kingdom and ascend its throne. Jayavarman had invested me with godlike stature. He would not be disappointed. I would descend on Angkor like an avenging Siva.

I would pulverize the gates, scale the walls, and take from him the Khmer king's impregnable fortress city. All who opposed me would be put to the sword. Imre would mount the Khmer throne as my viceroy.

As for Banteay Samre, all within its walls would die lingering deaths and the temple would be pulled down stone by stone. Prince Indra would die in agony—very, very slowly.

I brooded almost constantly on this plan of conquest. I took the first steps by ordering stepped-up recruitment and intensified training for the army and set the foundries of Vijaya humming with the fabrication of engines of war.

I divulged nothing of these inner thoughts to either Mohammed or Golden Dawn. I would do so, I thought, when my plans were finalized.

In the tenth month, the Month of the Boar, in the Year of the Dog, Ong Ansaraja died unexpectedly. Accompanied by Ong Dhamapatigrama, Golden Dawn and I journeyed to Panduranga to attend her father's funeral rites. While there, on my instruction, the viceroy installed Prince Phanra, Golden Dawn's half brother, in the seat of authority vacated by his late father.

It was during our visit to Panduranga that I reached my firm conclusions concerning the monarchies of Champa and Kambuja. When I did so, I felt as though a great weight had been lifted from my troubled mind.

One evening, in our quarters in the palace at Panduranga, I broached the subject that had not been mentioned by me earlier.

"Would it suit you," I asked, "to be queen of this realm in name as well as fact?"

Her face wore a worried frown. "Have you decided, then, to ascend the throne?"

"I have given it considerable thought."

"And the throne of Kambuja . . . do you intend to take that, as well?"

Her perception surprised me. How had she divined my thoughts? "I have given that thought, as well," I answered gravely.

"You have governed my land wisely and well for many years. It could have no more capable ruler than you. If you wish to now ascend the throne, none would gainsay you that right, and I would sit proudly by your side as queen consort. But . . ."

"But what?"

"I have watched you grapple with your inner turmoil. My heart went out to you, but I could not intrude. You have been eaten up with a desire for revenge against those who have wronged you in Angkor. This I can understand. But if it is your intention to plunge Champa into war—to use it as an instrument of vengeance against Kambuja—this I cannot support."

"Such were my thoughts," I admitted candidly. "I intended to march on Angkor with a combined Khmer-Cham force, wrest the throne from Jayavarman, and seat my son Imre in his place. I have examined my conscience on this score, and I find I cannot undertake the conquest."

"Why not?"

"From childhood, respect for authority has been an integral part of my being. I have given my allegiance to Jayavarman. Until he no longer rules in Kambuja, I find I cannot break that trust."

"And when he no longer rules?"

"When that happens, Kambuja will be a troubled land. Its empire will be slowly eroded. Its long-oppressed peoples will probably rise in revolt. I find I have no desire to guide its destiny at that time, nor have I the right to inflict it on my son."

Her face wore a look of profound relief. "And Champa?"

"In effect, I have ruled this realm for twelve years. I shall continue to do so in the same manner while Jayavarman lives. When he dies, Champa must become again an independent kingdom. I will admit that it is a great temptation for me to take the throne at that time, but I have altered my views on this, as well. To govern as a 'gray eminence' is one thing, but to assume the mantle of a monarch is quite another. A king must devote much of his time to ceremonial functions and affairs of state; he has little time to devote to his family. And that family is inevitably caught up in court intrigue." I paused, then continued with a smile. "And I was swayed by another selfish reason. I am nearing fifty-four. I would like to spend the autumn of my life with you and our children with my time not divided between you and the state. It is better that younger hands guide Champa's destiny. I fear, my love, that you will have to forgo the pleasures of being the royal consort."

Golden Dawn's face was suffused with happiness. She came to me, pressed herself to me, encircled my waist with both arms, and smiled up at me. "It is no wonder that I love you so," she said softly. "What woman could resist a man who would forgo a throne for the pleasure of her undivided company?"

"Since your country is to be deprived of our royal guidance," I said banteringly, "we must find it a suitable substitute." Then I added in more serious vein, "There is much to be done. The realm must be prepared for its independence. This must be done in strictest secrecy . . . and we may not have much time before the Khmer king dies. I believe your brother Phanra has both the lineage and qualities to suit him for kingship. He is the candidate I suggest."

Only the inner circle—Mohammed, Ong Dhamapatigrama, General Chun, Golden Dawn, myself, and, of course, Prince Phanra—was privy to my plans. A happy, if somewhat overworked, band of conspirators, we slowly shaped the state-to-be. Since we believed ourselves working against time, we put in long hours in the formulation of plans and the execution thereof.

On the military side, my vengeful aberration of some months earlier worked in our favor. The wheels had already been set in motion to strengthen the Cham component of the Army of the Jade Banner and to make available to the army sophisticated engines of war. Recruitment was increased even further. Nor was the Cham Navy neglected. Under the direction of Admiral Mohammed, assisted by his oldest son, Hasan bin Mohammed, who was senior captain of the fleet, naval recruitment was increased and a program of shipbuilding was embarked upon.

Chun, Mohammed, and I restructured the Cham Army into three commands: an Army of the North, based at Indrapura; an Army of the Center, based in Vijaya; and an Army of the South at Panduranga. In addition, a high command was structured at the capital. Designated as Commander-in-Chief of the High Command, Prince Phanra was brought to Vijaya in the rank of general of the first rank. By this move, Phanra was included in our planning and became familiar with the officers and units designated to comprise the three armies when they were activated.

For the moment, the new commands were skeleton structures with only enough officers and men to supervise the construction of barracks, stables, and elephant stockades. Slowly, at the northern and southern cities of Indrapura and Panduranga, military supplies were stockpiled.

This increased military activity did not escape the notice of King Jayavarman's spies. The Army of the Jade Banner grew in size and strength with each passing month. I hoped this was causing anxiety and fear in the heart of Prince Indra. It was certainly causing uneasiness in the Khmer high command. I received official queries concerning the buildup to which I replied that I deemed the expansion prudent in view of unsettling indications of renewed Annamite military activity.

Our preparations were not confined to a military buildup. Under the viceroy's able direction, without resorting to edicts and decrees, the military governors were quietly stripped of much of their authority, which slowly became vested in the civil administration. On the economic front, I directed my attention to increased trade with China and to the annual levy of forced labor sent to Angkor. In the latter case, I had for some years been decreasing the numbers gradually. I now decreased them sharply. I expected an outcry from Angkor and was prepared to state that this was necessitated by internal military demands. I received no complaints and assumed that, since the orgy of construction at Angkor was all but at an end, the requirement for conscript labor had diminished considerably.

In the Year of the Boar, I reinstituted my practice of annual visits to Indrapura and Panduranga. As before, Golden Dawn accompanied me. I took with me my two oldest sons, Mohammed and Jaya, now aged twelve and ten, respectively. We were accompanied as well by Prince Phanra in order that he become acquainted with the administrators who would serve him in the years ahead. We had good reason to be pleased in our selection of Phanra. To a marked degree, he possessed the qualities that so endeared Golden Dawn to the Cham people—quiet dignity, charm, and the magnetic quality that attracted people of all walks of life.

Without a doubt, those were the happiest years of my life. Golden Dawn and I were not separated for more than a day or two at a time. There was much laughter in my house. Happiness and contentment reigned beneath my roof. The sexual attraction between Golden Dawn and myself had not diminished. We found complete fulfillment in my bedchamber and rose to face each day with renewed vigor and confidence.

Our children were a source of pride and enjoyment. To the unconcealed delight of the old seadog whose name he bore, young Mohammed, early in his teens, announced a preference for a naval career. Jaya, when he reached that age, indicated a preference for the cavalry. From his interest in ships and seafarers, it looked as though young Anan would follow in Mohammed's footsteps. Vivacious young Lavender Jade grew lovelier with each passing day, and little Dhama was the darling of the entire family and the household staff.

Golden Dawn was still of childbearing age and radiantly healthy. I, apart from the minor afflictions I have mentioned, enjoyed excellent health. That Golden Dawn did not become pregnant during those years I attributed not to her, but to the beatings administered to my genitals during my confinement at Banteay Samre. The fact that no new life quickened in her womb did not seem to disturb Golden Dawn, so I put it from my mind.

I heard from both Trac and Imre during those years, as well. Trac announced the birth of two more sons. Hsien was rising in his chosen career. The family moved to Canton, where Hsien became the administrative assistant to the governor of the prefecture and city. Trac's scrolls indicated that she was a happy and contented wife and mother.

The news I had from Imre made my heart swell with pride. He was promoted to general of the second rank and given command of the Cavalry of the Golden Banner. It was obvious that the Khmer high command had no knowledge of the part Imre had played in spiriting me from my cell in Banteay Samre.

Trac, as well as the Khmer envoy at Lin-an, kept me advised of the activities of Genghis Khan. At the time when I was presenting my petition in Angkor—the winter of 1213–14—the Mongol had accepted heavy payments of tribute and withdrawn from the gates of Peking. The Chin emperor and his court retreated to what they believed to be the safety of Kaifeng. Genghis Khan returned to sack Peking and put thousands of its demoralized inhabitants to the sword. Then, with the Chin state within his grasp, he unaccountably turned his attention to conquest in the far north and beyond the mountains to the west.

What I found most intriguing about the Mongol warlord was that the population of his entire nation numbered little more than the population of the Sung capital of Lin-an. The force Genghis Khan deployed against the Chin numbered little more than one hundred thousand—less than a quarter of the Chin forces opposing him. As far as I could ascertain, his forces at no time exceeded one hundred thirty thousand, yet with this force he ranged far to the north and followed the caravan routes to the west with nation after nation falling to his mounted bowmen.

His horsemen lived in the saddle. They fought ruthlessly

and gave no quarter. They swept everything before them, living only by the *yasa*, the code of law of their blood-thirsty champion. The tactics they employed were the two-column advance and the swift encirclement I had used so effectively with my cavalry. The one thing they seemed not to have mastered was siege tactics. This, I felt, would come in time. I felt as well that China had not seen the last of the horsetail banners of the Mongol horsemen.

The one serious dispute to arise between Golden Dawn and myself during those years concerned Lavender Jade. As the child neared puberty, I gave thought to the local practice of defloration. I had been raised to consider chastity a virtue—that a bride should come to her husband's bed a virgin. I voiced these sentiments to Golden Dawn.

With her eyes smoldering, she said heatedly, "Did you expect I would come to your bed a virgin?"

"Well . . . no."

"No more would any Cham in whose eyes our daughter finds favor."

She pointed out that, in the relaxed sexual atmosphere of Cham custom, were the deflowering not performed by Brahman rites, it would be achieved fumblingly by others. Since the sexual education of our daughter was Golden Dawn's province, I gave way to her in this matter.

When the ceremony was carried out with clinical detachment in the temple in the Year of the Hare, it was accepted as the normal course of events by Lavender Jade. I found that it did not bother me as I had thought it would. Many of my former prejudices and beliefs, I thought wryly, had become blurred and indistinct through my long exposure to conflicting cultures.

In 1218, the Year of the Tiger, Admiral Mohammed retired from active naval duty at the age of sixty-seven. He retained his advisory capacity with the council. The cape of authority of Admiral of the Fleet was donned by his oldest son, Hasan.

Mohammed's retirement reminded me that I, though ten years his junior, was not growing any younger. It served me well to remind me that King Jayavarman had reached the incredible age of ninety-three and still held the reins of power firmly in his grasp.

I was convinced that Jayavarman suspected what I was doing in Champa. That he had not stayed my hand lent substance to Prince Surya's contention that the king now had implicit faith in my loyalty. In his warped mind, Jayavarman may have derived a good deal of enjoyment from the consternation my activities must have stirred in Khmer court circles. I hope that was the case, but I shall never know.

I need not have been so concerned that we would not have time to prepare Champa for independence. Although totally paralyzed during the last year of his life, King Jayavarman clung tenaciously to life until the age of ninety-five—six years beyond my escape from Banteay Samre.

chapter 52

A MASSIVE SEIZURE STRUCK KING JAYAVARMAN IN THE eleventh month of the Year of the Hare News of this, stating that the king was totally paralyzed and that Prince Surya had assumed the duties of acting chief of state, did not reach me until the second month of the Year of the Dragon, 1220 My interpretation of this was that the king no longer ruled and I, therefore, was no longer under an obligation to exercise his mandate. The king may still have lived, but his game on life's chessboard was at an end.

I moved without delay. The forced-labor levy was abolished, as was martial law. The Khmer component of the Army of the Jade Banner, including military governors and garrison troops, was ordered to assemble at Vijaya. The country reverted to Cham civil administration. The Cham units of the Army of the Jade Banner were directed to the Cham commands to which they had been designated. In the third month of the year, auspiciously the Month of the Dragon in the Year of the Dragon, Ong Dhamapatigrama stepped down as viceroy and Prince Phanra. assuming the dynastic title of King Jaya Paramesvaravarman II, ascended the Cham throne with all due pomp and ceremony.

The officers and men of what remained of my Army of the Jade Banner were given the option of remaining in Champa with their Cham wives and children, or returning to Kambuja, taking their families with them in the baggage train. By the time this was satisfactorily sorted out, it was the middle of the third month.

With myself, in the full trappings of my rank and riding my caparisoned war elephant, in the lead, the army that had occupied Champa for seventeen years was withdrawing peacefully. It was reduced to about one-sixth the size it had been when Vijaya had fallen to us.

Golden Dawn did not accompany me. There was much to be done in Vijaya. We were vacating the palace we had occupied for almost seventeen years and moving to a smaller residence within the royal compound. Golden Dawn was supervising this move to quarters more suited to my station. On my return, I would be an adviser to the Cham king, but without rank or title.

I intended to lead the Army of the Jade Banner only as far as the Mekong. At that point, I would relinquish my command to General Chun, and with a strong escort of Cham cavalry attached to the army for that purpose, I would return to Vijaya.

We were still in the central highlands when I received an unexpected visitor from Angkor. A dust-smeared officer, wearing the insignia of a general's rank, was ushered into my command pavilion. I did not recognize him until he spoke.

"Honored father" were his first words.

I rose and strode to him, grasping him in a warm embrace. "Imre, my son. it has been so many years, I knew you not. . . . But what brings you here?"

His face was drawn with fatigue. His shoulders drooped. He looked as though he had been riding long and hard. He had, as his next words indicated.

"I came as fast as I could to warn you. The king is dead. It is Prince Indra who has ascended the Khmer throne as King Indravarman the Second."

"I expected as much," I said dryly. "But come, you look exhausted. Share a cup of wine with me. Then get some rest. You can give me news of Angkor in the morning."

"Father," Imre said impatiently, "you don't understand. Indravarman's first proclamation declared you a traitor for having placed a puppet monarch on the Cham throne and for marching against Angkor. You have been stripped of Khmer rank. You are to be arrested, taken to Angkor Thom in chains, and publicly executed. A courier bearing this news cannot be far behind me."

I smiled "Indra is inconsistent. If I march against him with an army intent on conquest, does he expect me to submit meekly to arrest and execution?"

"No. Units of the armies of the South and West are marching toward Angkor to strengthen the Army of Angkor as a force of sufficient strength to oppose you. I have come to offer you my services. I have come with all possible speed because, though the Army of the Jade Banner is loyal to you, there may be paid assassins in its ranks The courier that rides behind me may well have been instructed to arrange your death."

There could be truth in Imre's surmise concerning assassins. It would be Indra's method of choice. I summoned the captain of the guard. My orders were that any courier approaching the encampment during the night was to be detained until mornig and allowed to speak to no one other than General Chun. I had the guard around my pavilion doubled as a precautionary measure, and I sent a request that General Chun attend me.

While we waited for General Chun, I explained the situation to Imre.

"This is no army of conquest. Had you caught up with us by day, you would have been astonished by its numbers It is all that remains of the Khmer army of occupation. I am returning it to its rightful owner. It is not a gift of much consequence; like its commanding general, it is old and tired."

Chun arrived and was introduced to Imre. I then briefed Chun on the situation. He listened without interruption, his face clouded with anger.

"Do we return to Champa and assemble an effective force?" he questioned.

"No. I here and now turn over my command to you. You will continue your westward march Tomorrow morning, assuming the king's courier has arrived by then, return him to Angkor with a written message pledging the allegiance of the Army of the Jade Banner to Indravarman As it nears Angkor, it will be apparent you lead no army of conquest."

"What of you? What do you intend to do?"

"When my son has had a few hours of rest and is

provided with a fresh mount, we will ride toward Vijaya. We will leave before dawn. I request that you delay tomorrow's march until midday. At that time, return the Cham cavalry to Vijaya."

"Why not have them accompany you as an escort?"

"It is unlikely, but there may be would-be assassins in their ranks, as well. When you reach Angkor, you will report to the high command that I must have received a warning . . . that I fled in the night, and you know not where. From this day onward, you must disavow me."

"That I will never do," Chun declared angrily.

I flung my arm over his shoulder and embraced him. "I cannot order you to do so, Old Stallion. It is for your own protection. Indra's hatred for me will embrace all those who stand by me."

I had not used that nickname of endearment since the death of Horse-master Chang. Chun knew not the accolade I accorded him.

With Chun gone and Imre bedded down in my pavilion, I had one important task left. I summoned my sergeant at arms. He listened intently to my instructions.

He was to leave at once and ride to Angkor. There he would proceed to the trading community at the head of the Great Lake and contact a Chinese merchant by the name of Wu Shing. Through him, the sergeant was to arrange sea passage to Vijaya for a party of twenty. Once this was done, the sergeant was to contact my wife, Princess Sita. My wife, my sons, and my daughter and their respective families were to embark secretly on the chartered vessel. They were to take with them only a few trusted servants and no more possessions than could be carried.

With that matter attended to, I stretched out on my sleeping mat Sleep eluded me.

I thought of the tortured egomaniac I had served for two-thirds of my life. I hoped that now, in death, his mind was at peace. I had given him my loyalty, but not my affection. He had, however, my awed respect. In his madness had been genius. He had brought the Khmer empire to its zenith of power and glory, yet, in so doing, I feared he had planted the seeds of its eventual destruction.

It had been a long game, but the king, at last, had

been toppled from the chessboard. And, as Apricot Blossom had once surmised, while I was a threatened piece, I was still on the board at the game's end. In Jayavarman's game, I had been a piece of some importance. But the chessmen were being assembled for another contest. In this one, I would be a mere pawn.

My thoughts turned drowsily to Temujin. In my arrogance, I had once challenged him to match my feat. He certainly had done so. My name was known, respected, even feared in the kingdoms of this region— but the whole world trembled before the name of Genghis Khan. I was sure he would live in history. Who, I wondered, would remember the victories with which the name of the Tartar was associated?

I must, I thought just before sleep claimed me, chronicle my life for the benefit of my sons and grandsons.

We reached Vijaya without incident. Imre was made welcome in my household.

Events had not stood still during my short absence. No sooner had the dry season come to Champa than it faced a threat on its northern frontier. Li Hue-Ton, emboldened by the withdrawal of the Army of the Jade Banner, had sent Annamite forces into Champa. There had been a number of clashes between the Annamites and the Cham Army of the North, but there had been no decisive battles. I discussed the situation with Mohammed. We agreed that the skirmishes indicated a probing action on the part of the Annamites. We also agreed that —if not this year, then the next—Li Hue-Ton would mount attacks in strength. We advised the king that the Army of the North should be strengthened against this contingency.

I had, of course, reported the situation in which I found myself to the Cham king immediately upon my return. My brother-in-law had expressed dismay and concern. There well could be assassins within Champa instructed to murder me or abduct members of my family, he averred. He insisted that my household guard be augmented by an armed detachment drawn from the palace guard. Mohammed heartily endorsed this precautionary measure.

While I told Golden Dawn there was no danger, I was not as easy in my mind as I pretended. Indravarman's hatred of me was such that I felt he would have me hounded relentlessly. In truth, I welcomed the additional guards. I did not know what form Indravarman's pursuit of me would take. but I had dire forebodings that he would be infuriated by my escape and would act promptly.

I was surprised, therefore, when it took some months for news to reach us from Angkor Thom.

I welcomed the opportunity to get to know this son of mine who. at grave risk to himself. twice had come to the assistance of a father he scarcely knew. I found Imre intelligent and a man of principle He had. I soon discovered. a command of cavalry tactics equal to my own. Our views were remarkably similar. I undertook to instruct him in the wider aspects of tactical command and was delighted by his ready grasp of the essentials I had learned from General Dom and from experience.

In turn, Imre became an instructor. He spent a good deal of time with his half brothers, riding with them, competing with them in archery, and picking up their instruction in the martial arts where I had left off.

Imre adjusted easily to life in my household I could tell he was much impressed by the atmosphere of harmony within my household and by the chatelaine who directed it with quiet efficiency. Both Golden Dawn and I were amused by the shy reverence with which he treated her.

One day I asked him casually if, now that he was almost thirty he had given consideration to marriage He answered gruffly that he had been too busy furthering his military career to give much thought to the taking of a wife. Then he added glumly that since his military career seemed at an end, he might think in terms of matrimony Innocently, I asked him if his plans centered around Quiet Breeze, the young niece of Golden Dawn to whom he seemed attracted. Believing his budding romance to be a secret, he colored.

His answer to my question was that he could not consider marriage seriously when his prospects seemed so unsettled. Then, falteringly. he added that Quiet Breeze was very young Eighteen, I observed, seemed a suitable age for a girl to marry. As for his prospects. I broke the news to him that the Cham king had appointed him to command the newly expanded Cavalry of the North.

Before Imre left for Indrapura to take up his new

command, he and Quiet Breeze were married in a ceremony befitting his bride's royal status. She was one of
the king's four daughters.

King Paramesvaravarman requested my presence. When
I appeared before him, he wordlessly handed me a message he had just received from the Khmer king. It was
couched in the form of an ultimatum.

Indravarman stated that he had been advised of my
presence in Vijaya. If I was not surrendered to Angkor
Thom to answer for my crimes, Indravarman stated that
a Khmer army would march against Champa. The message ended by stating that my family in Angkor was
being detained as hostage.

The latter part of the ultimatum came as a jolt to
me.

I handed the message back to the king and asked him
what he intended to do about it. He answered that to
surrender me was unthinkable. He stated that, in his
estimation, Indravarman was bluffing. The Khmer armies
had their hands full with the Shrivajayans in the south and
the Siamese in the northwest. Indravarman could ill afford
to divert forces to a third front. In any event, it was now
too late in Champa's dry season for the Khmer to consider an attack. It would give us many months to determine whether the threat was serious.

The king suggested that, for the time being, we not
disclose the contents of Indravarman's ultimatum. To do so
would cause needless speculation in the kingdom and
anxiety within my house. I agreed about this. I left the
king's presence with a sorely troubled heart.

That Indravarman was not bluffing I learned from
another source. A week after my interview with the king,
my old sergeant at arms returned to the Cham capital.
What he told me left my heart leaden within my breast.

On his arrival in Angkor, the sergeant had found my
family already placed under house arrest. So heavily were
they guarded that escape seemed out of the question.
Indravarman, it appeared, had anticipated my probable
reaction to his proclamation.

The sergeant stated that Angkor seethed with military
activity. The Army of Angkor, doubled in size by units
from the other Khmer armies, had been renamed the

Army of the Golden Banner and was being readied for war. Evidently Indravarman feared me more than he did his belligerent neighbors to the south and northwest. His threat of war had not been an idle one.

The sergeant bore as well news concerning the Army of the Jade Banner and General Chun. The army, on its arrival at Angkor, had been disbanded and its units had been attached to the armies of the South and West. No units likely to defect to my cause were within the makeup of the new Army of the Golden Banner. General Chun had been seized and imprisoned. It was rumored in Angkor that he was to be executed for complicity in my alleged plots.

I knew I must advise the king of this situation. I would have to confide in Golden Dawn, as well. I did not do so immediately. I needed time to think.

chapter 53

WHILE THE RESOLVE WAS STILL WITH ME, I EMBARKED ON this chronicle a week after my return to Vijaya. Retiring each day to the seclusion of a small pavilion adjoining the main residence, I worked at the task for several hours. Golden Dawn, who knew of the endeavor and considered it would be a valuable legacy for our family, insisted I have strict privacy during these hours of writing. It is just as well that she did, since I found the chore more arduous than I had anticipated, and, at least with the early scrolls, I would have welcomed distraction.

When I received the news brought me by my sergeant at arms, I spent more time in the pavilion than formerly, but I was not engaged in calligraphy. I paced up and down the confined space and grappled with the dilemma that confronted me.

My initial concern was for Golden Dawn and our family. Even though our residential compound was well guarded, it would not be an impossible undertaking for a determined assassin to gain entrance to our grounds. But my greatest fear, as my mind returned to my ordeal in Banteay Samre, was abduction. Neither Golden Dawn nor the children were confined to the compound. At any time, as they walked the streets of the city, they could be seized and carried off as I had been in Angkor.

I thought of Champa. There I had found happiness and fulfillment as I had never dreamed possible. During the long years I had shaped its destiny and prepared it for its return to an independent monarchy, I had grown to love this country. More than China, Champa was now my true homeland, its people my people. I had bequeathed its present king a prosperous and militarily strong realm, but unless the entire kingdom became an armed camp, it could not survive a war on two fronts. I knew full well that if Indravarman attacked us in the west, Li Hue-Ton would fall upon us from the north. Tens of thousands would die to no avail. The realm would be ripped apart in the same way two hungry tigers fight to the death. Could I allow that to happen?

My thoughts turned to Sita and my sons and daughter trapped in Angkor Thom. If the Khmer king was thwarted in his demands, or if he suffered a setback on the battlefield, my family in Angkor would pay with their lives. Of that I had not the slightest doubt. I felt only pity for Sita and had little affection for our children in Angkor. But could I abandon them to their fate without sacrificing my honor at the same time?

My inclination was to take Golden Dawn and my family and flee to the sanctuary of China, but if I fled I would be condemning Champa my family in Angkor to certain death.

I gazed with unseeing eyes at the unfinished scroll and at the brush cup and ink stick on the low table. With a heavy heart, I knew I had no option. Only one course was open to me—my death to ensure the safety of my families and the country I had come to love. I was resolved in only one thing: I would die by my own hand rather than return to Angkor in chains to face a degrading death.

Before communicating my proposal to the king, I discussed it with Mohammed. His face was dark with anger.

"The king owes his throne to you . . . the country owes its very existence to you. Surely we can be asked to sacrifice some lives to discharge our debt to you."

"Could Champa survive a war in the west *and* the north?"

"We . . . they . . ." The anger drained from Mohammed's face, leaving it haggard.

"Could I live with myself if I abandoned my family in Angkor to Indravarman's mercy?"

Mohammed looked at me bleakly. "If I could do so, I would trade places with you, Lao Hu, Old Tartar."

"I know you would, Old Pirate," I said softly. "But it cannot be. If this is to be my fate . . . Insha Allah."

The king's first reaction was much as Mohammed's had been. The kingdom, he declared, would defend me on the battlefield if need be. Would that, I pointed out, save the lives of the hostages in Angkor? Would war remove the threat to my family in Vijaya? Would not a two-front war destroy Champa? Reluctantly, the king had to agree that, for me, flight was out of the question, and for Champa, war with Kambuja must be averted if at all possible.

My proposal gave Indravarman an alternative I felt he would find acceptable. I would submit to public execution, but subject to certain conditions. Firstly, the execution must take place in Vijaya. Secondly, my wife and family in Vijaya must be guaranteed safe conduct to China. Thirdly, I must be allowed sufficient time before the execution to complete my memoirs, during which period I agreed to being placed under house arrest. Fourthly, my wife and family in Angkor must be released from custody as soon as my execution was carried out. And lastly, I must be given funeral rites in accordance with Cham customs.

The proposal was forwarded to Angkor in the tenth month of the Year of the Dragon. An answer was not received until the second month of the Year of the Snake. King Indravarman accepted the terms, his only condition being that a Khmer emissary witness the execution.

It was only now, whem my fate was sealed and I could rule out suicide, that I told Golden Dawn of the situation. I think, however, that she had already guessed part, if not all, of the dilemma that had confronted me and the decisions I had reached. For many weeks prior to my confirming disclosures, she had been quiet and withdrawn.

In the seclusion of my bedchamber, I explained what had led to my decision, the proposal I had advanced through her brother, and its acceptance by Indravarman. She did not interrupt. She did not protest. She clung to me desperately. My chest was wet with her tears.

It was agreed between us that the children not be told that I was to die. They were told that I was to make a journey to a distant land and present my credentials to its emperor. It was not untrue. They were not told that the land was the Celestial Realm and that the emperor to whom I would present myself was the Emperor of Jade.

Golden Dawn and I did our best to act as though nothing had changed. It was not, I fear, an entirely convincing performance. As the months progressed, bringing the family nearer and nearer to its date of departure, the atmosphere in my household grew increasingly tense. There was now little laughter under my roof. I am sure that at least my two oldest sons, Mohammed and Jaya, knew of the fate that was to befall me.

The ship sailed four days ago. It was a ship of the line of the Cham Navy. The arrangements were made on my behalf by Admiral Hasan bin Mohammed.

I did not accompany the family to the harbor. I feared it would be too painful an experience. Our good-byes were said the morning of their sailing day.

The servants that would go with them took their leave of me. Next, the Cham and Chinese tutors who would accompany the family came to pay their respects. Then, one by one, my children came to me.

Eighteen-year-old Mohammed stood before me, his face rigidly set. I told him that, until I rejoined the family, he was to be the head of the house and responsible for the well-being of his mother, brothers, and his sister. I told him that although I could not accompany the family on its journey to Canton, I would be with them in spirit. I gave into his keeping three scrolls. One was for Trac, who would receive the family on its arrival. The second was for an admiral of the Sung Navy, commending Mohammed to the naval service. The last was for my steward in Lin-an, instructing him to turn over my accumulated wealth, my holdings, and my property to my oldest son.

As we parted, Mohammed betrayed his emotion by the strength of his grip upon my wrist. He turned stiffly, then strode from my presence.

My partings with Jaya, Anan, Lavender Jade, and ten-year-old Dhama were shorter, but no less painful for me. I fixed each of their faces in my memory.

The previous night, Golden Dawn and I had talked at length. She had promised me she would not grieve, that she would think only of the joys we'd shared and the children with whom we'd been blessed. There was no need for words between us when she came to my chamber.

She knelt before me and placed her head on my lap. The sunlight streaming in my window imparted a coppery sheen to her raven hair. I stroked her hair, then gently raised her head to gaze on her face.

Her eyes glistened with unshed tears. A smile trembled on her lips. I was reminded of the shy but determined girl who had stood before me so many years ago to pledge herself to me. Today, in her mid-forties and the mother of five children, she seemed little changed to my eyes. I was much moved and could not suppress a sigh.

She rose and, as she had so often done in the past, brushed my temple with her lips. Then she turned from me and, without a backward glance, left my chamber.

For a long time, I sat and stared unseeingly at my tightly clenched hands. The square of sunlight slid slowly from my lap.

I have advised King Jaya Paramesvaravarman that my memoirs are all but finished. The ceremony has been fixed for high noon the day after tomorrow. I have specifically requested that none that I hold dear—Mohammed bin Abdullah, Ong Dhamapatigrama, or their respective families—attend the execution. Fortunately, Imre and his wife are safely absent in Indrapura. It is not an event I wish to live in the memory of those who love me.

This is the final scroll. In a few more brushstrokes my task will be done. This evening, Mohammed bin Abdullah will come to say good-bye and take from me the sandalwood-and-ivory box that will hold this scroll and its companions.

It is strange, is it not, that all the predictions made by the blind monk half a lifetime ago have come true? I have sometimes wondered if he existed only in my mind. Yet, can that be possible? How could *I* have foreseen all that has befallen me?

His words come back to me as though just spoken:

". . . *you will attain greater years than did your father before you . . . and you will die with honor.*"

My father was fifty-eight when he perished in the flames at Angkor. It is now the Year of the Snake, almost the fifth cycle since the year of my birth. On my last birthday, some weeks ago, I reached the venerable age of sixty. I have lived two years beyond my father's allotted span, and there is no question that I will die with honor.

I specified that my funeral rites should be in accordance with Cham custom. The Cham king has gone well beyond that request. He has decreed that my rites be by royal custom, as befits one who has ruled the kingdom. When the embers of my funeral pyre cool, my ashes are to be sealed in a golden urn.

I will be with my family in more than spirit. My old friend, Mohammed bin Abdullah, will forward not only the box containing these scrolls, but my funerary urn, as well, to China.

I close this chronicle with personal messages to those for whom it is intended:

To my beloved wife—May these writings shed light on any dark corners of my life that may have been hidden from you. May they remind you of the love I hold for you and help you to relive the years of happiness we shared.

To my sons—May you find guidance and inspiration in my words. May they remind you of your proud heritage such that you do honor to me and your ancestors, whom I shall soon join.

To Lavender Jade—It is my hope that you grow to womanhood resembling your mother and that you bring to your husband all the joy and warmth she brought to me.

To Trac, should these memoirs reach your eyes— Be not distressed by the disclosures concerning your mother or your childhood. Think only that I have loved you since the day of your birth and that you have brought me great pride and happiness.

Grieve not for me. I bear malice toward none. I regret nothing in my life—least of all the manner of my leaving it.

Lao Hu

(Ḥsü Yung)

Epilogue

IN THE GLARE OF THE NOONDAY SUN, THE MAN THEY called the Tartar walked toward the market square with measured tread. At a respectful distance, his escorting guards matched his pace.

There was about the man an aura of quiet dignity. He held himself proudly erect. His limp was scarcely noticeable. He wore no adornment, but the hem of the *sampot* of jade-green silk that sheathed his loins was richly embroidered with gold.

The spectators lining the street and square were hushed; the silence was broken only by muffled sobbing. The air was still. There were no sounds of drums or gongs from the nearby temples.

The guards stopped at the edge of the square, leaving the Tartar to stride alone toward his waiting executioner. In mid-square, the Tartar paused. His gaze swept the throng of spectators. To his left, above the heads of the crowd, he saw the top of the pyre, which had been decorated in his honor. He smiled faintly before resuming the few remaining steps to a circle chalked on the hard-packed earth near the headman.

The Tartar dropped to his knees within the circle. With his hands clasped behind his back, he bowed his head.

Fortunately for his peace of mind in his last moments, he had not seen the woman standing proudly at the base of the waiting funeral pyre. Like the Tartar, she wore a sheathing *sampot* of green silk embroidered at the hem with gold. She should have been with her family on board a Cham warship that was now halfway to Canton—not here to play a role in his rendezvous with destiny.